Haim Be'er

THE PURE ELEMENT *of* TIME

Translated from the Hebrew by BARBARA HARSHAV

BRANDEIS UNIVERSITY PRESS

Published by University Press of New England

Hanover and London

Brandeis University Press
Published by University Press of New England
One Court Street, Lebanon, NH 03766

Published by arrangement with the Institute
for the Translation of Hebrew Literature

Originally published in Hebrew as *Havalim*
by Am Oved Publishers Ltd., Tel Aviv, 1998

Published with the support of the
Jacob and Libby Goodman Institute
for the Study of Zionism and Israel

Printed in the United States of America

5   4   3   2   1

Library of Congress Cataloging-in-Publication Data

Be'er, Haim.
The pure element of time / Haim Be'er ; translated from
the Hebrew by Barbara Harshav.
    p.   cm. — (The Tauber Institute for the Study of
European Jewry series)
ISBN 1–58465–277–2 (cloth)
I. Harshave, Barbara, 1940– II. Title. III. Tauber Institute
for the Study of European Jewry series (Unnumbered)
PJ5054.B374 H3913 2002
892.4'36—dc21   2002013141

THE
TAUBER INSTITUTE
FOR THE STUDY OF
EUROPEAN JEWRY
SERIES

JEHUDA REINHARZ, General Editor
SYLVIA FUKS FRIED, Associate Editor

The Tauber Institute for the Study of European Jewry, established by a gift to Brandeis University from Dr. Laszlo N. Tauber, is dedicated to the memory of the victims of Nazi persecutions between 1933 and 1945. The Institute seeks to study the history and culture of European Jewry in the modern period. The Institute has a special interest in studying the causes, nature, and consequences of the European Jewish catastrophe within the contexts of modern European diplomatic, intellectual, political, and social history.

The Jacob and Libby Goodman Institute for the Study of Zionism and Israel was founded through a gift to Brandeis University by Mrs. Libby Goodman and is organized under the auspices of the Tauber Institute. The Goodman Institute seeks to promote an understanding of the historical and ideological development of the Zionist movement, and the history, society, and culture of the State of Israel.

Gerhard L. Weinberg, 1981
World in the Balance: Behind the Scenes of World War II

Richard Cobb, 1983
French and Germans, Germans and French: A Personal Interpretation of France under Two Occupations, 1914–1918/1940–1944

Eberhard Jäckel, 1984
Hitler in History

Frances Malino and Bernard Wasserstein, editors, 1985
The Jews in Modern France

Jehuda Reinharz and Walter Schatzberg, editors, 1985
The Jewish Response to German Culture: From the Enlightenment to the Second World War

Jacob Katz, 1986
The Darker Side of Genius: Richard Wagner's Anti-Semitism

Jehuda Reinharz, editor, 1987
Living with Antisemitism: Modern Jewish Responses

Michael R. Marrus, 1987
The Holocaust in History

Paul Mendes-Flohr, editor, 1987
The Philosophy of Franz Rosenzweig

Joan G. Roland, 1989
Jews in British India: Identity in a Colonial Era

Yisrael Gutman, Ezra Mendelsohn, Jehuda Reinharz, and Chone Shmeruk, editors, 1989
The Jews of Poland Between Two World Wars

Avraham Barkai, 1989
From Boycott to Annihilation: The Economic Struggle of German Jews, 1933–1943

Alexander Altmann, 1991
The Meaning of Jewish Existence: Theological Essays 1930–1939

Magdalena Opalski and Israel Bartal, 1992
Poles and Jews: A Failed Brotherhood

Richard Breitman, 1992
The Architect of Genocide: Himmler and the Final Solution

George L. Mosse, 1993
Confronting the Nation: Jewish and Western Nationalism

Daniel Carpi, 1994
Between Mussolini and Hitler: The Jews and the Italian Authorities in France and Tunisia

Walter Laqueur and Richard Breitman, 1994
Breaking the Silence: The German Who Exposed the Final Solution

Ismar Schorsch, 1994
From Text to Context: The Turn to History in Modern Judaism

Jacob Katz, 1995
With My Own Eyes: The Autobiography of an Historian

Gideon Shimoni, 1995
The Zionist Ideology

Moshe Prywes and Haim Chertok, 1996
Prisoner of Hope

János Nyiri, 1997
Battlefields and Playgrounds

Alan Mintz, editor, 1997
The Boom in Contemporary Israeli Fiction

Samuel Bak, paintings
Lawrence L. Langer, essay and commentary, 1997
Landscapes of Jewish Experience

Jeffrey Shandler and Beth S. Wenger, editors, 1997
*Encounters with the "Holy Land": Place, Past and Future
in American Jewish Culture*

Simon Rawidowicz, 1998
*State of Israel, Diaspora, and Jewish Continuity:
Essays on the "Ever-Dying People"*

Jacob Katz, 1998
*A House Divided: Orthodoxy and Schism in Nineteenth-Century
Central European Jewry*

Elisheva Carlebach, John M. Efron, and David N. Myers,
editors, 1998
*Jewish History and Jewish Memory: Essays in Honor
of Yosef Hayim Yerushalmi*

Shmuel Almog, Jehuda Reinharz, and Anita Shapira, editors,
1998
Zionism and Religion

Ben Halpern and Jehuda Reinharz, 2000
Zionism and the Creation of a New Society

Walter Laqueur, 2001
*Generation Exodus: The Fate of Young Jewish Refugees
from Nazi Germany*

Yigal Schwartz, 2001
Aharon Appelfeld: From Individual Lament to Tribal Eternity

Renée Poznanski, 2001
Jews in France during World War II

Jehuda Reinharz, 2001
Chaim Weizmann: The Making of a Zionist Leader

Jehuda Reinharz, 2001
Chaim Weizmann: The Making of a Statesman

ChaeRan Y. Freeze, 2002
Jewish Marriage and Divorce in Imperial Russia

Mark A. Raider and Miriam B. Raider-Roth, editors, 2002
The Plough Woman: Records of the Pioneer Women of Palestine

Ezra Mendelsohn, 2002
Painting a People: Maurycy Gottlieb and Jewish Art

Alan Mintz, editor, 2002
Reading Hebrew Literature: Critical Discussions of Six Modern Texts

Haim Be'er, 2002
The Pure Element of Time

Yehudit Hendel, 2002
Small Change: A Collection of Stories

Thomas C. Hubka, 2003
*Resplendent Synagogue: Architecture and Worship
in an Eighteenth-Century Polish Community*

Those were holy books filled with content.

Day after day Father grew wiser by a word,

Mama — more understanding by a smile.

Little by little their words came together

And took on meaning.

— "Snowy Harvest," Jacob Glatstein

foreword

During the last few decades of the twentieth century, Israeli fiction has enjoyed an unprecedented growth in sophistication and scope. Novels and short stories, many now translated into English, were produced by a dazzling variety of talents who succeeded in rendering the complexities of Israeli life in compelling narrative forms. The horizons of Hebrew fiction, hitherto primarily the domain of secular men, expanded to include new categories of writers: women, non-Europeans, and religious Jews. These new voices have presented insights into worlds that had rarely been visible to the average reader. Haim Be'er is one of the most prominent examples of the new expansiveness. His first novel, *Notsot (Feathers)*, published in 1979 — and soon to appear in English — dealt not with secular Tel Aviv or the kibbutz, but with the religious community in Jerusalem of his childhood and adolescence in the 1950s and 1960s. In it we meet a fascinating gallery of characters, often pious Jews or Jerusalem eccentrics, who contribute to the sentimental education of the young hero. The moods of the novel swing wildly from hilarity to the macabre, from familial warmth to the loneliness of adolescence. Political events and social strains inform the plot, but are always kept in the background, even the Yom Kippur war which occupies the closing scenes of the novel.

While *Notsot* established Be'er's reputation, his popularity was enhanced over the years by his many newspaper articles which often presented the historical background to Israeli public life. His second novel, *Et Hazamir (The Time of Trimming)* (1987), is also marked by its marginality to the mainstream of Israeli fictional topics: though it does take place in the Israeli army, its characters are again religious Jews, not the usual soldiers one is accustomed to in Israeli fiction. Five years later, Be'er published

Gam Ahavatam Gam Sinatam (Both Their Loves and Hates), a loving, semi-biographical re-creation of three of the leading modern Hebrew authors who were clearly formative in his intellectual development: Haim Nahman Bialik, Yosef Haim Brenner, and Shmuel Yosef Agnon.

Be'er's versatility—novels, poetry, popular history, journalism —has allowed his move from the marginal to the mainstream. The subtle, continued expansion of the horizons of Israeli literature has blurred the distances between center and periphery. This shift has enabled Be'er to attempt his most daring novel to date, *Havalim* (1998), whose title is translated as *The Pure Element of Time*; it is a study in self-reflexivity, "post-modern" in its concept. The book involves a reflection on previous stages in the writer's career and logically presupposes some familiarity with it. Part memoir, part novel, the work derives much of its fascination from its relationship to Be'er's previous works, particularly to his first novel, *Notsot*.

Read against the background of the works that preceded it, the book assumes a narrative density which justifies the double meaning of the title, *Havalim*: bonds and pains. For what Be'er has created is a complex story of his growth as an artist within the seemingly hostile atmosphere of his religious Jerusalem family between his birth in 1945 and the publication of *Notsot* in 1979. The narrator is none other than Haim Be'er, the author of *Notsot*; the bonds he describes with an abundance of narrative detail are those of his conflicted pious Jerusalem family in which he has to forge his own self-consciousness and identity as a writer. From the very first chapters, the power of stories and storytelling is the dominant theme which both lends the book its variegated narrative density and constitutes the psychological cocoon in which he grows and must eventually escape. His ultra-pious maternal grandmother, for instance, still a resident of the Batei Ungarin in the old Meah Shearim district, smothers him with her tales of her pious and learned ancestors going back to R. Yisrael of Shklov, who settled in Eretz Israel at the beginning of the nineteenth century. Her daughter, the narrator's acerbic mother, escaped the suffocating religiosity of her mother's house and moved to the Geula quarter which, in the 1940s and 1950s, was not yet the ultra-orthodox neighborhood it is today. The narrator, Haim

Be'er, grew up in that neighborhood where his parents ran a Tenuvah dairy shop; it is one of the central locales of the narratives of this memoir/novel. Both the mother and the father had had painful previous marriages and were poorly matched: she was an acerbic, astute observer of human behavior, a voracious reader who had broken the bonds to her ultra-orthodox background; he, considerably older than she, devoted much of his energy to a local synagogue and the pious, often eccentric, men of the neighborhood. All these characters either told or inspired scores of odd tales which populate the imagination of the young boy who is to become the author Haim Be'er.

And yet, it is from the author Haim Be'er and in his voice that we hear all these stories that are strategically, novelistically ordered and detailed for maximum effect. The narrator is ever conscious of the enduring relationships between these bizarre stories, the world they embody, and his growing sense of self as an author. He refers repeatedly to other novels, often those his mother read and discussed; he repeatedly compares his act of writing this book to Nabokov's *Speak, Memory,* also an evocation of family memory by a maturing author. The reader cannot escape echoes of Joyce's *Portrait of the Artist as a Young Man,* a religious environment from which the young author must escape; the religious institutions and rites; the attempt to forge in the smithy of the individual soul a coherent, expressive consciousness.

The narrator relates the adventure of his painful yet exhilarating emergence as a writer, his "havalim." He writes from the perspective of Ramat Gan to which he had moved from Jerusalem once he married and began a career as a journalist. This geographical move supported the perspective he gained over the period from his childhood in Geula in the late 1940s to his maturity in the Tel Aviv literary world in the late 1960s.

The appeal of *Havalim* derives from its rich Hebrew, its evocation of a period and world which are past but, perhaps even more so, from its fascinating hybridity: part memoir, part novel, it challenges the reader's imagination. For while we are aware that Be'er is writing a memoir based on his experiences, his technique is that of the experienced novelist, in its construction of individual scenes and larger units of discourse. The tensions between the technique of the memoirist and that of the novelist are perennial and, if handled properly — as they are here — aesthetically productive. The novelist can readily speak through an unreliable narrator, while the memoirist must attempt to be reliable, to be true to his efforts to re-create the past. Be'er is relentless in his efforts to re-create and interpret the experiences which have made him who he is and often devotes lengthy passages to the problems of the narrator's struggle with memory. This tension, nevertheless, does not corrupt the integrity of his text or his style. Like similar "post-modern" texts which defy easy categorization, and fuse and confound traditionally disparate types of narration, *Havalim* demands of its reader an attention to its internal tensions which enrich it measurably.

Arnold J. Band

The Pure Element of Time

Grandmother was afraid of death.

She didn't admit it — and would even say, with a modesty al-
loyed with more than a trace of arrogance, that she was afraid
only of the verdict of God when she'd stand before Him on Judgment Day — but I discovered that fear when a peacock stood like
a devil in our path at the Bible Zoo.

Father and I had already been to visit the zoo on the Sabbath
when it first opened to the general public, but Grandmother
heard about it from our neighbor Reb Yitzhak Bak, the artist
who drew naïve Sukkah decorations and images for the "Eastern
Wall." "Just like real life," she praised the four animals he had
drawn on the ceiling of the temple in the advanced yeshiva in
Meah Shearim, to illustrate for the students the commandment
to "Be bold as a tiger and light as an eagle, run like a deer, and be
brave as a lion to do the will of Our Father in Heaven," and she
said that, in her eyes, he was a wise-hearted artist, a real Bezalel
ben Uri of our day. "But great are the feats of Our God," stated
the pious Bak humbly, stroking his pointed beard and running
his fingers through his graying hair, as he told her that instead
of marveling at his wretched imitations of flesh and blood, she
would do better to go to the zoo and see with her own eyes the
handiwork of the Lord, for who in the heaven can be compared
unto the Lord? Who among the sons of the mighty can be likened unto the Lord?

Afterward, Grandmother regularly visited the small Jerusalem
zoo that settled on the northern crest of the city when it was
exiled from Mount Scopus after the War of Independence. Now
and then, on an ordinary weekday morning, she would come to
our house and take me there, accompanied by Mother's explicit
blessing, for Mother didn't think anything bad would happen to

her son if he were absent from school a few times at the end of third grade.

The zoo's founders wanted to collect all the animals mentioned or alluded to in the Bible, from the serpent more subtle than any beast of the field and the big crocodile lying in the midst of his streams, to the hoopoe, the legendary wild chicken that went as Solomon's emissary to the Queen of Sheba bearing his threatening missive in its mouth — all that stirred Grandmother's imagination. She fell, unwittingly, under the lunatic charm of the Zionist dream that wanted to reunite the real objects of biblical fauna and flora, which had been dried for generations between the pages of the Book of Books like a cyclamen or the sloughed-off skin of a snake, with the concrete, semi-wild landscapes of the Land that opened its eyes onto the world.

Grandmother loved to wander around there with me, among the cages in the small pine grove skittering down to the barren wadi marking the border with Jordan. With a varying blend of fear and amazement, she watched the Syrian bears waging a battle of bites and trying to geld one another, and then she intoned the words of Solomon, the wisest of all men, who could tell the difference between a braying ass and a chirping bird: "Let a man meet a she-bear robbed of her cubs, rather than a fool in his folly," which were printed alongside the scientific name of the animal. She looked for the badgers hiding in artificial crevices, and there she read: "The badgers are a people not mighty, yet they make their homes in the rocks." Or she lingered at the ostrich pen, gazing for a long time at their big eggs laid on the earth, and then she solemnly recited the words of God replying to Job out of the whirlwind: "The wings of the ostrich wave proudly . . . for she leaves her eggs to the earth, and lets them be warmed on the ground." And she said that her father, head of the scribes of the Austro-Hungarian consul in Jerusalem, had trained in Vienna to do miniature artistic writing on ostrich eggs.

On our way home, Grandmother would avert her eyes from the menacing church spire of the Schneller Orphanage, ignoring the German Lamb of God striding there, with a proud foot on the heights of the Land and a Crusader banner held aloft in his tail, and would say that we Jews should be proud of our forefathers, who gave the world the Bible — everything is written in that book and nothing is more wonderful, neither in the heavens above nor on the earth below.

There was in the zoo only one animal Grandmother used various unconvincing excuses to avoid meeting face to face — the peacock. That bird, a member of the pheasant family, is not really mentioned by name in the Bible, but the founders of the Bible Zoo relied apparently on the King James and the Vulgate, which translated parrots — the birds imported by Solomon in ships from Tarshish along with herds of monkeys — as peacocks, and took them in under their aegis. The mature peacocks who walked around freely in the zoo did prefer solitude in remote places, unfrequented by visitors, but sometimes, especially in the morning, they would come out of hiding and amble along the paths.

One morning — in retrospect, it would turn out to be our last visit together to the zoo — a peacock suddenly burst out at us. Grandmother tried to hurry to another path, but I stood stock still, fascinated by the bird whose long regal tail dragged behind him heavily in the mud. The peacock fixed his little eyes on us and then, as if on an internal command, he raised his tail with an astonishing movement and opened it like a fan with countless gleaming eyes, blue, green, and yellow, spread out before us in a bold display. Grandmother covered her face with the lace shawl on her shoulders, like the prophet of Tishbe in Gilead at the mouth of the cave of God in Horeb, but when the bird fluttered his tail and his wings, gaped his beak open and uttered a shuddering shriek, she grabbed my hand and pulled me away, muttering in terror, "We've got to get away."

We made our way in silence, almost running, among the stone houses with red roofs, the houses of the Schneller teachers, and only when we were in the heart of Makor-Barukh and the peacock's shrill mating cries were drowned out in the sounds of life, only then did Grandmother break the silence, and with her hand still clutching mine, she said, "Did you see the thousand eyes he opened on us?"

That night, when I told my parents what happened, Mother's judgment that Grandmother saw the peacock's fan of eyes as the Angel of Death annoyed Father. "Stop that," he protested. "The child doesn't have to know everything." But Mother, who always refused to hide anything from me, explained that the Sages of the Talmud pictured the Angel of Death as a creature full of eyes like a peacock, whose eyes roam from one end of the world to the other, and when a person passes away, he stands at the head of his bed with a drawn sword in his hand.

Grandmother did not bring up that embarrassing episode again — "the incident with the *paveh*," as Father put it — but a few weeks later, as we were returning late one morning from Petah Tikva, the day after the wedding of Nathaniel, Aunt Nehama's son, the repressed thoughts rose to the surface. The bus was crawling on the narrow mountain road going up to Jerusalem. Grandmother, who didn't like to sleep in strange beds, even if those beds were in the houses of her own children, was dozing next to Father on the seat behind us. Mother was impatient. She was afraid that when our regular customers saw the locked door of our grocery shop, they would desert us for our competitors, and so she was prattling on nonstop.

Mother surveyed the forsaken stone houses of Lifte, clutching like stubborn goats to the steep slope on our left, and she asked if I knew that the name of the Arab village, whose inhabitants had fled in '48, preserves the ancient Hebrew name of the Waters of Nephtoah mentioned in the Book of Joshua. Mother, who saw travelling as a necessary waste of time to be used in disseminating knowledge, went on to explain that the Waters of Nephtoah were apparently named after Pharaoh Merneptah, who got this far on his military campaign in Canaan, in the period of settlement of the Hebrew tribes, and gathered up this village and the spring at its foothills, along with many other villages as if he were gathering up abandoned eggs.

Grandmother, who heard the word Pharaoh in her sleep, opened her eyes in terror and asked if Passover was already at hand and she hadn't yet made any preparations for it, hadn't even bought eggs. Mother chuckled and said that if this slow trip of the GMC went on endlessly like this, we would indeed get home just before the holiday.

Right at the entrance to the city, Father cast a long glance at the elongated, barracks-like structure stretching to the left of the road, where the Central Bus Station now stands. The low, barred windows, half sunk into the ground, looked out at us with veiled eyes. Behind the crumbling, dusty window blinds, the tenants of the United Old Age Home for Men and Women, many of them Grandmother's friends and acquaintances, ended their days waiting for death. Then he shifted his eyes right to the place where the telephone company had recently erected a modern office building, while the gloomy low building that stood there back in those days, hidden by a high stone wall and a locked iron gate, housed the mental hospital for women. On a veranda stretching along the whole second floor, screened like a cage above the height of a human being, abstract figures in pajamas flitted back and forth, shouting and weeping in terrifying voices. After Father had sated his eyes on the lunatics, he burst out, to my great embarrassment, in a cantorial wailing as on the Days of Awe. "Do not abandon us in old age, when our strength is spent do not forsake us," he sang in a weepy voice, waving his hand left toward the old age home and then turned it right with a grandiose gesture to the lunatic asylum, "and the spirit of Your Holiness do not take from us."

"This time your father's right," Mother said to me in a voice louder than necessary. "The fate of old people waiting idly for death and the shouts of lunatics bursting out of that cage should frighten a person, not the shouts of mindless wingèd creatures doing stupid mating dances." And then she glanced back to see if Grandmother got the hint.

"Blessed is the person who is always afraid," Grandmother gave as good as she got, and added righteously that we human beings, who live in clay houses, should also be afraid of the hour when we are visited by labor pains and of birth itself.

"I could never understand why you always cloak death in parables of birth and life," grumbled Mother.

"Stop it now, I'm coming back from my grandson's wedding," Grandmother cut her off, and to change the subject, she asked why the bus was still going so slow.

"Because a truck broke down near Wallach," Father explained on his return from the front of the bus. And indeed, next to the funeral hall of Sha'arei Tsedek Hospital—the hospital of *der meshuggener daytsh*, as we called him—was a truck loaded with chickens, and another truck was backed up to the back of that truck, and porters were quickly moving the chickens' cages from one platform to another.

"You see, my boy," said Grandmother as Father and Mother were busy preparing to get off at the Mahane Yehuda police station, "when one automobile breaks down and can't move anymore, a new automobile needs to come to it and take off the birds so they won't die." And after she examined my face to see if I had caught her meaning, she added in a whisper that she'd be very happy if I could come to her that evening, "since we've got to make some transports, too."

2

Grandmother loved to tell stories.

She'd start in the morning, sitting erect at the table as if that were her work, and read with an insatiable lust all the printed matter that fell into her hands. "I'm like a bee," she'd say, with a blend of apology and pride, when someone came to visit her and wondered at the heap of books, pamphlets and newspapers piled up during the weekdays on her round dining-room table, covered with a flowered oilcloth, and fully extended to make room for them all.

Mother addressed this issue the day my first prose piece, the opening chapter of *Feathers*, was published in one of the literary supplements. Her sharp eye wouldn't miss the eclectic nature of my writing, a quality she regarded as inferior, and she felt obliged to comment on it to me. After praising and encouraging me to the skies, for some reason she started talking about her mother. "Blood is thicker than water," she asserted and said that no one would deny that I inherited my narrative talent from Grandmother, but that I should be careful not to make her my model. "You have to look for your own materials inside you and not in the world of others, to hew them, as the poet says, from the cliffs of your heart." Grandmother's reliance on the outside world Mother could understand, since somebody who was forced to sit in one place most of her life would have to walk with a cane if he wanted to venture out in old age, but a young person should trust his own forces and strive to walk on his own. "You surely remember that Grandmother compared herself to a bee." To avoid the embarrassment evoked by her candor, Mother said that a Symbolist poet would probably write about Grandmother that she'd secretly bring the nectar she gathered so diligently to the hidden hives of the soul and concoct the honey of charms that sweetened her waning days.

At first, Grandmother read the random collection of books in her house—about fifteen books, crammed on the top shelf of the pantry, mostly the remnants of the book collection she and Grandfather inherited from their forefathers. During the famine years of World War I—the worldwide war, as she put it—they were forced to sell most of the books they had for pennies, including rare books printed by the first Jerusalem presses, to buy rye bread, a little corn and a measure of Portugals, as oranges were called back then, so they'd have something to feed the children.

After Grandfather's death, other books disappeared, including copies of the *Humash, Midrash,* and a few tractates of the Talmud, which, according to Grandmother, were taken by his brother during the seven days of mourning, the *shiva,* when she was all confused. She was left with only a woman's prayer book, *Korban-Minha,* that she had received the day she got married, bound in olive wood, with an image of Rachel's Tomb etched on it; a book of supplications for women, whose pages were yellowed with teardrops, and *Menorat Ha-Me'or,* written by the Sephardi sage, Rabbi Yitzhak Aboab. The book with greenish pages, that still showed traces of the water they had absorbed in Slovita in 1828 to prepare them for the printing press, was accompanied by an *Ivri-taytsh* translation, intended to instill reverence in the hearts of the women it was written for. And the cabinet also contained two volumes of the Maskil book, *Paths of the World,* which Grandfather, who thirsted for wanderings and journeys, purchased with his last pennies. But since he was fated never to leave the bounds of Jerusalem, not even for Jaffa, he'd find solace in his few free hours in poring over those Jewish Baedeckers from the end of the previous century.

There was also a thick German medical book, printed in Gothic script and replete with colored diagrams of the human body. That was used by my great-grandfather, Rabbi Moshe Yules, a self-taught physician, who was known in Jerusalem as the supporter of the hernia of the Gaon of Brisk. Rabbi Joshua Leyb Diskin, rumor had it, suffered from a hernia that got caught now and then, "playing at propitious times" in Mother's golden tongue, and because the elderly Jerusalem sage refused "to go under the knife" because he didn't trust surgery, the pious physician was summoned to him from time to time to extricate the trapped intestines with awe and reverence and to set them free. After the death of "the doctor from Pressburg," the book lost its importance and it was deposited with his son, and his widow, that is, Grandmother, so that her grandchildren would find entertainment in it, inasmuch as they came to visit her largely because of it, for in its pages they saw for the first time in their lives the anatomy of the human body and slaked their curiosity about breasts and genitals.

Beside the "red book," as we called the secret medical book, a few of Mother's old books were also kept in Grandmother's old cabinet, to Mother's dismay. These included Waldstein's pocket Hebrew-English dictionary, whose words she had memorized devotedly when she still believed she could elude her fate and emigrate to America, and that there, in the "new world," she could turn over a new leaf; volume two of the writings of Scholem Asch; an old translation of *The Soul Enchanted* by Romain Rolland; and Flaubert's *Salambo,* a gift from the cursèd husband of her youth when they were engaged. Those books, and a few other objects she took from her husband after her first marriage collapsed, were brought after her to her parents' home, where she fled. After she married my father they all stayed where she had left them. She probably had a souvenir of sin from that chapter of her life that she wanted to erase from her memory. Only two books from those days, *Anna Karenina* and *Madame Bovary,* did I find in our house. I guess that was because of the solace they provided in her days of affliction and because she identified with the lives of those two heroines.

Grandmother, who was about eighty years old at the time I'm talking about, didn't know how to read and write until she was fifty, except maybe for some ability to follow the obstacle course of the leader in the synagogue with a hesitant finger in the prayer books. Even today, many years after her death, it's still hard for me to utter the words "Grandmother was illiterate." With the force of their faith, the zealous and pious men who ruled her life, first her father and then her husband, deprived her of the right reserved solely for them, the right to acquire knowledge. From the day she knew her own mind, in the 1880s, in the Jerusalem of those lost days, illuminated by the splendid light of the Ottoman decadence, they drummed into her ears the words of David, the sweet psalmist of Israel, that the king's daughter is all glorious within, and sealed off her world at the borders of the women's section of the synagogue, the kitchen, and the nursery. Her name, Hannah, she once told me, was an anagram for *H*allah, *N*o relations during menstruation, and lighting *H*oly candles, the three commandments women have to observe strictly lest they die in childbirth. Mother used to say that Grandmother's limited world began where the desires and demands of the men in her life ended.

But after she was widowed and four of her eight surviving children emigrated to America, and the others, except Mother who stayed in Jerusalem, moved to Tel Aviv and Ramat Gan, her life opened like a late-blooming rose. Secretly and without anybody's help, she started teaching herself to read for real and not just to follow the prayers and the Torah reading, and especially to write. Mother said that in those days she wondered what the books of Flaubert and Romain Rolland were doing on her table and what the mysterious ink spots on her fingers meant, and when she asked her, Grandmother blushed as if she had been caught *in flagrante delicto* and said that old books needed to be aired out from time to time, otherwise the moths ate them, and the ink spots she explained as an unsuccessful attempt to dye the sweaters and the wool jacket from America black or dark blue, since a pious old woman living in the Hungarian Houses couldn't possibly go out into the city with loud colorful clothes like a New York girl.

Mother, who knew that was a lame explanation, held her tongue until the eve of Rosh Hashanah, when all of Grandmother's offspring, from the oldest daughter in Wilmington, Delaware, to her great-granddaughter in New York, were surprised to get a "new year's" card from her written in her own hand. The paper was scratched and bruised, and the handwriting was angular, shaky and inept: she hadn't gotten the hang of controlling the movement of the nib and couldn't figure out just when to dip the pen in the inkwell, so the writing alternated between thick and thin. The style and the lack of mistakes in the writing showed that Grandmother had obviously copied the letters verbatim from an old correspondence textbook that had wound up in the house from the days when Grandfather still secretly cherished the hope of becoming a successful merchant and sent a lot of business letters to Odessa, Pressburg, and Vienna.

Grandmother herself played down the importance of her achievement and explained it as a practical matter: the desire to keep in touch with her children, who in troubled times had scattered to all the ends of the earth, and not to depend on someone else to write her letters for her, letting family secrets out of the bag. But Mother saw it as a triumph of the human spirit over the circumstances of her life and the triumph of the aspiration for education over the ignorance and backwardness that had been an inherited disease in our family from generations back. She rejected Grandmother's explanation out of hand, and saw it only as part of the cunning and sophisticated female technique she had acquired in her youth to curb dissension, to keep from waking the villains who sought to hurt her from their lair and to ward them off with a soft reply, a proven device for repelling wrath. "Take very good care of Grandmother's letters," Mother ordered me shortly before her death. "They're a wonderful human document, maybe even more than the letters of famous authors that you keep like the apple of your eye in your archive."

After she mastered the art of writing, Grandmother would write two or three letters every day, letters that over time were copied almost whole from the dry and standard formulations of the correspondence textbook and became personal essays in which she expressed her view of the world and were the creation of her soul and her life.

But she became especially fervent about reading. "This is my comfort in my affliction, for thy word hath quickened me," she would sometimes quote from the Book of Psalms, which she made sure to read from start to finish every morning when she awoke, and only then did she turn to the non-religious books. When she finished reading the books in her house, she started borrowing books of ethics and Hasidic tales from neighbors and relatives, and she even used the money she saved from the monthly allowance her children sent her to buy more books in the gloomy shops of Meah Shearim, where, in that male fortress, her presence was an extraordinary phenomenon that stirred their curiosity. "Your grandmother was a spitfire," Rabbi Abraham Rubenstein once told me. He was one of my acquaintances among the booksellers, and with a smile that couldn't conceal his admiration, he added: "If she had lived in the days of the judges, she would have sat under the date tree and the Children of Israel would have come to her to be judged."

She asked Mother to borrow reading books and popular scientific pamphlets from the turn of the century from the B'nai B'rith Library on Ha-Habashim Street. She herself wouldn't set foot in the library. "Because it wouldn't look right for her," said Mother, who lovingly filled her requests, "to enter the library her forefathers had sealed with the ban of the ancients, threatening with coals of fire the transgressors who dared visit it." From me, Grandmother would take volumes of the youth encyclopedia *Source* with information about remote tribes in Borneo and equatorial Africa and the inhabitants of China and India, and popular books about scientific discoveries, from the discovery of steam and electricity to the invention of the telegraph and radar. She was especially entertained by the Yiddish newspapers my uncle Isaac, the son of her old age who lived in America, started sending her every month, by surface mail, where Isaac Bashevis Singer under his pseudonym, Varshavski, published his stories in serial form. She was like a child who discovered the magic of reading, and she soon became an expert on the legends of the Talmud and adventures of the Jews in the Middle Ages, astronomy and alchemy, the marvelous animals of the continent of Australia, the voyages of Marco Polo, Columbus, Vespucci, and Vasco da Gama, and even the route of the Trans-Siberian railroad.

What she weighed and investigated in her ardent reading, she didn't keep to herself. In the afternoon, Grandmother would place her chair in the doorway of her house, facing the long narrow yard, enclosed between the two rows of the Hungarian Houses, and all her aged and dejected lady friends from the "Old Yishuv" would sally forth from their apartments, each woman with a chair in hand, and sit around her. Like a tribal storyteller, she would tell them the parable of the prince who imagined one day that he was a chicken, the annals of the construction of the Great Wall of China, and the unbelievable story of the Pygmy tribes in Africa. Nor did she spare them the deeds of the hypocrites (charlatans, as she put it), who take pity on little worms and are careful not to tread on them as they walk on the road, but are corrupt through and through. Afterward, in the short time between afternoon and evening prayer, when the men were in the synagogue, she would divulge some current events: about the war in Korea and the atom bomb, about the Rosenberg trial in America, about the Finaly children, whom the Catholic nuns refused to give back to their people after the Holocaust, and about the quarrels in the top ranks of the Kremlin after the Georgian Ham kicked the bucket — things she read in the year-old *Forverts* and *Amerikaner*. Inadvertently, in her own special way, she'd distort the names of the leaders and the politicians: she made Ben-Gurion's name sound like a sedative for those afflicted with nervous disorders or like a flower, and she mangled Winston Churchill's name until it sounded like some accursed intestinal parasite.

Once I caught her in the act. Grandmother, like Grandfather, who had never been outside the borders of the Land of Israel, and hadn't even gotten to Safed or Tiberias, resurrected the capital of the lost Austro-Hungarian Empire in the heart of the enclosed and modest courtyard of the Hungarian Houses. With expressive words and a hypnotic force, she thrust between the cobblestones the pure gold sword that Maria Theresa strapped to her thigh when the Hungarian crown was placed on her head, and from that she stretched the strings of the imaginary Vienna. She took the women up the spiral staircase of 753 stone steps to the heights of the tower of the Stefankirche to view the temples of splendor and the internal city, surrounded by a canal; then she took them down, trembling and frightened, to the chilly and gloomy cellars of the Capuchin tombs, where, in ornate, gigantic palaces, the bodies of the Habsburg emperors are buried, with Franz Josef first; she roamed with them in the parks and streets, crossed bridges, lingered at the statues of the lords of the land, and finally brought them into the depths of the Schweizerhof, the lodging of the Emperor and Empress, that palace of perfect beauty and great splendor, with the house of exquisite delights.

The tour of that city, which Grandmother, the last of the faithful subjects of the Austro-Hungarian Emperor, made from the old travel book published by Abraham Mendel Mohr in 1880 in Josefon, ended at the corner of Graben and Kertnerstrasse. There, at the corner of the house, she said, a thick wooden beam was nailed, seven feet high, all full of pegs and rusty iron nails, with a big lock at the top. Many years ago, Grandmother told her slack-jawed listeners, a locksmith had come here, hung a big lock on the top of a tree in the square, and announced that he had thrown the key into the Danube and would shower gold crowns upon anyone who could open the perfect lock he had made. Many artists tried their hand in vain, and before they withdrew in shame, they stuck a peg or a nail into the board as a memento. The women adjusted their kerchiefs, raised their eyes to Grandmother, who smiled sweetly and dismissed it casually, "wisdom of Gentiles, believe, Torah of Gentiles, don't believe," and they said to one another that a person could sit here, in the Holy City, and see castles in Spain.

About thirty years later, late one night, I took my wife there right after we arrived in Vienna for the first time in our lives. Without a map and without asking any of the passersby for help, we walked quickly in the streets of the foreign city, with the December skies hanging low and heavy over them, and near the Stefankirche, at the crossroad, in the doorway of the bank, we stood still. Two bald young men, wrapped in orange sheets, politely offered to sell us the books of their sect. "This is the place," I said with no hesitation; I raised my head and pointed to the corner of the house. The ancient wood board was indeed there, in the center of it was a big lock, and around it were countless nails, illuminated by the pale silvery light of the street lamp. And the only thing that was new for me was the round fiberglass covering the board, to protect it from the ravages of time.

3

In the evening, when Grandmother remained alone, forsaken as a stone in the field, and the dark and the dread of destruction besieged her little room—where the life of generations stood still in a strange blend of immortality and crumbling, as Gershom Scholem wrote of his encounter with the "Old Yishuv" in Jerusalem—the stories were her only allies.

Beyond the two big windows facing Saint Paul Street, behind the one-story house, stern and restrained in its modesty, the first house of Doctor and Mrs. Ticho, beyond the Romanian church with its pink walls, whose octagonal tower has been lopped off by an enemy shell, the border flickered in the white light: A field covered with a carpet of white-yellow chamomile flowers. "Don't let the apparent serenity mislead you." Mother would warn me that among the gigantic Herodian stones—stones of the third wall of King Agrippas—lying there in ditches hidden from the city, land mines were buried. A straying mule once wound up between the barbed wire fences in his search for a pasture, and his mashed limbs were scattered all over. The roars of the explosions that sometimes horrified the late-summer afternoon serenity, when fires suddenly spread in the thorns, confirmed her remarks.

Outside, shadows rustled in the thicket of abandoned houses caught in No-Man's-Land, bumping into facades pocked by bullets and shrapnel: the evil spirits of Jordanian Legionnaires, their faces covered with red-and-white Kaffiyas, or of menacing infiltrators. And inside, the fear of the siege shakes the crowded room smelling of a smoky kerosene lamp, camphor ointment, and the sour taste of unaired bedclothes, and it sinks into sleep.

Sometimes I stayed there overnight.

Grandmother would lie shriveled up in her place, like old Eli in the house of God in Shiloh, burrowing into the ashes of memories, taking handfuls from it and casting them straight ahead to appease the demons of night and to mollify the terror. She even called on her dead forefathers—rabbis, whose "pillar of light" was seen emanating from their body when they passed away—and she told the story of her old, crumbling family, a proud and pedigreed family, that lost its importance as the generations declined, an incoherent story with many twists and turns, a sequence of marvels and tribulations, miraculous guests, barons and kings.

Shadows strolled on the thick stone walls, darkening the family pictures one by one, and she'd talk to me from the distance, before the candle of God went out, and I, as Nabokov writes in *Speak, Memory*, would feel as if I were thrown all at once into something radiant and moving, which was simply the pure element of time.

An excessive affection, almost a familiarity, did Grandmother feel for Bonaparte.

"Who was Napoleon, do you know?" she asked one evening when I stayed overnight at her house, and since she never put much stock in the education I was getting in school, she didn't wait for my answer, and immediately went far back to the remote regions of the past.

In strong, expressive words, the woman, who as I said never left the Land of Israel, described the endless, snow-covered plains of Russia, where the remnants of Napoleon's beaten and hungry units plodded on in 1812, retreating west, after the defeat they had suffered on the outskirts of Moscow, with the Cossack cavalry cutting off stragglers and pursuing them in forests and villages.

One day, Grandmother told, a rich Jewish merchant from Mohilev, Reb Yosef Yona ben Ya'akov Aharon Luria, went to his big warehouse near Smolensk, and that day, he lingered in the isolated warehouse at the edge of the forest, something he usually didn't do. He stayed until afternoon, and recited the afternoon prayer all by himself. And as he was reciting the Amidah prayer, a solitary cavalryman rode out of the forest on a tired horse, stopped next to the Jew who was absorbed in prayer, and waited in the doorway of the warehouse for him to finish.

"Good-hearted Jew, I, Napoleon Emperor of France, place himself in your hands. Save me," Grandmother would cling to the plea of the retreating commander. "Show me the way to go to my country and my kindred."

The surprised Jewish merchant immediately showed him the way through the dense forest, but the quick response itself evoked fear in Napoleon's heart lest that was only a tactic, and he started pleading with Luria not to turn him over to the Russians.

Here, Grandmother would break off the story, both to increase the tension and to stir respect and admiration for the scion of our family, and she'd say, "Reb Yosef Yona was one of the offspring of the Maharshal, Rabbi Shlomo Luria, author of the book *Sea of Shlomo*. And you, if you ever swim in the sea of Talmud, I have no doubt you will also reach his bay."

When she talked about her mother's family, the Luria family, you could hear a kind of regal pride in her voice. The roots of the family reached back to early medieval Mainz. About a thousand years ago, the Jewish community there in the heart of the vineyards, near where the Main River pours into the Rhine, was led, she said, by the ancient patriarch of the family: Rabbi Kalonymus ben Rabbenu Meshulam ben Rabbenu Kalonymus of Lucca, who was brought to Mainz from Lombardy in Italy, according to ancient tradition, by the Emperor Charlemagne.

"You don't believe me?" Pain permeated her voice. And then, in the dark dominated by longing and yearning, as her distant forebears put it, "Who remembers all that was forgotten. You will open the Book of Chronicles — it will read itself," from the prayer "Let Us Now Relate the Power," attributed to Rabbi Amnon of Mainz. On the third day after his martyrdom at the hands of the bishop of Mainz, she said, Rabbi Amnon appeared in a dream to Rabbenu Kalonymus and taught him that liturgical poem and ordered him to send it all over the Diaspora to be a memory forever, and the words were written in the prayer books for Rosh Hashanah and Yom Kippur.

The first time I returned to that story of Grandmother's was about forty years later, one morning in early spring 1995, in the ancient prayer house attributed to Rashi (who, by the way, was also one of the descendants of Rabbenu Kalonymus) in the heart of the Jewish quarter of Worms. A small group of Israeli and

German writers had gathered there, and I ascended to the stone Bima, where men had been called up to the Torah for many generations, until the building was destroyed by the Nazis on Kristallnacht, and in a trembling voice I read that liturgical poem. And a still, small voice was heard and the echo that came back to me from the Gothic arches was the voice of Grandmother. When the poet Friedrich Christian Delius ascended to the Bima after me and read the Hebrew text in the German translation, I seemed to hear from the walls the voice of his father, the Protestant minister of Hesse, and of his grandfather, who had been the bishop of Mainz.

"Are you still awake?" asked Grandmother, who was so pleased by the description of the humble condition of the fleeing Corsican before the descendant of Rashi and the Maharshal — Gentile and Jew facing one another, as she thought proper. And for another long hour, she detailed the words of the Law imparted by the merchant of Mohilev to the unexpected guest. Luria calmed the Emperor, convinced him not to worry, for those who are well-versed in the Law are enjoined not to turn over one king to another, and a pious Jew will not deny what the sages of his faith commanded.

He also invited Napoleon to rest in the warehouse, gave him food and drink, and when night fell, led him seven leagues into the dense forest until they came to the road leading west. When they parted, Grandmother went on, Napoleon took off his greatcoat, the green velvet greatcoat, held it out to the merchant and said he was giving him the cloak as a sign of gratitude for the goodness he had shown him, and Luria, who was moved by the imperial gesture, took off his Jewish cloak and placed it on the shoulders of the Frenchman who was trembling with cold and dread.

And what always happened in stories also happened to him, and on his way home in the forest, robbers assailed him. They wanted to steal his greatcoat, but he managed to persuade them to take only the gold letters, NB, on the lapels, and the gold buttons, and they left him the cloak. He hid it in his house, because if it was discovered that he had saved the Emperor, not only would he pay for it with his head, but he might also bring disaster onto his family, the Jewish community of Mohilev, and perhaps all the Jews of Russia. Only three years later, when the tempest of war subsided, did he take the cloak out of hiding, make it into curtains for the Ark of the Covenant and swore to bring it up someday to Jerusalem, the city of the great King, as befitting a royal garment.

"And what embellished an earthly king," said Grandmother with the humility of the victors, "now becomes the beauty of the Heavenly King."

When the son of Rabbi Yosef Yona, Rabbi Ze'ev Wolf Luria, ascended to the Land of Israel in 1851, he took the Torah Curtain with him, wrapped around his body, and brought it to Jerusalem. His son, Rabbi Nathaniel Luria, gave it first to the "Menahem Zion" synagogue of his father-in-law, Rabbi Isaiah Bardaki, in the courtyard of the Hurva. When Nathaniel Luria and his wife Hannah moved outside the Old City walls, to Yemin Moshe, they took the Torah Curtain to their home and would bring it to their neighborhood synagogue on important Sabbaths and holidays.

"And as you know, Rabbi Nathaniel Luria was my grandfather," Grandmother wanted to conclude the story, "and I'm named Hannah after his wife."

By now, Grandmother wanted to withdraw to the world of sleep, but as someone who was taught to cast doubt on everything, I pestered her with a series of questions. First of all, I said, maybe the man Grandfather met wasn't Napoleon but one of his generals; second, I added another layer of appeal, what language did the two of them speak and even weave in the sayings of Our Sages of Blessed Memory; and third, maybe the real reason the Frenchman gave the greatcoat to the Jew was that he wanted to get rid of the garment that might give him away on his flight to the west. And to conclude the series of appeals with a crushing argument, I said that I didn't believe anything except what I saw with my own eyes, and could she show me the Torah Curtain someday or at least tell me where it was.

Here, Grandmother's voice became angry and turgid, and she said that the grandson of her grandfather, the son of Jacob Aharon, Mr. Isaiah Luria, took the green velvet Torah Curtain embroidered with gold and silver with him when he went to manage the Carmel Mizrahi wine shop in Port Said, and nobody knows what became of it after that.

"At least we've still got the story," she said and got out of bed to turn off the lamp and open the window a crack. "And if any of my grandchildren ever becomes a writer, he'll return to our family the Napoleon Torah Curtain embroidered with words which, as we know, lengthen your days more than any other fabric."

And only years later did I find out, almost by accident, that Mr. Isaiah Luria, whom Grandmother could never forgive, didn't take the Torah Curtain for himself, but deposited it for safe-keeping in the Museum of Anthropology and Folklore in Haifa. The curator sent the Torah Curtain to France, and there it was determined that the green velvet and the splendid embroidery was indeed the style during the Napoleonic period.

In 1985, the Torah Curtain was exhibited in the Israel Museum in Jerusalem, as part of an exhibit called "Ascent to Holiness — from Secular to Holy, Second Use in Jewish Art." When I stood before the lost Torah Curtain of my childhood and looked at it, I saw that it was indeed sewn from parts of a greatcoat, and I could even make out small strips of fabric like those under sleeves. And the dents left by the buttons were also there, the big gold buttons of the imperial coat that remained more than 170 years after the donor Joseph ben Ya'akov Luria of Mohilev May-His-Light-Shine was forced to tear them out and consign them to hands of the robbers in the forest.

"The cloak and faith to whoever for eternal life," Grandmother's triumphant voice passed through the lighted, airy hall of the Jerusalem Museum, as clear and fresh as the morning wind.

4

My mother couldn't bear her mother's compulsive preoccupation with the family chronicles, and so my attraction to Grandmother's nocturnal stories made her angry. "Who were those forefathers of ours that you and your grandmother are so proud to share your beds with?" Mother accused me when I went overboard, in her opinion, and spent more nights in the small room in the Hungarian Houses than in our house. "Obscurantists, and if by the stroke of fate, you were, God forbid, put in their tyrannical control, you'd curse your days." At best, she saw me as a naïve fool falling into a trap set for him by nostalgia, and at worst, she asserted sharply, I was an irresponsible boy, whose desires could bring disaster down on him and others. And to illustrate her words, she said that when she played in the moldy cellar extending in the depths of the earth all along the Hungarian Houses, among the Sukkot walls stored there, she found thin gold threads, shining and quivering, a real delight to behold, and only the shouts of her older sister Rachel warned her that they were simply day-old snakes. "Your forefathers were a coil of vipers and everybody who reaches out his hand to their hole risks his life," she said, and harshly enumerated their iniquities.

The main sinner, according to her, was Rabbi Isaiah Bardaki — Grandmother's great-grandfather and the son-in-law of Rabbi Israel of Shklov, the patriarch of our family in the Land of Israel — who led the Ashkenazi community in Jerusalem five or six generations ago and waged war against every manifestation of the Enlightenment that popped up in the city. Rabbi Isaiah was a conservative leader, resolute and charismatic, and served as a consular agent of the Russian Consul, and afterward as a consular agent of the Jews of the Austro-Hungarian Empire — posts of great power in the corrupt and crumbling Ottoman Empire. Because of his position, he won the official recognition of the Turkish authorities and was given an interpreter, that is, a private secretary, and a liveried bodyguard who preceded him, banging a silver-knobbed staff to clear the way for him in the crowded, narrow alleys of the Old City. Rabbi Isaiah, Mother told, led the intransigent battle against the Viennese Jewish poet, August Ludwig Frankl, who came on behalf of Alice Herz to establish the first modern school here in memory of her noble father von Lemmel. "And instead of putting on his Sabbath clothes and going down to Motza to welcome the distinguished guest, who brought the Enlightenment to Jerusalem, with bread and salt, he set his seal at the top of an excommunication decree against him, and even ordered the writs to be tied to the tails of stray dogs who were run through the streets of the city to increase his disgrace." And Mother took a breath and said with bitter mockery that we — Grandmother and I — would do better to admit that if, God forbid, Rabbi Isaiah and his cohorts had triumphed, I wouldn't be attending a progressive school and preparing myself to be a modern person, and she would never have come to read books and newspapers or to write letters. "The only thing that interests her and you are stupid anecdotes about holy relics, like those Christians who yearn for beams of wood of the Cross or Moslems who preserve the hair of the beard of the Prophet in silver lockets," she laughed, meaning in fact the quill pen and the pillow brought by Sheindel, the daughter of Rabbi Israel of Shklov, as a dowry to her bridegroom, Rabbi Isaiah — a story Grandmother loved to tell.

It's a tale of a woman from the city of Selets in Lithuania, who once crossed the bridge over the River Romanovo holding her baby daughter. Suddenly the mother stumbled, and the child fell into the river with the pillow she was lying on. The terrified mother and the passers-by watched helplessly as the child sank in the water, and then, to everyone's surprise, the pillow rose on the flow, which changed course, and slowly approached the bank. The name of the baby who was saved from drowning was Trayna, and she was the mother of the Vilna Gaon. That pillow was given by the family of the Vilna Gaon as a gift to the wife of Rabbi Israel of Shklov, who was his student, just before she ascended to the Land of Israel so that she would be borne on it in the waters of the Mediterranean Sea, and she gave it as a gift to her daughter

Sheindel to bring as a dowry to Rabbi Isaiah Bardaki. Rabbi Israel himself gave his son-in-law the quill pen as a wedding gift, a feather from the wing of a goose that he got from the sons of the Vilna Gaon. With this quill pen, said Grandmother, the Vilna Gaon wrote the *Letter from Elijah* when he parted from his family and friends to ascend to the Land of Israel, an ascent that did not take place, as we know, because of hidden impediments. Rabbi Isaiah never used it, except one single time, when, as head of the sages and rabbis of Jerusalem, he signed the awful excommunication imposed on the poet Frankl and the school where foreign languages and sciences were taught, and ever since then, the quill pen vanished and its whereabouts are unknown. Mother, who was disgusted by that story, which she was forced to hear over and over, couldn't help adding that even the moth that ate the hundred-year-old goose quill, praise God, was more modern and progressive than those dark Orthodox humbugs.

"Ye shall know them by their fruits," Mother would quote, maybe unintentionally, the Christian verse, and conclude the description of the procession of the wickedness and foolishness of her family following the path of Rabbi Isaiah, with Grandfather's brothers. "You don't know them, the sons of the Wallace family, Tefillin makers and ritual fringe plaiters, who by day bind the angels with threads of blue cloth and holy strips of leather, and who before dawn would sneak into the house of their widowed sister-in-law, wife of their dead brother, and pour a chamber pot of slops on the threshold or smear the door with tar to protest that her children were disobeying the authorities of the 'community,' that they cut their sidelocks and took off the black clothes, the garments of the Exile, and dared go to the teachers' seminary of the Mizrahi to acquire knowledge."

According to Mother's descriptions, Grandmother was trying to be borne by the turgid flow of the life of her forefathers, which floods the tortuous caves of Jewish time so as to reach eternity. "Your grandmother is afraid of death — you've known that ever since the day you saw the peacock spread his tail — and with her cunning naïveté, so characteristic of women who live under oppression, she thinks that under the aegis of time, she'll succeed in reaching the End of Days, or at least, evading death and postponing it for a while."

"With the Angel of Death, no one has yet signed a contract," declared Mother. Ever since the death of her two little daughters from her first marriage, she had looked it in the face, refused any deal or negotiations with it, and came to the conclusion that only art can extricate a strip of life from its bony fingers and give it eternal life.

That view of the world, which she considered revolutionary and painfully bold, she owed to Anna Ticho.

One Saturday, Mother took me to the exhibit of her paintings in the pavilion of the "Artists' Union," south of the King David Hotel. For a long time we walked in silence past the huts with roofs of whitewashed, galvanized tin that housed the government offices at the end of the Mandate, and looked at the paintings that captured the outskirts of Jerusalem; following the invisible movement of the ridges — the landscape of terraces in the rocks of the mountains and on the mouths of deep valleys, the slow and diligent interference of man building "fences of living stones," and, without mortar, capturing within them the aspirations of stones to rejoin the incessant flow of nature, down down, with the force of floods sweeping away to the riverbeds, returning to their sisters, which even then, in ancient times, were swept up in the flow of water and turned into oval river pebbles. After we pored over the black-and-white pages where countless experiments were accumulated to decipher the secret of the Jerusalem existence, to break the code that directs rocks to converge with crabapple trees, a solitary olive tree, and light for a whole section of unprecedented landscape, Mother said that Anna Ticho was the hope of the scarlet thread in the weave of her childhood.

When we left the exhibit, we sat down on the bridge of the splendid hotel, the stone angel with six wings before us, as in Isaiah's vision, frozen on the YMCA tower, and Mother told about herself: a modest, shy girl from the Hungarian Houses, whose whole world was constricted among the staircases, the arches, the long balconies, and today, in the dark light of dusk, they remind her of DiChirico's metaphysical paintings. In melancholy and in the secrecy of the narrow passages, shadows lengthened in the doorways of the houses, and in a window, she, a pure maiden, rising from the bath, would plait her hair and look gloomily at the stone house across Saint Paul Street, home of the wonderful eye doctor, who saved many people from blindness, and his delicate painter wife, with soft eyes. In Mother's world, permeated with fanaticism, suffering, and hunger, the name Anna Ticho had a tinge I cannot express more precisely than a pleasure-of-culture.

In that house, for the first time, she encountered another world, a world that won her heart with its spirituality, its transparency, and its beauty. Sometimes, when her mother had a laundry day and the house was like a cauldron, she'd sneak to the yard across the street, to the building that now houses the ultra-Orthodox "Daughters of Jerusalem" school — where young maidens now come and go, reminding her of how she looked in her youth — pass among the bushes of the garden, rosebushes, if memory serves me right, and peep inside, through the window, to the private wing of the Viennese couple. Once Mrs. Ticho — as Mother insisted on calling her all her life — found her there and invited her in. And ever since, she became a welcome guest in the home of the painter who didn't have any children of her own. There her heart opened to the sweetness of culture, to the broadminded European home, with its carefully chosen carpets and furniture, and to the paintings hanging on the walls, paintings that tore open a window for her to expanses infinitely rich in sights. Mrs. Ticho would pour tea for herself and her little guest with the thin chestnut colored braids, in china cups painted with lavender flowers whose eye is like the eye of smoke, slice apple cake for her, and then invite her to the studio to see her paintings and to be there as she painted them.

"She even gave me a piece of charcoal and some paper that came from abroad and taught me to draw a tree," Mother stroked her fingers, wiping off invisible black spots, wetting the end of her handkerchief with saliva and cleaning my chin, and as her eye roved among the dusty cypresses in front of the YMCA, she said, "What I'd like most in the world is to be a painter."

5

On those long nights, Grandmother anointed me as the one to draw my family tree, and to prepare me for that responsibility, she wasn't satisfied with the long complicated chronicle she unfurled in my ears, but over and over, she also recited the annals.

"Look unto the rock whence ye are hewn and to the hole of the pit where ye are digged," she'd invoke Isaiah's injunctions to the children of his nation. "A Jew has to know who were his fathers and his fathers' fathers, as far back as he can go."

I heard the same kinds of things a few years later in Rabbi Abraham Rubenstein's bookstore from a person who shaped my literary world perhaps more than any other Hebrew creator. The store, at the end of Meah Shearim Street, next to the big flour mill that was destroyed and is replaced now by a yeshiva of the Bratslav Hasids, across from the houses of Naytin, was where I spent most of my time between my bar mitzvah and my wedding day. The dark store, with only a narrow doorway to the street, was called "The Light," as indicated by a square tin sign with black Scroll letters already rubbed out by rain and sun. Rabbi Abraham himself was a character out of Dickens. He'd sit scrunched up behind the counter piled high with books, and only his head was visible. He incessantly twirled his sidelocks which were wet with sweat or from bathing in the ritual bath, and was always sucking on mints, and his small and turgid eyes seemed to ask their owner what he was doing here in this Vale of Tears. From the very first day, he was fond of me and loved to play practical jokes on me, the practical jokes of a Talmud scholar. Once he put before me a wooden box crammed with books he had bought that day, and said that if I pointed to the most expensive book in the stack, he'd give it to me as a gift. To this day, my library contains *Merkava Shlema*—the basic book in the esoteric Heikhalot and

Merkava literature — which was published by Mr. Shlomo Mussai-
off in the year one thousand, nine hundred eleven as proof of
the greatest quiz I ever participated in. On one of my visits to that
store, a man was crouching in a corner. He wore a suit and hat
and looked like a well-to-do merchant, a former scholar, who
now, at the end of his days, was returning to his youthful love.
Hearing our lively conversation in Jerusalem Yiddish, the stranger
straightened up and asked me who I was. I replied. He asked me
who my father and mother were. I replied. He went on asking
me the names of my forefathers. When I came to Rabbi Israel of
Shklov, who was my grandmother's great-grandfather, I told him
that, as Rabbi Israel of Shklov wrote in the preface to *The Edge
of the Table*, he was the son of Rabbi Shmuel, the son of Rabbi
Ezriel, the son of Rabbi Moshe Brakha, the son of Rabbi Menahem Mendel the religious judge of all the provinces of Russia.
"And who were the forefathers of Rabbi Menahem Mendel the
presiding judge of all the provinces of Russia?" asked the stranger.
I shrugged and said I didn't know. He glanced at me and said
that a man had to know the pedigree of his ancestors at least back
to the First Adam. When the stranger said goodbye and disappeared around the corner, Rabbi Abraham Rubenstein told me
not to get too excited by the Galitzianer jokes and asked if I knew
who the man was. It was Agnon.

One winter Sabbath, when Grandmother was forbidden to use
the Biro — the ballpoint pen that was rare in those days, which
she got from America and guarded like the apple of her eye — to
write the names of the forefathers and mothers on the pages she
tore out of the daily calendar and lined up in front of me like
cards, she illustrated the dynasty in a way that didn't desecrate
the Sabbath. She took a handful of peanuts and diligently removed the shells enveloping the fetuses, thrust her fingernail in
the crack between the lobes and split them in two. The smooth
lobes she gathered in her hand, and those that had the bud of
the seed and the rootlet sticking to them at the top she arranged
on the white starched tablecloth, her Sabbath tablecloth, on
their convex side, careful not to damage the corpuscles where
the seed sprouts and blossoms if you don't roast them and cas-
trate the charge of life poured into them. A row of busts, tiny
heads sharpened with a beard, grew long before us, a committee

of elders whose lives froze at the start. "That's you," she pointed to the shriveled lobe at the left end of the row, and she went along like that, named our forefathers and the forefathers of our forefathers backward. And at every single one of them, she added the smooth lobe and gave the name of his wife. (Later on, when I wrote *The Time of the Singer*, I foolishly transformed that scene to a sleepy Sabbath afternoon, close to the time of the Six-Day War, to one of the half-abandoned rooms of the hostel on the grave of R. Simon bar Yohai, Rashbi, in Meron, and only now do I have the courage to redeem it from bondage and return it, albeit belatedly, to its natural existence.)

The image of a tree that Grandmother found in genealogy books of other ancient families, which she often pored over, excited her so much that she often clung to it. At nightfall, when the small flame lent her wrinkled face a dull gold tinge, Grandmother would burrow into the recesses of the past. The moldy aroma of the distant earth invaded the dry desert air when she'd track down the roots thrust in the dark depths that suck their moisture from proximity to the abyss, until she was stopped by an impermeable stratum of rock that human memory couldn't break through. And that, as I said, was Mainz of the early Middle Ages. The roots of our family tree were the forefathers of our fathers: rabbis, rabbinic judges and community leaders, Hasids and mystics, commentators and liturgical poets—people who for more than a thousand years had all of Europe, from Italy and the depths of the vineyards of the Rhine to the poor towns of Russia, lost in mysterious birch forests and wafting rot, an expanse of searching and wandering. Not searching for inspiring landscapes or for an easy life, but for a place promising calm, where they could study Torah, serve their occult God modestly and form a normal human community, as they liked, characterized by grace and charity. The branches are the generations of local natives, of which I, her grandson, am one of the young leaves, aspiring to the bold glow of the eastern sky. The trunk was always her great-great-grandfather, Rabbi Israel of Shklov, who sailed in a light clipper ship along the shores of the Mediterranean in late summer of 1809, until he reached the ancient fishing port of Acre. He ascended to the Land of Israel with his whole family, including his aged parents and his married daughters, along with a group of young and enthusiastic people; and as soon as they came, they joined the small community of students of the Vilna Gaon, who had ascended earlier and had been living for some two years in the small holy city in the Upper Galilee.

The Safed Rabbi Israel saw in his imagination was probably a celestial city with clouds of glory tied in its firmament, surrounded by orchards of pomegranates and groves of oranges and trees of the spheres whose fruits radiate perfumed splendor of secrecy far and wide. That was the image of the Galilean city of the Kabala, the city of the mystics Cordovero, Luria, and Alkabetz. But in truth, Safed in those days was a miserable Arab village, whose houses of wild mountain stones were packed together in heaps on the rocks of the steep summit, and the roofs of the lower houses served as streets for the houses above them. "The entrance to our great grandfather's house, which stood on the edge of a cliff with its windows facing the deep abyss," Grandmother sailed on her descriptions even though, as I said, she had never visited the Galilee, "was through the roofs." And she said that once, a ceiling collapsed under a camel passing through and it fell into the house of somebody from Rabbi Israel's group and broke its leg. "The homeowner demanded compensation from the camel owner and the camel owner demanded the value of the camel as compensation from the homeowner," she said. "And the cadi ruled, of course, in favor of the camel owner who was a Moslem like him."

Before Rabbi Israel could adjust to his new city, his friends asked him to go back out to collect money for the distressed community. And after Purim, he gave in to their pleas and traveled overland to Istanbul since the sea lanes to Europe were closed because of the Russo-Turkish war, and after many adventures, he reached Lithuania. The dispatch he took with him was definitely one of the most exciting documents ever written in the Land of Israel in the nineteenth century, in the days when the Land was still a neglected and God-forsaken district at the edge of the Ottoman Empire. It is a kind of manifesto of the new community, which was still very small, but that had a splendid future in store for it. Magnificent and brilliant is the rhymed opening of that letter:

The Land is on its way,
The Land wakes to a new day.
What does the Land say?
Nothing lacking here, don't dismay,
Torah here we study and obey.
The pious hold sway,
The soul in me is free and gay.

All over Eastern Europe our grandfather roamed, and although those were the days of the Napoleonic Wars, he succeeded in his mission, and in Minsk, he even managed to print his book *New Money* about the Tractate Sheqalim in the Jerusalem Talmud. Grandmother, who was very proud of him, added that, in fact, he was following the path trodden before him by his grandfather Rabbi Ezriel. That grandfather had ascended to the Land of Israel about three decades before him, tried to establish an Ashkenazi community in Jerusalem, but had to go on a mission to Russia, and on his way back, died in Izmir, where he was buried. Her grandfather, she said, changed his route, and on one of his trips to Vienna, he stopped in Izmir in a vain attempt to find the grave. "Like Our Rabbi Moses, May-He-Rest-in-Peace, whose grave is unknown, so the graves of Rabbi Ezriel and his grandson Rabbi Israel of Shklov are also hidden from us." Rabbi Israel, who added to his name the nickname, "Dust of the Land of Israel," returned to the Galilee in the summer of 1839 to meet with Sir Moses Montefiore and used the opportunity to bathe in the spa of Tiberias, where he met his death in an epidemic. For more than a hundred and forty years, the site of his grave was unknown, and only a few years ago, after exhaustive searches, it was found by one of the descendants of his descendants, a member of Kibbutz Ashdot-Ya'akov, in the ancient graveyard of Tiberias, who restored the wiped out and crumbling tombstone.

Grandmother apologized for getting ahead of herself, as usual, and said that three years after he set out on his journeys, Rabbi Israel returned to his home in Safed, but by the time he rested from the tribulations of travel, an epidemic of cholera erupted in the Galilee. He quickly hired pack mules and fled with his family to Jerusalem. On the way, his wife died and was buried in Shfaram, in the burial ground of the ancient Jewish community that resided in the Arab village. "Just like Jacob buried Our Mother Rachel on the way to Efrat," said Grandmother, who was wont to attribute to our own patriarchs the glory of the ancient Patriarchs of the Nation. The epidemic pursued them to Jerusalem. That summer his two sons, his two daughters and their husbands died there. His aged parents, Grandmother recalled, when I asked what became of them, had taken sick and died even before that and were buried in Safed. Both he and his little daughter Sheindel, the only one he had left of all his offspring, were afflicted with cholera. And then Rabbi Israel—"our own private Job," as Grandmother said—vowed that if he recovered, he would write a book about the Commandments concerning the Land. And indeed, that very night, he saw in a dream a man standing above him and whispering vague words in his ear: "Hit and heal," and the next morning, he and his daughter woke up and were recovered.

"See how many graves of our forefathers cushion this bitter earth we sit on." It was hard for Grandmother to stop the tears that flowed over her cheeks. "At least you, not like your aunts and uncles, don't ever leave this land. The Land of Israel is won by torments." Outside, from the blue-black velvet square, spread like a Torah Curtain over the pair of windows, from the direction of the minefield of No-Man's-Land, came the stubborn wailing of an abandoned jackal. Then a single shot was heard and the wailing stopped all at once.

When the epidemic came to a halt, Rabbi Israel and his daughter returned to Safed. Rabbi Israel took a second wife, "the daughter of the rabbi of Jampoli," Grandmother took pains to emphasize to me, the one she had chosen as the future chronicler; and when his daughter Sheindel grew up, her father married her off to one of the immigrants, a young widower with two small children, who had ascended to the Land from Pinsk, named Reb Isaiah Bardaki.

On the eve of Sukkoth, when she'd clear the books and newspapers off the table and craft handmade chains and *royzelekh* to trim the Sukkah, as she cut out the colored paper, Grandmother loved to tell about the miracle that happened to Reb Isaiah when he ascended to the Land. He made his way from Beirut to Acre on the eve of Sukkoth, with his son and daughter, on a rickety barge that was transporting cedar wood from Lebanon to build the palace of a rich effendi near Acre. Soon after they set sail from Beirut, the sailor lost his way in the sea because of the winds, and Reb Isaiah, who feared he'd be forced to celebrate the holiday on the barge, built himself a temporary Sukkah from the cedars. Meanwhile, the winds blew harder and a fierce storm hurled them about so much that the barge landed on a shoal facing the coast of Acre and started sinking. And Reb Isaiah hoisted the little boy on his shoulders, clutched the little girl to his chest, and tied himself to one of the walls of the Sukkah which had miraculously turned into a raft and brought them unharmed to the shores of the Land of Israel.

More disasters and troubles embittered the life of Reb Israel. Abdallah Pasha, the tyrannical governor, who lived in the half-ruined Crusader fortress overlooking Safed, threw him into prison to force his community to pay dearly to redeem him, his two sons from his second wife died, and one winter night, when the narrow streets of the city looked like branches of a mountain stream and heavy rain poured onto the flat roofs, his house collapsed on its inhabitants. Reb Israel, according to Grandmother, saw the repeated and recurrent disasters as a reminder from Heaven that he had to fulfill the oath he had made that night in terror in Jerusalem and to start writing the book.

One of the most secret affairs he set in motion was the mission to the Ten Tribes. "Beyond the Sambatyon River that spits crystals all week and rests marvelously on the Sabbath from its fury, in distant lands, that the eye of no living person had looked upon, live the children of the Ten Lost Tribes and wait for the call of their brothers for help. Free Jews they are, who gallop on mighty horses wrapped in tefillin, and wave burnished swords and stamped on their blade are the words, 'Who is like unto thee our God,'" Grandmother would try to astound me, with one of the most exciting Jewish myths. And after she observed the impression her words made on me, she said that about twenty years after Rabbi Israel came to Safed, a rumor was circulating among the Jews of the Galilee that the lost children of the tribe of Dan had an independent Jewish state in the southern half of the Arabian Peninsula, beyond the dreadful boundary of Hadhramaut. Like his teacher the Vilna Gaon, Rabbi Israel believed that before the coming of the Messiah, there must be "the stirring from below," which will be expressed in building the Land and the Ingathering of the Exiles, and he was very excited by the possibility of finding one of the Ten Tribes at long last, and as was his wont, he quickly translated his excitement into acts. He was eager to send a special emissary to them and for this mission, he chose his student, Rabbi Barukh ben Shmuel of Pinsk, a bold and valiant physician. Rabbi Barukh left from Safed for Damascus, from there he traveled to Aleppo and from Aleppo to Kurdistan and from Kurdistan to Baghdad and from Baghdad to Aden and from Aden to San'a. From the capital of Yemen, he tried to go to the Haydan Desert to look for the Lost Tribe, but in the end he deviated from his plan and returned to San'a where he became the physician of the Imam el-Mahdi, and as usual with the personal physicians of despots, he took care not only of their illnesses, but also of affairs of state and in the end was executed by his masters. And thus the dream of finding the Ten Tribes and bringing salvation once again passed away.

Here I cut off the torrent of her words and asked with a soupçon of mockery if the immigrants from Habban with their long bold faces, fearless look, and plaits that adorn the heads of the men like the locks of Samson, who was also, as we know, from the Tribe of Dan, if they were those lost Jews that Grandfather sent to look for. "You ask questions that are beyond my understanding. The Ten Tribes are those they'll always look for and never find," Grandmother lopped off my inquiry and said she'd better tell me only the things she was an expert in.

In the end, Rabbi Israel finished writing his book, she said, and he called it *Edge of the Table*, a name with a double meaning: to hint that this is the completion of the *Set Table*, the *Shulhan Arukh* of Rabbi Yosef Caro, and also to hint at the commandment of the edge, leaving the uncut edges in the fields of grain for the poor to gather the gleanings and the forgotten sheaves — which is one of the commandments of the Land, which is what the whole book is about. Rabbi Israel meant to go to Russia and supervise the printing of the book himself, but meanwhile Rabbi Israel Bak, the grandfather and ancestor of Bak, the "naïve Eastern painter," settled in Safed, and in a small room, he set up the wooden press he had brought with him from Berdichev, and opened the first

Hebrew printing press in the Land of Israel in 250 years. Rabbi Israel gladly gave him the manuscript, but in the middle of the printing, a revolt broke out in the Galilee — the fellahin rebelled against Ibrahim Pasha, the Egyptian ruler, who had conquered the Land two years before. The heathen are come into thine inheritance, say the chronicles of those days; they killed men and children and raped women on Torah Curtains they tore off Arks of the Covenant, and from the parchment of the Torah Scrolls, they cut bands for horses and made shoes. Our grandfather, Rabbi Israel, fled to the cemetery and hid in the cave where the rioters found him and stabbed him in the eye. They also burst into the printing press, attacked Bak, burned the books he was in the middle of printing, pillaged the tools, and cast the lead letters into rifle bullets. "Only the proofs of the books of our great ancestor were miraculously saved," said Grandmother, and a year later, when the printing press was restored and Bak cast new letters, more perfect and more beautiful than the previous ones, he completed the printing and published the *Edge of the Table*.

"I want to see the book," I asked, and Grandmother got up reluctantly, and from the depths of the closet took out an ancient, moth-eaten leather binding from out of a pillowcase. "Whenever one of the descendants of the author got sick or when one of his granddaughters had a hard delivery, they tore a page out of the holy book and made it into an amulet to hang on the neck of the sick person or over the bed of the woman in labor, and after all the troubles that befell us in the last hundred and twenty years, this is all we have left — an empty binding." Grandmother returned the holy object to its protective covering and said that we had to wash our hands carefully, and not only because books defile the hands. And only this year, after constant efforts, did I succeed in acquiring a rare copy of the book from an antiquarian dealer in Jerusalem at a price that could have financed the whole printing of the book.

A year after the book was published, a strong earthquake shook the Galilee. "Safed shed its houses as a fig tree sheds its leaves in the fall," Grandmother described the earthquake of 1837, a description surprisingly similar to the description of the shock in the writings of the Dutch traveler Van de Velde. Safed, which was close to the epicenter of the earthquake, was completely wiped out, and the houses, built on steps, collapsed and buried one another. Anyone who didn't die in the avalanche, starved to death. "One man, who tried to get his family out from under the rubble," Grandmother said, "found all of them dead. His wife lay with her skull crushed under the roofbeam, one of her children under her arm, and the baby at her bosom with the nipple of the breast still in its mouth."

On that awful day, when the abysses roared and the earth, staggering like a drunkard, gaped open, Rabbi Israel was in Jerusalem on a mission from his community, and his daughter Sheindel, her husband and their grown children went to Tiberias to warm up a bit from the cold in Safed.

"When you grow up, you'll get to go to Tiberias for me, too," Grandmother promised, not only to dissipate the choking sensation brought by the gloom of the past into the crowded room, but also to moderate the drama of the story a little, and she said that the mute demons of King Solomon's slaves are bound on the bottom of the Kinneret and warm its springs, because it's not sand that's scattered on the shore of its sea, but stones smooth and round as ostrich eggs and her houses are built of black stones, basalt stones from the time of Lot. And still talking, she rummaged around in one of her big purses, overflowing with photos of her offspring — farewell photos at the port of Tel Aviv, photos of circumcisions and weddings and photos of babies baring their first teeth — and came up with a negative of the Jerusalem house, the background her children were photographed on before they went abroad. "If I look at this strip of celluloid in the sunlight," she said, "I can taste a taste of Tiberias in it, as we taste a taste of death when we sleep."

In Safed, Grandmother picked up the thread of the story, only the baby was left, since her mother wanted to spare her the hardships of the trip, because anyway she wouldn't bathe her in the hot spring waters of Tiberias. Everybody was sure the little girl was killed in the earthquake, along with the thousands of Jews of Safed, "but my grandmother, Bubbe Hannah, was saved by a miracle, and the One-Who-Sits-On-High, Who performs His missions with a bee and a spider, this time performed the mission with a *kessele*," said Grandmother and dragged out from under the bed a deep copper laundry tub, with a long crack all along

the shriveled and banged bottom. The basin fell on the baby and
sheltered her, and through the crack, which was torn by one of
the stones, she got air and could breathe. "For in the time of
trouble He shall hide me in His pavilion: in the secret of His tabernacle shall He hide me," Grandmother raised her hands in
gratitude to the One-Who-Sits-On-High, and said that two whole
days later — two "from one time to the next," as she put it —
when they came to dig out the rabbi's house, they found the
neighbor's daughter, who was taking care of the baby, stretched
out with no sign of life under the wood beams and the rocks, and
under the overturned basin lay Bubbe Hannah, weak and whining, but safe and sound, swaddled in a blue-green wool sheet that
protected her soft body from the bitter cold.

From the strip of fabric, woven and dyed indigo by the delicate
and proper hands of some anonymous woman of Safed, Sheindel
sewed a swaddling cloth for the Torah Scroll and dedicated it to
the "Solace of Zion" synagogue, established by her husband in
the Hurva courtyard. "In the War of Independence, when the
Legionnaires set fire to the synagogues in the Old City, that swaddling cloth was also burned as a sacrifice for the sin of Heaven,"
said Grandmother.

"All of us owe our lives to that basin," Mother declared when
she came to help Grandmother clean her house for Passover and
her foot struck it. "Just as all Russian literature came from the
folds of Gogol's overcoat, so our whole family burst out of the
crack in its bottom." But Grandmother scolded her and said that
clowning is one of the cunning features of the evil instinct and
that we owe our lives solely to the One Who inspires a pure soul
in us and preserves it in us. With an obvious effort, she lifted the
basin, angrily pushed aside Mother who wanted to help her, put
it on her bed, ran a wet rag over it, and said that she had gotten
it when her mother's legacy was divided because she was named
after the miraculous Bubbe. And in the future, she added, the
basin will be bequeathed to the first granddaughter or great-
granddaughter to be named after her. In northeastern New York,
there does live a woman named Hannah, the only great-granddaughter to be named after Grandmother, but the basin isn't in
her keeping, because one of the heirs, who didn't care about the

basin or didn't know the tale connected with it, threw it out while clearing out her things after her death.

After the chain of disasters—"the black pearls of the family, that Grandmother wore around her neck on holidays," as Mother put it—which befell them from the day they ascended to the Land, Rabbi Israel of Shklov and his son-in-law, Rabbi Isaiah Bardaki, came to the conclusion that Heaven was punishing them for preferring Safed to Jerusalem, and along with the whole small community of Perushim, they moved out of the Galilee to Jerusalem to build their house next to the site of the Temple.

"And in Jerusalem, Hannah married Rabbi Nathaniel Luria, and Gittel-Leah, their daughter, married Rabbi Eliezar David Ha-Cohen, and I, your grandmother, am their daughter," said Grandmother, gathered up the rows of male and female lobes and held them out to me. "Say a blessing and eat the peanuts, so you'll have strength to draw the tree."

6

In Grandmother's eyes, the family photos were more beautiful and interesting than any cinema. In other eyes, more skeptical and curious ones, they can become a window to look through to the labyrinths of her soul, which weren't always understood even by her.

She stood the photos of her offspring on the cabinet, leaning on empty jam jars, and against a Japanese vase with a picture of a white-faced Geisha with opaque eyes, sitting shrouded in a kimono on the horizon. Every Friday evening, she persisted in replacing in the vase a branch from the fragrant rue bush, to protect her offspring from the Evil Eye. To the right of the Geisha, on permanent exhibit, stood the picture of the beloved son of her old age, Isaac, a photograph that was taken the day he flew out of the nest and went to America, and on the left, a photo of him about ten years later in Philadelphia when he was more sedate and settled, with his wife Connie and their daughter Alice. The place of all the rest of the photos would change every day, to indicate which one she brought close and which one she pushed away, who sent her a letter and who neglected her, who made her sad with too much talk and who made her glad with a sweater or a woolen kerchief.

On the walls she hung the pictures of the dead, and invested quite a bit of thought in that, too.

For ages she harbored hatred for her mother-in-law, and she expressed that hostility by hanging her portrait on the wall, over the buffet, next to the portrait of her father-in-law. In the picture of her mother-in-law that she selected, the woman was in her final years, after she had grown very old and her cheeks were shriveled, and not a single tooth was left in her mouth; on the other hand, the photo of her father-in-law, Rabbi Moshe Jules, a self-

styled physician, as I said, was taken in his youth—a young yeshiva student, with black hair and smooth skin, who was still
studying in some yeshiva in Hungary. "Who are those two?" asked
everybody who came into her house and saw the strange couple.
"My husband's parents, may-they-rest-in-peace," Grandmother
would reply, swallowing a smile. "That doesn't make any sense,"
the guests would be astonished. "He's young and handsome, a
fine young man, and she's old and ugly. She must have been a
bitch who drove him nuts." And Grandmother, with ostentatious
piety, would answer, "Who can fathom the depths of a person's
soul, it is the Holy-One-Blessed-Be-He Who sits in the refuge of
His Holiness and makes matches."

"Why is Grandmother still so hostile to Bubbe Rivka?" I ques-
tioned Mother one Sabbath afternoon as we returned from the
Hungarian Houses, walking home through the empty streets in a
heat wave; and as an old child who shows an excessive understanding of grown-up affairs, I added, "Is it because all daughters-
in-law hate their mothers-in-law?" Mother suppressed a smile,
and led us out of Father's hearing. He was lingering at a display
window of the silver shop of "Herrenthal and Partners," his eyes
looking covetously at spice boxes in the shape of churches. And
she whispered, "Because there was in her, in Bubbe Rivka, as in
her father, the cunning of foxes and the thievery of cats and the
boldness of a dog and the deceit of a bear lying in wait." Mother
was silent a moment, seeing what impression her accusation in
the style of Alharizi made on me, and then she said that if I really
wanted to know who Rabbi David Jules and his daughter Rivka
were, I should hear how the two of them set a trap for Rabbi
Moshe when he was still a lad and took him captive in their family. One day, at the end of the 1860s, three Hungarian lads from
the city of Vac appeared in Jerusalem. They told the leaders of
the community that they had fled from a Europe afflicted by the
Emancipation, had walked for ten days to the port of Trieste,
boarded a sailing ship and sneaked into the port of Jaffa without passports or visas. Rabbi David Jules, son-in-law of the Gaon
of Kobersdorf and a quick-tempered zealot praised for the war of
excommunication he waged against the French archaeologist
de Saulcy, who had then exposed the "Tombs of the Kings" in
Jerusalem, invited the bold young men to his house and quickly

took their leader, Moshe Wallace, under his wing. "He didn't do that out of altruism, because he took pity on the lonely fellow," Mother explained. "But because he saw him as a fit son-in-law for his oldest daughter, the *alte moyd* who sat drearily in his house. To make sure the sensitive lad, weary from his journey, wouldn't have time to change his mind, he made a wedding ceremony that same week and persuaded the bitter, ugly virgin to change her ways for a few days and put a smile on her thin lips, and to make sure the Turks wouldn't expel him from the Land, he gave him his own family name." Only after they were married did the sons of Rabbi Moshe, including her father, return to their original family name, Mother concluded her story and said that she was amazed that I never thought to ask how a father and son came to have two different family names.

Above the pair of pictures of the father-in-law and mother-in-law, for many years, there was a slightly pale square of wall around it. Here the portrait of the Gaon of Kobersdorf, Rabbi Abraham Lion, was hung, the patriarch of Grandfather's family, and underneath the picture sparkled his curlicued rabbinical seal. When Grandfather, who was named after the Gaon, passed away, one of his brothers came after the week of mourning and took the photo by force. Grandmother, who refused to be consoled, left the white spot on the wall as a "memento of the destruction," and whenever she recalled the despicable act of her thieving brother-in-law, and not-to-be-mentioned-in-the-same-breath, the wonderful beauty of the lost picture, she'd repeat the wonders of the great man among giants, whose face was a torch and his mouth most sweet.

Grandmother especially loved to tell about her relative the rabbinical judge Rabbi David Ha-Levi Jungreis, the story of the annunciation when the Angel of God appeared to the mother of the Gaon of Kobersdorf and announced the birth that was in store for her. One evening a mysterious guest appeared at the home of the head of the community in the Hungarian town of Freistadt, Rabbi Yehuda Leib Lion (the original family name, however, was Zwebner, but when the "Noda bi-Yehuda" [R. Ezekiel ben Judah Landau] ordained him as a rabbi, he declared: "The lion hath roared, who will not fear?" And from then on that name stuck to him and his offspring) and closed himself with him in his room.

When midnight came, and the two of them hadn't yet come out, Yehuda Leib's wife peeped through the keyhole and saw a scary sight: the guest, blazing like an angel, sunk in stormy Halakhic negotiations with her husband. Frightened, but also curious, the woman waited at the locked door, peeping inside from time to time, and at dawn, the stranger came out and found the woman lurking near the door. She apologized and said that she longed to hear words of Torah, but didn't come in because she didn't want to disturb them. "How shall I bless you?" asked the man in order to calm her. "Bless me that I will have a holy son like you." "Your wish will be granted you. At this time next year, you will give birth to a son with the face of an Angel of the Lord of Hosts." After the guest went off and the woman told her husband what he had foretold for her, Rabbi Leib quickly mounted his horse, chased after the guest, and when he was outside the city, he saw him standing at the top of a high mountain and a halo of light surrounded his head like a wreath. "What name shall we give the son to be born?" asked the father. "Call him by my name," said the stranger. "But I don't know your name," the father was terrified. "Call him Abraham, the name of the first Jew," the thunder rolled on the wooded mountain.

"A Christian legend converted to Judaism by the idlers in the study house in Pressburg," laughed Mother when she heard the story of the annunciation and explained that such motifs wandered from place to place faster than silver coins, and yet, she added, there is a seed of truth in the story: the fair and transparent skin of the offspring of Rabbi Abraham Lion, which easily tended to turn red and to blaze. "It's enough for your father to make me mad or for me to be in the sun for fifteen minutes and I look like one of the seraphim or the holy animals."

One day, about a year before Grandmother's death, I expressed my opinion about the fact that Grandfather's picture, which naturally should have been next to the image of his parents and the patriarchs of his family, was exiled to the back of the buffet. Over the shoulders of his smiling sons and daughters, in the postcard-size photo, which was isolated and enlarged from a family photo taken a year or two before he became paralyzed, my grandfather, Rabbi Abraham Halevi Wallace, rejected and embarrassed, looks at me.

One Sabbath, when I got up late and didn't go to the synagogue with Father, I dared to share my new revelation with Mother. And Mother was unusually silent for a long time until you could almost see her hesitating about whether to tell what she intended or to dismiss my words with empty words. "I'm glad you noticed that," she answered me at last, maybe because Father wasn't home. "The time really has come for you to start getting interested in human beings and the complicated relations between them." And then she sat down on the edge of my bed, gathered me close in her arms, and as the smell of her body mixed with the steam from the morning coffee and the aroma of hand cream enveloped me, she said that for a long time she'd been afraid I'd be one of those people who are captivated by the charm of legends and have no desire or curiosity to expose the hidden psychological mechanisms of the soul that motivate human beings and their acts.

From the quiet Sabbath street rose a wonderfully sweet song, whose monotonous sadness was violated now and then by a raging joy that immediately flickered out. I extricated myself from Mother's embrace and stood at the window. Yearnings and longing, softness and determination throbbed in the small group of Hasids. All of them were like desert princes, in their rough gold caftans and their brown camel-hair coats. They walked in the middle of the street, escorting to the synagogue a young man with a thin chestnut-colored beard, and a silver silk scarf at his throat. With his embarrassed look, his heavy, downcast eyelids, and the blush that spread on his cheeks, he looked like the Savior in Italian Renaissance paintings more than a bridegroom marrying a woman this week, who's now walking to the synagogue to ascend to the Torah. I hummed the heavenly melody with the Hasids and said that, according to Father, that's the song of the angels who accompanied Our Father Jacob when he left the Land of Canaan to seek a wife in Horan. "That's a tune of Gentiles from the Carpathian Mountains," Mother dismissed his words. "And the little shepherd girls would sing it to the geese when they'd bring them in from the reeds at night."

Mother, who stood behind me, also watched the group going off, and when the tune died out, she said that Grandfather was also like that boy, with milk still on his clenched lips, when they led him to the marriage canopy with Grandmother, back then, at the end of the last century. A weak Hungarian youth, scared and cowering, ruled by his mother who was as ignorant and rigid as the peasant women in the remote villages of Zibenbirgen where her family came from, and in the hands of the secessionist and fanatic tradition of his father's family, the students of the students of the Hatam Sofer, who was known for his motto: The new is forbidden by the Torah.

"So you'll understand who the Hungarians are, I'll tell you a story," she said. "Once, in the days of the Hatam Sofer, one of the rich Jews of Pressburg donated a clock to the yeshiva and hung it over the doorway facing the Ark of the Covenant. Within a few minutes, a group of yeshiva students armed with sticks and hammers entered the hall, and as the excited students watched, they smashed the clock to smithereens. You understand the meaning of the act?" she asked, and without waiting for my answer, she said, "They were fighting against the new time. They wanted time to stand still. So they fled from central Europe, which was flooded with the light of the Haskalah in the middle of the last century. Here, in the heart of the East, under the aegis of the backward Turkish rule and in the slothful Arab life, they believed they could set up forever the thousand-year-old ghetto. So, don't let Grandmother come and tell you stories and tell you you should be proud of your ancestors who ascended to the Land of Israel long before the Biluim and who were the true Zionists."

Grandmother, unlike Grandfather, was a proud and beautiful girl. "Her beauty was never to my taste. In her youth she had a full, pinkish body and a round plump face — the face of the sun when it's full," said Mother. "Like the faces of all the women in her family; but that was the ideal of beauty of the Jews at the turn of the century; and if that wasn't enough, she was also pedigreed and took pride in her family tree which went all the way back to King David and Ruth the Moabite."

"Now, imagine a maiden, whose cradle stood in a noble house, whose father walked around with foreign consuls and Oriental governors, as I walk around with the milkmen of the Tnuva farm cooperative, who spoke pure German he acquired in the imperial school in Vienna, who conducted a correspondence with the house of Rothschild and Sir Moses Montefiore, a maiden who looked like one of Rubens's women, who — not out of choice and not because she fell in love, but out of the cold calculation of her father who wanted to link his pedigree with the Hungarian elite whose status quickly rose — is put without much ceremony into the arms of a timid and provincial fellow, and before she knew her right hand from her left, her belly was swollen and the children start bursting out one after another, one-two-three."

Mother poured herself another cup of coffee and went on guiding the sharp scalpel with a brutal cold-bloodedness. "Grandmother in fact never loved Grandfather," she decreed. The spoiled girl, who had grown up in a house where nothing was lacking couldn't appreciate her husband, who really risked his life to earn a living, with exhausting work, first as an apprentice to the Ashkenazi butchers in the Old City, then as a ritual slaughterer in the abattoirs in El-Azaria, at the Jericho crossroad, and then he got fed up dealing with four-legged cattle and exchanged them for two-legged ones — customers in a small grocery store he opened in the market in Meah Shearim. He found refuge, said Mother, in the company of the gravediggers. Grandfather volunteered to be the standard-bearer in the Burial Society and was entrusted with nocturnal funerals. "When he'd come home at two in the morning from the Mount of Olives with a smell of the crushed limestone earth and death still in his clothes, we could hear Grandmother's grumbling rejection of him when he thrust himself into her bed." Mother looked straight at me and said, "That's how it is when all of them, parents and grown children, sleep in one room."

Mother wiped the steam off her glasses, and with a face glowing like the face of the Gaon of Koybersdorf, she said: "Grandmother in fact didn't love us children either. She gave birth to us. Like a cat. She took care of the babies with the vital maternal instinct, and when they grew up a little, she pushed them away. She never talked with me, didn't try to understand what was bothering me. She never talked, just got orders from her father and her husband and gave orders to us children. An obsequious subject and a merciless ruler." Only many years later, when she herself lost the two little girls, did Mother understand that Grandmother's inability to connect with her children apparently stemmed from a sense of self-protection, not to let the expected and routine death of the babies be bound around her. "Once, between Haya and Isaac, we had a baby girl, and when she was two years old, she died of pneumonia. Understand, there was no penicillin back then. Grandfather hastily buried the little blue body in the dark of night. They sat *shiva* in silence. They didn't even put a tombstone on the grave. After the month of the memorial period, Grandmother sewed up the rip in her suit as if the baby had never existed. In fact, they had one less mouth to feed."

The footsteps of Father returning from the synagogue were heard in the yard. "Nobody is to know what we talked about," Mother decreed and went into the bathroom to wash her flushed face.

All week long, Mother's words oppressed and upset me. I saw her candor as pure cruelty, a bitter settling of scores stemming, I thought, from the fact that Grandmother took Mother—the only one who took care of her all the time and supplied all her needs—for granted, not worthy of appreciation or thanks; never did she praise her, but on the other hand, she plied her with the virtues of her sisters and brothers, especially the virtues of her young son, Isaac. An external expression of that treatment was her place on the buffet—next to Grandfather's photo.

All week long, I waited for the Sabbath to talk to her and prove to her how wrong she was. On the Sabbath, after Father went to synagogue, I woke Mother up, and without waiting for her to get out of bed, I said that what she had said about Grandmother didn't fit the woman I knew, who was warm and kind and understanding.

"A great change really has taken place in Grandmother since those days," Mother admitted. "When Grandfather died, twelve years after he lay half-paralyzed at home, Grandmother felt an enormous relief that she ultimately translated into the spiritual freedom she acquired by teaching herself to read and write and devoting herself to books."

"But Grandmother talks about Grandfather with open love and great longing," I interrupted her.

Mother smiled and said that after a person dies, those left behind tend to reorganize not only the furniture in the house, but also their relation to him, and to place him on a higher spiritual level than in life and to attribute to him noble qualities he didn't have. In every world picture of the past a revolution took place then, said Mother, and asked me why did I think his prayer books and *Humash* and holy books didn't remain in Grandmother's house. I replied that Grandmother said that his brothers came to her when she was still wounded and in pain and plundered them. Mother chuckled sadly. "After Grandfather passed away, Isaac and Zachariah went and stored the books that weren't fit for use because they were porous or rotten from the saliva that drooled from his twisted, paralyzed mouth when he'd study and pray from them, fulfill the lovely words of the songs of Israel, 'unless thy law had been my delights, I should then have perished in mine affliction.' So you see, the past is the most unexpected thing, even more than the future."

After she removed that obstacle from her path, Mother said that now that Grandmother was rid of the dread of her husband, who was unsuccessful in her eyes, and from the eternal pregnancies and the demanding, suckling babies, the need awoke in her, the need that seems so natural to us, to connect with a child, and so she became close to me. "Now she can love you, but in her own way, without feeling that she's exploited. But that's a belated contact, it's only a taxidermist's dummy of such a contact. In the end, she behaves like a princess—does she take care of you? Did she sit at your bed when you were sick? Try to remember how she touches you, when she does touch you—always pulling or pushing, as if she were touching something that nauseated her. Did she ever give you a kiss?"

"Grandmother says that kisses can spread diseases," I tried to plead her cause.

"To treat kisses like that is definitely not a good preparation for life," Mother didn't let me finish and argued that the only contact Grandmother made with me was through the stories. "She never asks what's upsetting you or what you like. And she doesn't show others her real feelings. She knows only one thing: To tell stories, and in the end, stories are a pretty sad imitation of life."

Mother fell silent, testing whether I could take another blow of her battering ram in the crumbling memorial of Grandmother, and then she said that, in fact, Grandmother treated me like a bridegroom. "She's trying to impress you, maybe even seduce you, and the only means she has left in her old age are the stories.

She's like the charming brides—and that's the only model she knows—who, in their furtive encounters with their destined bridegrooms, brag about their pedigree."

Mother, who saw the panic in my eyes, got out of bed and said that, in conclusion, she wanted to tell me two more things. First, only someone who can give himself the finger—she said *fayg*— can also give it to somebody else, and second, I had to get it into my head very clearly that our parents are not only Father and Mother, but are also human beings—sons and brothers and husbands and even lovers who had the door slammed in their faces—and as human beings they have many different aspects, and that's also true of Grandmother and, of course, of her.

"And yet—who does Grandmother love?" I didn't let Mother off the hook.

"Grandmother admires her father; she's still in love with him," she decreed, and said, as if to herself, that tomorrow she'd go to the B'nai B'rith Library and check the psychology books to find out what they call the Oedipus Complex if you change the sex.

7

At dusk, when Grandmother's gloomy room with shuttered windows was filled with perfumed steam, like the cloud of incense covering the Torah Curtain on the Ark, I knew that her forefathers would soon appear. She bent over the wick in the kitchen corner in the corridor, poured a boiling tea of medicinal herbs and said that if you prepare the spices properly and ground them very very small, those who drink the tea would behold the beauty of the House of God and would visit His Tabernacle.

Grandmother gathered the small, yellow-white chamomile flowers and rosemary leaves on spring mornings, at dawn, when the dew still covered the ground, among the lush hills between the Hungarian Houses and the border station of the Mandelbaum Gate. As she put it, they weren't only hills but the remnants of the ashes of the victims collected by the Levites from the base of the altar in the Temple and thrown into the uncultivated fields outside the city. Mother, who had heard that legend over and over again ever since she was a child, couldn't help saying that if they took a sample of dirt from there and sent it to be examined in the university labs, they'd find that there was nothing in it but the trash from the soap workshops in the Old City. But Grandmother didn't concede the point and said that on rainy days, the wildflowers growing there suck the remnants of holiness caught in the ashes of the victims and absorb them in their leaves and flowers, and when you pour water on the dried flowers, they come back to life, and the hidden smell of the distant past is released, expands vigorously and surrounds everything with an unimaginable sweetness.

"The Temple, excuse me, it was nothing but an abattoir," Mother blurted out, as she was at the pinnacle of the vegetarian chapter in her life, "and the smell that rose from there was a disgusting smell of the dung of slaughtered livestock, the blood and sweat of the Priests, gorging themselves on roasted meats from morning to night."

"There shall no stranger come to the holy thing," Grandmother silenced her and said that it did not befit a person from the seed of Aaron to speak evil in the Tabernacle. "The big and holy house where the name of Our Lord was called, was full of celestial, pleasant smells, which a mortal of our day can't imagine because his understanding can't reach so far."

"And you, how do you know," Mother asked knowingly. "Were you there?"

"Of course I was there," her words were measured. "Aren't I the daughter of a Cohen, a Priest." And she raised her glance where reverence and a plea for forgiveness for profaning the Holy Name were blended, to the portrait hanging on the wall, across from where she always sat, and muttered as if to herself: "Oy, *tate, lieber tate*, like a wreath on the brow of a king is the appearance of a priest."

When her father, Rabbi Eliezar David Ha-Cohen, chief scribe of the Austro-Hungarian consulate, returned at night to his house on Dynasty Street, he'd take off his official imperial clothes and reveal underneath them, as it were, seven priestly garments of gold and blue and scarlet, artistic work of crimson yarns and woven linen. Behind the locked door, in the narrow and roofed passage, where tens of thousands of Moslems streamed to the site of the Temple every Friday, he would leave the bodyguard who carried the scepter, push aside the Torah Curtain covering his secular character, the one that sent letters on the stationery of the Austrian Kaiser, stamped with the seal of the two-headed royal eagle, and reveal a new portrait, created by the force of a profound faith that knows no compromise, the resplendent icon of a Priest serving the Holy One. He was a Priest in a generation when the face of God was hidden, lived the almost desperate attempt to live to the end the unattainable, marvelous past of a family of servants of God, who stand in His house and speak His faith at night, as they recite His grace in the morning.

The priesthood is not fresh water streaming like a bold and fresh mountain brook, said Mother, but holy water, stagnant water, slowly growing moldy in copper basins in the gloom of the

Temple Court. And after she drew breath, she said that if my teachers in the Mizrahi school, those aging German Jews, graduates of the rabbinical institute in Breslau and supporters of "Torah and a secular education" would gird themselves with courage and dare to teach us the "Priest and Prophet" of Ahad Ha-Am, then I could acknowledge the distinction between the Priests who preserve what exists and restrict it, and the true Prophets whose spirits are exalted above the borders of nations and states and who preach justice and righteousness for all mankind.

One evening, the day after I returned from the annual field trip to Rehovot and Rishon-le-Zion, when, drunk with excitement, I told Grandmother about going down to the chilly cellars of the Carmel Mizrahi wineries drenched with alcoholic fumes, she poured me some of her herb tea even though I hinted to her that I'd prefer the cocoa she got in the Script package from America — and said with open pride, "My father didn't drink wine in the middle of the week."

From the wall, her father looked at us, leaning his downcast head on his withered hand, with an infinitely sad gesture. Many years later, in Amsterdam, I would stand before Rembrandt's "Jeremiah Mourning the Destruction of Jerusalem," and the more I looked at the old Prophet of destruction, sitting depressed at the entrance to the ruins of the cave, with a few gold vessels rescued from the Temple next to him, and a light of a gold terror cast by the flames enveloping the plundered Holy City illuminating his brow, the silhouette of his face and the back of his hand, yes, the more the image of Jeremiah ben Helkhihu of the Priests that were in Anathoth joined the image of my grandfather Rabbi Eliezar David Ha-Cohen.

"Grandfather didn't drink wine because he was mourning the destruction of the Temple," I was glad to reveal my expertise and told Grandmother that our teacher, Mrs. Leah Bachrach, told us, as we came out of the winery, about the mourners of Zion who refrained from eating meat and drinking wine and said: How will we eat meat from which sacrifices were offered on the altar and now it is cancelled, and how will we drink wine that was poured on the altar and now it is cancelled.

Grandmother smiled and said that an improvement she considered desirable was indeed taking place in the Mizrahi education, but the reason for her father's custom was different. The Third Temple, the future Temple, would descend from heaven all at once, perfect and complete in its glory. "Morning and night, Father would recite to us: the Temple will be built soon, and when it stands in its place, at the time of the end of wonders, they will seek throughout Jerusalem for Priests who can enter immediately to serve the Holy One." She checked to see if I had understood her and said that a drunkard, as I had certainly learned, was forbidden to participate in divine services.

"All his life he was ready and waiting for that moment," she boasted and added that her father studied the laws of sacrifice and recited the order of the service, and when he put down his Talmud for a little while, he would stand up and go to the window, look yearningly at the mosques in the courtyard of El-Harm a-Sharif, and know for sure that that was only the House of God and that was the Gate of Heaven.

"And when he adjusted the wick in the kerosene lamp on the table, he would stand again in the twenty-four watches of the priesthood and adjust the lamps," Grandmother's voice was choked, and as if à propos of nothing, she added: "They never sat at the table in our house, for eating is like the sacrifice and the table is like the altar."

Grandmother gulped the rest of the tea, sucked the water-soaked chamomile flowers, and let the distant past live again in her heart. "Listen, a voice came out, as it were, to give force to my words," she said and signaled to me to be still. In the silence of the night, from one of the neighboring houses, rose a hushed prayer, full of yearnings and hope, sung over and over to himself by an old man: "May the Temple be rebuilt; the City of Zion replenished. There shall we sing a new song, with joyous singing ascend." For a long time, she looked out the two dark windows where the shape of the house sank, dimmed the light in the kerosene lamp and whispered: "In front of him he still sees the holy area standing and waiting, like a candle peeping from between the windows."

A week later, when I brought her the essay I wrote about the field trip to the winery, Grandmother said that her father studied calligraphy at the imperial school in Vienna, and when Franz Josef's teacher wanted to examine them, he put a sheet of paper in a basin of water and the students had to pass the quill pen over it quickly and lightly — quickly, before the paper absorbed water, and lightly, so the paper wouldn't sink. And then she examined my sloppy handwriting, cast her eyes at the invisible future, and

said: "Try to write like your great grandfather, quickly and lightly." But I, unfortunately, could do neither one nor the other.

And because it was a good time, I asked her if, perhaps, she had an example of his handwriting. Grandmother didn't make do with the regular kerosene lamp, but lit the polished copper Sabbath lamp, and then from the depths of the closet, she took out a roll of linen and from it she carefully and delicately pulled out an ostrich egg, with tiny Scroll-type letters densely written on it. She had gotten the egg from her father, who wrote the Song of Songs on it especially for her in marvelous micrographic work, the book of eternal love between Israel and their Father in Heaven. "That's the gift Father gave me on the day I married your grandfather," she said. "And to you, of all the grandchildren, I have chosen to leave it."

Later on, when she left the Hungarian Houses and came to live near us, the ostrich egg was broken during the move. "That's my share of all my toil," lamented Grandmother, rolling up the brown hairy bundle in her fingers. And when she reconsidered, she buried it among her winding sheets prepared in a drawer of the cabinet for her day of visitation and whispered that after the washing women scour her body with the linen skein and sing sadly, "No weapon that is formed against thee shall prosper," they would dress her in a white garb, like those linen clothes donned by the High Priest on Yom Kippur before entering the Holy of Holies.

8

At the end of winter 1959, after the grief of a week-long visit of
the son of her old age—"She waited impatiently for her lost
pet, and instead, a tired American in checked trousers came into
her house" was how Mother summed up the essence of the disappointment—Grandmother lost interest in reading, and the
books and newspapers were left lying in a tall pile on the Viennese straw chair in the corner of the room; she also stopped
telling stories, and as spring approached, we knew that her days
were numbered.

"*Tate, lieber tate,*" she cast a last glance at her father, and before
she closed her eyes, she passed a transparent finger in an arc
from the walls to the cabinet. "Take away the pictures, I don't
need them anymore." Aunt Nehama whispered to Mother that
"*di mame* doesn't want her forefathers and her children to be
present when she gives birth." Mother nodded, but when the two
of us went out to the yard to dust the portraits of the dead and
the living, she said in a choked voice: "You're the only one who
knows why she wanted that. She doesn't want to see eyes now."

From that hour, she lay curled up like a fetus in her bed and
refused to open her eyes. On Saturday night, after the Sabbath
Queen departed, Father held the Havdalah service at her bed,
hoping she'd open her eyes to see the light of the fire. He held
out his hands to the candle, letting the flame shine through his
fingernails, like the First Adam who found consolation in light
after he first experienced the dark, and then he signaled to me
to put the shriveled citron with dozens of cloves stuck into it to
her nose so she'd smell the fragrance of the spices and be restored. But even before I could pick up the citron, Grandmother
suddenly opened her eyes and shuddered as if she saw someone
standing at her bed. Never again have I seen eyes gaping like that.

Aunt Miriam shrieked and wanted to run and call Dr. Israelit, but Mother put her hand on her big sister's shoulder and said: "There's no need for a doctor. It's all over now."

"Don't be afraid," Mother whispered and didn't let me flee from the room. "That's exactly the same Grandmother you loved, only now she's dead." And before she covered her face with a sheet, she said in a quiet, restrained voice: "Look very carefully at the face of the woman who loved you so much. You won't see it again."

The next morning, the women came to cleanse her body. Mother gave them the bundle of winding sheets, and they closed themselves in the room with Grandmother. The two of us stood at the locked door, and Mother hugged me. I remember only the smell that was there — a smell of valerian blended with the smell of burning paraffin candles, accompanied by the sharp aroma of mothballs, reeking like the train of white linen cloth that was brought into the room.

Suddenly the door opened, and for a fleeting instant, I saw Grandmother laid naked on the cleansing board, but Mother covered my eyes and turned me around. The woman who came out holding a bucket of water waved it and poured its contents onto the paved entrance and the patch of ground, where in the autumn I had grown onions and radishes, and now it stood desolate. "Human beings are like the herbs of the field," said Mother, "some sparkle and some wither." And the water seeped between the cobblestones and on the ground under the casuarinas a skein of water-soaked linen lay like an abandoned swallows' nest, brought down to the ground by the winter winds.

Squatters' Rights

1

To write about Mother means inevitably to write about the past. And from the incomprehensible distance, as I try to set a trap for words to catch misleading memory, first her hands stretch out to me dripping blood, holding a carp for the holiday meal. From its split guts, she'd pull out the bladder and ask, and answer, whether I still remember that Naomi Kaplan, my girlfriend in kindergarten, who loved to play with them during the time of rationing, used to call them "Dov Yosef's white balloons," after the marching song.

Mother's words bring a smile to the face of Mrs. Ruhama Weber, who came to our house to borrow a cup of matzo meal, and she said that, for some reason, with its long smooth form, the fish bladder reminded her of his eminence the Graf Zeppelin, that went across the skies of her youth in a wink. "When, do you think, that was?" Our pesky neighbor narrowed her eyes, and ran her fingertips over the smooth back of the bladders that trembled and recoiled, rolling in their mucous; ignoring the tremor that passed over Mother's upper lip, she said that, as far as she could figure, it was in '31, more precisely, on the Sabbath after Passover. All those years, the airship had not pierced the walls of her memory, and now all of a sudden, now of all times, a few days before the anniversary of that Sabbath morning in spring, when her parents took her and her little brothers to see the celestial wonder from Germany, the Zeppelin returns and bursts forth from the edges of the firmament. She stood there, next to the flour mill in old Montefiore, and looked slack-jawed at the tiny apertures of the passenger cabin attached to the belly of the enormous balloon, envying those who dwell above, who get to look upon the world from on high, while the boys dance at the Zeppelin with sidelocks waving, and demand confirmation for their assumption that that big air fish is the Leviathan prepared for the feast of the righteous in Paradise. The older brother is now an aeronautical engineer in Michigan and the younger one rules a kingdom with Einstein at Princeton University, laments Ruhama softly, while she, whose dreams rose upwards even then, is stuck here at the end of the world, with her ne'er-do-well of a husband. In her foolishness, because back then she was led astray by his beautiful handwriting, and melted when she read his love letters, and in the end, he barely makes a living from writing curlicued addresses on begging letters of the Weingarten Orphanage. That's life, our neighbor summed up gloomily, just as it came, so the Zeppelin went—a few moments the silent gigantic bladder circled over the Old City, and immediately ascended to the heights and slowly vanished to the north, beyond the ridge of Neve Samuel, leaving a strange emptiness behind, in the blue sky.

Strangely, Mother remained stubbornly oblivious to Ruhama Weber's words, as if they had absolutely nothing to do with her, and she went on carving the carp and cutting off their heads. To my great amazement, she didn't chase Father out either when he stuck his head through the narrow window connecting our apartment to my parents' small Tnuva shop in the same house, and took advantage of the lack of customers to amuse our guest with the stale joke about the child who went to the bathhouse with his father and there, for the first time in his life, he saw the most honorable hernia of all in the groin of the head of the community. "What's that?" Father chirped, imitating the question of the child at the sight of the *killeh* floating on the water. "That's a Zeppelin, my son," his father taught him. "Why doesn't it fly in the air like all the other Zeppelins?" asked the child. "Because the captain is a shmuck!" Father burst into wild laughter and was quickly swallowed up in the store again, after a groan of protest was wrung from Mrs. Weber's mouth, and she asked Mother, half-angry and half-offended, when it was that her husband, who had studied in a scientific institute in Kiev, had stopped behaving like a gentleman and started telling tasteless jokes like one of the empty-headed characters who gathered around the gramophone in Weissfish's newsstand listening to cantorial chants.

Mother went on digging silently, and Ruhama Weber, who couldn't bear that anymore, started asking her in a nasal twang that covered her embarrassment where she had been when the German Zeppelin visited Jerusalem, and if she had also gone out to the mountains to greet it like everybody else.

"He stood there, on the slope near Augusta Victoria, in a field of blood-red poppies and smiled his damned smile of death," answered Mother, à propos of nothing, reciting her words as if she had had them ready for a while after she had repeated them countless times, and added that if she hadn't given into Nehama Wallenstein's coaxing and joined the group of girls from Miss Landau's who went to Mount Scopus, she wouldn't have seen him standing there, with a poppy stem in his fingers like a whore having a smoke, and her life wouldn't have become an endlessly overflowing goblet of grief.

Mother's hatred of poppies was one of those riddles I didn't dare ask her to solve. Two years earlier, when I came home from wandering in Schneller Grove holding a bouquet of wildflowers I had picked there, Mother snatched them out of my hand, and from among the buttercups, the chamomile, and the last cyclamens, she pulled out the poppies with ostentatious disgust, and threw them outside, into the yard. "I'm allergic to them, they hurt my eyes," she explained the violence she couldn't repress. But her face revealed hatred and pain which burst out again a few months later, one winter night, when we made a great ceremony of opening a Hanukkah package from her brother in America. In it were sheets and tablecloths, including one especially colorful cloth, decorated all around with wreaths of poppies. "We don't need this disgusting rag in our house," she tossed out and before our amazed eyes, she stuffed the cloth in the back of the shoe closet in the passage to the roof of the house. "As far as I'm concerned, you can take it to your synagogue," she said to Father. "Cut herring or kugel on it." She was in a foul mood, her upper lip puffed, and she claimed that despite our poverty, here, in Israel, we don't need the largesse of American moguls who send us whatever goes out of fashion and goes on sale at the end of the season. "Are you also allergic to painted flowers?" I asked insolently. Father stifled a laugh of embarrassment, and Mother, who froze on the spot and moved her eyes uneasily among the ashamed gifts, immediately recovered and told me in a composed voice that not everything has to be remembered and certainly not everything should be recalled. Later, when Father went off to the "Akhva" synagogue for a daily lesson in Talmud for heads of families, Mother clutched me to her, surprisingly, and said that someone who is blessed with a memory has no choice but to develop his ability to bear pain, but the meaning of her hatred of poppies she didn't reveal. Now, I knew, the mystery was deciphered at last.

"Who stood there, the Zeppelin?" Ruhama groped cautiously. She still didn't understand why Mother was so furious.

"*A Shvartz Yor*," she hissed. She kept her eyes down and she kept on preparing the fish. Never did I hear the name of Mother's first husband pass her lips, except for that one and only time, when she told me, after exposing a bunch of cut-up photos, that she'd tell me about them some day, about her first marriage in great detail and the annals of its brief life and the death of her two little daughters. The sentence of excommunication Mother had issued on his name was so total and uncompromising that it also included her own name when she took his family name. In all the books extracted from the destruction of that house and brought to her parents' house, front pages were torn out at the upper left margin, where her name would have been written. Moreover, after the Six-Day War, when we discovered the graves of the little girls on the Mount of Olives and cleaned the little tombstones, I realized that even there, their father's family name had disappeared, replaced by their grandfather's name. The gravedigger, Rabbi Ele Mintz — "I'm an old friend of yours from years back, I buried your whole family," he confessed to me one day with a great intimacy that was innocent of all irony — told me when I came to order a tombstone for her, that he "remembers like today" how "Mother may-she-rest-in-peace" fought like a wounded animal against all the sextons of the Burial Society and threatened them that if they didn't grant her request not to carve the name of the damned good-for-nothing on the little girls' tombstones, she'd go to the graveyard and slaughter herself on the graves with her father's slaughtering knife.

Ruhama Weber who vaguely knew about Mother's failed first marriage, sat annoyed in the "Electric Fauteuil" — as Father called the sunken armchair where Mother would sit him down when she'd lay down the law to him — and her fingers roaming among the lilies woven into the upholstery fabric created an imaginary maze of interlaced hoops.

"That same night he invited me to a rendezvous," said Mother and screwed the meat grinder to the edge of the kitchen table with the ardor of Torquemada's lads preparing the instruments of torture of the Inquisition: "You should know what a rendezvous is," she addressed me because, ever since Naomi Kaplan's name was mentioned she hadn't seemed to pay attention to me. "Back when I was a girl, that's what they used to call a romantic meeting with a man. And at the end of the evening, when we returned from Cinema Zion, suddenly, at the entrance to the Italian hospital, *A Shvartz Yor* pushed me to the fence and gave me a kiss."

One winter Sabbath, as we returned from a visit to Grandmother's house, we passed by there together. A soft sun, peeping out for a moment between tatters of clouds, poured down on the waterlogged walls of the Italian hospital and on the carpet of bunches of red flowers of the pepper tree plastered on the flooded sidewalks by the storm the night before.

Mother grumbled about why we had to take the long way home, but Father insisted, saying it wouldn't hurt us to take a little walk in the fresh air after we'd been shut up all morning in Grandmother's little room, breathing the kerosene vapors of her Sabbath paraffin stove. At the intersection of St. Paul and Prophets Streets, Mother suddenly hugged me and kissed my head, and said that before the war, a statue of Mary carrying her Son in her arms had stood in the stone alcove at the corner of the building. "So much love and maternal warmth were in the way she bent her hooded head to her baby, that my heart was really torn with pity." But Father hushed her and asked why a Jewish child, and on the Sabbath to boot, had to hear those Christian legends about the bastard and about his mother who went astray, and thus, borne on a wave of Jewish enthusiasm, he said we had to give praise and thanks to the shells of the Arab Legion for accomplishing their mission with a precision that wouldn't have shamed even the Italian surgeons who had worked here before the RAF ruled the place.

"He gave me a kiss on the mouth," Mother repeated, and her upper lip, shaded by a soft down, was puffed up as if she were about to cry. "And ten years later, at three in the morning, in the pediatric unit of Bikur Holim Hospital, when I came out of the little girl's room, I saw him. He was standing at the end of the corridor, in the dark, hugging a student nurse in his arms, and he was kissing her. Here's little Tovele dying, gathered in the arms of the Angel of Death with dreadful torments, and he's giving a kiss to that little slut. Less than an hour after dawn the little girl was finished, and I had nothing left. Nothing. Like a drunkard I went to Mother, to the Hungarian Houses, because there was no reason to go back to that house. And I never wanted to see *Shvartz Yor* again ever."

My cousin Yehuda, who saw her climbing up Chancellor Street alone that morning, her hair disheveled, pushing her dead little girl's empty buggy, told me many years later, on the day we buried Mother's tormented body in the earth, that he'd never forget that awful sight. Only now, when I can no longer force myself to accept the restraint that prevented me from writing about her all those years, and I try, for the first time in my life, to describe Mother's upper lip as I saw it then, during the week of Passover, puffing up with intense humiliation, repressed bitterness, and unimaginable pain, I put my mouth on hers and let that weeping she blocked with her clenched teeth burst out.

Ruhama Weber sat with her head bowed, blew her nose and blotted her eyes with her handkerchief.

"You'll never understand that, Ruhama," said Mother, and she picked up a few pieces of carp and started pressing them into the maw of the meat grinder. "Ever since then, I haven't allowed anyone to kiss me on the mouth. Only the Angel of Death himself will do that."

"Stop, the child mustn't hear such things," Mrs. Weber nodded slightly toward me, and whispered the words in Yiddish so I wouldn't understand. "When women at last start feeling close to one another and reveal the burdens of their heart to each other, this child should be outside, with children his own age."

"On the contrary, let him hear," Mother ignored the neighbor's reprimand, turned to me, and said: "I'm telling you that on purpose. You have to know everything. Maybe someday you'll make something of it."

The flesh of the fish was pressed out through the holes in the iron disk like pink earthworms peeping out of the soaked earth after the rain, and Mother who was about to finish grinding, said that, after many years of reading, she had almost no doubt that authors often base their works on real life tragedies, especially those that happened in their own families. "If you want to know the source of Chekhov and Balzac's strength and emotional force," she declared dramatically, peeping at me out of the corner of her eye, "get thee to their country and their kindred and their father's house."

Ruhama Weber didn't note the amusing mating Mother made of the Pentateuch with Bialik, but she quickly took advantage of the strange and quick change in Mother's mood to get out of the "Electric Fauteuil" and at last achieve the goal she had come for. "Give me a little matzo meal, for God's sake," she injected a pleading tone into her voice. And she held out the empty cup, announced that if she didn't make *kneydlach* as big as goose eggs for her dumb Hasid, who restrained himself all Passover and didn't eat food soaked in water, he'd turn her holiday into mourning. But Mother, who didn't intend to stop halfway through her lecture on literature and life, ignored her and went on and said that both Balzac and the wife of Rabbi Tiktin, who sits on the big porch of the Hungarian Houses in the evening and gossips with her neighbors, ultimately collect the same materials. And then Mother fell silent a moment, and examined our neighbor's face to see what impression that comparison had made on her, and Ruhama, as expected, did twist her mouth and said that to compare the French Goy and the widow of Reb Mottele is a very serious thing bordering on profanity, and that now wasn't the time, when her kitchen was turned into a kind of Sodom and Gomorrah, to discuss that.

The only difference between them, Mother decreed, was that with Leahke Tiktin, people's troubles turn into slander, while in *Père Goriot*, they miraculously become an eternal work of art.

"You're not yet finished talking, women?" Father mocked, coming in from the store for a quick lunch, and happily quoted the words of the Sages on nine measures of conversation that the women took from the ten measures that had descended to the world. "There is no wisdom for a woman except at the distaff," he tossed tyrannically at Mother, gave Ruhama what she wanted and said that even professors at scientific conferences take a break in the afternoon.

Mother turned her back to Father and asked if I'd bring her four or five onions from the pantry. "Life is like an onion," she said as she arranged the purple onions on the cutting board. "You peel layer after layer, and in the end, there's nothing left." That parable, she said, she had read in Ibsen in *Peer Gynt* and also in one of the stories of Rebbe Nahman of Braslav, and it's amazing how two people, so far apart in time and space, saw life the same way. And yet, there is one difference between them: Reb Nahman said that although, when you peel the onion and in the end nothing's left in your hand, a tear does remain in the corner of your eye. Mother put on the old sunglasses so she wouldn't cry while she chopped the onion and said that authors dip their quill pens in that tear and write. She waved the knife over the onions and said that, someday, when I come to write about her, I'd have more than enough ink.

Over the years, the words "my life is a book" became the solemn and demanding elipses she'd often put implacably at the end of conversations we chanced to have, both in the days when we lived in Jerusalem and some time later when she moved out of Jerusalem and came to live near us in Ramat Gan, conversations when she was so good at dispossessing herself of her life, as if it were already a closed chapter, and she let her memories hover above it, with a distant, lucid light illuminating it like the last light of day pouring on a section of a street twisting between two walls, touching their top layers and the hairy, tainted flowers of the yellow henbane a moment, holding on between the stones while emphasizing the elongated shadows of a lad, who is already out of the range of vision, running down the slope of the street, chasing a rolling cartwheel.

After the death of her two little girls, Mother lost her faith in God ("He lies there dozing, in the coop of His heaven, on a featherbed of angels, like a cat after tearing the chicks to pieces"), and didn't trust human beings much either. So all she had left were books, her only allies ever since she had discovered them in the B'nai B'rith Library, where she'd slip off at dusk for fear of her father's zealotry. She laughed at herself for that, and said that she found herself foolishly putting her trust in words that hold onto paper like flies caught on the strips of sticky paper dangling from the ceiling in her father's shop, and yet for her, books were life that separated from its hold on reality in the mysterious process of art and ascended to the stage of metaphor — unfortunately I can't recall her simple and unpretentious formulations — and granted her some degree of consolation, peace, and perhaps even an abstract sense of infinity.

"I'm about to turn over a page," she declared to me one evening, and that was at the end of the final remission of her illness, before the great outburst that proved to be too much for her. She gathered the open book to her, which she put on the pillow face down (a copy of *Promise at Dawn* she had found on my bookshelf) and added in a voice that blended depression and grandeur — two moods that often appeared together in her — that the more books she read, the more she realized to her great joy, that even though the author draws his inspiration from life and seems to be writing about it, he is definitely not obligated to the truth, that is, to what did indeed really happen, but only to accuracy. The request of such a formal and limited truth, she said, choosing her words carefully so as not to offend me, is especially dangerous for an author who has obsessive tendencies. And then she was silent a moment and afterward she said that an exaggerated effort to discover what really happened is liable to make his writing too restrained and controlled and instead of trying to decipher the world, such an author — and she meant me, of course — is liable to find himself imposing his rigid rules on reflections of reality. "When I took a swimming class at the YMCA after you went to the army," she told me and noted that she was 59 years old at the time, "they taught me that when you dive or jump from the diving board, at the critical moment, you have to let go of control. That's exactly how an author should behave and when he wants to grasp the world, he has to be spontaneous, and without prejudices or ready-made conceptions, something that's especially hard for somebody who's compulsive."

Never did Mother hide the fact that she never went to school ("The house I was born into prevented me from getting a formal education," she looked straight at the student who came to interview her for the census and who didn't understand how the woman engaging her in such a cultured conversation hadn't even completed eight years of grammar school. "But despite that, you can't say I'm an ignoramus"), and she was proud that she had acquired her education at night school, correspondence courses, and mainly by constant and diligent reading. Preparing for a trip to America, an escape that didn't come to pass, and that will be discussed when we get to it, she wanted to improve her knowledge of English. She had taken her first steps in the language as a girl by a comparative reading of the Bible in its original Hebrew and the English translation she got in the Christian missionary store. Now she memorized Waldstein's English-Hebrew dictionary and took a Berlitz correspondence course, until she could carry on a friendly conversation in the language and could even read the *Reader's Digest* for pleasure. But after my poems and writings began to be published in magazines and the literary supplements of the daily newspapers, she discovered literary criticism and was especially fond of the essay. The height of her interest came, as I recall, in the first remission of her illness, some time after the publication of my story "Circle Circle Cranes," which subsequently became the first chapter of *Feathers.* She bought *The Art of Fiction* by Henry James from Pollak, the antiquarian on King George Street, and for a few months she read it with admirable persistence, penciling in the translation of words she didn't understand. When I expressed some resentment and may even have grumbled about that, amazed that she was so sated with prose that she had gone over to the "competition," she giggled and said that she couldn't let herself see me go down to play in the lot without at least watching me from the upstairs window.

Now she waved Romain Gary's book like a fan and declared that the books that were dearest to her heart were those where the characters were described honestly, but lovingly. The desirable balance between those two contradictory demands is very complex, even though it looks quite simple, and anyone who wants to decipher the secret of the complicated relations between human beings and the depth of the repressed forces that impel people into each other's arms and then separates them, has to teach himself to observe them courageously and steadfastly, and mainly he has to be careful not to go overboard with honesty and not to be swept away by love. Anyone who writes out of absolute, brutal honesty, ends up falling into a pit of sterility, so characteristic of music (Mother hated music, seeing it as impersonal expression pretending to be feeling), while someone who writes out of obligations of love is easily liable to be a victim of the demands of his fellow man. "If you read Romain Gary without yielding to his charming French sentimentality, you'll understand how paralyzing and castrating love is, and how here, in this pleasant and sticky novel, the mother and son, maybe even reluctantly, become tools in each other's hands."

A quiver of pain passed over her forehead and stirred up the waves of wrinkles that had grown dense ever since the illness intensified. She shut her only eye—the other eye, the left one, was surgically removed in an attempt to excise the cancerous tumor that had developed in its socket—and said that someone who writes must not forget, not even for a moment, the solitary tear left in the corner of the eye. Shutting her eye and straining her scalp as the quiver of pain passed through her emphasized even more the three blue veins starting at the bridge of her nose like the three arms of the letter "Shin." ("When the angel-of-death comes and sees that I lay tefillin-of-the-head, he'll think twice about whether to take me," she'd tell me a few weeks later, when she'd come out of her suicide attempt and want to see her face in a mirror. "Aside from Michal the daughter of Saul and a few wives of Conservative rabbis, up there, in the women's section of heaven, you don't find many specimens like me.") When the pain passed, she slowly opened her eye and asked if I could recall when I first heard her tell the parable about the onion peel.

I reminded her of that distant afternoon on the day before the holiday in Jerusalem, the smooth fish bladders and our prattling neighbor Ruhama Weber, and to lighten the serious tone of the conversation a little, I tried to tell her about an article I read in the paper about a stamp collector who bought an airmail envelope stamped with the seal of the Egyptian post office in the city of Suez, and the envelope was on the deck of the Graf Zeppelin when the airship hovered in the skies of Jerusalem, an envelope that apparently came from the stamp collection of King Farouk and was auctioned for the fantastic sum of sixteen thousand dollars. Mother smiled and said that the Zeppelin, with the thousands of letters and postcards it carried, must have been worth ten times more than the fish in whose belly the pious Joseph found a gem.

"But to pay the yearly salary of a high school teacher for an envelope?" I asked.

"There are all kinds of fish in the sea," said Mother and took off her wig ("I'd rather look like Yul Brynner than wear a *sheytl* like some Poylishe dripke from Krakow," she hissed at the wigmaker who measured her skull after all her hair fell out from the radiation and chemotherapy treatments) and then she added, "and it looks like there are bald fish among them, too."

Mother sank into silence and her fingers fluttered aimlessly in the pages of *Promise at Dawn*, as if they were counting a bundle of bills, until she suddenly said in a dreamy voice, "Our house was like an aquarium back then."

I asked her if she meant the walls of our living room, which were painted deep turquoise, the hue of a calm sea, and studded with multitudes of fish scales. During one of Father's inexplicable outbursts of love — which infuriated Mother — he wanted to please her, and without consulting her, he sent for a Cyprian *kinstler*, a master artist, who went from house to house handing out flamboyant business cards — a phenomenon previously unknown in Jerusalem — boasting that he was a master painter in the European style. For about a week, he took pains with the walls and promised my skeptical mother that his handiwork would give our house an English splendor and glory and it would look like one of the rooms in Hampton Court Palace or Windsor Castle and all our friends and acquaintances would come to gaze at the wonder and would leave green with envy. But before long, when the UN water tanker taking water up to the small Israeli post on Mount Scopus or the Tnuva milk truck passed by on Geula Street, the walls would shake and scales would fall off and cover the sofas and the cupboard with a whitish scrim, and because of that she'd claim that here in this world, thanks to the good deeds of her husband, she was already sitting in the molted skin of Leviathan.

"There you go again with your sentimental childhood memories," Mother grumbled and said that our house was like an aquarium because Father, terrified of arguments, tried to impose silence on her. "As far as he was concerned, I should have been as mute as a fish," and after she inhaled, she added, "And besides, you know very well how much I hate fish."

2

A few years before I was born, Mother and her brother owned a modern fish shop downtown. I learned that by accident, one of those times when she couldn't resist my pleas and took me with her when she went to buy fish from Mr. Mattityahu Rapoport.

Matthes High Priest—as he was called with a trace of humor by the Horowitz brothers, the pair of Levites of our synagogue, when they poured water on his hands. He led us into the inner sanctum with an affectionate gesture, to Mother's deep sorrow. She grumbled that even without that, for my age, I tended to see the world too much from the point of view of store owners. But Reb Matthes ignored her, swung me up in his arms, careful to keep me away from his stinking rubber apron, so I could see the fish swimming around in the small pool in the back. As his assistant pulled the carp out of the water, the old fish seller sang "For man also knoweth not his time: as the fishes that are taken in an evil net," in the gloomy, bewitched melody Engineer Brinker used to chant Ecclesiastes on Sukkoth. And then, maybe to distract me from the thumping that rose from the porous tin laid on the scales, he asked if I'd like to feed the carp in the pool. "That thou givest them they gather: thou openest thine hand, they are filled with good," he declared when I scattered the handful of breadcrumbs on the surface of the water and the fish rushed up from the depths and devoured the food. He stole a glance at the wife of Rabbi Sorotzkin and her daughter-in-law, who were waiting in line, and said in a voice filled with pseudo-reverence, that even the fish increase and multiply in seas without end, they sing to the Holy-One-Blessed-Be-He, but our dull, uncircumcised ears cannot hear such soft voices.

Like Father, Rapoport was a ritual Jew, who was drawn to the synagogue mainly for reasons of form and not content, and because he longed to hear the singing and the prayer. The two of them would often slip off together for secret journeys to acquire well-known cantors and novice cantors, who were reputed to have a glorious future in store for them, and they'd coax them to put on a guest performance, for free of course, in the synagogue they had founded. (Mother, who loathed cantors and the fools who tagged along behind them, once remarked with bitter mockery that Rapoport's soul detested the song of the fish he was compelled to listen to all week long and so he chose to spend his Sabbaths and holidays in the company of slaughtered bulls bleating as in the abattoir.) But during the Torah reading, Rabbi Matthes found no reason to stay inside the synagogue and he'd slip out to the broad front porch. There a regular group of idlers was already waiting to hear his tales of the days when he and his comrades, sons of poor piece workers from the Bronx, volunteered for the Hebrew Brigade and served under Colonel Margolin. And so, every single Sabbath, the old Priest would regale them with stories about The Fourteen, those fourteen wonders, the elite youth of the New York underworld, who served in his company and were dreaded by the whole battalion, the New Zealand cavalry that fought shoulder to shoulder with them for the Jordan passes in September '18, and about the practical jokes that Braverman and Vinifer played on the major of the Royal Fusiliers in the camp near Jericho. Now, as I'm held in his arms over the edge of the pool and smell the odor of old age bubbling up from him, it's hard for me to believe that Reb Matthes was once like Yermi, the curly-haired gallant from Zikhron Moshe, who was a paratrooper, according to the older kids.

Reb Matthes put me down, warning me to watch out so my little foot didn't get caught in one of the spaces of the slippery wooden footboard on the floor in front of the counter, and then he asked Mother if she might want to spoil her husband with some fresh sea fish that had just recently been caught on the shores of Jaffa. "Pick out the best of the best for her," he whispered instructions to his new assistant so as not to make the impatient rabbi's wife and her daughter-in-law envious, and then he added as if he were revealing a secret, "You should know, Corporal Epstein, this lady is one of the *Brancha.*"

On our way home, when we passed by the Sephardi boys'

school, where Father's synagogue was lodged on the top floor, I remembered the opaque words Reb Matthes High-Priest had whispered to Epstein about Mother, and I asked her why she had never told me she served with Rapoport in the Hebrew Brigade.

"Me, in the Hebrew Brigade?" Mother stood still and put her shopping bags down on the sidewalk on both sides.

"That's what he told Corporal Epstein."

"What are you talking about? Did you forget that I'm from the Hungarian Houses, and anyway, back then they didn't take girls in the army like today —" and suddenly she burst out laughing. "Do I look that old to you, like Reb Matthes. When the English entered the Land, I was thirteen years old, only five years older than you."

"But he said you were with him in the *Brancha*," I persisted, and the unfamiliar, foreign word refused with all its might to be cut off from the torrent of English words that Rapoport brought down on the heads of the deserters who gathered around him during the Torah reading.

"He meant that we've got a common profession," she explained to me in a good mood and said that she and Uncle Isaac had a fish store on one of the little streets near King George, right next to the Knesset. "That was long before you were born, even before I was even sure I'd have you," said Mother, and became pensive, and I knew, maybe without being able to put that feeling in words, that there were regions of time I'd never ever set foot in, and even if I wanted to very much, I couldn't, not even if she held my hand, as now, and took me there with her.

When we were close to our house, Mother licked the end of her handkerchief and annoyed me by cleaning the remnants of the sweetened coconut roll she had bought me at the entrance to the market off my chin and lips, and said that nobody — meaning, in fact, only Father — had to know I ate sweets. "And anyway, you don't have to be so disgusted." She didn't hide her disappointment. "After all, it's only mother's saliva." And to appease me before we entered the house, she promised that some day, when the time was right, when the two of us were alone again, she'd tell me about that shop, and then I'd understand why creatures with fins and scales were revolting to her. "Only to please your father do I bother making him fish that he loved," she said sadly. "But he can never appreciate what I've done for him ever since I've been with him."

That opportunity was afforded us only four years later, one Sabbath when Linda Ben-Attar invited the class to celebrate her bat-mitzvah. Mother suggested that I first go with her to the exhibition of a new artist at Bezalel and from there, I'd go to my classmate's house in Nahalat Shiv'a. (I remember clearly that it was an exhibition of wood carvings by Steinhardt, because Mother said there that at the magic touch of his chisel, the stone houses of Jerusalem turned into a herd of dozing tigers, "and in another moment they'll get up and disappear beyond the horizon.")

On that Sabbath, the two of us were once again alone, far from home and from the constant oppression brooding in it, freed from the gloomy, paralyzing presence of Father sitting at the table, with his long, stubborn silence, staring at us, Mother and me, with a sealed face, barren of expression, as it were. When I look straight at him, now, from the sober distance, lacking the recoil of the present, and try to straighten out the life that was wrinkled between the walls of that house, the house that doesn't exist except in my awareness ("Houses are condemned to crumble, houses are condemned not to stand," Alterman's lines pop up unbidden) my heart is torn with pity — the pity felt by someone who is himself now a father of grown children for that forsaken man, my father, sitting idly on long evenings, feeling over and over the arched scar at the base of his thumb, a souvenir of his failed attempt to open a bottle of liquor at the bachelor party his friends made him in Kiev before he married Luba Bat-Tsion, the wife of his youth (I won't remember if it was the right thumb or the left, but what difference does that detail make, now, after his body has been consumed long ago in the dust) or busy by himself in the kitchen, helpless, preparing miracle potions for the afflictions of old age (garlic cloves cooked in milk) that smelled revolting when they boiled over onto the stove, filling the house with ostentatious opposition. And more than pity, maybe it's sadness that will never find redemption, for the father who sees his only son, born in his old age, becoming alien and even hostile to him, a son who formed an alliance with his inconsolable mother, a secret alliance against the whole world, but also against him, and he doesn't have a hint of how he sinned and why he was condemned to have the two go far away from him. Sometimes, Father would reconsider and taking advantage of Mother's absence, he'd succeed for a little while in finding the way to me, but then she'd appear and cleverly restore the situation in a wink. His violent outbursts of rage, I tend to think today, were unconscious attempts to breach the wall of solitude that was built around him, mainly because he was tender-hearted and pliant, which was even intimated in his name ("Our name is Rakhlevski, soft-hearted," I heard him explain to the director of the Tnuva cooperative, one of the foolish followers of Ben-Gurion, who came to persuade him to change the non-Hebrew family name to a Hebrew name. "My forefathers didn't have enough money to buy themselves a nicer name from the Ukrainian lord and the convert who served him, but at least we took care not to be faint-hearted, just tender-hearted.") That wasn't just an attempt to get out of the isolation imposed on him, but also to remake the intimate triangle of father-mother-child, which Mother made every attempt to destroy. One winter night, when Father was sitting and warming himself at the "Ideal" Stove that emitted a hissing, bluish light all around, his hands clasping the steaming enamel kettle, Mother paced from wall to wall, like a caged wild animal, and stirred up an old injustice perpetrated on her by Mrs. Shlang, who, six or seven years earlier, one Purim, had borrowed the gorgeous ivory-handled cowboy pistol I had gotten as a gift from America, for her soldier son, who was about to go to a costume party, and when she returned it the next morning, the revolving cartridge drum was broken. Mother, who could bear a grudge against her for years, slandered Mrs. Shlang, what is she, a serpent by the way, an adder in the path, and her husband, even though he's a high official on the staff of Hadassah, and all the doors of the hospital are open to him, didn't grant her request and get her an appointment with Professor Beller sooner, and her son, who's a gambler and a skirt-chaser. Father, who sat mute all evening, burst out, without any warning, in a medley of furious, unclear words, in Hebrew and Yiddish, studded with Russian curses, and when he finished he banged the kettle on the floor. In the silence that prevailed after the sound of metal striking the floor tiles died out, Father stared at the puddle of water with the slivers of brown enamel scattered in it, and said that what was was and what

75

Squatters'
Rights

advantage would come from her ugly custom of constantly explaining the past all her life, especially when children should
grow up facing the future. And then, passing his hand over his
mouth with an obliterating gesture, he said, "*Geshtorbn, bagrobn,
arop fun mark.*" Mother, who froze on the spot at first, pulled me
into the kitchen and closed herself up with me there, waiting
until Father went to bed, and her lips kept muttering over and
over, "At least I've got you."

So we were standing at the gate going out of Bezalel, after a
visit that went on too long for my taste in the chilly rooms of the
old museum. Mother leaned her foot on the thick roots of the
eucalyptus that occupied almost the whole width of the sidewalk
to retie her shoelaces and said that the grief poured on my face
indicated, even if I didn't come right out and say so, that I had
suffered quite enough today for her love of art, and that now
I had the right to decide how we'd spend the time left until
the bat-mitzvah. I guessed she'd be happy to wander down Ben-
Yehuda Street past the shop windows, but I surprised her and said
that I wanted to stroll in the City Park, where my school was
enclosed, at the northwest edge, beyond the natural stone fence
and the thicket of bushes. "I've never seen it on the Sabbath," I
said. "I'm curious to see the playground when there aren't any
children in it."

"No objection," laughed Mother. "I've not yet managed to see
the Sambatyon dozing on the Sabbath either." But many years
later, when the two of us sat side by side on tiny school chairs,
waiting for the start of the Hanukkah play, in which her granddaughter was to play the role of a candle, she suddenly explained
that scene and said that I had touched her heart in the sophisticated but in fact painfully open way I had tried to stage my life
and fix the entrances and exits of the actors to my will. "On the
one hand, you wanted me, like all the other mothers, to come to
school with you and share your experiences there; and on the
other hand, you didn't want to expose me to the investigating
and mainly mocking eyes of your classmates. So going to school
like that, when it was sunk in a deep slumber, and you made up
an acceptable excuse, maybe you didn't even know why, was a
solution to your distress." Mother waved to her granddaughter,
who huddled with her classmates at the foot of the stage, and the

little one, with a paper candle wrapped around her forehead, quickly threw her a kiss, and then with an effort and firm as a needle boring its way through a thick fabric, Mother added, "Maybe you don't remember, but I won't forget how one winter day, when you were in the second or third grade, the sky was covered with black clouds, and it started pouring rain, and you didn't have galoshes or a rubber poncho. I left Father and the store full of customers and ran to you without changing clothes, and I even forgot to take an umbrella with me. I waited for you, soaked to the skin, in Mr. Reich's dreary restaurant lunch counter. You certainly don't remember his narrow corridor, where he and his wife used to make tea and sandwiches. The smell of hard-boiled eggs and melting margarine, and the roar of primus stoves was hard for me to bear. And at long last, came the bell and you all came out of class, but you ignored me and ran away from me like a lunatic until I caught up with you at the Eden Hotel, because the police were blocking the sidewalk to let Ben-Gurion go inside. I never saw you so ashamed. And at home, only after I promised you on my word of honor that I would never again set foot in the school, except for parents' assemblies I had to go to whether I wanted or not, did you tell me with downcast eyes that the children from the other class burst into your class and shouted to you that 'your maid' came with galoshes and a poncho and was waiting for you at Reich's. They were right, the children. That afternoon, in the clothes from the store, I really wasn't pretty or well-groomed, and certainly not young, like their mothers, who sat all day, morning and afternoon, in Café Hermon and Café Saviyon and treated themselves to coffee and apple strudel. I couldn't even get my hair done every week. Unlike them, I didn't have a regular monthly salary of professors or high officials. You were ashamed of me in front of your friends —" The lights went out, the vice-principal banged the cymbals, and as the human candles went up on the stage, quivering like flames and lined up there in the form of a Hanukkah lamp, Mother managed to finish what she had to say to the high-pitched sound of "My Tiny Candles." "And nevertheless a living mother is preferable, even if she's depressed and sick and works like a contemptible slave in a grocery store, to a dead mother. It's much harder for Vardit Hiel." And mentioning in the present tense the family tragedy that befell one of my classmates, whose mother died in the early 1950s, gave the events she was talking about that dreaded dullness that undermines the borders of tenses, where we try in vain to imprison the past behind their fences.

When we crossed Shmuel Ha-Nagid Street and turned to Be'eri Street, Mother remarked that for many years she had avoided crossing that street, but now, accompanied by her Eldad the Dane, she felt protected and sure that no evil would befall her on her way to the Sambatyon River.

"Grandmother didn't tell you about him, Eldad the Dane?" Mother was amazed at my silence. "That's the Jewish Marco Polo." And she added that on Sunday, I better ask Judith, the librarian of the B'nai B'rith Library, to find me a book in the library so I could read about the legendary traveler who came to the land of Havilah nine hundred years ago seeking the lost Children of Moses, but was forced to turn around and go back when his path was blocked by the enchanted river vomiting boiling rocks.

Behind us, in the yard that was slightly above street level, in the shadow of deserted tin huts, a lot of tombstones were crammed together, leaning against one another. I sneaked frightened glances at the tombstone workshop, furtively reading the names of the dead abandoned in the middle of carving. Mother knelt again to tie her rebellious shoelaces, and said that the tombstone industry would at least make a considerable capital of the *apfol* of the Sambatyon. ("Your father's friend, the proofreader, would most likely translate that as 'the rubbish of the river,'" remarked Mother seeing the amazement on my face.)

"You were afraid to cross here because of the tombstones?" I tried to find out.

"Listen carefully. On the other side of the street, right next to the grocery store of Mr. Eisland, Assie's father, was our fish store, mine and Uncle Isaac's," Mother shot out her words, wanting them to be engraved deep in my heart, and with a strange mixture of repulsion and attraction, she stood, her back to the tombstones, and surveyed at length the worn doorsill, the lowered barred shutter and the dusty window behind it, and said that only now, when I was here at her side, could she look straight at those awful years.

On that bitter and impetuous day, the day Tovele's little body was buried in the barren earth of the Mount of Olives, alongside her sister Yael, who had died three years before, the silence of Job spread over the house, her parents' house in the Hungarian Houses, where Mother had returned from the hospital. The consolers, who came to mourn with her, sat down with her on the ground, and none spoke a word for they saw that her grief was very great. The silence was broken from time to time only by Grandfather's cracked bleating. He was laid on his bed, his limbs paralyzed, his head supported by pillows to keep it from slipping down, and his eyes gazed at those who came in or at the book of Psalms open in front of him, and the saliva dripping from his twisted mouth was absorbed in the paper and destroyed the words. On the third or fourth day of the week of mourning, after those who had come to recite the morning prayers had disbanded, and Haya, Mother's younger sister, got up to feed him some porridge, the sick man pushed away the hand approaching his mouth, and with his healthy hand, he pointed to his bundle of books and muttered "Rus, Rus." "I think Father wants the Book of Ruth," said Uncle Isaac, the only one who understood him and deciphered his wishes. Grandfather blinked his healthy eye and Isaac opened the book and ran his finger along the lines, reading the chapters in a low voice, close to his father's ear. Grandfather made an effort to listen and when Isaac came to the words of Naomi at the top of the third page, the sick man once again blinked quickly, signaling to him to read aloud. "And she said unto them, Call me not Naomi, call me Mara; for the Almighty hath dealt very bitterly with me," Isaac read in a sobbing voice. "I went out full, and the Lord hath brought me home again empty: why then call ye me Naomi, seeing the Lord hath testified against me and the Almighty hath afflicted me." Grandfather's twisted mouth gaped open like a dark well, and his cry of despair drew after it the wailing of all those who sat in the room. "And only I sat hugged in the arms of Nehama and was silent," said Mother after we had gone away a bit from the bored watchman, pacing back and forth along the circular wall and the high latticed windows of the Knesset building. "And as through a curtain of tears I saw the two little girls, in the blue and white checked pants I made them, scattering seeds for a small flock of swallows who glided like a fan from the old cypress in the yard of that house on Zefaniya Street, and imitating their chirping."

Her physical need to feel the bodies of the little girls was so strong in those days that she'd sometimes imagine slipping away to the Mount of Olives, climbing the steep path among the tombstones in the dark, scrabbling in the mounds of dirt, pulling up the stone tablets covering the little girls, and a brief moment when she'd feel their pulse. She found her consolation in their clothing, which an invisible hand toiled to remove from the destroyed house. And when nobody except her father was at home with her, she'd kneel down next to the bed, open the suitcase underneath it, where they were concealed, hidden from all eyes, and bury her face in the little dresses and stockings, inhale their breath she imagined was still stored up in the orphaned fabrics. One day, as she was doing that, she felt that that vital longing would drive her out of her mind, and with a resolution that terrified her, she went out to the fallow field that stretched east of the Hungarian Houses in those days, to the place where the foundations of the Third Wall were discovered, placed the precious bundle on one of the Herodian stones that was half-sunk in the earth, poured kerosene on it and set fire to it. As a souvenir, Mother kept only two festive Sabbath dresses, trimmed with muslin ribbons, Yael's white one, and Tovele's pink one. "You know them, you saw them back then, when Dov Yosef's inspectors burst into our house and searched and threw out on the beds whatever they found in the closets," she said.

Less than ten years after Mother slammed the door of the house where she was born and blindly followed her lover, imagining she had gotten away forever from her father's fanaticism and her mother's ignorance, that she'd divorced herself from the curse of their lives, she was forced to return there defeated and humiliated. And the house she returned to, where she requested shelter because of the treason of the man she had trusted, was then many times worse than the house she had left, never to return to. Most of her sisters and brothers were scattered and weren't there to support her. Her father, as I said, was bedridden, a broken vessel who had to be taken care of twenty-four hours a day. But the main thing was her disappointment in her mother.

"Your egotistical grandmother, with the primitive feelings of an ignorant but cunning peasant, discovered that my forced return home could work to her advantage," said Mother with her direct speech that didn't discriminate in favor of anybody — a quality I would learn to admire only years later — and told that the submissive and obedient woman, who practically hadn't left her house until then, discovered the pleasures of freedom from the dictatorship of her paralyzed husband and began going off for hours, explaining her behavior as her desire to work for the little souls and for the sick man may-he-live-long, and left Mother by herself to cope with Grandfather's despair and demands. Every Monday and Thursday, Grandmother would go to the Wailing Wall, on the evening of the New Moon, she'd go to Rachel's Tomb, prostrate herself on the graves of her forefathers on the Mount of Olives, and mainly lingered in the synagogue and responded "Amen" and "May His great name grow exalted" after the Kaddish, "since, after all, there's nobody to say Kaddish for the soul of the little girls, Heaven Forbid."

For that she might have forgiven her, said Mother, if she hadn't returned one morning from the Yeshiva Ha-Matmidim, and hiding behind the curtain spread in the corner of the room, that enclave of privacy for changing clothes, and shaving her head, said that, according to Rabbi Shlomo Zalman Brizl, the yeshiva teacher, the death of her two granddaughters was a punishment from Heaven because her daughter showed the flesh of her arms and legs, didn't cover her hair according to Jewish law and walked around in colorful, arrogant clothes. "The children of harlots don't have guardian angels that accompany them on the road and save them from all trouble and distress," Grandmother quoted the words of the rabbi, who was the life spirit of the "Guardians of Modesty," and she didn't hear Mother slip out without a sound. All day long she trudged through the streets, crossed roads without looking, praying that a car would hit her, but when darkness fell, she returned to the Hungarian Houses, to her father sobbing silently in the dark and calling her name and to her mother wringing her hands with worry. "I am like a pelican of the wilderness: I am like an owl of the desert. I watch, and am as a sparrow alone upon the house top," said Mother and stopped at the corner of King George and Narkiss Streets. In a small glass box fixed to the wall, left of the entrance to "Beit Ha-Ma'alot," Alfred Bern-heim, owner of an artistic photographic studio, was presenting his portrait of Agnon this month. For a long time, Mother ex-amined the writer's sober, ironic look and said that if she had listened to the cracked voice between the lines of his stories, she would have known that such a return was destined to failure from the beginning. "I should have gone to a kibbutz, rented a room for myself, or if need be, slept in abandoned laundry rooms on roofs, but should not have gone back to the Hungarian Houses, not even for the week of mourning."

"In those days, I lay with my limbs crushed on the bottom of a well," said Mother as we crossed King George Street, which was steeped in the Sabbath slumber. "And the only one who came down to me, risked his life to let himself down through the nar-row opening, fearing neither avalanche nor poison gas, was Isaac, when all the others stood around and wrung their hands." And she added that, now that she sees the events "with a bit more per-spective," she can say that her brother was the only one who related to her and not to the disaster that befell her. ("You're an only child, and you'll never understand that," Mother would answer me later on, when I'd come to her with questions about the complex system of relations—a skein of love and hate and jealousy and friendship—that prevailed among the children of Grandfather and Grandmother. "Take eight boys and girls, and of course a mother and father, and imprison them in thirty-eight square meters, let them sleep together, two to a bed, or on the floor, next to one another on mattresses, and don't let a single one of them have anything private of his own, not a garment, not a book, not a drawer to hide something in, and that's how they're forced to spend all the days of their youth, dreadfully crowded, going through adolescence in public, the first menstrual period, the first nocturnal ejaculation, and if that weren't enough, some-times they wake up in the middle of the night and hear Mother's bed moving, and Father groaning, and then the awful silence— nothing normal can come from such a dense human existence." And she would always add that it was luck—Mother never used the word miracle—that they didn't come out even worse.) Isaac volunteered to help her, Mother explained, because of the secret spiritual connection that had taken shape between them ever since the day he was born: she was seven years old, seven and a half at the most, when, one day at dusk, without permission, she watched him being born. Scared, but looking directly ("as I did all my life," she emphasized) from her hiding place under her father's bed, which had been moved to a corner of the room, she watched her mother lying with her bare legs up in the air. She had never seen them before, ("and those enormous white legs had a life of their own, because I didn't see her face.") She heard her groans and curses, saw the feet of the midwife and her sister Rachel running, bringing in pots of hot water, saw the bandages dripping blood ("I thought all her blood would flow out of her any minute and she'd die"), and finally she saw the little doll, its face wrinkled and shriveled, that was wrapped in a white sheet, heard the midwife call out "Hanneke, *a zun, a lebediker zun*," and heard her sobbing mother's sigh of relief, "*danken Gott.*" "From then on, I was his little mother," she said and described how she amused him and diapered him, and especially how he became attached to her when her mother got pregnant again and again, and was bothered with miscarriages and delivering a baby who died at birth. "Now, when everything was shattered to splinters and I cried out for help, he came to my aid like a son." And Mother's eyes rested on my face, carefully examining every nod or tilt of my head, in a touching attempt to decipher the secrets of the future, which was destined to fail.

Soon after Mother's return to the Hungarian Houses, her brother quit his job in the Mandatory Electric Company and rented the shop near King George Street to open a fish store. Like everybody else, Grandmother couldn't fathom his intention and claimed that he was throwing away his chances in life. ("Look at Ravinek and Zelinker. Like my Itsikl, they also climbed on poles in the rain and the sun and repaired *kurzshluss*, but they had patience," Grandmother would still lament many years later, when Isaac had succeeded in America. "And after the English left, they went into the offices and became officials who get the salaries of ministers, and every day they take a hot bath, because electricity flows in their house like water, while my dummy went to sell fish.") According to his secret plan, the fish store, as Mother put it, was to be a lifeline he'd drop down to get her out. Only years later, did she understand that his delicate soul and his wisdom kept her brother from revealing his plan lest she reject his outstretched hand. "On the contrary, he didn't tell me that I needed his help, but rather that he desperately needed my help, and if I wouldn't come and be his partner in the store, the business would collapse."

And so, to assist Isaac, the closest person she had left in the world, in the adventure he had gotten into, Mother gathered up whatever was left of her strength and followed him into the fish business. "Every morning I had to get up, comb my hair, smear lipstick on my lips, get dressed like a normal person—Rehavia isn't Geula or the Hungarian Houses—and go out to life." And so, reluctantly, she started breaking away from her father who tyrannized her with his wretchedness, and from her mother, who along with all her previous acts of piety took to going to the miracle worker in the old Beit Israel neighborhood whenever she had a bad dream, and there she'd reinterpret her dream to make it come out better. And she even got away from herself a bit. The work was back-breaking, and she suffered mainly from the gills of the sea fish whose sharp points scratched her hands until they bled and left ugly scars on them. And sometimes, when the fish was polluted, she was also afflicted with severe blood poisoning. ("That's exactly how my hands looked when I worked with fish," she remarked once, out of the blue, when she was leafing through an art book and came on a painting by Jackson Pollock.)

And yet, being with constantly changing strangers worked its effect during the day ("I simply couldn't burst out before the customers," Mother explained. "If I didn't keep up the façade they'd stop buying from us. After all, nobody wants to salt the Sabbath fish with tears") and the great fatigue worked its effect at night. "The enormity of the pain didn't decrease, but its bulk went down a little," said Mother when we sat down on one of the new benches the city had put up along the concrete wall that was hastily erected during the war to protect passers-by from getting hit by Arab snipers sitting on the Old City Wall. "It didn't shrink, but it got scrunched, like a spring, and when it was released, it sliced my chest, and like a dum-dum bullet, it shattered me inside."

That usually happened during the noon break. Her brother used the break to take care of business with the wholesalers, while she'd stay in the store, behind the half-lowered grate, to clean up and get ready to reopen in the afternoon. In the silence that would descend on her in the empty store, her life would once again scatter into slivers, and she'd see little Yael sitting in front of the aquarium Aunt Ayala had given her, putting her little lips to the glass case and imitating the way a pair of guppies moved their mouths. Mother would then drop the fish she was scraping and cover her face with her filthy hands that smelled of death and abysses. "I couldn't stand it, and I'd flee to the streets, walk like a shadow along the walls and ledges," her hand stretched out, sketching the orbits of destruction of her life.

"Sometimes, when I couldn't bear my life anymore, I'd sneak up to the roof." Mother who kept opening and closing the clasp of her purse, suddenly fell silent, took hold of my hand, clutched it hard, and said that people would probably say that all that talk was liable to cause me serious emotional damage and I'd be better off growing up in a healthy atmosphere, "but from my experience, I know that a person can smother the past and bury it very deep in secret places of the grave, but its shadows will keep walking around, many times stronger and bigger, on the walls of his life." And furthermore, she said, who knew me and my soul better than her, and she had no doubt that the things I was hearing here, today, from her mouth, would shape me and prepare me for life.

Once again Mother fiddled with the clasp of her purse, and asked if I knew that every young woman gets a period once a month and menstruation is the indication that the body is preparing itself once again for pregnancy. Not only didn't I understand the strange turn in her talk, as if she were planning to begin a lesson in sex education — like a school nurse — but a blush also rose onto my cheeks. My embarrassment was compounded when Mother remarked that a boy who was invited to his classmate's bat-mitzvah should be grown up enough to listen to such things naturally and without fidgeting uneasily.

"I knew all the roofs here, from three stories and up," Mother returned from the slight deviation from the track of her story, a deviation whose meaning became clear only later, and looking up, carefully combing the skyline of large buildings facing us and next to us, she said, "You understand, I wanted to take my life.

Whenever I went up to one of the roofs, I dared to take one more step to the edge of the building, to glance with a sweet, hypnotic yearning into the back yards and streets that were so close beneath me. I practiced so that at the crucial moment, I'd have the strength to take the last little step to liberating destruction, and after it there'd be no more grief or longing."

Today, as I write these lines, forcing myself to make a futile effort to restore the full picture with maximum precision and not to make do with noting selected moments preserved in the disorder of memory, in its fondness for details, the question that has preoccupied me all these years — of where Mother got the strength to expose her internal world to me so openly and transparently back then, on a Sabbath afternoon, as we came out of the Bezalel Museum — bothers me less than the much more tormenting and cruel question of why she did that. And to give a reasonable answer to that question, not only do I have to breathe life into Mother's portrait, as it is preserved in my memory, tended with the diligence of love and yearning, and to resurrect our relations, but I also have to recognize that a mother also has selfish needs, that Mother wasn't aware of them, and projected them on me. Did she realize that she might need me to fill her narcissistic desires and that in fact I was subjected to unconscious manipulation, and like every child who is exploited by his mother, I developed the sensibilities to absorb the feelings of others. But putting these words on paper seems to prove that writing as the work of mourning achieved that blessed release, and exposes that known quantity of personality that managed to survive beneath the layers of pretense, denial, and self-alienation. Nevertheless, I won't easily give up the feeling that, unlike the character of the exploiting, perhaps even destructive mother, described here with so much repressed anger, Mother succeeded in freeing herself from her past and overcoming it, and so on that Sabbath she was able to feel empathy for me, to consider my needs as she understood them, and to treat me with respect as expressed in a conversation between us. And perhaps that stubbornness of mine is really the definitive proof that I still go on absorbing what Mother wanted from me, responding to her and adapting to her demands by giving up my own needs.

As I bend over the unconscious body of that distant Sabbath

afternoon in an effort to restore its spirit and revive it, I realize
how recalcitrant memory can be. You can coax it to talk until it
consents and tells what color Mother's silk blouse was (misty bluish, lacking any sweetness, like Wedgwood pottery), what smell
greeted us at the entrance of King George Street (the stench of
police horses that had galloped past shortly before on their way
to disperse a demonstration of Neturei Karta, leaving their droppings on the street, blended with the perfumed fragrance of the
Spanish broom blossoming in the nearby park) or what my fingers were busy doing while Mother spoke (I was folding the ex-
planatory papers we had gotten at Bezalel and making fans of
them, annoying Mother, who remarked "you decided to open a
workshop for pleated skirts," and asked me to stop it because it
disturbed her concentration). But memory will altogether refuse
to answer the question of what you were thinking or feeling at
that time. Those details — the best thing to open the eyes of this
world you're trying to resurrect — are also the hardest to achieve.
Thoughts and feelings, which are abstract and ephemeral, are
apparently the first to be crushed to death under the waves of
forgetting, and only when they're trapped in the concreteness of
words and phrases and tales do they preserve the likeness of their
model, like that bee or beetle down on its luck and trapped in the
stream of resin flowing onto primeval forests, and for that choking death they're condemned to eternal life imprisoned in transparent amber in pendants on the breasts of rich ladies.

And so, as Mother stands at the edge of the roof in her story,
the strong wind blowing there striking the back of her neck and
pushing her toward the abyss gaping at her feet, tempting her
with vain promises of eternal serenity, I start ripping the sheets of
paper wildly, fiercely, and mainly with an awful feeling of insult,
"You're crazy, crazy, what are you doing, if you fell, I wouldn't
exist now either."

"But you are alive," she stroked my head. "And so am I, only
because of you." And then she glanced at her watch, got up from
the bench and suggested we go see my school as I wanted, and as
we walked she told me that the last time she went up on the roof
to seek her death, on the roof of the nearby Beit Ha-Ma'alot,
when she almost saw the sidewalk beneath her and already saw
the treetops, so close was she to the edge, she suddenly felt that

she had gotten her period. "And all of a sudden, like a bolt out of the blue, I knew I wasn't lost, that I was still young enough for a new life to sprout in me, that if I only wanted to, I could be a mother to a living child again." She said that and took the lipstick

out of her purse, glanced at the oval mirror I had bought her for Mother's Day, painted her upper lip very precisely and then,

with the light movement of a kiss, pressed her lower lip against it. Flooded with a cold sweat, said Mother, she then retreated, with all her might, she gripped the rusty water barrels lined up along the roof, until she came to the entrance to the staircase and started going down, very slowly, one floor after another. When she came out to the street, flooded again with the strong afternoon light, she buried her face in her rust-covered hands and burst into heaving sobs, the first time she had wept in her life. "And from then on, life for me is the smell of rust mixed with tears."

3

Up to now, choosing the moment this chapter opens had seemed so obvious that only in retrospect, when I starting teasing out the first thread of that skein of events enfolding Mother's two daughters, did I realize how foolish and naïve I was to fix the search of our house by the inspectors of the Rationing Office, not only as a proper starting point for the chapter, but as the precise date when the two little girls burst without warning into my life. I never did deny the hidden but significant role the little girls played in my life even before that, since their little hands reached out to me from the vague phantom world where they dwelled. Not only had they preceded me, but according to the geometry of the dead, whose relations with the living don't end anywhere, they were also the ones who drew their circles around my cradle, and those invisible drawings will never be wiped out. And yet I discovered how mistaken I was to think that reality first rolled up the screen Mother had pulled down over their lives and their deaths to separate them from me, that afternoon when she and I returned from visiting a friend of hers, and our neighbor, who was afflicted with a goiter, stood there polishing her windows and announced with obvious joy that a gang of rioters of the military governor Bernard Joseph had invaded our house and made a pogrom.

At home, we found Father sitting and gazing among the mountains of clothes and wide-open closets. Mother froze on the spot, and then she wrung her hands and asked in a whisper how this was different from the sights of destruction in Hebron, that were described in the newspapers after the riots of 1929. She wandered around aimlessly among the beds, where a lot of things were heaped up, and then she dropped onto one of them and cursed that anonymous and ungrateful customer who informed on them to the authorities, accusing her and Father of engaging in black market activities. Father, who sat forsaken at the window, with strange and delicate lattice shadows resting on his face and shoulders, kept muttering over and over that at the end of that very thorough search, all the loot the *khaleriyas* got was a tin box with a pound of unshelled almonds Mother had gotten at the Vegetarian House, in exchange for the portion of meat and fish she didn't eat. I leaned on Mother who buried her face in the wreckage of her dresses and my dread slowly turned into curiosity at the unexpected treasures turned out of their hiding places. My eye was drawn especially to a small cylinder like a lipstick, swaddled in a white sheet carefully sewn around it, and two children's dresses, one pink and one white, lying on top of one of the heaps of clothes. "Whose is that?" I asked Mother, pointing to the dresses and picking up the strange object. Mother glanced at me as through a crack and immediately recovered, got up and without a word, hung the little dresses on a hanger and piled three dresses she had stopped wearing long ago on top of them, and quickly buried them all in the empty clothes closet. Then she asked me to give her back the little cylinder and promised that in the evening, after she had straightened up the house, she would tell me about the amulet hidden in it, an amulet she had gotten from an old Babylonian Kabbalist, an expert in palmistry, the day the university opened on Mount Scopus. "And the dresses — did you have little girls?" I didn't relent, and a vague, old memory lying in the depths started floating up to the domes of consciousness. But Mother, like a trained and bold chess player willing to sacrifice a less important piece to save the queen, ignored my interrogation, beckoned me to follow her to the kitchen, where she whispered, so her words wouldn't steal into Father's ears, that I should be proud she had found me grown up enough, and fit, to reveal to me those concealed and sealed secrets she hadn't wanted to share with anybody before. In the end, that evening I didn't hear what the Kabbalist palmist saw on her palm that made him tell her what would happen to her in the future. Shortly after Father shut himself up in the kitchen to work on his miracle potions, a smell of valerian bubbled up through the closed door. "Father's heart," Mother raced there and found him shrunk in a corner, his gray frightened face blurred by tears. He was holding his chest and muttering "Gefu . . . Gefu . . ." Mother led him to bed and said he should thank God that the apparatchiks of *di yiddishe medineh* didn't take him along to prison in the Russian Compound and she signaled to me to go get Dr. Israelit.

This scene was the first thread I pulled out of that tangled skein of the past, intending to attach other threads to it, every single one separated, in order to weave them into the fabric of life constantly flowing dark and changing. But I had already used it many years ago in my first book of prose, where I embedded it, distorted and adapted to the needs of the plot. Now, when the person in me rebels against the story teller, as Nabokov confessed, and I came to redeem it from captivity and restore it to its original place, I realized, like the author of *Speak, Memory* after he borrowed the portrait of his nanny for the lad in one of his stories, that the scene had been swallowed up in the artificial world where I had placed it without much hesitation, and there it was assimilated into its new place, an assimilation more complete than in the previous reality, where it had once seemed to be protected from the interference of the artist.

And then, when I thought I had succeeded in the work of extrication, which was accompanied by an oppressive sense of shame for my frivolity and extravagance during the writing of *Feathers*, one of those blessed moments came to me when spacious plains of life are suddenly opened before you and you see with bold clarity sights that speak in the direct present tense, even though they were meant for other times.

From the distance of time, from days whose memory was lost and hours that seem wiped out, I saw myself sitting and dozing next to Father, squashed on a bench, between men leaning around a long table, a coarse, bare wooden table, in the depths of the big synagogue of the Akhva neighborhood, in the morning dimness of the day before Passover. Their heads leaning on their flaccid, naked arms, whose flesh was still stamped with the imprint of the tefillin straps that had just been removed, the bedraggled burghers were listening to Reb Moshe Leyb Black who was teaching them the issue that closes the Talmud tractate Pessahim. I myself sat looking back, counting one by one the green, blue, and red puddles of light pouring on the stone floor, and the sheaves that burst through the colored glass panes of the eastern windows, prancing between them. Father, who had woken me up that morning at dawn to take me with him to the feast of the firstborn, told me as we passed through the deserted streets, that we, the firstborn, had to torment our souls on that day and fast, as a sign of thanks to the Lord of Hosts for distinguishing between us and the Egyptians, a fast that can be broken only by a feast of commandment held after finishing the study of the tractate. And when he described that dreadful moment of midnight, when God came out and smote all the firstborn in the Land of Egypt, from the first born of Pharaoh sitting on his throne to the firstborn of the servant behind the millstones, Father withdrew to the mythic time sealed with the stamp of eternity. And I, too, who woke up with the firstborn of Israel to life and peace, I became with him one of those myriads reflected, and no one knows who they are and in what generation they live and the last of them looks at us from the big marble tablets set on the walls of the House of God, from the names of our forgotten forefathers engraved there in a confusion of times. "We shall study you again, Tractate Pessahim," Reb Moshe Leyb Black's face beamed, and the many generations echoing in his voice lent his countenance a secret exaltation, and we answer after him like an echo "We shall study you again, we shall study you again," promising to return here in other times. The call of the reader made Mr. Rivkesh, the sexton, jump out of his alcove. He had been lying in wait for this moment, he tightened the old tie wound around his neck like a hangman's noose, and sent his two boys, his adjutants, to set up bottles of liquor and cups and to bring plates of herring from the pantry, as he himself passed among us and passed out the traditional cakes, eaten at this feast of commandment — round cakes that look like pincushions, with coarse sugar sprinkled on them. When he came to me, Rivkesh pinched my cheeks with his skinny, rheumatic fingers that emanated a sweetish, disgusting fragrance of vanilla intensified by the smell of medicinal cognac and the juice of chopped fish, and said that, according to the law, he didn't have to give me any cake. "Thou are not a firstling," he explained in biblical language, and when he realized that I didn't understand, he said in simple words, "You aren't your mother's firstborn. They didn't tell you that she had children who died before you were born?" Father chased him away with a furious gesture, warned him not to gossip in that holy house, broke off half his cake, and said—and I don't know if his voice was choked from the cake or from grief—that for him I'd always be his first-born. When we came out of the prayer house, Father, who had recovered by then, advised me not to pay attention to the impetuous things people say, and to emphasize his words, he said that ever since Rivkesh's young daughter was burned to death when the fire from the Sabbath candles caught her nylon robe, the sexton's mind was muddled and his whole world was populated by dead little boys and girls. But when he realized that his attempts to tighten the bond of silence he and Mother had tied around me had failed miserably, he said that human beings shouldn't indulge in vain investigations and shouldn't rack their brain with questions about what is found above and what is hidden below, and especially shouldn't try to decipher the tempting but meaningless secret of what happened before they were born, but rather should face forward bravely, toward the future. And after he pondered, he added that he was counting on me to forget the stupid incident in the synagogue, and mainly not to ask Mother anything, for she was busy enough with the store and the holiday and her mind wasn't free to give me answers to such questions.

I don't have a satisfactory answer to the question of why I didn't protest then, when Father quickly and firmly moved me away from the pit gaping at my feet between the colored puddles of light, or simply, why I repressed my curiosity and didn't persist in clarifying what the deranged sexton meant. Was the abyss he exposed so menacing and tempting that I yielded without resisting to Father's hand holding me and obediently retreated from the rim of the pit so the void wouldn't draw me into it? Or was the answer enfolded in another question, a harder and more complicated one, emanating from the previous one, like a box from a box, the question of how the repression of that incident, as Father called that scene, was so successful that only now does that distant memory return and come to stand before me so vividly? In the essay, "In a Room and a Half" about his years in Leningrad, Joseph Brodsky writes that the common element of memory and art is the skill of choice and the sense of taste for details, but this discernment, which apparently even flatters art, especially the art of fiction, is an offense to memory. Yet, the connection between the mechanisms of preference and the surrender of art and memory, which Brodsky pointed to, may, I hope, help me understand to some extent that blocked process of rejecting the memory of that event in the synagogue for the later memory involving the search of our house by the inspectors of the Rationing Office. The preference for the one memory and its persistent cultivation by careful repetition, which evoked words about it and led to a certain crystallization of it, and especially to an artistic shaping, might be what blocked the earlier, vivid but shapeless memory, and prevented it from floating up. And who would guarantee me that that memory itself, an act that surfaced at long last, even before the flesh of the words was closed beneath it, won't ward off what it now wants to destroy from those internal places that never know peace. And the hand that wants to hold onto those abstract things, that no longer have shape but essence, as they were back then in fact vibrations, an eternal and direct present — that hand will return empty.

The time for the little girls to enter my life openly will arrive, inadvertently, in the summer vacation between the sixth and seventh grades, on one of those calm days, with no obligations, that always pass idly without being engraved in memory, when I'll take advantage of the absence of Father and Mother, and with a sudden impulse will reach into the depths of the clothes closet and find the photos of them.

"Strange things are liable to happen when you leave a child at home alone," I heard Aunt Nehama scolding Mother that night as she lay next to her in the dark, and tormented her for adding a sin to a crime and daring to tell me things a child my age shouldn't know.

A few times a year, always on Tuesday, when businesses aren't open in the afternoon, Aunt Nehama would hide in a secret place the "portable shop" — a leather bag crammed with post-office and Knesset stamps, bills and lottery tickets, that she carried up and down neglected staircases in south Tel Aviv on her swollen legs, to plead with lawyers, accountants, and customs agents — would prepare meals for Uncle Jacob and her stepson Issur, and would go to Jerusalem to visit Mother — "my own private Wailing Wall," as she put it. On those nights, Father would give up his bed and sleep next to me, and the two women, as in the days of their childhood in the Hungarian Houses, would lie in the dark, each one telling her troubles to her sister until their eyes shut. When I'd eavesdrop on them sometimes, I'd hear Aunt Nehama delivering a long tortuous monologue to Mother always about constantly coping with the hardships that befell them ever since they lost the big wholesale dealership they had owned, about the uncle who had to pass by the door of the shop now run by strangers every single day in his old age, about the treason of relatives and friends, and about the shame and disgrace, her constant companions as she trudged between the offices, needing the pity of donors who still remembered her from the good old days. *"Ober meh tor dokh nisht zindikn,"* was the repeated refrain she'd recite devoutly and confidently. On the outside there was acceptance of the judgment, but inside there was a suppressed mutiny.

And so, that day, as Aunt Nehama put it, I was left alone. Ever since the Sabbath, Father had been staying at his brother's house in Nahalal. He went there, as every year, to visit the grave of his mother, Bobbe Mindl, whose memorial day fell on Sunday, but he stayed in the Jezreel Valley another few days to see his relatives and fellow townsmen (Father uttered the word *shtotike* with such intimacy as if he were hinting that it was a private territory that none of us, that is Mother and me, could set foot in). Mother herself used the afternoon until Aunt Nehama came, to take part in an activity of the "Federation of Vegetarians and Naturalists," which was held at Beit Ha-Halutzot in Rehavia — the weekly yoga lesson, and a lecture by Dr. Netsakh, the guide to the perplexed from Mishmar Ha-Sheva, who explained ecological issues, extolling the preparation of domestic compost and warning of the danger of fruit and vegetables sprayed with insecticides, and taught his audience to understand the innovations in combining different foods. Before she left me alone, Mother did urge me to finish what I had to do to prepare for the new school year, but the do-it-yourself workbooks for the vacation bored me and it was much nicer for me to use her absence from the house for rummaging in the closets to see what I could find.

"Father's side," as Mother used to call his part of the triple-door wardrobe, was a land of unlimited opportunities for me. The soul of a collector was latent inside Father, but was almost never actualized. Once, when he noticed the spark of desire kindled in my eyes at the sight of an airmail envelope Mrs. Melitz got from Argentina with three stamps of different values with the image of Evita Peron, he sighed and said that as a person who roamed and roved in the world all his life, he was forced to brutally subjugate his instinct for collecting, and even now, in his old age, when he had reached the last stop of his wanderings — *di letste statsia* — his steps were constricted. "Your father was an exiled collector who had to seek political shelter in a land ruled by functional realism," said Mother many years after his death, and in her voice I thought I heard a thin tone of regret, even though she never expressed her grief openly.

First I checked the shoe box where Father preserved family mementos: an antique silver goblet, his great-grandfather's Kiddush goblet which was put on the table for holidays. It had come to our house from the flickering steppes of the Ukraine, where two sharp medieval villas were etched, with towers and a river flowing between them; the Soviet passport, a deliberate series of blunders that got him out of the Soviet Union (the bearded face of a student from czarist times, so different from the beaten, wounded, and lost face of the man I knew, an immigrant in a land that did not requite his love, glared at me whenever I leafed through the red-covered passport); the page from the 1945 calendar, where he recorded my birth with a pencil stub; my drawings from kindergarten and the first essay I wrote about the jet of oil that burst in a well in Israel. In that box, Father also kept ten war bonds (he bought them in a burst of patriotism to Mother's dismay. She claimed it was better to buy new down quilts and prophesied that those bonds would end up like the bonds of Franz Josef that her grandfather bought out of trust in the rock of salvation of the Emperor of Austro-Hungary and his great-granddaughters used them to wipe their doll's bottoms), a license to keep "a wireless instrument (radio)," and a curl of my hair that was cut the night before I went to Rivka Strikovsky's kindergarten.

Then I peeped into the innards of the Zionist sarcophagus — as Mother called the cardboard box where, as she put it, Father buried the bones of the state after its meat was eaten. His admiration for the Jewish state that rose from the ashes after two thousand years like the phoenix, the admiration that was demolished with the visit of the agents of the Rationing Office in our house, made him a diligent collector of the various expressions of the resurrection: the first paper money issued by the temporary government, "Hebrew post office" stamps and envelopes of the first day of the State, copies of newspapers reporting on historical events like the liberation of the Negev and the fall of Gush Etsion and the Old City, the declaration of the State and the declaration of independence of the State, legends for Independence Day, and menus for holiday feasts. The items he loved most were the pages of the battle in the south and a delegate's card to the first Zionist Congress held in Jerusalem—he got those from Yoske Sorek, the son of old Sirkis, who was an officer in the Negev Brigade, in exchange for eggs and butter in the days when food was rationed.

But Father's main glory was his collection of Seder plates. Collecting them was an open declaration of revolt against Mother, who remarked time and again with haughty contempt that she didn't understand how many plates a person needed for a feast that takes place once a year. Father ignored her, and now and then he'd drag out from under the sofa the wooden Valencia Orange crate that still smelled of the sweetish chemical solution used to disinfect citrus fruit. He'd take the plates out of it and display them. And as he examined them fondly, he said that the organizers of a "hobby exhibition" showed how stupid they were not to respond to his invitation to come determine whether to include his collection in their exhibition. There were a Yemenite copper plate brought to Israel from the British crown colony of Aden by an Irish officer, who served in the Shneller Camp close to our house and who needed cash; two black bitumen dishes, the handiwork of some anonymous Jerusalem artist; and a brass plate he bought from a Holocaust survivor from Poland, with a snake stamped in its center and the words "For out of the serpent's root shall come forth a cockatrice." Only many years after Mother got rid of Father's collection of plates, selling it for pennies to an antique dealer on Princess Mary Street, did I realize that that plate was an extremely rare Sabbatean dish, used by one of the followers of the false messiah (Natan He-Azti called Shabbetai Zevi, "the holy serpent." And a collector of Judaica, who wrung his hands when he heard, told me he'd be willing to pay a king's ransom for that popular artistic expression of the

Midrash the Sabbateans adopted, attributing the prophecy of Isaiah to the Messiah ben David, and that the numerical value of the letters of the serpent in Gematriya equaled that of the letters of the Messiah). Aside from the antique plates, Father also acquired new ones that expressed the Ingathering of the Exiles, the settlement of the Land and its resurrection; and the place of honor was accorded to the patriotic Seder plates that were hammered out by our neighbor Mr. Har-Sheleg in his little workshop for ritual articles. Mr. Har-Sheleg was one of the leaders of "Brit Hasmoneans" and one of the regular worshippers at the "Ahdut Israel" synagogue, a stronghold of those from the right-wing Etzel and Lehi organizations. In the center of his plates were the portraits of Herzl, Rav Kook, Lord Balfour, and Jabotinsky in their scene of action — from the balcony in Basel, through the Western Wall and placing the cornerstone for the university on Mount Scopus, to the Mandatory prison where the British imprisoned the "Protector of Jerusalem." Mrs. Har-Sheleg, who wasn't daunted by her husband's artistic pretensions, would complain to Mother that in their house on Passover they were forced to gather crumbs of bitter herbs from the beard of the visionary of the State or wipe the Haroseth from between the unclean lips of Balfour, and with another wink, that Efraim-Fishl, her brother's son who was studying at the Tree of Life Yeshiva, refused to taste the sweet mortar, arguing that the English goy made the wine in the Haroseth forbidden. One evening, during the Sinai Campaign as Father was bent over the radio, accompanying the regiments invading the Sinai Peninsula, Mother came in from the shop and said that, according to Mrs. Har-Sheleg, her goldsmith had started hammering out a new dish which was to show Moshe Dayan standing at the foot of Mount Sinai and Our Teacher Moses holding the Tablets, and the two of them stretching out a hand of peace to one another, and above them the words "From Moses to Moses None Like Moses." When Father heard of the new initiative of the goldsmith with a sense of current events, he giggled and remarked that on the next Passover Seder, if two eggs were placed in the lap of Abu-Ghilda of Nahalal, his arm would salute. But the next day, Mother found out that Father had ordered a victory plate from Har-Sheleg and even agreed with a solemn handshake that someday he'd also purchase a plate etched with the glorious

98

HAIM
BE'ER

image of Menahem Begin waving the flag of Israel on top of the Temple Mount.

But even though Father's side was rich and varied and hid surprises like an antique shop, my heart yearned for Mother's side. There was something exciting about the unpretentious simplicity there in the jumble of the few pieces of jewelry and the bundle of random documents that survived after all the sorting and destruction, singing a paean to her contempt for imaginary possessions. Mother, I assume, would have a few reservations about the way I formulated the end of the last sentence and would have wanted me to choose the words from a more careful and modest scale of language, for example: expressing (or maybe better, demonstrating) her indifference to objects.

The secret of the charm of the objects and the combinations created on her side didn't have to do with what they were — although even today I tend to accept as self-evident her esthetic taste in jewelry, a taste I internalized in my childhood — but with the meaning they were known to have in the various contexts of her life. A payment book recording the monthly sums she paid for the sewing machine she bought after the fish store closed became an exciting document to me only after I heard her tell Haika Kipnis what an effort it had cost her to purchase the Singer and how for two whole years she couldn't buy a new dress or even a bra, so that she could keep up with the payments. "If you've got ten fingers and good tools and you're not afraid of work, you'll never starve," she said, and she told that some days she drowned all her grief in sewing until the winged sphinx painted on the neck of the machine in black and gold looked to her like the twin of the Shekhina with broken wings mourning for the Destruction. Mother's coral necklace won my heart not just because of the purple light trapped in the beads, which are the most beautiful in the world, but because of the thin fragrance of memory that escapes from the coral when they rub against one another. One Purim, I dressed up as an effendi and took the necklace to the costume party at school to use as worry beads, even though Mother wasn't happy about it. And, while rolling the beads between my fingers, as Moslems count the names of Allah, the thread holding them was torn and they scattered in the playground. You can imagine how scared I was when I returned home with the beads gathered up burning with disgrace in the pocket of the effendi's suit, the remnant of his foppish beard wiped out with tears. Mother clutched me to her, kissed my cheeks (never will I forget her lips turning black) and said that nothing had happened, ultimately the corals wanted to return to the bottom of the Tethis Sea, and didn't I know that there's no stopping someone who wants to return to his homeland with all his heart. "If your geography teacher didn't sell his soul to the obscurantists, someday he'll teach you that millions of years ago, all Jerusalem was covered with a primal sea."

Mother enlisted some of the documents and jewelry as improvised educational aids to illustrate her opinions and beliefs. The gold bracelet, in the petit-bourgeois taste of the early 1950s, a bracelet made of hollow cubes coupled together like railroad cars (once Mother gave into Har-Sheleg's coaxing and gave him her old jewelry, which she didn't like anymore, to be melted down into a new fashionable bracelet). It didn't fit her wrist and she never wore it, but whenever she wanted to prove to me how capricious and absurd people's taste was, she would deliver a sermon on it. Like a magician, she'd open the blue cardboard box where it lay on a bed of cotton, and say that the golden calf that came from the hands of Har-Sheleg was only a proof of how quickly tastes change and what was just recently considered modern craftsmanship was now old-fashioned kitsch, but it also taught us why gold was superior to human beings: "Gold can be recycled over and over again. And when you get married, your wife will be able to melt down this miserable bracelet and make some new piece of jewelry that will suit her time. But human beings are good for only a single use, like a cotton ball you use to wipe pus."

The affidavit her sister and brother sent her from America (I could attach no literal meaning to that foreign word Mother frequently wove into her stories. But she pronounced it with such respect, gravely parting *affi* and *davit*, stressing them individually like two first names, that the pair of those mysterious American guys became very powerful because they determined whether she'd be able to make her dreams come true) and the Mandatory passport she applied for right after she got the American document (I loved her transparent face in the oval porthole, trapped between two pages of the passport, with the word Palestine printed diagonally across it, her erect, bare neck, her open gaze into the distance, and mainly her lips clenched proudly, but without any contempt or arrogance, as if to say: Thank you, but I don't need encouragement or consolation, I'll find my way on my own) proved to Mother that a person is not the master of his life, that it is directed in advance by an ancient decree of fate. Mother slapped together those two invalid documents and said that in spite of everything, the prophecy of the old Kabbalist who read her palm when she was twenty years old had come true, that she would never leave the borders of the Land of Israel. And indeed, two weeks after she had all the papers, and the ship that was to take her to America, to a new beginning, was rowing here on the sea, Father appeared in her life and confounded all her plans. "It looks like you insisted on being born and you turned a deaf ear to the dim sirens of the *Abraham Lincoln* entering the harbor." And then, tying up the passport and the affidavit, she added that if I ever remember that conversation again and wonder how those two opposites—fatalism and the demand for a supreme self effort—lived together harmoniously, I shouldn't forget the "constructive pessimism" she learned from the workers back when she worked for Esther Kalko, at the Histadrut, making blankets. For her, that phrase was the key to understanding the absurdity.

The only jewelry Mother was really attached to was a silver pin she had bought early in the spring of 1945. When I was two months old, she took me for a first walk in downtown Jerusalem, drawn to the life she had been cut off from when she was confined to bed during her pregnancy. In the little display window of Merayon, the refined antique and jewelry shop in Zion Square, she was enchanted by a rectangular silver pin with rounded corners that looked like steel. A hint of a branch was welded on it. The minimalist beauty of the lone branch, of the three elongated leaves like willow leaves bending down, either weeping or bowing in gratitude, and the one tiny fruit, a little ball at the end of the branch, was like a metaphor of her life. For a long time, she stood at the window, rocking the baby buggy, and couldn't take her eyes off the pin, until at last, the saleswoman, Mrs. Rebecca Merayon, came out and invited her in. And so, on the spot, she dared to buy herself the jewelry. She and Father had no money, and the price of the pin was enough to support a couple with a child for two weeks, but Mrs. Merayon said that the flash of joy kindled in the eye of the discerning customer was worth more in her eyes than making a profit. "Objets d'art should belong to those who deserve them," she said, and gave Mother a handsome discount and even allowed her to pay the sum in installments, whenever she had money. "I have no doubt that you'll pay me what you owe. The baby's wide-open eyes are an excellent guarantee."

"This is the gift I bought myself in honor of your birth. The only gift. No one thought of giving me a gift after I got you as a gift from Heaven," said Mother as she put on the pin for the last time in her life, a few months before her death, on the way to her sister's grandson's wedding. In Merayon's tiny, narrow shop, Mother put the pin on her chest, between her breasts that were once again producing milk ("From the day the little girls died until he was born, I hated them. As far as I was concerned, I would have been willing to have them cut off me," she once told Aunt Miriam, who, while waiting for her to finish getting dressed, remarked that she had breasts as handsome as a girl's), and set out on a triumphal journey, pushing the baby buggy on the Via Dolorosa she had walked many years before from the hospital to her parents' home, pushing the empty buggy of her dead little girl.

The main attraction of Mother's side was the collection of family photos in her leather purses. The illusion of the camera drew the eye to these outmoded purses. All those people who were scattered in all directions by the vicissitudes of fate and were gathered together here, once again, with no barriers, the living and the dead, the near and the far, those who hated and those who loved, images from distant times that for me were mythological darkness and images still illuminated by the light of memory, ostensibly joined in an intimacy with no reality. On rainy Sabbaths, Mother would pull bundles of photos out of one of the purses and paint complex family miniatures for me, replete with envy and greed, wretchedness and pain: telling about her cousin, an ignorant woman, who married an educated and scholarly teacher, and her intense jealousy of her husband and his world drove her so crazy that one day, in a fit of madness, she poured kerosene on his library and the notebooks of his female students he had brought home, and burned them up, slapping her face and shouting that this was the end of his romantic trysts with them; about her sister-in-law's sister, an American old maid, beautiful as the night, who bought a delicate Jerusalem boy with a Green Card and dragged him to Brooklyn with her, where he spent his life as a tailor when here he would have become a respected instructor in the Mizrakhi Teachers' College; and about her cousin's stepson, a heartless swindler who moved to America and opened an illegal casino in the Midwest, and every night, after he counts his ill-gotten gains, he pledges his troth to another waitress, a seductive Gentile with smooth yellow hair like the silk of the corn growing there as far as the eye can see.

Now, without Mother's convoluted stories, as she sits on the floor of Pioneer House in Rehavia like a lotus flower, the photos in her purses are nothing but faded strips of paper, smelling old and musty, and the images—a random collection of blurred, unidentified faces.

In the depths of the closet, behind embankments of mattresses and carefully arranged bedclothes, my hand, blindly scouting unknown regions, came upon another purse. Its shape was different and its leather was softer and felt better than the other purses of photos I knew. I carefully took it out through the space between two piles of sheets so that I could put it back in its place before Mother came home. It was an elegant leather purse, the kind that are carried under the arm, and it was the same scarlet as the lipstick Mother used. The distant, sweetish fragrance of roses enveloped me when I opened it, overpowering the fresh, washed breeze wafting from the lavender soaps Mother scattered in the closet. Never in my life had I seen the small bundle of photos it held.

In many of the photos, some of them damaged—either half of them was removed or some part was cut out—a young woman appeared. That was Mother, but much younger, easy and smiling, like a girl with the soft and wonderful face of a bird, whom I knew from the portraits of her youth, more than from the tense, gray-haired woman with an eternal pain etched in her face—my mother.

But the little girls Mother was hugging, holding them in her arms or taking their first steps with them, wasn't me, the way I looked in the photos from my childhood, just as the yard where they were taken wasn't the yard of our house and the shutter in the background wasn't the iron shutter on our window. Those were two strange girls on an unfamiliar background—one of them touching in the hesitation and fear expressed in her long face that looked so much like Mother's, who sucked her thumb or held out her two little arms to be picked up, and the other one, mischievous and smiling, pounding on a drum with both fists or bending like a little mother over a shabby teddy bear and feeding him devotedly.

I don't know how long I was absorbed in the photos, but in every one of my reflections which suddenly looked at me when I raised my eyes—the closet was wide open and I was standing between the two doors with mirrors on their inside panels—I was at the same time both observer and observed in the billows of this discovery that froze on my face. Feelings gather and evaporate, ignite and go out, glow and are lost, madly accelerate into a one and only moment, and if I want to talk about it today, all I can do is spread it out, static and lifeless, like a hide stripped from an animal carcass. Feelings that change into a dread of betrayal, Mother's awful betrayal of me, her only son, when she dared lavish her love on other children, gather them to her bosom, bend over them at night and murmur whispers into their ears that drive away bad dreams, put her lips to their temples, and pity for Father, who was also betrayed, pity turning into an immediate standing at his side and forming an alliance of wretches against her, and jealousy of the little girls for the young mother they had whose face was hearty and carefree, who wore sleeveless, flowered summery dresses, and her arms were as handsome as the arms of a girl, and vulnerability from the deceit Mother wound around me, dragging Father into that move, hiding her most precious secrets from her child who trusted her, and the dread returning again and again, that not only was I forsaken, but that Mother, just like Father, was now in fact nothing but an endless line of women who wear the same external identity and one name, and they move one after another on a conveyor belt, like the sour cream jars in the dairy where I went with Father, she appears for a little while and vanishes as soon as she's pushed by the one behind her, who looks amazingly like her—and so on into infinity.

The storm that had rocked me didn't escape Mother's discerning eyes as soon as she came in, even though I did my best to pretend to be calm. She froze on the threshold, tried in vain to catch my evasive eyes, and asked why I was so angry at her. "You can't fool a mother's heart," she decreed and repeated her question.

"You're not my mother at all," I burst out. "You're just a liar and a cheat."

"What happened, *kind meyner*?" She wanted to hug me, but I slipped away from her roughly, hitting her with my fists.

"And I'm not your child," I screamed and added that now I knew the real truth. "You've got two other little girls and your real husband is a stranger, not Father."

Stunned, Mother asked how I knew all that.

"I found their pictures hidden in the closet, in a red purse, behind the sheets."

To my amazement, my words neither angered nor surprised her. Nor did she deny them, but remarked in a quiet voice that she did indeed admit she was wrong to listen to Father, who argued that, for my own good, they should hide from me the fact that both of them had been married before. "You're right, and I'll tell you everything," she said as if a heavy rock had been lifted off her heart.

And so, putting another package of seaweed she bought in the Association store on her lap (in those days, she strictly followed the recommendation of one of the lecturers at the vegetarian committee meetings to add dried seaweed to her salad, since it constituted an excellent substitute for fish, because of the iodine in it), Mother sat down on the sofa, and in a matter-of-fact, somewhat distant voice, almost without including details, she enumerated the major stations in the secret chapter of her life: falling in love with the fickle, young printer who made her head spin with his heretical acts and his infectious laugh ("He was a saving angel with brilliantine on his hair and soft moccasins, who came to deliver me from the living tomb of the Hungarian Houses. He took me dancing at the Menorah Club and to the movies at the Zion Cinema and promised to get me the golden bowl from the sky if I wanted it"); the hasty marriage, despite the warnings of her girlfriends who claimed that the match was doomed from the start because of the fellow's treacherous nature, his pathological lying, and his love affairs with women ("But I stood on the roof, under the wedding canopy, and I thought I was the Thomas Alva Edison of love"); their life together in the room and a half they rented on Zefania Street; the birth of Yael and Tovele and the quick ruin of the marriage ("Even when I was pregnant with the little one, I knew for sure it was all over. The *Shvartz Yor* would disappear from the house every night and come back at dawn with his shirts reeking of women. The truth was that I wanted to rebel, but for the sake of the little girls, I restrained myself, and stubbornly held onto the façade with what was left of my strength, because inside there wasn't anything anymore"). And then death appeared, brutal and unexpected. First they discovered a serious lack of iron in the older girl's blood, and when liver injections didn't help, the doctors decided to try a blood transfusion; but by mistake they gave her the wrong type of blood and the little girl died in a few minutes. Soon after, the little one got diphtheria, and even though they put her in the hospital, they couldn't save her and she choked and died in torments. "The two little girls slipped out of my hands. Each one died of something. But I know they caught the viruses of death from the cursed walls of that eroded and crumbling house." Mother, who kept fiddling with the bag on her lap, thrust her fingernails in the wrapping paper and all the seaweed scattered around her. "That's how I was then," said Mother. "As if drowned on the bottom of the sea."

And I sat withdrawn in the "Electric Fauteuil," listening to Mother as I had never listened to her before in my life, my eyes staring at the closed wardrobe, where the few indications of those young lives ended by inexcusable violence were hidden. The plywood on each of its three doors looked like veins of wood, like a tasteless hybrid of sharp triangles distorted into half oval rings, one inside the other, shrinking as they move away from the edges and approach the center. Halfway up, the covers of the doors crossed an almost invisible but sharp break line, that turned the bottom half into a precise mirror image of the top half. And my thoughts, holding on to the clear contours and going beyond them and climbing them, back and forth, stumbling and falling to the bottom of narrow channels and once again scaling the slopes and escarpments of the mountains to the heights from which there is no return, only a bone-crushing slide down to the abyss.

"Apparently here too, the Sea of Tethys didn't yet say its last word," Mother suddenly lopped off her story, and bent down to gather up the scattered seaweed, and as she did, she asked if I still remembered the extemporaneous geography lesson I was forced to hear from her back then, on Purim three or four years before. Apparently seaweed, just like coral, Mother remarked, and I didn't know if she was giggling or serious, even when they're removed from the source of their vitality and every drop of sea water in them is dried up, they preserve in some of their atoms the ancient memory of the big and spacious sea, and they try to find their way to it.

The speed of the change in her and the transition from re-strained lament for her failed marriage and the death of the lit-tle girls to the joke about the beads, was so scary that its strong impression on me wasn't lost on Mother.

"You don't have to be scared, I haven't gone crazy," she wanted to calm me. She straightened up and stood on her knees and said that, from the moment the bag was torn until the moment she bent over to gather up the seaweed, she had had time in her thoughts to rock the little girl's lifeless body wildly, to see the grayish light, the light of dawn coming up, touch the face frozen for eternity, hear the scared running of the doctor on duty in the hospital corridor, catch sight of *Shvartz Yor* kissing the night nurse and Father's shoes, forgotten under the sofa, next to the geography notebook Hannah Grant had lent me, to leaf through *Discoveries in Science*, which she had taken out of the B'nai B'rith Library and to get angry at the vandals who drew hearts pierced with arrows on its margins, to thread the beads that had been scattered on the playground and to feel on her lips the charcoal crystals of my effendi beard. The thoughts gather together and rise from the immeasurable depths, bump into each other, burst and combine, and move on different and opposing planes. And even though the speaker is attentive to them all, with their many facets, and can contain them in his thoughts, he can't control how part of them, a random tiny part, finds its way to the surface and not to the imaginary harmony where thoughts are lined up in single file and take on the form of speech.

Mother said I'd have to live with the paradox that thoughts multiply inside in a geometrical progression, while speech, no matter how fast, comes out in an arithmetic progression, usually cut off, and that words almost never succeed in catching up with thoughts, even though they always start out in the same place. And then she added, innocent of all didacticism (which might be implied from the way things are presented here), that when I went to high school and studied mathematics, I would certainly understand that parable properly.

Even though Aunt Nehama was supposed to come any minute, Mother answered my questions patiently and only when I asked why she had poured her wrath out on the photos and carefully burned every souvenir of her first husband, did she try to hide her disappointment from me and said she was sure I'd understand that by myself some day. And besides, she added, gnashing her teeth, "the *Shvartz Yor,* may he be crushed to death like a cat," was the last creature in the world she wanted to see during those moments of panic when she suddenly thought she couldn't remember how the little girls' faces looked, and then she'd lock herself in the bathroom with the bundles of photos and memorize every one of their curls and every fold of their little legs. "And who do they still have left here in the world, except me?" said Mother after a silence. And so, sitting on the floor, crammed into the narrow space between the bathtub and the wall, with the photos in her lap, she'd thrust her teeth into the flesh of her arms until she drew blood, and would choke off her wailing so it wouldn't disturb the peace of the house. "From now on, at least you'll know why, even in summer, I often wear long-sleeved dresses."

I saw the portrait of Mother's first husband for the first time only five years after Mother died, when Aunt Ayala called and asked me to come to her alone because she had something for me. Ayala was an amazingly brave and candid woman ("The leaders of the rebels," Mother called that sister with more than a trace of admiration, and said that she was the first one to disobey her parents, shook off the name Hinda and chose a modern Hebrew name for herself, cut off her braid and wore her hair short like a boy, and enrolled in nursing school — all acts of rebellion no girl in the Hungarian Houses had dared do before. "Only if you've got a universal profession are you free to do what you want." That was her motto and she was always full of surprises:

she was a conscientious vegetarian, practiced yoga, insisted proudly on her atheist and suffragist views; and most important, she would never accept anybody else's authority). And yet I had to discern a slight hesitation in her voice when she handed me an old envelope and said it had been deposited with her for nearly fifty years. Back during the week of mourning for Tovele, she told me, it was she who boldly accepted the mission of reaching an agreement with Mother's husband and dismantling the ravaged home: packing up the diapers and the bedclothes that still smelled of death and giving them to the orphanage, destroying whatever she had to destroy, and taking Mother's clothes and things and a few mementoes. For some reason, she kept these two items for herself: a picture of Mother and her husband, which was taken right before their wedding and a card game called HOF — Hebrew Original Flirt. "You'll know what to do with them," said Ayala. "At any rate, they do belong to you." For a long time, I stared at the image of the cursed man whose face had been restored, and at last I remarked that the reserved, somewhat aloof posture, next to Mother, even though he had his arm around her shoulders, shows something about the future, as did his hollow, unfocused look, and the cruelly clamped jaw. But Ayala didn't let me go on and said that Mother's voice was still talking from my throat. From the table she gathered up the cards of the game, with affectionate and teasing words printed on them that lovers used to play in the 1930s when they started courting. She shuffled them and stated that the time had come for me to see things as they were, and with my own eyes, and for me to know that they're much more complicated than the simple, one-dimensional picture Mother took care to plant in me at an early age. "Your mother's first marriage was doomed from the start," said my aunt. Everybody on the roof at that distant dusk, looking at the couple standing under the wedding canopy, between the clothes lines and the rusty water tanks, felt that. Without Father and Mother, without old and young relatives, surrounded only by about fifteen friends their own age, the bride in an everyday dress and a veil concocted from a handkerchief, the groom in a borrowed hat, and the rabbi struggling with the wind that was trying to snatch the wedding contract out of his hands — they looked like denizens of an orphanage or a refugee shelter rehearsing a

Purim-shpiel. When the groom broke the glass, some woman whispered that the whole deal was a fly-by-night affair that wouldn't last from the Fast of Esther to Purim. She didn't imagine that her prophecy would come true in a few years, but vice-versa, from Purim to the Fast of Esther, and in such a tragic way, said Ayala. She shuffled the cards faster, added that she had also felt that, but not because of the grotesqueness or the orphanhood of the scene, but because of Mother's nature. She glanced at me and at the cards spread out like a fan in her hand, and went on pounding: "When you look at her, you look at her as a son looking at his mother, and so you always miss the essential thing. If you really want to understand her, you've got to ignore your connection and think about her as a woman. As a writer you must know what I'm talking about." In her opinion, the destruction of her first marriage and the wretchedness of her second marriage with Father, resulted from her nature. "Your mother wasn't capable, by nature, of creating a real bond of love with a spouse. Love in her had nothing to do with sharing and cooperation, but with exploitation. Often, when we'd walk and talk about men and women, she'd say; 'You trust your spouse, believe him, entrust your secrets and your weaknesses to him, and in the end, you'll always find yourself exploited, betrayed, blackmailed, thrown out like an unwanted instrument. If you want to preserve your life and your freedom, you've got to behave cautiously, to seem reserved, and most important, to watch out and be suspicious.'" According to Ayala, there is only one channel for the love amassed inside women like Mother — "love is like the milk that overflows from the breasts. If you don't get rid of it by sucking, pumping, or placing cold cloths on it, it causes infection and fever" — my aunt recruited a parable from her nursing area of expertise — that is, to grant it to a child. The child is the ideal, non-threatening incarnation of the lover. "You don't give your love to someone else, to a barbarian stranger who invaded your life, but you invest it in yourself, in your own reflection. That is, in fact, a very sophisticated kind of narcissism." So, she makes the child an ally, a confidante, a bearer of hope and love, pure, as it were, a child who gains all that is withheld from the neglected spouse. "From the day the girls were born, just as from the day you were born, she didn't need a husband anymore. He had filled his function and he should have disappeared, vanished, dropped dead, like the male that impregnates the queen bee," said Ayala and explained that if Mother had been brave enough, like women like Tsiona Tagir and Hanna Rovina, she would have brought a child into the world without being married. "But your mother was conservative and to maintain the stage set of family life for the child-who-needs-a-father, she was willing to pay the price and serve as housekeeper for the father of her children, to cook and wash and clean. But thus far and no farther." Ayala put the cards down on the table, examined my face, to see if she had succeeded in tearing up the image of the world I had drawn for myself or at least dulling its colors, and then she whispered, like a person confessing in the dark, "I'm talking about things I know very very well. The inability to love is an inherited trait in us, passed down in the family like a disease," and to persuade me she presented other examples. Aunt Ayala shuffled the cards again, and without lifting her eyes to me, she said that if I compared Mother's two systems of marriage, her life with my father and her life with her first husband, without prejudice, I'd find that in both of them, she followed the same pattern. But whereas my father was old and wounded, too tired and despairing to insist, and was reluctantly forced to accept the conditions of surrender Mother dictated to him, her first husband was a young man with a lust for life, who insisted that his wife go on being his spouse for pleasures and enjoyments and not just be the mother of his daughters. And when Mother entrenched herself in motherhood, and rejected his advances and invitations time and again, the man rebelled and went to parties and dances by himself, and from there, there was no return. Despite my efforts, I couldn't restrain myself and cut off her ardent plea for the defense and told her that it was beyond me. "I always was the devil's advocate," my aunt didn't give up and claimed that only if you were brave enough to let go of your traditional positions for a little while and look straight at things from the other side, would you reach a fuller understanding of reality. "Don't be afraid, they're all dead now anyway. You've got to take the frozen portraits of the past apart into their tiniest components and put them back together in their full ambivalence and vitality. A grown-up can't go on holding onto the truths of a child all his life." And Ayala sat up straight again, and for a long time, she looked at her sister holding the lover of her youth in her arms, and then she gave the photo back to me and said: "And now try looking at him with different eyes. Every person has another face, even M.G."

That name was never uttered in our house, not even on those distant afternoon hours, after I found the photos in their hiding place. Mother, who unfurled the story of her life to me, went to great lengths, and so did I, to keep from saying his name. But because she promised never to hide anything from me, she found her own way to circumvent the ban. She wrote the name of her first husband on the back of the bus ticket folded between the watchband and her wrist, and after I saw it, she put a lighted match to it and threw it into the ashtray she had prepared for Aunt Nehama who was late. The fire lapped the small strip of paper, and Mother, tensely watching the devoured letters, hissed: "May his name be wiped out."

One single time, in the summer of 1974, about two decades after it was devoured by fire, the forbidden name flew up like a flame that had never died. Every day, at dusk, I would come visit Mother, who had moved to Ramat Gan by then, and bring her the evening newspapers. She had an amusing technique of reading newspapers: she'd put them aside for two or three weeks and only then would she sit down to read them. That way, she explained, she got rid of all the nonsense, the tempests in teapots and failed prophecies, because the passage of time was the best way to classify them. But before she sentenced the journals to temporary hiding, she'd glance at the obituaries — "the only truths you can't argue about," as she put it — to know who passed away. That time, too, in the summer of 1974, Mother was browsing through the names of the dead, when suddenly she froze, stood up immediately and went to her bedroom. When she hadn't come back in a while, I followed her and saw her pacing there, in the aisle between the bed and the wardrobe, like a pent-up animal. I tried to ask whose death had upset her so much, but she kept me away with an impatient gesture, something she had never done to me, and said, "A mother is also entitled to a certain degree of privacy." And she asked me to go and leave her alone. Right after I left her house I bought another copy of the paper and carefully went over all the obituaries until I came on the announcement of the death of M.G. His wife and sons announced with dismay and profound grief the untimely passing of the beloved husband and father, who was killed by a car while crossing the street. The next day, Mother was back to normal and didn't mention the matter, didn't even hint at it. A few months later, she was afflicted with awful headaches and the sight in her left eye quickly became blurred. Those were the first symptoms of the malignant tumor in her skull, which began penetrating her brain and her eye socket. But it wasn't until seven years later, when I came out of Aunt Ayala's house holding the photo, that I remembered what I had read back then in *The Magic Mountain*: the symptoms of a disease are nothing but exposed revelations of the force of love, and every disease is only love that changed its shape.

4

Regretfully I must admit that it is not within my grasp to create
an image of Mother. This hope that I toyed with when I began
writing — I now see it more and more clearly — was doomed from
the start, because, by its very nature, life sentences the person to
facelessness and every one of Mother's facets that I've presented
here commits the sin of symmetry and balance I observed so
meticulously, an unforgivable sin against the chaos of her existence. In the end, I am also forced to give up the more modest
attempt — to lend a delusion of wholeness and continuity to all
those details of events, feelings and conversations memory pro-
vides me — because Mother's hesitations and instincts shake off
this literary device like a skittish filly. But even the intention of
observing the ups and downs of her life, and revealing them
inadvertently, is likely to come to naught if I don't take heart and
burst through the fence to expose what's hidden deep inside,
that concealed flicker that grants meaning and elusive unity to
the maze of contradictory acts and conflicting wishes. Apparently
the restrained understanding Mother was graced with and her
amazing self-control — qualities that helped her succeed so often
in imposing a firm logic on the tempests and tossings she encountered and then to escape from them — evoked a dim suspicion in
me which in time became a certainty, that behind that manifest
rationality, there was a dark, thoroughly irrational foundation in
her that never rested and that constantly nourished her.

In the beginning, going to the fortune teller was within my
grasp.

One evening, Mother came home agitated from the parents'
meeting she was summoned to by a personal letter in a sealed
envelope. I shut my eyes and see her bursting into the house, her
flushed face and disheveled hair indicating that she was forced to

sit there, in the school, on one of those low, back-breaking chairs, and to listen with a skeptical expression to the teacher's verbal attack of my perverse behavior and my contempt for the rules of the institution and indirectly on her too because she supported me. "The Berlin *kurva* didn't even raise her eyes from the grade book when she talked to me," Mother stood planted in the middle of the room, her fingers still wringing the handkerchief that had absorbed her tears all the way home. After she made sure that Father hadn't yet returned from his daily Talmud lesson, she opened the wardrobe with a melodramatic gesture and pulled out the red purse. The time had come for me to hear the one and only opinion worthy of me, she said, scrabbling among the photos of the little girls until she found the amulet she got from the old Kabbalist, and I'd be immune once and for all to anybody who would ever try to persecute me for my ways.

Once upon a time, there was a young woman. Before she reached her twentieth birthday, sometimes, when she found her newly-blooming life loathsome, she'd turn her back on needle-work in the Shoshana handicraft institution, which Mrs. Heller had opened on Mellisande Street, and on the evil winds blowing from her parents' house, and would go wherever her feet took her. Ignoring the lustful looks of the passers-by, their faces worn out and dusty, she'd search curiously for life pouring like shallow waters in rooms whose low windows face the street, glancing at unmade beds overflowing with bedclothes, fragments of closets and tables where forsaken old people were sitting. She was often accompanied on her journeys by one of her girlfriends and their conversation always revolved around the books they avidly read, indulging in imagining regions that exist only in the kingdom of words, regions where men in hats embrace maidens and women bearing the burden of their love throw themselves under the wheels of a passenger train. They incessantly practiced cutting themselves off from a world with no turns, a shrunken world shriveled like the geranium bushes tended by unhappy hands on window sills to mark the distinction between public and private property.

She talked about those days and about events whose memory is now lost forever, but the glowing pleasure and the affection in her stories about the people who died or disappeared and about the houses and streets that were wiped off the face of the earth, made those distant days, before I came into the world, an inseparable part of my present tense, and it was as if the events were taking place even now.

On the day the opening ceremony of the university was held on Mount Scopus, while wandering aimlessly, that young woman came upon the maze of alleys near the market of Mahane Yehuda. Like a butterfly that had lost its flock, she couldn't make up her mind between the fronts of the houses that besieged the street from both sides, now and then she went down to the recessed curbs of the road meant for rain water, to get out of the way of a vegetable cart or a pack mule. Over one of the entrances, flapping in the wind, was a sign with a hand painted in the middle, and underneath in scroll letters, "Wisdom of the Hand." She was captivated by the uncompromising lines that crisscrossed the hand, arching and stretching, and finally all of them lost in the rises surrounding them, an uncompromising web of roads of a lost city, but she was charmed even more by the words whose individual meaning was so familiar, but whose combination took on a new, almost metaphysical meaning in her eyes. She fiddled with the little bundle of money she had earned from the mind-numbing needlework, and with the sudden resolution of a person who decides, no matter what, to peep behind the screen placed in front of him by the future, she pushed the half-open door and went in. A clean emptiness stood there in the room, where no one was seen. The afternoon sun, rubbing against the wall of eucalyptuses in the yard, cast a rectangle of light inside through the wide-open window. Its upper part rested on the naked, white wall where it sketched the shape of an opening to a world of wonder; and its bottom half spread at its feet on the stone floor that had just been washed, like a carpet of radiance. (Many years later, when I shall leaf through an American magazine of modern art, and come upon the work of Edward Hopper, "Sun in an Empty Room," that sunset room, as Mother described it, will be resurrected.)

A soft voice called her two or three times, until she discovered where it was coming from. At the end of the inside room, on a kind of divan in the corner, lay an old man who looked like one of the Sephardi Sages she had often seen in the alley leading to the Kabbalist Yeshiva in the Old City. He beckoned to her with his shriveled hand, invited her to come in and sit on the stool. The kerosene lamp on the stone shelf poured a dim yellow light on his silhouette, and deepened the wavy softness of his aged beard and the backs of the old books in the alcove. "And ere the lamp of God went out," she described that distant vision, and the Bible verse, she chose very aptly, lent the scene something of the mystery and fate surrounding the serving lad lying in the Temple with the Ark of God and the old Priest whose eyes were beginning to grow dim, on that night in Shiloh, when the word of the Lord was heard from the dark now and then.

The old man raised the flame and then took her outstretched hand and tilted it to the light. For a long time, his transparent airy fingers hovered over the lines of the hand trembling in his. The man shut his eyes and the girl, who saw his eyebrows stretched into an arch, fearfully followed the battle spreading on the mountain ridges of his brow and his shut eyelids. And then, when he opened his eyes, the eyes of a person willing to take on every dread and pain, the words crossed the tremendous plains and made their way to her, sad and pensive as warriors returning to their base after a defeat. Abysses will call to you — he spoke as if to himself in the gloom — and many times you will want to throw yourself into the depths, and at the edge you will retreat; there will come a day when you will decide to flee from them to the ends of the earth, but your soul bound with a chain to Isaac may-he-rest-in-peace will stand before you and won't let you do that, like the bound son you too are condemned never to leave the Land of Israel. The girl was on the verge of fainting, but his voice, which suddenly became clear, supported her and stood her on her feet. He couldn't uproot all her fears, but the precise formulation of the words she didn't forget until her dying day: "A precious and special son you will have and with his birth he will fill the house with light. Blessed is the Lord who gives unending salvation and refreshes your soul and supports you in your old age and when you see it, you will rejoice." The Kabbalist, whose name Mother didn't know, let go of her hand and she dropped it onto her lap languidly. "I'll write you a *shmira*," he said and bent over a small strip of parchment and wrote combinations of letters on it quickly and quietly. Then he rolled it up into a scroll, bound it with a strip of cloth, and with every single stitch he made, his lips trembled, "For this child I prayed; and the Lord hath given me my petition which I asked of him." He refused to take the coins Mother wanted to pay him and said that in exchange she had to promise him that to the last generation, neither she nor her offspring would undo the wrapping and read the amulet lest the blessing hidden in it vanish.

This savoring and melding the two scenes—the mystery-shrouded encounter in the house of the Kabbalist and Mother's agitated entrance from the parents' meeting—even though they're vital for discerning what's hidden beneath the surface of her revealed life, evokes in me an oppressive shame now, as I write these words. First, because simply presenting the fortune teller's words, embarrassing words because they're about me, has an arrogance or at least an immodesty that doesn't suit a person who has chosen to tell a story in the first person. But if you preferred to ignore the warning that this first person aspect is destined from the start to be sloughed off in a long story, don't demand consideration when you're hit with it full force at the impassible frontiers posted by the autobiographical novel. But the major source of embarrassment and uneasiness is the insight, albeit belated, that the encounter with the fortune teller of Mahane Yehuda shaped not only the course of Mother's life and nourished it, but shaped and nourished my life, too. And the things she told me when she returned humiliated from school exposed that truth that was hard for me to see, and it seems I even refused to see it until then. By dint of foggy words of prophecy, I was forced to live my life as an echo, and maybe it would even be more correct to say that I was imprisoned in a fictional image of myself that was preordained for me from the day I was born, and in fact long before, to be the realization of a document I didn't choose and that I wasn't free to accept or reject, bearing on my shoulders a cursed cloak whose exterior is grandiose and whose depressed lining corrodes.

And maybe it's better to leave these strange and improper thoughts and go back to the night Mother removed the last partition between us, and to follow the course of her life without being disturbed by the wisdom of the retrospective observer. In the bruising of the years, the amulet sank into oblivion, was shoved farther and farther into the depths of the small closet where Mother kept her few items, just as the Kabbalist prophecy was repressed in the recesses of memory. At first, especially when she passed by that house in Mahane Yehuda, her old terror would stir again, threatening to choke her, but after her first little girl was born, and even more after the second little girl came into the world, Mother saw those words as nonsense and wiped them out of her heart altogether. Even when she stood on the edge of the roof and the womanhood that suddenly stirred in her stopped her from throwing herself off, onto King George Street, even then the time hadn't come for the enchanted afternoon in the Kabbalist's room to be revealed again. When I learn history, Mother told me, I'll know that every personality, every idea, or every literary creation undergoes a long latency period, a time of waiting, between sinking and disappearing from view, when their memory seems forgotten and they no longer have a share in any-thing done here, under the sun, and their miraculous rise from the dead and return to the living to perform their activity once again. The yearning for motherhood returned to throb in her as she came down from the roof, as she had told me back then dur-ing that Sabbath stroll, on the day of Linda's bat-mitzvah, and she started meeting men. The taciturn, bitter waiters hovering like ghosts among the people relaxing and chatting in Café Zikhel and Café Atara were witnesses to her hesitant attempts to meet a spouse. But all the men she met looked like identical copies, more or less, of a *Shvartz Yor* and she quickly parted from them, sometimes even before she finished her coffee. Meanwhile, her brother realized his dream and sailed for America. Ever since she and her brother opened the shop, his thoughts had carried him far away, as Mother told it. And even when he stood at her side behind the counter of the little shop near Bezalel, his hands busy with fish and skillfully cutting the fins and tails, his eyes misted over as he talked about the unlimited possibilities open to them both on the big continent if only he could carry out his plan to prepare a bridgehead there and bring her to him. (I commented that it was apparently the sea smell of the fish that elicited travel fever in her brother, but Mother smiled forgivingly and said that that was certainly the thought of a poet, yet it was better to watch out for metaphors, because by the same token, cutting fins can be seen as a reverse parable.) Just before his departure, they closed the fish store, and Mother, who was unemployed for several weeks, finally found work in an "Office of Women Workers" clothing warehouse. For ten hours a day she stood on her feet in a damp cellar, around a frame table, making blankets. Her fingers, that had been scratched before by the fish, now became pierced like a sieve with needle pricks ("I had to feel the needle," she explained why she didn't use a thimble), but never had she felt wanted and loved as in those days. Esther Kalikow, the supervisor, discovered her talent for organization, her sense of responsibility and her loyalty, and quickly promoted her. First she put her in charge of the group of workers around the table, and then of the whole warehouse. "She trusted me and even gave me control of the money," Mother said proudly. "And whatever I did, I was successful. Esther Kalikow liked me, and she brought me up like Joseph was brought up in Egypt. The socialists treated me as their equal, they didn't look down on me and didn't rummage around in my private life. If I had continued there, maybe I'd be Golda Meirson's secretary today." Ever since then, Mother had supported the Labor Movement, remembered them for restoring her faith in human beings. In his letters, which came every single week, Isaac encouraged Mother and repeated his promise not to forget her, the promise he had whispered in her ear when she clutched him with all her might as they parted at the dock in Tel Aviv. (The photo showing Mother in the arms of the skinny, shy fellow, wearing a beret, against the background of the high wire mesh fence, with the small motor boat that would take him to the ship behind him, is my favorite of all her photos, and I sit now and gaze at it with tear-flooded eyes, here, in the quiet English village where I've been closed up for a few months now, writing her history, shortly after a phone call from Israel caught up with me, informing me that my Uncle Isaac gave back his soul to the Lord of Spirits in Wilmington, Delaware, where he had wanted to bring Mother almost fifty-four years earlier.) It wasn't long before Isaac really could keep his promise, and together with their brother Zechariah and their sister Rachel, who were already settled in America, sent her the affidavit and the Green Card. Mother quickly applied for a passport and even booked passage on a ship. And then, when all the papers designed to open the gates of the new world to her were in her purse, she chanced to meet the man who was to become my father. (Mother never told me how they met, and there's nobody left alive now who can.) And so, about twenty-five years after the Kabbalist passed his fingers over the lines of life and fate of her outstretched palm, after she made a sudden impulsive decision to cancel her trip and connect her life with the life of the stranger she met that day, that lost scene burst back into her consciousness. The few words of the old miracle-worker, stamped with the impression of eternity emphasized the existence of ephemeral time. The past, with its various times sliding into one another, and its lopped-off sequences hastily bursting up and down, dived all at once, formed and finished, into one solid point. All the events the Kabbalist had prophesied, Mother now learned, came true in full. The little girls, whose existence he didn't foresee, came from nothing and to nothing they returned, and their short lives and awful deaths left no memory at all, the despair that gripped Mother and tempted her to throw herself off the roof couldn't work, and the trip that was all arranged and ready, didn't come off. All the details of the first part of the prophecy were fulfilled, and now the time had come for the second part to come true. And when she threw off the burden of the past, she saw her future, and it was complete and clear and profound, glowing over the horizon of her life like the white disk rising over the Judean Desert. And so, the end became a new beginning, even though that wasn't her intention at all.

"What did I find in him, that foreigner, who was your father?" her voice was amazed and sank into silence, and her fingers stroking the amulet unwittingly tensed like the talons of a bird of prey. And only a few years later, when we would mourn for Father, would Mother be ready to reply to that question. It happened at night, after our house was empty of the last of the consolers and we were alone again, free for one of those long conversations, as in the days when Father was out of the house; but the two of us must have felt the bitter defeat evoked by the absence of interruption. Shortly before that, Mother had dimmed the lights and in the dark she washed the floor of the filth and dust the visitors brought in on their shoes. She was weary of following the religious Commandments and despised them, but she persisted in pretending, strictly maintained the details of the mourning customs, so the neighbors wouldn't slander us. Then she put the mattresses on the floor, but spread clean sheets on them and said, either apologetically or belligerently, that we had enough torments and we really didn't have to torture ourselves anymore than that. The fresh aroma of the bedclothes, blended with the dewy night air and the smoke of thorns burning far away that came through the open windows, stood in the room. Mother lay down on the mattress, and the light of the memorial candle flickering on the table among the tattered prayer books brought from the synagogue, spreading its shadows on the mirror covered with a pillow case and on the Torah Scroll wrapped in a Tallith, making the place look like a room of the dead, accompanied her choked sobbing.

"Father had nothing to offer me," her lips moved quietly, picking up where she had stopped herself back then, after returning from the parents' meeting, and at long last the words began making their way to me, tormented and pacified, laden with love that bloomed too late.

Father was an immigrant without a language in the Land of Israel in the mid-1930s and earned his livelihood from a thousand means that don't bring honor to those who possess them. A manufacturer of a magic potion for dissolving kidney and gall stones (in the "General Guide to the Land of Israel for 1940," in the list of producers of "seltzer and mineral water" in Jerusalem, his name appears along with the name of his factory: "Palm Laboratory, Mahane Yehuda, Yosef-Ben-Mattityahu Street 8"). When he came to the Land, he brought along in his meager knapsack a big-bellied and mucoid mushroom he had found in one of the caves of Manchuria and it would keep growing in jars of sweet tea that lined up on shelves in the storage room in his house. That cursed water, where the mushroom fermented, had a nauseating, shuddering sourness that later wafted from his skin, his clothes and every object in the house. Patients medicine despaired of were sent to him by well-known doctors, including Dr. Suessman Muntner, a student of the medical writings of the Rambam, and Father would pour the potion for them into individual bottles each of them distinct. Mother made fun of Father's "tincture of urine," but in the early 1990s, when veterans of reconnaissance patrols journeyed to the Far East in search of ancient Chinese healing methods, they rediscovered the secrets of the magic mushroom. The Kumbutsa mushroom used by millions of Japanese to make their Kargashuk tea is sold in health food stores today and is considered a potion to restore youth, making old men's hair thick and dark again, making them stand erect, and making their illnesses disappear. Father persisted in his illegitimate pharmaceuticals until the Mandatory Ministry of Health put an end to his activity and when his staff of life was broken, he moved to Geula Street, to the house where I spent my childhood and youth, and there he opened a dubious hostel for flotsam and jetsam, offered beds by the hour to low-brow, stammering Bukharans and to unfortunate women seeking shelter from their drunken husbands. And yet, to Mother's disapproval, he persisted in furtively supplying the potion to a select group of loyal clients, who kept his secret.

"He really didn't have anything, not even decent everyday clothes," Mother lamented, and for the first time, she pitied the weary, solitary man who looked older than his fifty-five years, who suddenly appeared in her life in his Sabbath hat and his only suit, which was worn out and too small on him, but was clean and neat, and the fumes of kerosene he had brushed on the fabric faded beside the fragrance of the eau de cologne that had been generously sprinkled on him in the barber shop. "He polished himself for the meeting like a bridegroom," Mother laughed through her tears, and a soft, warm pride rose in her voice. At any rate, when she sat across from him and examined his face, she took a strange delight in his clipped mustache, his cheeks flushed from shaving, and the short gray hair scattered on his broad shoulders and collar of his suit, since the barber's apprentice hadn't brushed them off properly.

With open, human curiosity, lacking any malice, he wanted to hear about her life, but when she quickly cut him off, frantically defending her privacy, he let go and started telling about himself. Innocent of all pretension, embarrassing in his innocence, he talked about how he missed his brothers and their families, who lived in the Jezreel Valley and worked the land, and his aged mother who lived with them. He yearned for them, but he didn't see them very often, since his aspiration to be a storekeeper or a

dairy worker in Nahalal had been thwarted. And then he told
about how hard it was for him to earn a living and about the distress of loneliness that had gnawed in him ever since his wife had
died, a loneliness that would have overpowered him, especially
on the Sabbath, if the others from his town hadn't mitigated it by
taking him in and lavishing closeness and warmth on him. "Ever
since my Luba died, I've been dying too." And Mother could feel
the intense emptiness in the pores of her skin when Father told
the woman he had just met about the wife of his youth. "She was a
pianist, and she played Schumann so beautifully," said Father,
swallowing his tears, and after she ascended to the Land of Israel
with him, to the land of yearning of her father, a member of the
Lovers of Zion from Kiev, who named her Ahuva Bat-Zion, she
quickly withered here. She, who loathed the harsh sun and the
eastern wind blowing from the desert that seared her silky skin,
locked herself in the house, tormented, sat for whole days in the
dark, behind heavy, scarlet brocade drapes, reciting "Yevgeny
Onegin" in front of her image in the mirror, or reading the Russian classics she toiled to collect here, and in the evening she
would entertain her lady friends with a cup of tea with verbena.
"If I could at least have bought her a piano," Father tormented
himself, but she stuffed cotton in her ears to keep out the noise
of the dogs barking and the neighbor children playing. And she
said that, in his deafness, Beethoven also heard the angels singing. "Come, come, death, take me in your arms," she would whirl
around the table, stretch out her bare, white arms, and the roses
she surrounded herself with would rot in the closed room, exhal-
ing a sweet fragrance of destruction and death, which indeed was
not long in coming.

Mother spoke from the dark and I lay in my place, my eyes staring at *shpin-lustra*—the name I gave the chandelier when I was
four years old— (Mother, who even then recognized my poetic
talent and fostered it, loved to tell how one winter night, when
the electricity in our house went out during a thunderstorm, the
chandelier looked to me like a giant spider dropping down from
the ceiling and stretching its black legs out to us), my mind
having trouble understanding wayward human nature. Two days
earlier, a few hours after Father's body was buried in the Mount
of Rest, Mother sat among the consolers and praised him to the

skies, told how he was quick to aid all the needy without any concern for his own health, the acts of charity she had once resisted, and she argued that his warmth and generosity were in fact at our expense, and he preferred strangers to his wife and son, only because he needed to be loved and accepted by people. Later that same night, when I foolishly remarked on that, attempting to reflect on the sudden change that had occurred in her, Mother claimed that that had always been her opinion about Father and she even scolded me for daring to come to her with vain charges when the sound of the clods of dirt and the stones rolling down were still echoing in her ears.

And yet the new image of Father, exalted and rising from the ruin of his body and hovering over it, pure and refined, accompanied by Mother's forgiving looks, was less surprising than the dramatic change that now took place in her relation to the forgotten existence of the wife of his youth. Luba, his real love, had been her grief. Whenever there was a crisis in his relations with Mother, his living wife, Father hid in the shadow of Luba's memory, where he found consolation. Like a ruler who quickly and systematically obliterates the memory of his predecessor as soon as he takes power, after she got married, Mother started a war to the bitter end against that woman, forced Father to annihilate her photos and letters at once, and to get rid of her few beloved books. She destroyed any trace of her that remained in the house, tore down the brocade drapes, claiming that they were old-fashioned and absorbed dust, got rid of the samovar, and the set of china plates trimmed with purple orchids, and banished the plates with the royal eagle of the Czar stamped on the back to the status of reserve Passover dishes and hid them in the attic so she'd be forced to see them only one week of the year.

Father, who wanted to avoid conflicts with Mother in any way, would light the memorial candle on the anniversary of Luba's death not in the house, but in the synagogue where he prayed on weekdays. Like many other things, I found out about this by accident, too, when I went with him to afternoon prayers in the "Akhva" synagogue one autumn day. Father, who evaded honor all his life and never wanted to pass before the Ark, asked to lead the prayers that day, and at the end of the prayers, he recited the Orphan's Kaddish. Afterward, as he lingered near the windowsill, at a dying memorial candle, I asked him who he was mourning for. He told me, while staring for a long time at a moth that had been destroyed the night before in the flame and was trapped in the dent of paraffin, and now floated embalmed on the bottom. The shadow of the declining day rested on his face as the man leading the evening prayer began singing in a reverent and devoted voice. "He, the merciful one, is forgiving of iniquity," and Father whispered, "I'm sure she would have loved you."

Mother's main struggle was aimed not at the synagogue Father founded in her memory and called it Bat-Zion, but at the group of Luba's friends who were an eternal souvenir of the iniquity of her life, and she tried with all her might to sever him from it. When they came to our house, after they filled their days of purification with honey and vinegar, as she put it, they fell on his neck and left behind a signature of lipstick and fox hairs that fell from their furs, and she'd glare at them. And once, when she came home unexpectedly and found Olga Parhodnik — the leader of the flock of Russian courtesans — freely hugging Father's waist and lapping his cheeks and earlobes with her lips, her wrath flared up, and she pushed the lady dentist out, slammed the doors and opened the windows wide to air the house from the myrrh oil and perfumes of the women, and flung rebukes in the direction of the kitchen where he stood ashamed. "The brothel of Kiev closed its gates forever, Gospodin Casanova!"

Supporting and rather embarrassing evidence that retrospectively reinforced the impression the child received of the way Mother treated Luba's friends fell into my hands many years after her death, and cleared up the meaning of some vague words she said on one of her bad days in our house before she lost consciousness for the last time. One evening, when Mother wailed with intense pain, shrouded like a nestling in her bed, Professor Shmuel Ettinger appeared on television and expressed his opinion on current events. Mother gazed at the bespectacled figure with silvery hair, and suddenly burst out, "That Communist was in our house." When I didn't respond — I couldn't imagine that the well-known historian would visit the home of the owner of a Tnuva branch in Geula — she repeated softly, very confidently, "Believe me, that fellow visited us with his mother a few times." I stroked her bald head and praised her memory, which didn't

give out despite her pains, but in my heart I knew that the clouds
were once again thickening around her crumbling consciousness.
Yet, I couldn't get her words out of my mind, couldn't dismiss
them as the delusion of a dying person, and as the years passed,
I felt that they were like a momentary lull, when a beam of life
bursts through the skein of death and illuminates it for a split second. But the riddle wasn't solved until I chanced to be in the
presence of the late Professor Ettinger. Near the conclusion of
the meeting, when the historian went off into memories of his
youth and hinted dimly at his activity in the Jewish section of the
Communist Party, I couldn't help asking if he knew my father,
without revealing that he was my father. Ettinger took off his
glasses, rubbed his eyes and his forehead, and then spread his
fingers and smoothed his hair, as if he were looking at a past that
would never come to an end. And when he put his glasses back
on, he told me that Luba, the first wife of the man I had asked
about, had been a friend of his parents in their youth, and often,
when he was a student, he'd go along with his mother to visit her.
They even went on visiting Luba's husband after he was widowed,
but a few months after he remarried, Ettinger's mother resolved
never to set foot again in the house on Geula Street. "The new
wife insulted and abused my mother for no good reason and
accused her of clinging to her husband. But because the woman
was pregnant, my mother preferred not to answer her," he said
and a smile he didn't know how to end lingered on his very
expressive lips. And then, while his mind went on plunging into
those days, which he thought he was describing to himself, and
his hands were busy straightening a bundle of reprints, his eyes
caught my inflamed look, and my eyes caught the gift of making
connections that shone in his eyes — the gift of absorbing the
details of things and connecting them with one another — and
granted them a revelation that ended in a wave of his hand, and
the hand rose and fluttered and flapped and dropped, and then
the words burst out hesitantly, "So you're the one who was in her
belly, aren't you?"

The transformation in Luba's image that now occurred in
Mother's gasping awareness was bold and quick. The woman
who burst forth joyous and crowned with jewels from the grief-
stricken body of the night, slipping out of the arms of the spider-

chandelier and finally winding like a thin scarf around the new icon of Father, was celestial and glowing like him. And as if that weren't enough, in the three days since Father had returned to dust, not only did Mother toil to consolidate the position of Bat-Zion as her ally and confidante beyond the slings of time, but even took pains to persuade me that things had always been like that. And she persisted even after the days of mourning had passed and Father's image shrank back to its old dimensions in her consciousness.

"Luba is flesh of our flesh," Mother declared to Uncle Jacob, who came in late summer of 1969 for Father's memorial six years after his death, and afterward she invited him to join her in putting up a new tombstone on his sister-in-law's demolished grave. After the Six-Day War, when the extent of the Jordanian destruction of the graveyard on the Mount of Olives was revealed, Mother was assaulted by a rage to find the dead. At first she couldn't rest until she had located the graves of the little girls, and with the money she had set aside for a rainy day, she restored them. But even afterward, she kept making regular visits to the offices of the Burial Society in Jerusalem to do good for her father and grandfather, and after she found a proper resting place for the dead of the first circle, Luba's turn came to be visited. Mother's new devotion infuriated Aunt Ayala, who scolded her for sacrificing her last pennies on the gods of the underworld instead of treating herself to new clothes or buying gifts for her granddaughter. Mother extracted the waterlogged flowers from the chamomile tea and didn't answer. But when Ayala yelled at her sister that she was also one of the casualties of the Six-Day War and cast aspersions on the ritual of death that had spread among us ever since the roads had been opened to the cursed districts of the Bible, Mother couldn't help saying, "A rational person like you can't understand that things exist in the world that are deeper and darker than logic." "But you were never a pagan?" Ayala shrugged and reminded her of how the two of them used to make fun of those who prostrated themselves on graves and privately called them "The Worm of Jacob." And Ayala was certainly right. That had been Mother's opinion throughout the years, and she hadn't kept her thoughts to herself, and Father didn't get off scot-free either. When he came back from one of his campaigns for novice cantors, he told us excitedly of how he had joined a group of Betar members, proud in their dark blue uniforms, who marched in a parade to the roof of a house near Notre Dame, that looked onto the Mount of Olives. They were preparing to erect a miniature memorial to Feinstein and Barzani on the anniversary of their heroic suicide in the Mandatory prison in Jerusalem. The boys and girls, who were equipped with binoculars, looked at the place where they assumed that the two who were condemned to death were laid, who deceived the British wardens and all Albion, and sang "From the Pit of Rot and Ashes." Mother imitated the Betar anthem and said, "Maybe those little fascists need a fetish to remember their two underground heroes, I don't—my dead are kept here with me," and she tapped her breastbone.

One day in late autumn, a date Mother set, a small group of family members followed her on the slope of the Mount of Olives, with pebbles and fragments of stones rolling down. She navigated her way nimbly on the winding path, as if she were at home, and then she pointed to a new tombstone prominent on the slope, white and firm, among all the crumbling tombstones half-sunk in the ground, and declared: "Here's Luba!" Mother leaned her hands on the marble tablet, her fingers drumming on the edge of the tombstone, the way Father used to stand behind the counter and wait for customers, and then she examined the thick clouds heavy with rain gathering in the west. The dramatic contrast between the black sky bending like a lord over the city and the frightened houses that looked ecstatic in the threatening, exposing light pouring down on them was so charged with tension that in a few moments, the storm was about to break with sweeping thunder and lightning. "Look, the atmosphere is just like in 'A View of Toledo,'" Mother whispered, waiting until the little group gathered. (That painting by El Greco was apparently her favorite picture. She framed its lousy reproduction, which she had found in some magazine Uncle Isaac used to pad the packages of food and clothing he sent us from America, and she hung it over her bed. "You'll get to travel in the world," she once told me. "When you reach New York, go to the Metropolitan Museum and see the original with your own eyes." And from the echo of her voice, steeped in yearnings that would never be satisfied, according to the prophecy of the Kabbalist of Mahane Yehuda, I could hear that if I ever stood before "The View of Toledo," she would stand there with me.) "We're finally going to get some rain today," Jacob's voice rejoiced as he examined the layers of stones on the tombstone. Mother cleared her throat in embarrassment and said that precisely because of the expected rain, she was grateful to him for accepting her invitation and leaving the farm at the height of preparations for the approaching winter, and coming up to Jerusalem. "We both did what had to be done," interrupted my uncle, who despised small talk. But Mother ignored him and said that this was the second time in her life that she had stood here, at Luba's grave. The time before was exactly twenty-five years ago. She remembered the date clearly because it was the day she married Father. On the morning of that day, Father, dressed up in his only suit, in which he would stand under the wedding canopy that evening, unexpectedly knocked on the door of the house in the Hungarian Houses, and invited her to accompany him.

"Like a gentleman, he opened the door of the taxi waiting for us near the Roman Church. And I thought he intended to go to the jewelry store to buy me a pearl necklace or a bracelet as a wedding gift," said Mother. But when the cab set out on its way, she learned they were going to the Mount of Olives. He wanted to say goodbye to the wife of his youth and to introduce his new wife to her, he whispered, and he fanned his sweaty face with his hat, even though it was cloudy that day and the air was chilly. Mother, who was surprised and even angry, sat apart from him the whole way, withdrawn, not uttering a sound, but when she saw her bridegroom standing here, at the grave of the forlorn wife, who had left behind no one in the world except him, burying his face in his hands and weeping quietly, she pitied him and felt a lot of love. "Only a delicate and noble man can do that," she had a hard time swallowing her tears. Uncle Jacob, who listened to all that in amazement, took her in his arms, hugged her warmly and asked why she hadn't told him about that until today.

"That's something between a husband and wife that you keep in your heart," Mother said on that long night, during the week of mourning, when she talked to me out of the dark. She got up to take the memorial candle out to the kitchen so the shadows wouldn't scare our sleep, and when she returned to her mattress, she said that what won her heart was not so much the way Father treated the memory of his first wife, but his love of children.

Her sisters and her handful of girlfriends didn't really understand her enthusiasm for him and tried to persuade her to realize the affidavit her brother had sent her and to sail for America which was not eager to open the gates of Ellis Island to foreigners, and even if she decided to postpone her trip for a while, they said, she had to be twice as careful and responsible and not repeat the mistakes she had made in the past and not rush into marriage with a destitute stranger.

And, indeed, the first year with Father was a very bitter year for her. Right after they returned from the home of Rabbi Auerbach, who married them, Mother shooed away the dubious guests who sat around the house and wanted a bed for the night. "I won't bring a child into the world so he can grow up among whores and sluts," she yelled at the man who had just made her his wife, and informed him that she had made up her mind to close the nocturnal bordello he was running in his house. Father buried his head in his hands and begged her to leave it alone, at least for now, because she was breaking his staff of life, but Mother blocked her ears and declared that the very next morning, before dawn, the lice-ridden, lechery-soaked mattresses would be thrown out, and then the house would be whitewashed and cleaned of filth to prepare it to raise a family. "The two of us are healthy and diligent people, we won't starve to death, all work honors those who do it," Mother tried to assuage him and asked him to help her spread the starched sheets on their beds, and to put a cover on the down comforter she had brought there in the afternoon, when they came back from the Mount of Olives.

Mother started her honeymoon the next morning in the office of the Tnuva district manager. What took place before she entered his room looks to me like a scene from an Italian film. A woman of about forty goes out the door of her house, her face resolute. The camera, waiting for her on the threshold, lingers on the comb she passes through her wavy hair, on her lips moving with a restrained sensuality to the movement of the lipstick, and her hand clutching to her breast the small purse hung on her shoulder, and then follows her from the side as she passes an endless row of shops, her eyes straight ahead. Finally, she turns and enters the spacious yard of the dairy, pressed between two apartment buildings, makes her way between distributors wrapped in aprons, loading trays of yogurt and cheese on pick-up trucks, and the bearded milkmen, waiting on tricycles loaded with jugs. She walks along a smooth concrete ramp, skips over puddles of crusted milk and a suction tube throbs, discharging the contents of a gigantic tanker; sudden bursts of steam from the filling rooms and streams of freezing air from the open walk-in refrigerators strike her, until she is swallowed up in the wing of offices, and the roar and the tumult are muffled by the thick stone walls.

"Comrade, you're not allowed to burst into the manager's office like that," an albino secretary tried to block her way; he brought his short-sighted eyes close to the contents of his salami sandwich. (Mother always took pains to tell that, at that time, in front of that janitor, one of the hoodlums of the "Labor Brigades," who was great at beating up Revisionists who came to break up the Mapai election rallies, stood a cup of coffee with milk.) But she, who knew how the system worked, from the inside, from the time when she worked in the "Office of Women Workers," ignored him, opened the door of the room without any hesitation, and went inside.

Mother lay her request before the manager: would he please give her and her husband a pole of eggs on consignment so they could earn their living by the labor of their hands. (Before I knew what an electric pole or a telephone pole was, not to mention a building pole or a polestar, I knew that a pole was ten gray cardboard pans that felt rough, somewhat soft, laid on top of one another, with thirty eggs in each of them, five rows of six eggs or six rows of five eggs, and only Father was strong enough and brave enough to pick it up in his hands).

"Who'll vouch for you?"

"The fields in the Valley, soaked with the sweat of my husband's brothers' brow," the answer was ready in Mother's mouth.

When he learned that she was the sister-in-law of Joseph Rakhelevski of Kfar Yehoshua, who had recently drowned in the Kinnereth with other members of the Livestock Growers' Committee, who went down to row a boat from Degania to Ein-Gev, the man relaxed in his chair, called the cherub with the flaming sword which turned every way and asked him to serve the guest some tea and told her that from now on, she shouldn't hesitate to ask for his help in every matter. "My door will always be open to you," he declared and called the manager of the egg department on the phone and instructed him to open an account for her. ("How can you forget a woman like her," the former district manager told me when I met him at a meeting of readers at one of the kibbutzim of the mountain on the way to Jerusalem. And then he slapped me affectionately on the cheek and added, "She had the head of a minister, your mother.")

And that very morning, the day after his wedding, Father showed up with his pole of eggs on the corner of Geula and Ashtorei Ha-Prakhi streets, next to the sign-making workshop of Reb Isaac Beck, and waited for customers. I once told that to an interviewer who wrote in her article that my father was a peddler and that caused me a lot of grief. Father, a third-year student at the University of Kiev, wasn't a peddler, I argued angrily, he sold eggs in the street. And yet how wretched was that man who had to flee with his pole of eggs on a rickety baby buggy whenever the elderly woman who collected charitable donations across the street warned him of the municipal inspector whose silhouette was seen next to Volga Ice Cream. Only his initiative and Mother's aspirations made him the respected owner of a "Tnuva Branch" the year she carried me in her womb. In exchange for quite a few bribes to one of the toughs of city hall, the store was opened in the front room of our house, which became a shop. My crib stood between crates of challah on Friday evenings and towers of matzo packages at Passover. A tormented chapter of my life and even today, as I write a few of its details here for the first time, it chokes my throat with tears of humiliation. Mother, on the other hand, saw that miserable shop as her life's work. On the night after one Independence Day, when we sat and listened to the Israel Prizes being awarded on the radio, she remarked as a joke that she also deserved a prize for establishing the shop, a shop that not only restored Father's honor, but also allowed them to build the nest to bring the baby who was about to be born, where they would protect him and bring him up right.

"You had nothing to offer me except your desire for a child," Mother called to him from the depths. A distant clock rang one

A.M., but she didn't stifle her lament. At their very first meeting, his defects were obvious to her, and she was sober enough to know that his irascibility, his impatience, and his lack of ambition would afflict their life together, and she certainly didn't need her sisters or her girlfriends to point out his poverty, his loneliness, or the fifteen-year difference between them. In her heart, she had already decided not to meet him again, despite his kindness and his warmth, and then a couple sat down next to them with a baby about a year and a half old in a stroller. "And you," said Mother, "instinctively turned your eyes away from me and started playing with the child." ("Never in my life did I see a man who was so attached to children. That's usually a quality of women," remarked Mother in the middle of talking to Father.) The child's transparent fingers fluttered airily over Father's big hand, but when the hand closed onto the little hand, the mother pulled her son away from the stranger and they stood up to go. Father turned his face to Mother, and when their looks met she saw that his eyes were full of tears. "To Abraham, too, a son was born in his old age," he whispered and a laugh glowed in his voice, and it seemed to Mother that she heard the voice of the fortune teller.

5

For many years I labored under the delusion that this was my earliest memory, caught like a bird in my hands.

I was three and a half years old. It was during the siege of Jerusalem and when the shelling would pour down on the Jewish city
without warning, we'd flee to the inside room of our house. We
didn't have an underground shelter, but my parents, who blocked
the high windows with sandbags, prepared the room as a refuge
from bullets and shrapnel. Later, after the bags were removed,
that room would be flooded with sun; but now, especially at dusk,
it was as gloomy and musty as the burial caves of the Sanhedrin in
the abandoned park next to the police academy. During the shelling, Mother would make me crawl under one of the iron beds
and lie there, protecting my head with my hands, while blocking
my ears. To this day, the cold rising from the floor along with the
smell of dust, cotton and seaweed jutting out of mattresses stir
feelings of danger and death in me.

We weren't alone in our house during the shelling. Customers
who were in the shop in the front room at that time and many
passers-by wanted to hide there, and rubbing up against random
strangers, uninvited guests, in the scariest moments of life is an
integral part of that accumulated memory.

That time, which memory is focusing on, slivers of a shell hit
the apartment above us. Later on, Mother said that Father, who
used to assign marks to the shells, distinguished between "ours"
and "theirs" by the way they whistled, almost smothered me in his
embrace when he lay on top of me during the explosions, and
afterward he burst into tears of relief.

When the shelling was over, I burst out from under the bed
and looked in amazement at the strips of whitewash and plaster
that kept on dropping from the ceiling one after another, illu-

minated by the thin tubes of light coming through the cracks between the bags and covering our floor of arabesques with a thin, whitish layer.

"*Vayse murashkes.*" "White ants," I shouted with foolish joy, the happiness of a child rescued from death.

"*Vayse murashkes,*" laughed the momentary guests, surprised at the image, and Mrs. Vine, the mother of Yosh Gafni, kissed Mother's cheeks that were flushed with fear, and said that her son would be a writer.

But it's precisely the crystallization of the memory, its ostensible perfection, and mainly the fact that it's sealed with the stamp of destiny that have made me suspicious over the years. And Mother, with her repeated attempts to express it in words so I'd preserve it in my heart and never forget it not only doomed to destruction the amazing, primal nature of the scene and its thin impression as envisioned by the child, with his fresh sight, but she also confiscated it from me. What could have been the quivering, forming shadow of a surrealistic fluttering of flakes became the white line homicide detectives draw in chalk around the body of a murdered man stretched out on the ground before it's cleared away.

Far away from there, in the heart of the demanding territories of forgetting, another memory still sprouts, maybe even before the first one, and unlike it, we didn't dare ever remember it again, and we let its illuminating streams go on undermining in the silent and shapeless depths of our being as long as they don't rise to the visible layers of real life and flood them.

Father has purple spots on his lips, and the spots become more purple whenever he puts the point of the pencil to his mouth. The paper tastes like medicine. Father leafs through his long book, the book where he writes rows of numbers from top to bottom every night. On the margins of the pages of the book are gold and brown feathers, like the wings of the golden hoopoe bird in the song Mother sings to me before I fall asleep. I want to stroke the feathers and I climb on Father's lap. His corduroy is warm and soft, but he puts me down immediately without even looking at me. "They'll put us in jail," Mother talks in a loud voice. "Dov Yosef's police will come." Father goes on leafing, and the purple spots kiss and part, multiply and add together all the time, and the feathers grow more and more pale. Now Mother stands in the door of the kitchen and weeps, and I run to her and grab her hand. Her hand is cold. Father gets up from the table, tosses his eyeglasses on the book and paces back and forth in the room. Finally, he stands still at the table and lifts his hand, and his big hand that almost touches the electric lamp turns into a fist. "*Zol zayn do shtil,*" he shouts in a voice I've never heard from his mouth and bangs his clenched fist on the table and demands silence. And then an awful quiet prevails, and in that quiet, Mother snatched me up and buried my face in her neck. She shook and kept whispering over and over, Chmelnitski, but I turn my head and look. The tabletop is split in the middle, and Father is kicking the table and tossing aside the fragments of Masonite top and everything on the table. "Mapainik, go to your Ben-Gurion," he shouts at her, slams his hat on the floor and tramples on it, and on the book and the eyeglasses and the oranges. "*Merder,*" she answers him and leaps over the broken glass and the crushed fruit, flees outside with me, and he waves the naked table legs at us, but I was the only one who saw the monster's eyes bulging out of their sockets and the shaved, bare skull chasing us and trying to catch us with her four gigantic arms. Mother runs in the streets with me and I lean my cheeks on hers, and thus, with the smell of my weeping blending with hers, I sobbed until I fell asleep. And the table, whose pieces were never mended, and it stands in the house covered with oilcloth until I'll give it to one of our children to burn in the Lag b'Omer bonfire, was not only a memento of an evil no one wanted to remember, but also proof that the flickerings of mystery, the ones that illuminate the cursed expanses I wanted so much to forget, are not made up.

Because on pillars of anger the foundations of our house were sunk, and on an incurable resentment was their cornerstone laid — "eczema," as Aunt Miriam, Mother's sister, with her sharp tongue, called that web of relations when she unfortunately stumbled upon one of those stormy fights that erupted between them — an eczema you sometimes scratch until it bleeds and sometimes it's dormant, but you can't ever get rid of it. The reason for the fights was haphazard — an argument about how to arrange the empty yogurt jars to be returned; Father's fancy, according to Mother, for a bow-legged customer ("the cunt of

Dudai of the VAT") and he saved a braided challah for her one
Friday; the royal food Father was addicted to in his old age, hoping it would restore his youth ("You'll never be a Don Juan," she
growled at him wickedly. "And instead of wasting money on quack

medicines you could buy the child a new blanket"), or the doors
of the kitchen cabinets he'd leave open. Like the laws of heaven

and earth, the fights were the single stable thing in their marriage and like a completely incomprehensible buzzing, for who
made a way for the lightning of thunder and out of whose womb
came the ice? Secretly, wrapped in frost, Mother would fan the
fire and spray its sparks with an innocence free of all malice, as
it were, and he would be kindled by them like chaff and would
burn and be devoured. And as he burned quickly, so he flickered
out quickly, trying to put things back the way they were and to
appease her — buying a used washing machine, surprising her
with a dining room table and four chairs he had ordered according to his own taste from a carpenter he knew, or bringing home
a Cypriot *kinstler* who would plaster the walls of our house with
fish scales. And she, instead of being reconciled, would cast forth
her ice like morsels, who can stand before her cold, and in the
day she punished him, enumerating his deficiencies, from first to
last, because of him our house had become a junk warehouse,
that every unwanted vessel the matrons of Rehavia wanted to
get rid of, found its way to us, that the table and chairs would
never go out of style because they weren't in style, and Abe Shapiro, the carpenter, better go on making coffins for the Greek
Orthodox, and instead of the walls smelling clean, they stink like
fish carcasses.

I realized how touchingly wretched were the borders of her
zone of maneuvers in her fights with Father on one of the anni-
versaries of Yael's death, when the little girls' existence was no
longer a secret. At night, Mother sat all by herself at the memorial candle, shooing away the moths circling around the small
flame, and suddenly she put her hands on her cheeks and abysses
flooded the restrained expression she took pains to achieve when
tempests racked her soul, converging with the pain and madness
peeping from her eyes. She takes pains to wash everyone's dirty
underpants, to iron their shirts, to cook their favorite food,
Mother spoke as if to herself, casting her words at Father, who sat

at the table and silently sucked the fish head left over from the Sabbath. For herself she doesn't ask for a thing, not to go to the movies on Saturday night, not a new outfit, not Parisian perfume, just a little attention, not for her of course, but for what was more precious to her than her soul. "Why is it so hard for him to remember the date and to say Kaddish. Everything I can do myself, just not that, and she's there all alone, so far away and lonely . . ." And without finishing her words, she got up and went out, slamming the door, on one of her nocturnal journeys. She'd return at dawn and find me sleeping in my clothes in the armchair, waiting for her, and she'd carry me to bed, take off my clothes, kiss my forehead with her cold lips and say, "In the end, Mother always comes back." Father moved the plate aside, bent over and wiped his lips on the edge of the tablecloth, leaving spots of brine and horseradish on it, and gave me a long, accusing look. But I got up and went off to the other room without a word, knowing I was sinning against him with my silence. A few months earlier, on the anniversary of Tovale's death, I was a hostile witness to his return from the synagogue. He put his hat on the bed, for a long time he looked at the flame of the memorial candle and said in a loud voice, so that his words would reach Mother, that he had prayed that evening for the elevation of the soul of the little girl and had said Kaddish. Mother burst out of the kitchen with eyes expressing disgust and blurted out, "Who asked you to do that? She's not your daughter. She's not his sister. She's only my daughter." She spoke and pounded her breastbone wildly.

When the fights between my parents grew stormier and Mother would throw up her hands and admit that all the tactics she tried to use in her relations with her spouse had come to naught — "I came to him with a prayer, with a gift, and with war," she once told her sister Nehama, who was unrolling the endless bandages from her legs — as a last resort, she'd recruit Uncle Jacob. In the morning after a big fight, Mother would leave with clenched lips for the post office on the outskirts of Meah Shearim and send a panicky telegram to Nahalal. Two things she knew clearly: that Jacob would leave everything and come to us with the first milk tanker from Nahalal to Jerusalem, and that Father would obey him without protest even though his brother was a few years younger than him.

Uncle Jacob, as Mother said, was the Priest Aaron of our house. Even though his head was uncovered and he wore standard khaki clothes, in her eyes, the Moshavnik was one who loveth peace and followeth after peace, whose very presence brought calm and peace to the little family that threatened to come apart.

All the bulbs were lit in the heavy bronze chandelier in our house and cast a dazzling, sobering light on the small room that was our whole world, when Uncle Jacob would burst out of the dense darkness outside and stand between the unmade beds like a saving angel, in his hand a leather bag crammed with Rome apples or queen-of-the-vineyard grapes, and his shining eyes and soft smile indicated, without a word, that he could encompass his fellow man in all his pain and distress.

As the sound of the air brakes of the Nahalal milk tanker that had brought him here at this pre-dawn hour were growing silent on the slope of Geula Street, as it approached the Tnuva Dairy, the guest would clasp his sister-in-law, Mother, to his bosom, stroke her cheeks straining with the effort not to burst into tears, cast a tormenting look at his brother who was muttering in embarrassment and rage, "Again she sent him a depeche," and would then bend over my bed.

He put his face close to me, a face plowed like the earth of his fields and still wet with dew, I awoke with a start, and he planted a wet Russian kiss on my sleep-stunned lips. He whispered my name, also the name of his son and his father, who was buried in a remote graveyard in Volhynia, and said, "Uncle Jacob came from Nahalal to give you a good morning kiss." And then he rubbed the bristles of his beard on my smooth neck, buried his head in my sky-blue pajamas decorated with blue anchors, and enveloped me in the smell of his body, the smell of someone who works the land, a blend of the aromas of clover, the sweat of mules and the dust of the open plains.

The three sat around the table and drank tea in a silence broken only by the sound of cracking sugar cubes and of sipping the scalding liquid. When the rising sun hit the windows of Dr. Meshulam Groll's office across from us and sent the reflection of its beams, Father would get up and go with a sigh of relief to the "Akhva" Synagogue for morning prayers, and Mother would go into the store along with her savior-from-a-far-country.

As she waited on the morning customers, Uncle Jacob would drag the jugs of milk in from the sidewalk and then arrange the empty yogurt jars in cartons by size and prepare them for Mr. Lerner, the Tnuva distributor. On one of those mornings, Mrs. Visski, the wife of the envoy who was sent overseas to raise money, came into the store and asked Mother what happened that her brother-in-law came all of a sudden, even before the time to say the "Shema" at morning prayers. "*Gute gest kumen umgebeytn.*" "Good guests come without an invitation," Mother answered, adding that whenever her brother-in-law came he purified the rancid air of the Jerusalem shtetl with a fresh breeze with the smell of the real Land of Israel. "What smell?" wondered Mrs. Visski. "The smell of the field," Mother fell into the trap the customer had set for her. "God gave thee of the dew of heaven and the fatness of the earth and plenty of corn and wine," intoned the wife of the envoy, "and as the Bible says, 'The smell of my son is as the smell of a field —' that's the smell of Esau," and she said that in terms of Yiddishkeit, Mother should prefer his brother to that Tovaritsch from near Afula, because he was the real Jacob of the family, who goes morning and night to the synagogues and the study houses and the smell of Torah rises from his clothes like the smell of the eternal offering. Mother waved away her words and went out to the yard in front of the store to pour milk for Mrs. Wein, and Mrs. Visski told me that our Jewish Muzhik walked around in the streets of the Holy City like a person plodding behind a pair of oxen.

That whole day, Mother would wait impatiently for the afternoon break. And then she'd put down the iron shutters, and the three of them would close themselves to talk. Jacob would listen patiently to her bitterness, mediate between her and Father, and smooth the rough places between them, until Mother would admit, albeit grudgingly, that she was appeased.

After the arbitration, especially if it took place during summer vacation, Uncle Jacob would suggest that I go to Nahalal with him. "It won't hurt the boy to get a little sun, drink some fresh milk, eat an egg right after it's laid, spend the day in the fresh air," he'd persuade Mother, and say that he and Sulka would provide whatever was lacking and protect me from all harm. "He'll come back to you a tough boy, with muscles and tanned skin," he'd repeat until Mother gave in and tearfully packed my clothes in a little suitcase, hiding chocolates and candy between the undershirts for the children of Ruth and Hanoch — my uncle's daughter and son-in-law.

In his house in Nahalal, among the heavy, dusty cedars hiding mobs of cooing birds in their depths, I realized that Uncle Jacob and Aunt Sulka embodied the new Land of Israel, whose skies are an all blue Zionist prayer shawl and a red and gold socialist sun shines above the runways of the military airport in Ramat-David and the cowsheds of the Dayan family and of the teacher Tsvi Liberman-Livneh, to illuminate a day of toil.

I'd cling to him and go with him wherever he went.

In the cowshed, during milking, he spoke affectionately with the cows, the way Father talked with the novice cantors when they went to the Ark. Jacob would pat their behinds, wash their teats with a sure hand, and then spray the stream of steaming milk into the bottom of the bucket.

Then we'd go to the yard, where, as Aharon Shabtai says, our culture is contained in a few tools and their objects, or to the lot (a word that took on a new meaning), where he'd teach me not to be afraid to pick a warm tomato, wipe it on my shirt tail and sink my teeth into it, or to gather cucumbers in a rubber bag and feel their spiky down I never knew before.

Once he took me to plow. The two of us walked in the field, with the sun shining behind us. He talked about the furrow that had to be as straight as a person, and then he walked in the traces of the pair of mules with stubborn silence, guiding them with a trained hand, straight to a secret spot on the horizon. When we got to the end of the field, Jacob pointed at the mountain rising in the west. "There's Keren Ha-Carmel, there on the summit stood Elijah," said my uncle as I stumbled among the clods of earth, skinning my white knees. "Yes, Elijah the Prophet, Elijah the Tishbi, from the song at the end of the Sabbath." And all at once, Elijah turned from a merciful Jewish grandfather who came to make up a *minyan* in the Old City, into a Hebrew prophet of rage, girt with valor and bravery.

"Maybe you should learn the Bible with Gordon's modern scientific interpretation," he advised me, as we sat that evening in his office, which was my room when I stayed in Nahalal. "The

Bible is a book of the Land of Israel, it grew here, from this sun-struck earth, waiting for rain, and not in the musty gloom of study houses in Eastern Europe." His bookcase was the key to his world: the Bible with Gordon's interpretation, "The Ascent of Shalom Layish," the stories of Dvora Baron, the writings of Brenner and A. D. Gordon and Berl Katznelson, volumes of *Ha-Tekufa*, the *Book of Legends* and the poems of Bialik, agricultural guidebooks for raising cattle, cultivation, and caring for brood hens, memoirs of those who fell in defense of the homeland, and volumes of *Gevilei Esh*.

Uncle Jacob was a member of Mapai, but he was never a Mapainik. Under the glass of his desk, among the family pictures, there was also a picture of Ben-Gurion. He respected him, obeyed him, but never admired him. "We're from a family of Hasids, but I never was a Hasid," he said. As I recall, he read only *Davar* and the party weekly magazine, *The Young Worker*, but washed his hands of partisanship. He was, in fact, a non-party party member.

And yet, he had a clear hierarchy of values — he distinguished clearly between good and bad: between the working settlement and the farmers in the Moshavot, between agriculturalists and the urban bourgeoisie, between someone he thought was willing to keep on bearing the yoke of national security and social missions without shirking, and someone who wanted to make his own home, take more than he gave, enjoy the fruits of the toil of others. At the top of the pyramid stood the Hebrew worker of the soil, one hand always holding a plow and the other a book and a rifle in turn. But he never spoke of that explicitly. It was heard from his priorities. Toward his fellow man he was endlessly tolerant. He never criticized anyone openly. He only praised what was praiseworthy, and the rest you have to learn. To anyone who violated that rule of behavior in his presence, he'd say only: "Blessed art thou in the city and blessed art thou in the field."

Obligation, responsibility, making do with little, volunteering — those were his outstanding features, a hybrid of the ideal of the "Protestant Ethic," as Max Weber defined it, and "all Jews are responsible for one another." Jacob and Sulka took young Holocaust survivors into their home, slowly restored their faith in mankind and in hard independent work, without concessions and without neglect, and when those youths wanted to go on their way, they'd supply whatever they needed, as if they were their own sons, and they'd make weddings for them in the court-yard of their house. Jacob was a patriarchal figure. He spread his protection over his family, especially over Sulka's sisters, who were orphaned in early childhood when the Hetman Kazir-Zirku, one of Petlyura's men, murdered their father, Jacob Biribis, in a slaughter of the Jews of Obruch on the fifteenth day of the month of Shevet in the year 1919. The nature of the man can be seen, for example, in the encouragement he gave his son Haim and his daughter-in-law Tamar to respond to Ben-Gurion's call to go down to the Negev with their little children and guide new immigrants in one of the settlements, even though their depar-ture placed a double burden on him; in the little notebook where he wrote down all the family birthdays and his expenses, from the purchase of a tractor and a harrow to a glass of soda he drank in a kiosk when he went to Haifa on business, and even in the stamps of "indemnify the Yishuv" glued to the back of their radio.

When his final illness had already lodged in him, he told me that he went to the Ministry of the Interior to correct the name of his hometown in his identity document, where it was smudged. I asked him why he had gotten out of his sickbed and bothered to go to Haifa. "What do you mean," he replied. "A person has to leave things precise and be as strict about the past as he is about the present."

I witnessed one of those peaks of quiet and restrained respon-sibility once when I was in Nahalal. One morning we got up and heard at the beginning of the news broadcast about the retali-atory raid the Israeli army carried out across the Jordanian bor-der. In the store in Jerusalem, when we learned of such a raid, the customers' responses ranged between a burst of patriotic enthusiasm and an attack of dread of hoarders of sugar, oil, and flour. In Nahalal, my aunt and uncle would bite their lips and walk on tiptoe, knowing that in the afternoon news broadcast, when the Army spokesman listed the names, they wouldn't be anonymous names for them, and they'd know what house had a gaping hole at that hour. And they also responded like that when trouble overtook them and Elhanan fell, and not long afterward, after Sulka's death, when Aki also fell.

Not only obligation, but also love and intimacy. Mainly love for

Sulka. In their bedroom stood a case of apples. A wonderful smell filled the room. Jacob took an apple, held it softly and intensely, offered it to me, and then he said with blushing shyness that he liked to put a case of apples under his wife's bed, and in the little room, steeped in the gloom cast by the old cedars in the yard, the chapters of the Song of Songs about "comfort me with apples for I am sick of love" came to life.

"How fair and how pleasant art thou, o love, for delights," giggled Mother, finding it hard to hide her disbelief in that biblical idyll I imparted to the relations of my aunt and uncle in the stories I told on my return from Nahalal. Indeed, Sulka's Hebrew name was Shulamith, like the name of the wife stayed with flagons, Mother opened the fetters of her tongue, and my uncle was named after the gentleman who rolled the stones off the well of Haran, but the naïveté of *Ahavat Zion*, which suited the time of Mapu and, with a stretch, could be accepted in the paintings of Lilien and his followers in Bezalel, and if they hadn't turned their hand to kitsch, they'd have starved to death, that prophecy certainly doesn't fit our generation and I'd better hurry up and wean myself from it. Of course, she wasn't sorry I had come home early, she said, anxiously observing the scratches and stings on my legs, but if I had managed to ignore the silence and introversion of "the aristocracy of the exercise shorts" — as she sometimes called my uncle's grandchildren — and stayed in the Valley another week, I would surely have sobered up from my delusions and would know that those were vain fantasies I made up out of envy and self-disdain at the intensity of the family clan.

Mother expounded on that problem again the next day when we passed by the scarred dining room of Kibbutz Ramat Rachel on our way to see the remnants of the biblical settlement that had been discovered there when defense trenches were dug during the War of Independence, and were now exposed in archaeological digs. She wove her desire to reward me for the truncated vacation with her longing for open space. With some apprehension, she entrusted the store to Father's hands and went for a half-day's outing with me in the south of Jerusalem. "Love really is a disease, as the husband of a thousand wives writes in his Book, but ultimately it's a childhood disease, like chickenpox, that passes quickly without leaving scars, as long as you don't scratch the sores," she said and started climbing to the roof of the catch basin, where we could view the ancient site. (About two months later, during Sukkoth, everyone glanced with rage and dread at that same place after a Legionnaire from the nearby Jordanian post opened fire on the assembly of "The Society for the Study of the Land of Israel and its Antiquities," killed four of them and wounded many others.) Mother watched the workers clearing out bags of dirt from between the low walls sunk in the earth, and at the archaeologist in the straw hat supervising them, and then turned her eyes to the soft white hills growing lower beyond the fence marking the border, and at the Mar Elias crest hiding Rachel's Tomb on the way to Efrat, which is Bethlehem.

"Even Jacob's great love for Rachel was a delusion," said Mother and sat down on the ground, crossing her legs, like a girl. She spread a cloth on the concrete floor, put sandwiches and fruit and a thermos bottle on it, and said that she herself would make do for the time being with some grapes I picked with my own hands in my uncle's vineyard. As usual in the last summer, Mother sliced one grape after another with a sharp knife, removed the pips, because one of the vegetarian guides decreed that the amino acids in them damage the stomach, and she said that the innocent Jacob who stayed in tents, who yearned so much for the wife of his youth at first, and the seven years he worked for her were but a few days in his eyes with his love for her, soon became, like all other men, a cock frequently visiting his wives and his servants and his concubines, and giving them fetuses. "In my eyes, love is exclusivity, while with men, everything is camouflage, as Aunt Miriam likes to say: you can't trust a man even in the grave."

"An eagle rises from the Dead Sea," Mother suddenly pointed with the knife in her hand to the place where the dazzling summer skies kiss the line of the convex firmament of the book of the desert. A little dot that quickly expanded approached us, soaring west on the invisible air stream, until it became a bird, with an enormous wing span. Mother got up and scanned the fallow fields around and said that behind one of the folds of ground there must be a fresh donkey or camel carcass, and if so, the solitary eagle would soon be followed by his companions. And indeed, soon after, a small flock of eagles was circling in the sky. The regal carnivores slowly glided, but when their feet touched the ground, the magic vanished all at once, and they looked like a congregation of bald turkeys, tottering heavily to their repast.

"That's how love is between a man and a woman," Mother resumed her parable. At first it's glorious and amazing, like the eagle with enormous wings hovering up high, and when it hits the hard ground of reality, it becomes a turkey who eats cadavers. "Everything deceives, everybody betrays, betrayal is the essence of human existence," her eyes flashed, and she wiped off the knife and put it in her purse. "You'll also be a man and will fall head over heels in love, not just once and not just twice. Who am I to tell you what to do? But you've got the instinct of a writer, promise me at least that you won't write love letters, so there won't be any incriminating documents scattered around."

On our way back, Mother lingered at the foot of the memorial to the defenders of Ramat-Rachel, who fell in the difficult battles that were fought here in the War of Independence. Frozen in the local mountain stone, her eyes raised proudly and defiantly to the fields of Bethlehem, a dreadful woman strove terrible as an army with banners to grasp a burning torch in one hand while her other hand spreads the wing of her dress over a small boy, holding a bundle of sheaves and clinging to her leg. "They turned her into a whore of the labor brigade," growled Mother and said that everybody sees the heroes of his nation in the image of his dreams, and the Rachel of the remnants of the labor brigade, who established the kibbutz, is a Soviet woman of valor, one of those comrades erect of chest and firm of limb who look out at us every week from the turbid greenish photos of the *Ogoniok* that Father pores over without seeing. Afterward, she read the prophecy of Jeremiah carved on the base of the statue and remarked that maybe it was no accident that the beloved, wounded, forsaken Rachel became a symbol of total motherhood — she who not only granted life to her son at the cost of her own death, but also the one who stands at the crossroads and waits endlessly for the return of her sons. "If there is love in the world, it's the love of a mother for her son," said Mother and added that, aside from that, she didn't know any other love that isn't crushed to dust and doesn't vanish with the years.

In the future, she'd back off from this firm judgment, casting aspersions on Grandmother, saying there are mothers for whom motherhood isn't an absolute value. But now, it stirred me to rebellion and I remarked that if, like me, she had lain in the dark and seen Jacob and Sulka sitting in the kitchen at night, after the turmoil of the day had subsided, talking softly and intimately, she wouldn't have been so quick to judge their love.

"They just didn't want to wake you up," Mother shrugged. But that evening, after Father, who had disappeared for hours on a hunt for novice cantors, sank into the easy chair and into slumber while listening to a political analysis on the radio and filled the house with his snoring, Mother woke him up shouting that maybe it was time for him to go back to Nahalal and take a crash course from his younger brother in how to live together so he could finally keep his promise to her at the wedding: to honor her more than himself.

Unfortunately for the successful Uncle Jacob, who didn't know the destructive role he played in our house, he became Mother's constant standard for examining and judging Father. "Look at your brother Jacob!" was often the opening of an indictment, and Father had no chance in that stringent comparison. There, in the "Electric Fauteuil," wrapped in a mantle of silence, he'd watch his birthright slipping away from him; there, during exercises in fractions in mathematics lessons with the private teacher their father had hired for them; there, in the woodshed next to the mill, competing to arrange wooden boards precisely in cross-hatched stacks with his brother and Zvi Arkes and Pini Katznelson; there, in a race to the ancient tomb of the kings from the time of Oleg, in the wake of the caravan of chariots of Nikolai II and his entourage, who came on a first royal visit to the district city of Volhynia—a world populated by failures and ruins, coalescing around the figure of the enviable younger brother who took his birthright from him.

Influenced by Mother, all through my childhood, through the fogs of everyday life, I didn't see his desperate desire to survive and his stubborn war against hunger and oppression. I was captivated by the myth of the Land of Israel, a child of the Labor Movement, embodied in the figure of my uncle, who maintained that only a farmer plowing his land and milking his cow, with a "girded" pistol thrust in his belt, especially if all those things were done in the Jordan Valley or the Jezreel Valley—only he was a whole person. I despised Father, the humble grocer, standing alone in the middle of the night in an empty shop and pasting "points"—as the ration certificates were called—onto government pages with rotten egg white, like a restorer mending a rare old painting. I despised him for his broken language, for being an immigrant, for lacking Zionist values and world view. Only many years after his death, in my uncle's library in Nahalal did I discover in *The Strokes of Salvation: The Book of Russian Zionism*, by Arye Zinziper (Rafaeli), the picture of the "Zionist Federation of Obruch (district of Volhynia), Passover 1913." There, my father was photographed with the thirty-seven local Zionists with the picture of Herzl in Basel, standing and looking at the Rhine, in the background. That year, in abortive attempts to resurrect his distinguished past, I met his friend and fellow townsman Pinhas Katznelson, who told me that Father didn't speak Russian, even though in his youth he knew Pushkin and Lermontov by heart and wrote pretty good poems and stories in that language, because, in the cellars of Lubyanka, the Bolsheviks murdered his two brothers for the counterrevolutionary sin of Zionism.

I despised him for the intoxicating magic exercised on him by cantorial music and mainly for yearning to be in the company of cantors and novice cantors. Indeed, one of my earliest and fondest memories is connected to his perfect devotion to the Jewish liturgy. (I'm in his arms. He spins around until he grows dizzy. A pleasant loss of senses. Father waves his mother's cane, Grandmother Mindl's, who came for her regular summer visit to us in Jerusalem, strikes the air with it and sings aloud, "On the rock bang bang, on the rock bang bang bang, on the rock bang bang and fresh water will come forth," and he brings my face close to his unshaven cheeks and kisses my head.) But after I grew up a bit, I turned my back on Father, and joined Mother's vigorous torments of the idolatry Father was addicted to with all his soul and all his might.

"Woe unto me! The treacherous dealers have dealt treacherously; yea, the treacherous dealers have dealt very treacherously," Mother would yell at Father on Friday afternoon, when the store was still full of customers concluding their Sabbath shopping, and he would hurry to the synagogue he had established in memory of Bat-Zion, to prepare it for the big audience that would gather there to hear the cantor's prayers. And it wasn't bad enough that he humiliated her to the dust by immortalizing the memory of her grief, argued Mother, but he also filled this house —and the words "this house" were emphasized in a venomous tone so everyone would understand what she meant—with young men whose stupidity was plastered all over their faces. "If he were willing to grant his only son, his own flesh and blood, one tenth of what he squanders on strangers' children, we'd have raised a splendid fellow here," she'd appeal to the customers, who'd nod to her and didn't say a thing.

During the week, Father was visited in our grocery by the novice cantors and their older friends, his foster children, who took their first steps in his synagogue and were now well-known prayer leaders throughout the world. These were the times of Dov Yosef, and despite rationing, Father would risk his life and give them eggs to drink and soften their vocal cords. And he would stand over them and smack his lips as they poured the rare eggs into themselves and would even serve them a bottle of *tsuf* for dessert. In exchange, the cantors would open their mouth and grant Father and the customers who assembled some exciting number: "Have Mercy," by Yossele Rosenblatt, "Is Ephraim My Dear Son?" by Malavsky, and "Reb Ishmael Purified Himself," by Kvartin, and sometimes "Lie Us Down," by Hershman. The neighboring shopkeepers claimed that Father and his cantors were stealing their customers.

The most generous of them was Velvele with the voice of a canary, who was a real midget, almost a dwarf, and to project his voice, he'd climb on the herring barrel or the sack of buckwheat, and trill his feminine voice. "He's got the voice of a betrothed maiden," Mother would say and cut the rolls of toilet paper into individual sheets, for the use of the pious who want to wipe their behinds on the Sabbath without violating one of the thirty-nine labors or one of their derivatives that are forbidden on the Sabbath.

At one of the appearances of the dwarf cantor, Rabbi Zevin, the editor of the Talmudic encyclopedia happened to come into the shop to pick up the kimmel bread his wife had ordered. He listened indifferently to Velvele's singing, and Mother, who thought she'd find support in that Talmud sage, told him her opinion of his canary voice. But the Rabbi, who didn't agree with her, said impatiently that the shout of the girl calling for help in the field with no one to save her isn't a joking matter, and certainly not an issue for frivolous women.

Years passed and rumors circulated that Velvele, with the voice of a canary, had gone to Germany, changed his name to Wolf, and appeared before the Ark as *Hoch-Kantor* in one of the synagogues of Frankfurt. I met him at a cantorial concert held in the early 1980s to commemorate the hundredth anniversary of the birth of Yossele Rosenblatt, a concert I went to impulsively as a person trying to find any road at all to his father twenty-five years later.

Two men stood in the raised square in front of the "Ohel Shem" on Balfour Street in Tel Aviv waiting for the concert to start. The lighted display window of the hall poured a sick, white light on them. The skinny man, in a raincoat from the days of rationing, rubbed his back on the tips of Max Pearlman's shoes, who was acting up on the poster of *A mazl fun a shlimazl*, while Monica, for whom *muzik iz ir lebn* — music is her whole life — leers at him seductively. Facing him, his throat extended, stood a stocky midget, waving his hands theatrically. "God save me, God save me," he trilled his voice, trying to give it the lightness of a coloratura, and after he swallowed his saliva, he made his voice thinner and even chirpier, like the voice of a woman, pleading until his Borsolino hat slipped off his head and rolled on the ground.

"*Zis vi tsuker*," the thin one smacked his lips, praising the sweetness of his prayer. "Got to get that falsetto of yours on records," he flattered him. "You're really Yossele Rosenblatt the second." "Yossele Rosenblatt the third," said the midget, put his hat back in place, and told his friend, who was amazed at his unexpected humility, that Rabbi Doctor Shmuel Rosenblatt, the son of the King of the Cantors, concluded the biography of his father with a story about a cantor who published an announcement declaring himself Yossele Rosenblatt the third. Why the third? the orphan asked him. And the cantor replied: because never will he have a second. "He is One — there is no second," the midget burst out in a mighty voice and pirouetted on his heels to show what an impression his song had made on the audience of people waiting.

Despite the lines on his face and his carefully dyed mustache, I recognized him immediately. It was Ze'ev Rosen, Velvele with the voice of a canary, one of Father's foster children.

"Velvele, you remember me?" I couldn't help addressing him. He seemed to review in his mind's eye the sons of the pimps and bar owners whose bar-mitzvahs he had done, and couldn't identify me.

At last, when I put an end to his distress and told him whose son I was, he hugged me warmly, kissed me, and muttered, "If only the father was alive, if only the father was alive," and sang the praises of Father, the patron of cantors, to the skinny man, who turned out to be the chandelier dealer on Wolfson Street in south Tel Aviv.

"If the only son of the spiritual father is interested in cantorial music," he said, "there's a future for the profession. In spite of everything you've been cured of your mother's venom. If she could, she would have drowned us all in a glass of goggle-moggle." And he invited me to come some Sabbath to hear him pray in the big synagogue in some Moshav in the south that turned into a city.

"But I live in Ramat Gan," I tried to get out of it.

"For a bit of good cantorial chanting, you're even permitted to drive on the Sabbath," decreed Velvele with the voice of a canary and said that it was time to go in.

The hall was full of retired teachers, most of them from the Mizrahi school system; textile dealers from Nahlat-Binyamin and food wholesalers from Kishon Street; Hasidim, Gur and Keretshnif Hasidim, for whom this was certainly their only amusement, aside from the quarrels between the Hasidic courts; and cantors — a lot of cantors. All the cantors of Gush Dan and the most remote provinces seemed to have gathered together and come here. If they brought an instrument into the hall to measure the intensity of the voice of stupidity, I hear Mother saying, the needle would have broken its glass covering. She would glance over the solid walls of "Ohel Shem," covered with decorative plywood, and say that it was no wonder all of Father's admirers congregated here, to hold the annual assembly of fools. "You know why cantors are fools?" she'd repeat her well-known taunt. "They always want the windows closed — so they don't get a draft and catch cold—and the air of the Land of Israel makes you wise as our rabbis taught us."

"By virtue of the fathers, you'll sit here the first in the kingdom," Velvele, who was one of the organizers of the evening, led me to the row of dignitaries, and sat me in the chair of the head of the leaders of city hall who had cancelled at the last minute. All around, cantors of little faith checked their tape recorders. (The *Brancha*, explained my companion, don't come here to enjoy, but to work, and at home they'll play the tapes over and over until "He looks down from Heaven and sees" and "He takes pity" will be like butter in their mouths.) Velvele leaned over to me and said that he owed Father not only his career, but a lot more. In the searches for musical talent, which he held at the Blumenthal Orphanage, Father noticed his "absolute *shtimme*" and accepted him in the boys' choir he had established with Cantor Kabetsky at "Heikhal Avinoam" in the Lemel School. ("You understand," Velvele tried to update his words. "He was like a training coach of a basketball team.") Three times a week he'd come and take him out of the institution, took him to a tailor who made him a suit that fit him, washed and ironed his shirts and even gave him food and drink, and when he'd appear in solos, as the youngest of the singers, he'd stand next to him and shamelessly wipe his tears. The boys of the chorus were like children to the childless man, while he himself, both because of his age and because of his height, he treated him like the youngest son, *"mayn Binyominka"*—my Benjamin—he would call him. Unlike other choir directors, Father didn't abandon the boys when their voices changed and they couldn't trill them, and he'd even sit with them for hours and console them and promise them that within a year or two they'd return to the reader's stand in the synagogue. Moreover, he had founded his synagogue not only to serve as a stepping stone for novice cantors, but also as a place where old cantors, whose voice had cracked, could also pray. The bell in the foyer rang again and again, and at last the emcee approached the microphone, like a bridegroom on his wedding day. And while he surveyed the audience with well-acted modesty, blinded by the spotlights, Velvele whispered to me that he could assure me that the master of ceremonies himself—the son of Ettinger of Hoshea Street—was also one of the lads of Kabetsky's choir.

"Your father, may your mother forgive me, was hardly an Orthodox humbug," Velvele told me in a hushed voice during the intermission. He was sipping a tepid Coke so his throat wouldn't get chilled, God Forbid, and he confessed that on the Sabbath and the holidays some of the singers, led by Father, would secretly gather in the home of old Biklis and enjoy the Sabbath around the gramophone.

"Why do you swallow a smile?" wondered the owner of the canary voice, but I nimbly steered the conversation to Rosenblatt's financial involvement with a group of swindlers, and because of that, he finally declared bankruptcy, so I wouldn't be tempted to produce the chatterbox in me and tell him about the religious war I waged with Father over that very issue one Sabbath. Every Sabbath afternoon Father would lie on the sofa and concentrate on what was going on in the neighbors' apartment, declaring that from now on no one should dare utter a word. It was no secret that he had a trade agreement with Mr. Zuckerman that, in exchange for the leftover chicken and the bones he kept for his gang of cats, the husband of the Pani would raise the volume of the radio so Father could hear "As Per Your Request for Cantorial Verses," which was broadcast on the radio at that time. I'd look contemptuously at Father glued to the "Gate of Mercy"— as Mother called the blocked door separating us from them— until one Sabbath, I couldn't help it anymore I protested. I yelled at him that he was a hypocrite who made a sham of the Law, and that didn't fit someone who just that Thursday painted *kippot* for the bare heads of Bialik and Ravnitsky in the drawing of them in the *Book of Legends* and who just now sat at the Sabbath table and sang "This day is honored from among all days" so yearningly, to violate the Sabbath and other holy matters as well—and the other absolute truths I was taught by my teachers in the Mizrahi school. But Father, who pretended to be asleep, didn't reply and went on enjoying the sweet voice of Goldele Malavsky who was singing "Is Ephraim My Dear Son?" or the melancholy of Yossele Rosenblatt singing "Look Down From Heaven and Behold That We Are a Scorn and Derision," and accompanied his Sabbath pleasure with light snores of disregard.

6

Father didn't believe in God.

He didn't like to talk about it, but that hump, as Grandmother called it, couldn't be hidden even by the suit handmade by Monsieur Shimen — that is, Shimon Schneider, the Parisian tailor of the Kerem neighborhood.

One day, when Uncle Jacob appeared in our house on one of his unexpected visits and was in a mood for memories, he set off for Obruch, and told about that bitter and impetuous day when Petlyura's pogromchiks attacked their hometown — and in the room there was once again the smell of charred human flesh, clouds of feathers flew, and Nehamka's Haim once again ran in the plundered streets, naked as the day he was born, raving to win favor from the stupid Ukrainians for someone with the halo of the holy fool on his head — Father put an end to the descriptions he wanted to erase from his memory, and said that the brothel we all call a world has no landlord.

Mother gave him an admonishing look, and Father corrected himself and said that, in his opinion, there was no leader in the capital. More than anything else, Mother hated obscenity.

And yet, every Friday afternoon, Father would shave, put on his best clothes — a cream-colored suit, brown-and-white shoes, punched with a flower pattern, the shoes of an aging Jewish gambler from Las Vegas, and a wide-brimmed straw hat — all that finery fell to Father's lot from a bundle of clothes we got from America during the days of rationing — and went to the synagogue.

At that time, he looked amazingly like Vittorio Gassman in the film *Scent of a Woman.* On the balconies along the way, women would stand and look at him, and smiling lasciviously, would say to one another that he looked like a man going to his lover. And there was quite a bit of truth to that because the synagogue he was heading for — the synagogue he and his friends had established when they withdrew from the "Shirat Israel" synagogue of the irascible Rivlin and from "Heikhal Avinoam," whose brilliance and splendor declined after the departure of Kabetsky — was named, as I said, after the wife of his youth, Bat-Zion.

The synagogue was in a classroom of the Sephardi Talmud Torah for the boys of "Beit Aaron," and Father would take pains to get there early while the day was still bright. Chalk dust mingled with the smell of almond paste, the sweat of adolescent boys and the mold of oranges forgotten in desk drawers would strike him as he entered. And he would air out the room, run a wet rag over the green walls and set up the Tent of the Congregation. On the ink-stained tables, he spread white tablecloths (which he cut from the sheets bequeathed by Luba and later from Mother's dowry and the head gravedigger buried a strip of them in his grave to be an advocate and tell his righteousness when he appeared at the trial of God at the Throne of Honor), dragged the lectern to the middle of the room and turned it into a *bima* for the cantor and the reader, and finally rolled the Ark of the Covenant on four wheels out of its hiding place and set it up at the Eastern Wall. When he'd open the wings of the doors of the Ark, which looked like an all-purpose cabinet during the week, and reveal the Torah Curtain with two catty lions supporting the Tablets embroidered on it, he'd say that the Children of Israel in their forty years of wandering in the desert would dismantle the tabernacle and reassemble it every time, but they never did it twice in the same place.

And then Father would shake the dust off his summer suit, and for the comfort of the cantors, would close the pair of windows facing Yosef Ben-Matityahu Street, where, across the way, in the house built on a crag, was the "Me'or Aynaim" Yeshiva of the Chernobyl Hasids (Grandfather, Father's father, had once been a follower of the Holy Grandfather, author of the *Me'or Aynaim*) and said that in theaters of the world there is a revolving stage and even if the actors ran fast on it, they'd stay right where they were.

That synagogue, where they'd pray only on the Sabbath and holidays, attracted a group of Jews who certainly had no place in the pretentious and humorless synagogues of our time.

For example, Mr. Brinker, the municipal sanitation engineer. ("I'll never lack a livelihood," he'd boast, as it were, and when his interlocutor was amazed at him, he'd add: "After all, human beings won't stop following the call of nature even in lean years.") The dignitary, whose violin song moan would rise at night over the houses of Pikiyin Street, was the purest reader of the synagogue. "Chaliapin," Father would dissolve when Shalom Gad Brinker put his narrow silk prayer shawl on his neck, a scarf, strike the tuning fork on the corner of the *bima* and begin with "Come, Let Us Sing." Over the years, a few of the religious riffraff that joined the synagogue complained about the use of musical instruments, because they were concerned that it might be forbidden on the Sabbath, and our friend would secretly strike his tuning fork, as if his ear itched, and would wink at us old-timers as he did. His great hour was on the eve of Yom Kippur, the night of Kol Nidre. When he came, he'd take off his shoes and put them in the next room, as the Moslems do in their mosques, and pray before the Ark in his stocking feet. In his opinion, Yom Kippur was not a day for sport when everyone has to wear white tennis shoes. Clusters of admirers would hang on the windows when he'd start his prayer, at first in a whisper, as if telling a secret, and finally in a mighty lion's roar. Even his son Menahem, who was famous even in those days as a Communist and a proclaimed atheist, would come to the synagogue at that time. (Many years later, between the New Year and the Day of Judgment, Menahem and I happened to be in Moscow as members of a writers' delegation. On Yom Kippur, as the hour of *Neila* approached at the end of the holiday, we left the Ukraina Hotel on the banks of the Moscow River and went to the central synagogue on Arkhipova Street. It was a freezing afternoon, and we made our way, wrapped in heavy parkas and caracole fur hats, through the gloomy streets of the crumbling empire, among the impassive mobs emitted from the doors of the metro, and the old woman peddlers gathering the muddy carrots and the rotten turnips they offered for sale, and Menahem sang aloud, into the wind battering our faces, "Open the gate for us at this time when the gate closes, for the day is fading away," in his father's distant melody, and those people went on walking among us as if they had never left us.) The serious man, whose silver hair was combed back severely and whose mouth was clenched, sober, had a subtle sense of humor, and when he wanted he would cheer his friends with it. One Yom Kippur, when somebody scolded him mildly for not praying at the Ark in a *kittel*—the white shroud-like garment reminiscent of the day of death, which is donned both on the Days of Awe and at the Seder—Brinker giggled and asked his interlocutor if he knew what the Sages meant when they said doing one transgression draws in its wake doing yet another, and said that the Sages aimed their words at some character who hid a slice of challah in the pocket of his *kittel* on Yom Kippur, and whenever they'd bow down to the ground during "We kneel," he'd take a bite of it and put it back in his pocket. When Passover came, the man donned the *kittel* again, and then, during the Seder, when he felt between the folds, he found the remains of the challah. But when that person went back into the synagogue, Brinker inhaled the ammonia fumes offered him by Shraga Feybl Griebovski, and said that our saint laughed in vain, since there are no pockets at all in the *kittel*, for what do the dead take with them except their acts.

Or, for example, Mr. Mordechai Rosenstein. The introspective man, with a wool scarf wound around his neck like an artiste, made his living by drawing posters for the Orion cinema: he'd sit in his tiny room in the garret of the cinema, overlooking the street, and paint Marilyn Monroe's eyes blue or add vermilion to Sophia Loren's cheeks. But his greatness came on the eves of holidays, when, with plywood and jute sheets, on the platform at the entrance to the cinema, he'd resurrect scenes from hit movies like *The Guns of Navarone* or *The Bridge Over the River Kwai*. In his house in the Vittenberg Houses, his internal life was revealed: a turbulent artist who wanted to express his soul—the soul of a Yeshiva student, who became one of the pupils of Professor Schatz of Bezalel—in oils and pastels. In the synagogue, he'd sit withdrawn in his seat, and his soft eyes were raised, outside, to the sleepy street corner or to the pepper tree with the twisted trunk twined around the stylish iron gate. And only on Yom Kippur, when he'd pray before the Ark and sing the verses of "Like the Clay in the Hand of the Potter," could you sense the confident soul of the artist, who sees himself as a god of his creation, he grasps it at will and smashes it at will, he makes it even at will and makes it uneven at will, he adulterates it at will and purifies it at will. And a charming sweetness of his voice, talking about one thing and meaning something else, would flood a child's eyes with tears, as once again he was shown the mystery of the art he had been unwittingly dedicated to from birth.

Or, for example, Mr. Babad, the heavy-tongued and heavy-bodied plasterer, who would leaf through the prayer book with fingers contorted by rheumatism, and under his fingernails and in the cracks of his skin you could still see the remnants of paint that neither turpentine nor soap nor hot water could destroy. Often I'd walk him home from the synagogue instead of waiting for Father who stayed to attend to his public affairs, and he'd talk to me about his loneliness. "You're the only person close to me in the world," he said in a rare moment of candor, and told me about Venice, whose name he pronounced like the name of a beloved woman he had lost back in the distant past. When he fell ill with the disease that was to kill him, he took me up to his room one day, the room of a man who lives alone, and gave me a small album of picture postcards of Venice. Together we leafed through the bluish photos, reading the names of the sites — Piazza San Marco, the Doges' Palace, Coleone Memorial, the Bridge of Sighs — and said that if I ever wandered over there and stood amazed at the buildings, whose lines blur in the reflected glow of the Lagoon, I'd remember him, who had wanted to go back there all his life and didn't make it.

That painful world, that says a thing and its opposite at one and the same time, that deliberately blurs boundaries and doesn't look straight at the truth, as it were, that world by its very nature doesn't appeal to young people who demand clear and cutting distinctions between good and bad, truth and lie, faith and heresy from their fellow man. Until one Sabbath, worried and scared, I plucked up my courage and refused to set foot in synagogue and instead got up early and went to the study house of the Bratslav Hasids, who clap their hands during the Amidah prayer in excitement and devotion to the flame of their Rebbe and afterward they drink brandy and listen to one of them tell tales of wonders that Reb Nahman told his students (on that Sabbath, one of the old Hasids told the tale of the moon who envied the sun and the sun sewed it a kind of garment as a gift).

"Wherefore cometh not the son of Jesse to meat, neither yesterday nor today?" asked Father, somewhat offended, when he came home from prayers.

Mother turned away to avoid seeing the clash she knew was coming, and I said to Father with the angry dogmatism of youth that I was fed up with that wishy-washy world of him and his friends, and that human beings their age had to take a stand: if they believed in God, they should pray like really pious people, and if they didn't believe, they should be decent enough to stay in their own houses and not trample the house of the Lord with their everyday shoes.

Father smiled, which wasn't like him, and said that after we ate, we'd study some Talmud together.

"A barrel which broke they save from it enough substance for three meals," Father read from the Talmud tractate Shabbath, discussed the legal issues deriving from it, went deeply into the discussions of absorption and squeezing, and split hairs over the difference between olives and grapes on the one hand and strawberries and pomegranates on the other. When we came to the words of Rami bar Hama about a person suffering from a venereal disease milking a goat, Father said we had already studied enough and he closed the *Gemara*.

"You understand?" he asked.

"No," I said angrily.

Father repeated the opening line of the problem, stressing every single stanza, and said that his faith had been broken in those distant days before I was born, the days after the Petlyura pogroms, like that barrel and there was nothing left of it except the hoops that don't let him do whatever he wants, and the substance of three meals in the synagogue is the main thing for them.

"Why didn't you look for a new barrel?" I grumbled.

"A barrel isn't stockings," said Father, wondering if I would ever understand him. "A barrel, even if it's broken, you don't change it every day."

Strange as it may sound, Father's lament for the rituals of the synagogue and cantorial chanting was a kind of echo, distant, late, and essentially distorted, of European Romanticism of the nineteenth century. Now, as I reflect on it, I see him as one of those dreamers and soft-eyed wanderers, whose soul longed for half-ruined castles and abandoned monasteries with caved-in ceilings, enchanted remnants, with pale moonlight poured on their collapsed towers, their demolished spiral staircases and their toppling walls. So, Father's cultural territory was also populated with the rubble of holy and liturgical rituals, and an ancient splendor was still poured on their desecrated stones. And God, whether He had taken off or was revealed or exiled, no longer dwelled within them. Father didn't seem to be bothered by that. On the contrary, he took advantage of the absence of the Lord of Lords to set up a department for man between the collapsing walls, even if it was only temporary. Based on that refuted parable, it could be asked why he didn't first destroy the remnants of the past and clear them away to prepare the place for something new. But he would probably have replied with a smile, "Let it stay like that, we'll get along," and would have added that in the end, that task would divert time and effort from what was essential.

One Sabbath in the early 1950s, I got to eat the forbidden fruit that grew in Father's garden. On that Sabbath, the Bible Zoo was supposed to reopen its gates to visitors after a long period when it was closed because of the war. All week a pickup truck with a loudspeaker went round the streets inviting the residents to come en masse to the grand opening of the zoo in its new permanent home in the Grove of Tel Arza. Father, who was standing next to me in the door of the shop and looking at the pickup truck festooned with posters of animals passing by him, promised me that this time he would give up the weekly lesson in the Maxims of the Fathers and we'd go together to see the lions and tigers, the deer and the eagles, which we had seen so far only in the drawings of Reb Isaac Bak, which decorated the ceiling of the tabernacle of the big yeshiva in Meah Shearim. When we got to the gates of the zoo, on the Sabbath afternoon, the guard stopped us and wouldn't let us in. Father froze. He realized that he had misunderstood from the announcement that entrance would be free of charge, and so he didn't bother to arrange for tickets. Father raised his eyes to the guard, to the barred box office and finally to me. I stood ashamed, my fingers grasping the fence and my looks accompanying the happy people sliding down the slope of the stony path toward the cages hidden in the depths of the grove. "Don't worry, we'll come back here again," Father promised and turned to go home. "But I want to go to the zoo today," I stamped my feet. "We'll go today, I promised you," said Father, and his words were accompanied by a lion's roar. Not far from there, one of the old stone houses that had once housed the German teachers of the Schneller Orphanage was now the home of Father's friend Mr. Kaminsky, owner of the fabric shop and father of the famous basketball player on the Jerusalem "Po'el" team. Father knocked on his door. Kaminsky came out to greet us in his pajamas, jolted out of his afternoon nap. They whispered together a little while and then Father went inside with him. When he came out, we hurried back to the zoo. Father turned here and there, went to the box office, and when he returned, there was a pair of tickets in his hand. For several more days, I still felt the sense of bliss I felt then, when Father led me over the threshold of the locked zoo. As a youth, I was angry at my sinning father for not keeping the Sabbath holy, and in vain I wanted to wipe out the memory of his awful transgression, but as an adult I'm filled with love once again for that man who, despite everything, didn't hesitate to break the holy rules of his life because he couldn't bear to see a child's tears of grief.

How sensitive Father was to others and how attentive to their needs, we heard one day during the week of mourning when Rabbi Arye Levin came to pay a condolence call. That sweet Jew, who was famous as the rabbi of the lepers and the prisoners because he used to visit them so often, entered our house with hesitant steps and sat down between me and Mother, on a low stool, like one of the mourners. He took my hand in his warm hand as soft as down, stroked it a long time and wept quietly. Everyone who witnessed that scene joined that simple mute weeping. Through his tears, the saint addressed Mother familiarly in Yiddish and said, "My daughter, you have lost a husband and your son has lost a father and I have lost a partner." And after a pause, he added in a soft, almost inaudible voice, "Yes, we did a lot of business together." Mother said that throughout the years she had often seen the rabbi enter the store and confer with Father, but she never dared ask her husband, may-he-rest-in-peace, what deals the two of them had. Just between the two of them, Rabbi Arye revealed to us then, he and Father together covered part of the costs of food for a widow, the mother of four children, whose husband died in a bad business. Like most of our customers, she'd buy on credit, but at the end of every month, when the time came to settle the bill, Father would take only half of what she owed without her knowing. "Real charity is not to shame the poor," said Rabbi Arye. "And your father, may-he-rest-in-peace, honored that with all his might."

About three months later, right before Sukkoth, I met Rabbi Arye again when I stopped into the old bookstore, The Light, in Meah Shearim. Like most of the bookstores in that neighborhood at the end of the month of Elul, Rabbi Abraham Rubenstein's bookstore also sold Ethrogs. And the small store, which stood in moldy dreariness all year, was now buzzing with thick-bearded men who stood against the light, each supplied with a magnifying glass, a jeweler's loupe and thin toothpicks, and examined the Ethrogs from the bud to the stalk. While I was standing apart from them, jammed into a corner, among the books, which were also jammed into a corner, and poring over a *midrash* from the Middle Ages, Rabbi Arye came in, made his way among the hosts in the doorway, bent over to the merchant and asked if he had had time to select an Ethrog for him. And Rabbi Abraham, who went on sucking his eternal mint, rolling it in his mouth like the words of the Torah, took out of his desk drawer a skein of linen and held it out to him without a word. Rabbi Arye, who didn't even glance at the Ethrog, buried it in the inside pocket of his coat and hurried out. I put the book back, ran after him, and called out his name. "What's up, my boy?" the Rabbi was amazed to find me here, and asked how Mother was. I told him that, as the son of the man who was his partner, I allowed myself to bother him with a nervy question. How could it be, I asked, that all the pious people examine the Ethrogs like precious gems, while he treats the Ethrog as he did. Rabbi Arye smiled and said that was indeed a question, and his reply to it was: the Torah warns us of only two Commandments that we should follow with zeal. One is the Commandment of the Ethrog, of which the Bible says, "The boughs of goodly trees—from the most goodly boughs," and the other is concern for old people, as the Bible says, "Honour the face of the old man." "Most Jews observe the former, while I, the small one, chose to observe the latter," said the short old man, and asked me to forgive him for not staying with me a bit more because he was hurrying to the Old People's Home to visit a solitary sick man who didn't have anyone to take care of him. And Rabbi Arye stroked my hand that was in his, wished Mother and me an end to the year and its curses, and suddenly he tensed and said he wanted to tell me something I didn't know. That man he was going to visit, Father, may-he-rest-in-peace, paid for his false teeth from his own pocket. "To some your father gave something to eat and to this one he gave what to eat with," he swallowed a sigh and left me. And I stood still and watched him, the old man who looked a chick, hurrying with tiny steps to the bus stop, and I couldn't take my eyes off his shoes worn out with so much walking, which barely rose from the ground he trod.

Naturally, Father's love of people and his devotion, a boundless devotion, to his fellow man didn't escape us even when he was alive, but, as Mother put it, she and I enjoyed only its dark side. Ever since his death, as I said, Mother abandoned her critical position, but one autumn evening, a little more than two years later, she broke her silence for a little while and lashed out at the trait of altruism, which she regarded as vile, and in the process, she castigated Father.

When I came home from the army in the evening I found her still in the shop, behind the closed shutters, arranging the empty egg crates for the delivery man, Mr. Schreiber. The radio was on and Mother asked me to wait and not relate my adventures until after the news. Before the end of the broadcast, the announcer said that in the yard of the central Mandatory prison in the Russian Compound, at dusk, there had been a gathering of the former members of Etzel and Lehi to honor the prisoners' rabbi, Rabbi Arye Levin, on his eightieth birthday. "That's your father's partner they're talking about," Mother giggled and said that all those saints, including the Thirty-Six hidden ones, as it were, have a dark side to their personality, a hidden side, that feeds the open side that's illuminated by the dazzle of the spotlights of splendor. "You see this egg carton?" she waved one of the cardboard cartons in the air. "Every bulge on the top always comes at the expense of a depression on the bottom. That's how it always is in life." The altruists are willing to sacrifice their own private good for others, not because they're really moved by love of their fellow man, but because they want to be like God, granting life to man at will and condemning him to destruction at will. "That song by Jabotinsky, the idol of Mr. Begin and Mr. Sheib, how does it go? 'Generous and genius and cruel,'" said Mother and added that I shouldn't forget the lust for honor that's always involved in the lust for power and rule and mastery. The altruists reward saints and do only good and in the process they sneak a look around, because even in their ostentatious modesty, they expect the applause of the masses. Otherwise, how could I explain to her Reb Arye's willingness to participate in the mass assembly in his honor.

Her bitter words made me angry and I couldn't help commenting that Father did what he did for Mrs. R and for the toothless old man from the Old People's Home not to get a prize, since nobody knew about it.

"But Rabbi Arye knew," Mother cut me off. "You don't understand anything. He didn't need us. The words of esteem lavished on him by the hidden saint were enough for him." And aside from that, she added, while he was performing those acts, he pictured in his imagination how the things would surface and become known after he died, and then everybody would admire him openly and would sing his praises and would glorify and laud his modest saintliness, and that thought was like balm on his old bones. Mother discerned the expression of disgust on my face and said that she had recently read about a Chinese comedian who stipulated in his will that after he died, he was to be dressed in his formal suit and his body was to be cremated at night, at the exact hour when he would come out and bow to the audience; and when the will was carried out and his body caught fire, the sky was suddenly filled with a shower of glowing stars that pleased the audience much more than all his appearances on stage. It turned out that the clown, who wanted to amaze his friends and admirers, stuffed the pockets of his suit with firecrackers.

But in truth the offense at Father's eager response to the unfortunates who knocked on his door and asked for help, and the envy, so miserable in retrospect, of those who won the competition for his attention, was merely one rather peripheral expression of the eternal hostility his altruism evoked in us. Our main grudge against him, and here my share equaled Mother's, was that he didn't ask us if we wanted to bear his acts of grace with him, but rather imposed them on us.

A mute man lurked in ambush for me at one of the first curves of the road of my childhood, poked his head out of his cave, a low basement apartment at street level, and terrified me with the wild and docile look he gave the world. Whenever we'd go to Grandmother's and come to the entrance of Meah Shearim, where the wide street suddenly turns into a narrow alley, pressed between houses, I would see him. A clean-shaven man he was, with a black velvet hat and a striped suit, well preserved, the way only proud paupers know how to preserve their clothes, the only indication of days that would never return, and he held out a hand for alms. Father would bury a coin in my hand and coax me to give it to him. Father wanted the act to be a model of compassion, but inadvertently it was a cruel ceremony of coaching. The mute would hold his hand out to me and his impenetrable look was the look of a hunted animal, bereft of memory. "Coward," Father would mock me when I'd snatch my hand back in panic. "What a coward you are." And he'd force my clenched hand to the repulsive hand of the mute, whose fingers with gnawed nails touched my fist. When the coin was in his grasp, the mute would spread his fleshy lips, emit a whine that was cracked at the end and be swallowed up in his room, which was carefully washed and smelled heavily of loneliness. And I would cling to Mother's leg and inhale her protective smell — a blend of fragrant soap with a slight breeze of sweat, absorbed in the silk fabric of her dress, a summer dress with big brown flowers.

The artisans Father brought for repairs in the house were chosen for their distress and not their talents, and often he'd even initiate work for them, which ultimately did us more harm than good. Our regular carpenter was a young man with a crazy look who had escaped by the skin of his teeth from a Soviet gulag in the far north, the father of an only daughter who was afflicted with infantile paralysis. The Sukkah he put up every year in our yard was calculated to collapse on our heads on the first night of the holiday, and the windows Mother bought from a demolition contractor in Talpiot for the porch she built in the entrance, he spoiled with his two left hands. Sometimes, when he'd dare to fill his mouth with nails, as carpenters do, he'd spit them out in panic and ask Mother to quickly make him some mashed potatoes so his stomach wouldn't be damaged. A discharged soldier, a Holocaust survivor, who lost his eye in the battle of Latrun, whom Father brought to make us a Sabbath clock, almost caused a fire when he misconnected the wires. Mother refrained from complaining about all those and reluctantly accepted Father's mistakes, but she couldn't help grumbling about the feats of the house painter Father picked up in the street. Every year, before Passover, we'd paint the kitchen, whose walls were always sooty. Often, Mother would put a pot on the stove, hurry to the shop and stay there until the pillar of smoke summoned her back to the dish that was burned. One year, Father's choice fell on a lunatic who was hospitalized most of the time in Ezrat Nashim Hospital, and when he was released, he'd wander the streets carrying a ladder and brushes looking for work. Mother pleaded with him not to do that, but Father didn't listen to her and claimed stubbornly that that's the greatest Commandment on the eve of Passover. The painter very carefully scraped off the old paint and Father teased Mother, saying that only a madman would do his work faithfully these days. The next day, when the painter stood at the top of the ladder, he called Father and asked for a bottle of milk. Why do you need a bottle of milk, asked Father. To give the paint a softer tone, answered the man standing at the top of the ladder. Father gave him what he wanted, but the painter didn't pour the milk into the paint. Instead, he gulped it down all at once and burst into dizzy laughter. Father took off in shame, but it wasn't long before he was called back. "What do you want now?" he asked. "With all due respect, Reb Jew, it's hard for me to come down, your ceiling is high, do me a favor and go pee for me." Father, who wasn't blessed with a sense of humor, smiled in embarrassment and answered that he was able to do everything, but not that. "You don't want to, Reb Jew?" asked the painter. "I want to, but I can't," said Father helplessly. And then, as mother described it to Uncle Jacob, the lunatic took out his family jewels, pissed into the paint, dipped his brush in it and started painting the kitchen walls. Mother, who heard about it from me, filled the house with her shouts. She threw the painter out, washed the walls with dozens of buckets of water, and declared that she was definitely "mad at" Father, and that lasted for weeks. That Passover the kitchen walls stood in the blaze of their layers from the days of King Shabetski to the days of Ben-Gurion, as Grandmother put it, until Father hired the Cypriot *kinstler* who made the desert bloom and turned it into a garden of brown daffodils.

Father's errors imposed long battles and mainly frustrations with the poverty-stricken artisans on Mother, but I was forced to put up with the yeshiva students he frequently invited to our house to disseminate knowledge to me. His compassionate heart was moved by the students of the Hebron Yeshiva near our house — those homeless *alte bahurim* who spent all their days on the worn wooden benches of the tabernacle of Torah, in monkish and filthy dormitory rooms, without any privacy, and wandering idly back and forth along Geula Street, from Sabbath Square to the gates of Mahane Schneller — and came up with the idea in agreement with Rabbi Meyer Hodosh, as Rabbi Meir Hadash was generally known. "Let him at least be a heretic who knows a page of Talmud, the main thing is we won't have an ignoramus growing up here," Father explained what he did to Mother the first time the yeshiva genius entered our house with the arrogance characteristic of the students of Slobodka, his tailor-made jacket hanging on his shoulders and a Borsolino hat at a jaunty angle. From then until just before Father's death, the sound of Torah reading was heard incessantly in our house. The daily lessons that kept me from registering for swimming lessons at the YMCA or the model airplane group at Camp Allenby, quickly disintegrated into theological debates on the existence of God, the nature of miracle and the reasons for the Commandments, or into marvelous demonstrations of expertise to impress me. One of the students, who sported ties appliquéd with silver threads and whose white shirts were stained with sweat on their collars and folds, had a phenomenal photographic memory. He asked me to stick a pin anywhere I wanted in the Talmud, poke a hole, and tell him the page number and the next page, and he'd promptly tell me the word written there. Another one, whose ruddy face and neck were sown with acne ("You see what happens when you eat canned goods and not fresh fruits and vegetables," Mother would admonish me) showed me how he wrote two letters at one and the same time with both hands. One letter was a complicated question of religious law addressed to one of the scholars of the age; and the other was to his fiancée. My last teacher was always

168

HAIM
BE'ER

going off into excited profane conversations about some sharp man who wrote a book of religious laws of latrines called *The Deep that Lieth Under*, about a Torah scholar, who would put a book of questions and answers under his pillow before he went to sleep and in the morning, when he awoke, he would know it by heart; and about a scholar who went out of his mind and cut out of the Talmud all the words of the Tosaphot that upset him, and when the jokers would mention that to him, saying "All right, the Tosaphot sinned, but what's the sin of Rashi who's printed on the other side?" He'd reply on the spot: "Woe to the wicked and woe to his neighbor." At rare times they would open their hearts to me and reveal their secrets, about the marriages they talked about, the quarrels between the heads of the yeshiva, or their loneliness. The saddest thing I remember from those intimate conversations were the words of a student who was exiled from his old mother's house in Afula and ascended to Jerusalem, the place of the Torah, and said in Yiddish: "In a place where there is a home there is no world, and in a place where there is a world, there is no home."

Mother did welcome them nicely, the forlorn and homeless students, would boil a cup of milk for them and slice them some onion *pletzlekh* and spread butter on them, but after they had gone, she carefully injected me with increased doses of antibiotics to counteract the charm they exercised to captivate me, and she'd say that those likable fanatics were steel fists in velvet gloves and she'd tell about the deeds of "the Cossacks of the Holy-One-Blessed-Be-He," who had made her and her siblings gulp gallons of torments.

A whole chapter in itself was my forced attendance at the funerals of the *gdoylim*, Father's overly familiar name for the famous rabbis. In that matter, he didn't ask Mother's opinion or agreement, but took me with him to those processions of death, to become, like him, part of that straying, black serpent that pursued the small, white body in alleys and then in open spaces outside the city, toward the cemetery, wanting to swallow it up like a rabbit, but it tramped on, retreating from it, until it would jump and disappear in its burrow in the ground. "Look around very carefully," he would shout at me, first when he carried me on his shoulders, and then, when I grew up, as I clutched his hand to keep from disappearing into the crowd, "you'll be able to brag to your children and grandchildren that you were at the funeral of the Gaon of Tashbin and of Rabbi Issur Zalman Meltser, and even of Rabbi Aharonio of Belz." But at that time, I saw nothing but the sweaty backs of the black clad men moving incessantly before me.

But Father's altruism reached the climax of its cruelty in the feast at the religious ceremony he conceived in honor of my bar mitzvah. Mother and I attempted to dissuade him, and she went out of her way to ply him with soft words, saying that the celebration was intended first and foremost to please me and establish my social status among my classmates. But father stamped his foot and said he had vowed to hold that thanksgiving feast when I was born and had sworn the vow again when I was three years old. "There won't be any going up to the Torah or any throwing of candy, no party for classmates and no magic lantern, not even a watch," he declared and slammed out of the house, shouting inside, "I have nourished and brought up children, and they have rebelled against me."

"Be a big boy and swallow your father's craziness as bitter medicine, and afterward we'll do what we want," said Mother, who knew that Father was implacable and wouldn't change his mind, and this time no one, not even Uncle Jacob, could remove his evil decree.

The scene in our house that winter night came from some Medieval painting of hell by Hieronymos Bosch or Matthies Grunewald. Because of Father's stubbornness, Mother had to spread new cloths on the T-shaped table and set it with china plates and silver cutlery, and even put in the center of it the pair of baroque candlesticks Father's grandmother got as a wedding gift. At the head of that table sat four eminent rabbis dressed in garments whose piety fit the scene. In the middle, between Rabbi Kipnis and Rabbi Zevin on the right and Rabbi Arye Levin and Rabbi Sandomirski on the left, sat Father and I. With a used bow-tie we found in some bundle of clothes from America, in the brown beret Mother put on my head so my pompadour wouldn't rouse the wrath of the rabbis against her, and with the new Dukes watch I wore on the sleeve of my sweater so everyone could see it, I looked like an innocent babe from the French province at a convocation of a holy synod with a forlorn and gloomy congregation.

The guests, whom we waited for, were about to enter any minute, and indeed, at the appointed time, the door was opened, and in the entrance stood Rabbi Leybish, the mighty herald of the Burial Society, walking around the streets and proclaiming in his terrifying voice the times of the funerals, and in his wake beggars and cripples, lunatics and paupers crowded inside one after the other, all of them gathered by Rabbi Leybish at Father's orders, in the public soup kitchens and the underworld, brought up out of a horrible pit, out of the miry clay. Like Reb Nahman of Bratslav's tale of "The Seven Beggars," Rabbi Zevin later mentioned in his sermon, the blind and the deaf and the mute came in, with the crooked and the hunchback, a beggar without arms and then a beggar without legs who hopped in on his stumps. And along with them, to complete the group, Levi Treger, the porter with the enormous pot belly, exposed both on cold days and hot, with the hernia of his naval on it, like a button on the holy lamp, who'd split watermelons to the delight of the children; the cantor Lufka Lufka, who had gone crazy from a punch in the brain stem during a drunken quarrel; and last but not least the musician who entertained the passengers at the bus station by playing a comb.

As soon as the jellied cow's foot was served, Mother's prophecies of disaster started coming true. The mute, who didn't want to wait his turn, snatched the portion from under the groping hands of the blind man with the pockmarked face, while Levi Treger stuck his tongue out at the man with no hands, who was waiting for Rabbi Leybish to feed him, picked up the cracker and the cube of jelly quivering on it in his enormous hand, stuffed them together into his mouth while emitting a contemptuous fart. When the time came for the soup, the cry of Father's pet children rose to the heavens like ten bathtubs emptied of their water. They gulped the soup straight from the bowls and ladles and plates, and Mother, who watched over the missing spoons, whispered to Father that all the silverware was disappearing. But he sat arrogantly at the head of the table, his hat tilted back, and said that the Lord would return us what was missing and glanced furtively at the rabbis to see what impression his words made on them. Each pair of rabbis was whispering words of the Torah to one another, eating small strips of jelly or fastidiously bringing the spoon to their mouth, as if they didn't regard food as important.

Between the soup and the main course, while Mother and two neighbors, Rachel Gruber and Priva Tshekonitski, who had been brought in to help her, cleared the table, the first pair of rabbis delivered a sermon. Rabbi Kipnis said that exactly fifty years before, my grandfather, the one I'm named after, along with the distinguished men of Obruch, came to the "kibbutz" of Rabbi Shmuel Noah Shneersohn in Bobroisk, and chose him, who was still a blushing lad, as the rabbi of their city. Rabbi Abraham Haim Sandomirsk, rabbi of the Bat-Zion Synagogue, who circled dizzily around the biblical verse "The glory of children are their fathers," told how Father gave his soul for the existence of the synagogue. "Never did I see our dear host sit still," said the Rabbi. "And not, God forbid, because he goes outside to talk of profane matters, but because he offers his seat to a guest." Both of them, of course, emphasized my obligation to continue on the golden path paved by my forefathers of Obruch until now. As the rabbis gave their sermons, the honored guests ate the soup nuts like sunflower seeds, tossing handfuls at one another, and the musician tried time and again to bring the comb to his lips but was repelled immediately by the sight of Rabbi Leybish's finger wagging at him.

As the main course was served, a melee erupted among the beggars over who should get the thighs and the giblets and who should get the upper parts and before the case could be decided, most of them even started snatching up chicken quarters and fried potatoes from the tray and stuffing them in their pockets. Lufka Lufka brandished the inherited candlestick and threatened his neighbor, Crooked Neck, with it. During the skirmish, the lighted candle fell on the table, and the cloth caught fire. Stammerer quickly poured wine on the fire and stuttered the song, "With joy shall ye draw water out of the wells of salvation, oh water, water, water." When things calmed down at the reprimand of the herald of the Burial Society, who threatened to send all of them to the cemetery in the first bus, Rabbi Zevin, editor of the *Talmudic Encyclopedia*, stood up to speak.

"The home of your grandfather in Obruch was always full of handsome Jews, misshapen by poverty," our neighbor addressed me, and added that he could testify to that first hand because he stayed in that house when he came to visit his friend at the "kibbutz" in Bobroisk, Rabbi Shmuel Kipnis, who then ascended to sit there on the Rabbi's chair. "When you grow up and read the tale told by Reb Nahman about the seven beggars who were gath- ered to rejoice the bride and groom, you'll find that just as the blind man isn't blind at all, simply that, since the whole world doesn't come to him in an instant and so he seems to be blind, because he doesn't look at the world at all, so looking and seeing for him aren't part of the world, so one who stutters doesn't stut- ter at all, simply that the speech of the world that doesn't praise the Lord May-He-Be-Blessed is not perfect and so he looks like a stutterer because he stutters the words of the world, but in truth he is a fine talker and a wonderful orator and can speak riddles and songs that are called wonderful Lieder." Our neighbor the Torah scholar looked at me a long time, and my sense of fear and disgust at the mad bacchanalia taking place before my eyes didn't escape him, and then he said that at the time when Our Master and Teacher Joseph Isaac of Lubovich was a little boy of four, he asked his father why man had been created with two eyes. His father replied by asking if he knew the Hebrew alphabet. When the child answered yes, his father asked him if he knew that there was **sh** and **s** and what the difference was between them. Joseph Isaac replied that **sh** has a dot on the right side and **s** on the left. Said his father: That's why you have two eyes, there are things that have to be looked at with the right eye and there are things that have to be seen with the left eye. You should always look at a Jew with the right eye, and at candy and toys—with the left eye. And from that time on, Rabbi Zevin concluded his sermon, the rule was fixed in the heart of Our Master and Teacher that every Jew, no matter who he is and how he is, he should always be looked at with a friendly eye.

Throughout the meal, I couldn't settle down: What would I do when my turn came to speak, and Rabbi Yankele the Milkhiker, the little *melamed*, who recited the *maftir* and the *haftorah* with me and even wrote me the bar-mitzvah boy sermon, hadn't yet ar- rived and was conceivably deep in the sleep of the just. For the six months before that evening, I regularly visited Rabbi Yankele's house on the border of Akhva and Zikhron Moshe (later on I'd realize that in that very house, the house of the widow Katinka, Brenner had rented a room the first time he came to Jerusalem) for Bible lessons. Rabbi Yankele would chant the biblical verse in his lush voice, like a person who pressed cake dipped in tea to his palate, and I'd have to respond to him. But as I made my way among the thorny labyrinths of the Bible verses, his head would drop onto the *Humash* and his snores would fill the poor room crammed with cots. Rabbi Yankele, who served as a reader on Sabbaths and holidays, was a milkman who got up at dawn every day and made the rounds of the houses with his jugs and so it's no wonder that when evening came, he'd be overcome by fatigue. His tall, plump wife would put an end to the embarrassment by lurking in the kitchen (because of the difference in height, we used to call the grotesque couple *Shabbos Ha-Godel un Kurts Fraytig*, the Great Sabbath and the Short Friday), and coming in and snapping her fingers in front of him. "Is it three already?" Rabbi Yankele would wake with a start and rub his eyes with fingers that always smelled of milk and metal handles.

When the prune compote, also accompanied by a few incidents, was passed around, my *melamed* at last appeared, but there was no need for me to worry. When I stood up to deliver my sermon, which I had learned by heart, and which, at Father's inspiration, centered on the Bible verse "Behold the tears of such as were oppressed, and they had no comforter," Lufka Lufka thundered in a mighty voice a cantorial verse accompanied by the musician's comb, and all the revelers applauded and didn't let me deliver my speech, according to tradition.

After the Grace after Meals led by the honorable Rabbi Arye Levin, Father leaned over to me, handed me a bundle of bills, lowered his voice and said that when the beggars came to congratulate me, I should casually thrust two bills into their hands. I implored him to do that instead of me, because I was disgusted by any contact with them, but he said that to welcome the outstretched hand of a Jew and to revive his hungry soul with charity — that was true love of Israel.

But even that was not the full measure of my torments that evening. Before they went home, Rabbi Kipnis declared that if a bar-mitzvah meal doesn't end with dancing, the whole thing was dubious. And so, a circle of wretches was formed around the

table. The mute and the stutterer held onto the belt of the arm-
less man, I gave my hands to Rabbi Leybish and the blind beggar,
and Rabbi Arye gave his hands in a private circle to the legless
beggar. A few times, we went round the table, which looked like
the cities of the plain after the Angel of God poured down fire
and brimstone on them, with Father standing in the middle and
singing as he did while dancing on Simhat Torah, "Helper of the
destitute, save now! Redeemer and rescuer, bring success now!"
And everybody responding: "Eternal Rock, answer us on the day
we call!"

When all the strangers departed, Mother finally broke her re-
sounding silence, handed me a towel and told me that, now that
Father's gala evening was over, I had to wash well in hot water and
soap and go to bed.

Father, who soon returned home after walking with the rabbis
a bit, came to me with his face beaming and held out both arms
to hug me. "Now you're really a bar-mitzvah, even Rabbi Kipnis
and Rabbi Zevin say so," he declared happily. But, standing in the
door of the bathroom clad only in my underpants, I burst into
tears, threw the new Dukes watch at him and shouted: "Don't
touch me! Don't touch me, you crazy man! I hate you!"

"You loved him so much when you were little," said Mother
as we stood at Father's bed at Rambam Hospital, watching the
hospital barber soap his cheeks. The nurses on the ward tried to
avoid that and asked why bother to shave a patient in a coma
after a stroke, but she insisted, and even made sure it was done.
Now she unwittingly twisted her mouth, following the razor going
around the gaping, drooling mouth that slipped to the side; but
when the barber put a steaming towel on his tormented face and
then kneaded it with cologne, she was satisfied and said she saw
the shadow of contentment pass over it.

"Stroke him," Mother suggested. "He must feel it." And she
reminded me that when he'd come home from the barber shop
on Thursday, after his weekly shave, I'd run to him with joy, ask
him to swing me in the air and plant noisy kisses on his smooth
red cheeks.

For the first time in years, I timorously touched Father, moved
my fingers over the paralyzed face. But the flaccidity and flimsi-
ness of the dying flesh that would soon become dust, was stronger

than any other feeling and my hand withdrew. Father opened his eyes and gazed at me and immediately shut them again.

"At least talk to him," said Mother. "Tell him something."

"What shall I tell him?"

"Tell him you love him." But the words came out of my mouth heavy and hard.

"When you first started walking you followed him around like a puppy, and I envied him so much," said Mother and told how when I clung to him, Father would put me on his outstretched leg and bounce me up and down over and over as he sang "Volga Volga" to me. "The two of us will now sing him that song. Maybe Mother Volga will come and carry him to the steppes of his childhood." We sang softly, devotedly, the song the Burlaks would sing while towing the ships up the river. Mother examined the expressionless face, watching for some sign, but I averted my eyes and looked outside at the barrier coming down and paralyzing traffic at the intersection until the evening train went on its way.

"You two had a special relation," Mother said afterward, when we went into the corridor during the doctors' visit. "And that relation, as you know, saved his life." During the siege, in one of the truces between the shelling, Father wanted to go to the Tnuva dairy on Yehezkiel Street and bring some produce (as the branch owners called the dairy products in their jargon), but at the age of two and a half, I grabbed his legs and begged him with heartbreaking weeping not to leave the house. Father removed me from him, but, according to Mother, I lay on the threshold and kept him from going out. "Father listens to you, Father will stay with you, Father won't go, and leave you alone," Father said to me, trying to appease me, rubbing the bristles of his beard on my face. Fifteen minutes later, a sudden salvo of shells fell on the city. One of the shells fell in the yard of the dairy, on a group of farmers, milkmen, and shopowners waiting there, killing and mortally wounding many of them.

In an attempt to decipher the destructive essence of the counterforce that infiltrated — perhaps more correctly, burst — into that sequence of feelings between me and Father and disrupted it beyond recognition, I force myself to run the sound track backward and listen to some of those distant explosions that left their eternal scars in the dust covered face of memory.

"That boy will remain illiterate," Father clapped and measured over and over with the hollow of his hand the distance between the pair of photos facing one another on the wall: Next to the kitchen door was the picture of the baby lying like a little lion, leaning his torso on his hands and turning his head to the pho-

tographer with a serious face and eyes gaping open in endless wonder and curiosity; and opposite, above our "Philips," the photo of a three-year-old boy, with long curly hair, laughing mischievously and holding a geranium branch. (Mother told how I was scared when David the photographer hid his head under the black sheet and I burst out crying and shouting, "I don't want him to take me away," and only the flowering geranium branch she hurried to pick and give me could calm my weeping). Two reflections mirrored in the shine of their glass, superimposed on one another and splitting apart again from one another, an infinity of revelations of face and soul moving back and forth in a never-ending movement, the movement of one whose image they captured in that blink of frozenness in time and who now wants to fathom their essence.

"He'll remain a boor and an ignoramus forever," Father raised his voice, wanting Mother's confirmation of his dogmatic determination. But she smiled, stroked my head and said: "Don't worry, in the end he'll make it, it just takes a lot of patience."

Hanukkah passed and most of the children in the class had already started reading while I still went on gazing at the alien letters, finding it hard to grasp the connection between the letters and the real objects I knew so well, each with its distinct color and smell and sound and solidity. So Father decided, with the teacher's approval, to try to practice reading with me.

Pointing to the page, he sat in front of me, and ordered: "Repeat after me and read 'Hanukkah Festival of Lights.'" But there was no connection between the four train cars of words and the flame of the *shamash*, the candle used to light the other ones, trying to light the wick of the candles and dripping boiling drops of wax on my fingertips, the fragrance of strawberry jam of the doughnuts, and the awful choking under the Roman elephant where I was stuck with Eleazar and couldn't remove the burden of hundreds of years of pressure.

"Don't dream," shouted Father bitterly. "Repeat after me

exactly. You don't have to understand what you read." And his finger reaches out and points to the words, turns red and bends and then is gathered into his big, hairy hand that turns into a fist.

After the fourth or fifth failure, Father made a big deal of closing the reading manual and stated his pedagogical opinion of me. In the end, it was Mother who did the unbelievable. It was on the Sabbath, in the afternoon, after Father had gone to a sermon in Zikhron-Moshe. She sat next to me, with one hand she hugged me and in the other she held *Robinson Crusoe*, which I already knew by heart, and she read it slowly and emphatically, as she usually did. And suddenly, the train of words jolted and started moving. The miracle occurred. "I can read, I can read," I shouted and jumped from one sofa to another, leaping over the space between them.

Preparations for dictations and reciting Torah verses by heart also became a battlefield between me and Father. Following the guidance of my homeroom teacher he consulted, Father made me repeat and read to him, a thousand times, Isaac's blessings of Jacob and Esau and Jacob's words to his sons before he died until the words finally broke through the stone crust of my brain.

I tried to evade Father's help, but he buttoned the top button of his shirt and said that when he was a boy, a student in the Gymnasium, he already knew all of *Evgeny Onegin* by heart. Whole evenings he sat and read to his grandmother, and she followed his reading. She didn't understand Russian and she held the book upside-down — just like Isaac Babel's grandmother I would read about years later in one of his Odessa stories — but that was how he became expert in the writings of Pushkin and the works of other Russian poets.

"Who's got to know poems and the Bible by heart today?" I rebelled.

"Got to, got to," grumbled Father. "A cultured person's got to."

"You don't understand anything, you're old," I yelled.

"O my soul, come not thou into my secret; unto their assembly, mine honour, be not thou united; for in their anger they slew a man, and in the selfwill they digged down a wall. Cursed be their anger, for it was fierce; and their wrath, for it was cruel," Father angrily read Jacob's words to Simeon and Levi, his rebellious sons, and even raised his voice so his words would reach the ears of Mother, who was standing in the distance, in the kitchen, and then, as usual, he slammed the Humash shut and left the house.

"Of course you'd want a young father like all the other children," said Mother and sat down to copy the blessings of Judah for me on five separate strips of paper so the billow of words wouldn't shock me all at once. "But there are children, like Eitan, for example, who envy you because you, at least, have a living father." And then she read verse after verse, emphatically, so I'd listen to the hidden melody that gave birth to the words and would hear how the first note brings the second, and the second the third, and all of them are harnessed together to the harmony, so memory can keep it inside.

The variant manifestations of that intensifying conflict between me and Father, seem to have one common source, and all the clashes that were apparently separate and independent from one another, were centered around it and drew their force from it. Looking back, it seems that whenever Father associated with an outside authority and decided to present it to me—either because deep down he doubted his own authority and wanted to reinforce it with outside support or because he identified with its goals and saw himself as its ally—that destructive force was reborn, undermining the foundations of the primitive force of love and subverting it irreparably. That's what happened when he gave into the coaxing of the supervisor of "Hebron" and brought a flock of yeshiva students home, bowing to the authority he denied in the depths of his heart. And that's what happened when he identified with the authority of the teachers and the school, and cooperated with them, unlike Mother who always defended her anarchistic savagery at great risk, shaking off every saddle and every yoke they tried to put on her.

And just as the exposure of his self-disparagement before the rabbinical world ultimately led him to the grotesque feast of the poor, so the series of incidents about learning, which family secrecy kept between the four walls of our house throughout the years, ended in a thunderous explosion outside, and to my deep sorrow, became common property one awful night of horrors in Poriya.

Shortly before the annual field trip to the Galilee, Mother was summoned to an urgent meeting in the nurse's office and the school doctor informed her with a grave expression, accompanied by the head-shaking of our local Florence Nightingale, that, because of the murmur he discerned in my heart at his examination at the end of the week, he was forced to stipulate that I could go on the two-day trip only if I was accompanied by an adult. Those tidings of Job could have confined me to bed for the rest of my life if Father hadn't taken me to Dr. Muntner, his old friend, who examined me thoroughly and decreed that the shoemaker with a stethoscope should wash out his ears, but the verdict was not to be appealed. At an emergency council held that very evening, Mother decreed that, unfortunately, I would have to choose between two evils: either to stay home for the two days of the field trip and enjoy sleeping late, going to movies during the day, and ice cream for dessert; or to let Father go on the field trip.

In his baggy khaki pants, pulled up to his breastbone, encompassing his pot belly, the old beret stretched on his scalp, and with the Korean War surplus rucksack reeking of rubber and the mustiness of a ship's hold, Father appeared with me at the gates of the school on the morning of the field trip. He looked like the double of Schweik as Josef Lada drew him. To my relief, the boys were wrestling in the trucks, struggling for control of the seats, and the girls were gathering around the women teachers who were wearing pants for the first time, and so nobody paid any attention to Father, who kept his promise not to interfere with the children. As Mother supposed, Father was welcomed warmly by the drivers, the Etik brothers, who worshipped in our synagogue, who even argued about which truck he'd ride in, and from the driver's cabin, he kept looking at me furtively throughout the trip, to make sure no evil would befall me.

Ill winds began to blow only at the end of that day, when we reached the youth hostel in Poriya for an overnight stop. The pair of brothers who wanted to rest a bit from the drive and the tumult of the children, entreated Father to go with them to a fish restaurant in Tiberias, but he insisted on staying with me in case I was stung by a scorpion or a spark caught my clothes.

From my place at the bonfire, I saw his stooped silhouette beyond the bursting and retreating flames, as he sat alone in the dark on the stone fence and quietly ate the sandwiches Mother had made him at dawn, now and then nibbling the hard-boiled egg held in his hand like a baby chick. He was so sad in his isolation and foreignness then, surrounded by thorns and the round and summery halo of the moon rising beyond the black mountains. That image of him comes back to life whenever I try to imagine his portrait in those decades of his life that are shrouded in mystery, the time before I invaded his world: A youth ran naked with his friends Aaron Rotblatt and Hillel Friedman on the slope covered with nasturtiums ("There was a carpet of nasturtiums there," one of the women from his hometown once told me) going down to the river, and a handsome lad going to fight the Russo-Japanese War, dressed up in a military tunic of the Czar's army and a Papakha — a tall fur hat — with a Makurka cigarette in the corner of his mouth, and the song of a Ukrainian beggar to the tune of the Kobza accompanies him on his way: In the bright field, in the wide space, viburnum is blooming. Oh, there a mother goes with her son to the army! So go, my son! So go, my son!

The plan was that Father was supposed to sleep with the Etik brothers, but when their car was late and the keys to the locked drivers' room were in their hands, he had no choice but to spread his blankets in the boys' dormitory and prepare to sleep there. At eleven o'clock, the flute teacher, Mr. Gula, declared lights out and disappeared into his room, giving a starting signal to the Destroying Angel. Obscene language and jokes, belches, farts, and dirty songs blended together into a mighty cacophony. Light beams from pocket flashlights secretly lit danced in the room like spotlights on Independence Day, crisscrossing and clashing, dying out and growing strong. A few surprise inspections by patrols of teachers finally managed to calm the tired children and a spirit of slumber began pouring over them. I curled up under the blanket, beseeched the Lord of my Father Abraham, that Father's snoring wouldn't attract the last ones who stayed awake waiting for the right time to rise against their slumbering classmates and paint their faces with shoe polish and chocolate sauce. In the middle of the night, when the phosphorescent hands of my watch showed ten after twelve, two figures rose from the gloom and went to stretch their hand over those who were stunned by sleep, to increase their marvels among the innocent. The shout of the tormented, who were awakened by the disgusting touch of polish on their faces, also woke the others. Once again the flash-lights were turned on and once again the packed dormitory was filled with a royal uproar and battle cries and victory hymns and the whining of the vanquished. Even the last of the sleepers moved and shook and naked bulbs were turned on and off with crazy speed. Within the horror my heart was paralyzed with fear at the sight of Father's enormous body. His identification with the morality of the teachers and parents overcame his promise to me, he got out of his bed and stood in the middle of the room trampling the kneeling and the lying and the prostrate as he walked — For the Lord shall rise up as in Mount Perazim, he shall be wroth as in the Valley of Gibeon, that he may do his work, his strange work, and bring to pass his act, his strange act. He stood there, lighted by the flashlights and in the electric strafing that went on and off, in his long underwear, his groin dark through the opening of his undershorts, and he waved his hand at the heap of ruins and the hairy routed carcasses stretched out on the floor, made a possession for the bittern and pools of water, and bore his unforgotten burden of the valley of vision, which gener-ations of students learned and recited long after:

> Turn out the light.
> Tomorrow is a day to work.
> Mary-Mary black or white,
> Not me and not some foreign jerk.

And after a very brief pause, he concluded his reprimand with an eternal pair of words:

Brothel of Bastards.

Many years later, in London, Father was once again revealed to me that in that long-ago evening in Ramat Poriya, sitting on the fence with the Kinnereth lying like a carcass behind him, but this time the rays of the setting sun fell straight on him and turned him gold. That day, one of the last days of the month of Tammuz, was the anniversary of his death, and I was looking for a syna-gogue to say Kaddish for the exaltation of his soul. I was plod-ding through the foreign streets and the map of the city became shredded between my fingers, but every synagogue was closed. It was a Sunday, and the Jews of London, apparently, had left the city for the weekend and left the doors of their prayer houses locked.

In the afternoon, my feet took me to the National Gallery. I walked around the halls for a few hours, and in the evening, in Room 19, in front of Rembrandt's self-portrait at the age of sixty-three, the miracle happened.

Through the age spots that speckle the skin, the awful weariness that drowns the eyes, the thinning hair, the drooping lips on the ancient toothless mouth, the slack brow and nose, the abject grief—I discover Father in his final years. An isolated man sunk into old age and death. Every week, sitting in the chair of the bald barber, he looks in the mirror while the depilatory ointment sears his face and plucks out the bristles of his beard in honor of the Sabbath, and sees a defeated, humiliated man, who hasn't achieved even half of his desires. All through his final years, he wanted to be buried on Shimron Hill near Nahalal, next to his mother. One summer day he went to visit his brother in the village, got sick, was rushed to Rambam Hospital in Haifa, sank into a coma and shouted, at long last in Russian, called out something, pleading for his life in the language of Lermontov, Pushkin, Beria, and Stalin. A week later he died. But because of the perversity of the village committee, we had to take him back to Jerusalem, his pitiless city. "Avrom, Avrom," Mother calls his name, but the gaping, toothless mouth shouts Russian words whose meaning we'd never know.

The Pakistani guard paces back and forth at the entrance. An amateur painter tries to copy "Baltassar's Feast." The king waves his hand, the serving maid pours the wine on the ground, the old man and the young man are terrified, the hand of the Angel writing Me'ne, Me'ne, Te'kel U-phar'sin won't finish the final N.

People pass by and compare the two portraits of Rembrandt—the self-portrait at the age of thirty-four and the self-portrait at the age of sixty-three, hung side by side—smiling, serene in the presence of the crumbling and old age, as if the writing on the wall weren't meant for them. No artist documented himself like Rembrandt—I read later in the museum shop in the introduction to a book with about a hundred self-portraits of the artist still extant, scattered in several museums all over the world, and if these portraits were collected they'd create a graphic biography or a restoration of a complete cycle of human life.

A father shows the frame to his son who's wearing a Beatles shirt and praises it: "Good craftsmanship." A woman in a tiger-striped body suit tells her friend that she's seen better paintings in Florence. A Japanese man takes a photo with a tiny camera of Madame Saskia van Alenburg, hanging nearby.

I can't take my eyes off the portrait of Rembrandt. And as I look, I become aware that the way the painter looks at himself is also the way to an appeased and reconciled view of Father — honestly and lovingly, as Mother put it in her declining days. This combination is the hardest and most complicated human combination in our relationship to our fellow man. What is more courageous than seeing things honestly, judiciously, with nothing but what the eyes see; and what is more gracious than seeing things out of love, love that usually spoils justice by smudging the shadows, the evil. And how rare and almost unattainable is that unique combination of love and honesty, free from all hatred and compassion. But how elusive, ephemeral, and essentially impalpable is the reconciliation, the supposed laudable results of that conscious and mature vision, as opposed to the eternal certainty of the grudge. From the basis of that malignant feeling, from the kingdom of the ghosts of the past bursts the young man, reappears on strange paths and in unexpected circumstances, and demands satisfaction from the grownups who ignored his existence and didn't include him in the solemn agreements they made with one another at his expense.

A vibration of association, a fabric of smell, a coarse step of the heart — those are the alarm clocks of that insane cerebral activity, that wrinkles days and years into skeins of pain beaten on the walls of the dream. To this very night the young man remains at the ford of the Jabbok struggling alone with the man in the khaki pants pulled up to his breastbone, refusing to let him for the day breaketh, wrestling with him in our kitchen in Jerusalem, pushing him to the big room. He whips the lad with a Lulav. From waving the date palm branch, it splits and an owl is startled out, circles around the chandelier and finally stands on the edge of the table. The table is covered with oilcloth, and half of a loaf of bread and an onion are in the middle of it. "Poke out his eyes," the young man calls for help, but the owl doesn't budge. He chases me and I gore him on the table. The owl falls to the ground and shatters. The table is split in two and Father shouts, "Get out of the house."

"In dreams you'll always come back here," said Mother, very carefully unstitching a narrow opening in the end of the pillow I slept on, and I pinch it hard and don't let go of it. Just before he hurried out of Russia, Father hid a bundle of gold coins in the pillows.

Most of the coins were taken out of there soon after he came to the Land of Israel, but even many years later the last vestiges of the smuggled treasure were discovered from time to time. Usually it was Mother who felt the small metal disk that pressed her head or her cheek and the whole house was awakened for the ceremony of bringing the Czarist coin to light. On the night I'm talking about, it fell to my lot to feel the touch of gold for the first time. Mother leaped out of bed and turned on all the lights. Father lay still, blinking in the bright light, and said that just a little while ago he was in Obruch, on the banks of the river, climbing the mulberry tree and filling his belly with fruit, and now he was back here in Jerusalem and a bitter taste was in his mouth. Mother, who was rummaging around in the depths of the pillow, laughed and said that she also came back again and again in her dreams to the long porch in that house in the market of Meah Shearim where she was born, and when she withdrew her hand covered with goose down and feathers, holding the coin in her fingertips, she said that I, unlike them, would return here, "For you this place will always be home."

7

Some years ago, while burrowing in one of the stands of Mr. Nissim, the gloomy *bouquiniste* at the corner of Allenby and Gurzenberg streets, my attention was drawn to a thin pamphlet with the pretentious and unoriginal title of "The Scout of the House of Israel — An Alarm Clock for My Nation," by Joseph Moshe Krumer, which had wound up among the piles of old books. This was a bundle of crazy letters that the character had sent in the early '30s to the high officials in Germany, newspaper editors, and mainly to Dr. Breslauer, director of the Jewish community in Berlin. A glance at the pamphlet made it clear that after all the efforts of the aforementioned Krumer to win the heart of the Jewish community for the honest way had come to naught — "a suckling infant knows his nurse, a baby chick knows who feeds him, and only the Jewish community organization doesn't know who is our God" — to his great sorrow, he was forced to advise President von Hindenberg to turn the government over to Hitler. "Because Hitler," according to Krumer, "is the best alarm clock to wake the Hebrew nation to repentance . . . In a word, Hitler has become the *Shulhan Arukh*, and is the man who, to our misfortune, has to come tell the Jews that a Gentile is forbidden to marry a Jew." And when his advice was accepted, Krumer immigrated to the Land of Israel in 1934 and addressed his ethics to local Jewry, arguing that "razor blades are sold in public on the streets of Tel Aviv and other cities of the Land of Israel and thus the nation is led astray to violate the explicit ban in the Holy Torah. If you plan to persist in these things, I promise you that what I wrote, 'This time you won't be exiled from the Land of Israel — but you yourselves will flee from here,' will all come true."

Logically, I should have washed my hands of that nonsense, but the grayish paper with the metallic gleam and the printed type that was slightly longer than usual seemed to burst forth as from a forgotten memory and didn't leave me alone. I see again the first printer's type I ever saw in my life, the letters the tall, quiet typesetter would assemble with tongs from the case of letters, and to the eyes of the watching child pressing his face to the display window their sequence could be read only backward. And indeed, at the bottom of the title page, in tiny Miriam letters, were the words: "Land of Israel Press Jerusalem." That small press not far from our house, in one of the shops under the "Etz Haim" Yeshiva in Sabbath Square (between Solomon's chandelier shop where we bought the spider chandelier, and the haberdashery of that short Gur Hasid, whose hand was cut off when he put it out the bus window on his way to celebrate Lag b'Omer at the grave of the Rashbi in Meron, and Mr. Morokhovitch's pharmacy), was the press where the invitations to my bar-mitzvah and Father's obituary announcement were printed.

But the most exciting thing of all wasn't yet revealed to me. At the end of the pamphlet, under the round, characteristic signature of "the place of our Temple," as usual in colophons of books published in Jerusalem, was the author's address: "Jerusalem, Geula, Beit Komil."

Beit Komil.

In the early '50s, when I started noticing my surroundings, the house we lived in was called Beit Komil only by the trustee, Dr. Alexander Amdur.

Once a year, in late December, Father would put on his Borsolino winter hat, which was kept for Sabbaths and holidays, wrap himself up in the synthetic mohair jacket that was at the bottom of one of the bundles of used clothes Uncle Isaac sent us from America, and set out for the Sansour Building in Zion Square, to the office of Dr. Amdur, and I walked beside him, my hand in his.

Year after year we'd stray in the circular corridors of the spacious office building, passing by the doors of lawyers, export-import companies, niches for repairing electric shavers and typewriters, and at last would find ourselves right back where we had started. After two or three rounds, Father would overcome his reticence, open one of the closed doors a crack, thrust his head inside and ask his question. Afterward, when he'd turn his face and slowly close the gray door, the light bursting from the window opposite would encircle his head with a halo, and he'd smile and say: "Just like last year—we've got the wrong floor."

When we stood before the office of the attorney and notary, Dr. Alexander Amdur, Father would adjust his jacket so the khaki

shirt underneath it wouldn't be seen, would check whether the money was still in his pocket, and would knock on the door. "Who do my eyes see? Isn't this the gentleman from Beit Komil," the heavyset trustee would greet Father, who took off his hat and clutched it to his breastbone and stepped inside with small, hesitant steps whose sound was swallowed in the rather shabby Persian rugs.

"Just look, look," Dr. Amdur would hiss between his fleshy lips. "How the time flies, a year has already gone by, and your honor comes to ask us once more to please renew his lease. Mr. Treasurer, what do you think?" he would turn to the Iraqi clerk whose hair was carefully combed and was slicked down and shiny on his scalp. "Should we grant the lessee's request?" "As you wish, sir," replied the treasurer who sat at a little table next to the trustee's enormous desk and filed letters. "Well then, take out the gentleman's file. Forgive me for forgetting his name . . ."

Year after year things recurred so precisely that I began to doubt whether time did indeed flow in a straight line. The money he and Mother scrimped and saved, Father would drop into the hands of the attorney and notary Dr. Amdur, who would transfer it with his fingertips, as if he were touching an insect or dung chips, to the treasurer, who counted the bills with dizzying speed like the cashier with hairy ears at Barclay's Bank, and buried them in a rectangular metal box with the words "Beit Komil" written on the lid.

And then the attorney and notary Dr. Amdur would pinch my cheek, ask my name, ask if I had yet learned the Talmud Chapter "you fortified the houses," and remark that the level of the schools had deteriorated remarkably in our generation, a poor and sinning generation, and that when he was my age—and I heard him say that from the time I was four to the time I was fourteen—he already knew the third chapter of Baba Batra by heart with the commentaries of Rashi and Tosaphot by the ROSH and the MaHaRSHa, and RaSHaSH and even The Wisdom of Solomon.

The walls of the office were paneled in walnut, and all around the diplomas and licenses of the attorney and notary Dr. Amdur were displayed in gleaming glass frames. "You want to be a lawyer when you grow up?" he'd ask me in conclusion, and without waiting for my answer, he'd end our annual meeting by saying: "Be whatever you want to be just as long as you don't write books. One author has already come out of Beit Komil, and even that was too many."

As we went down the stairs, careful not to bump into the bronze poles that once, in the glory days of the Sansour brothers, who now live as refugees across the border, held the carpet to the marble stairs that have been ground to dust since then, Father would put his hat back on and warn me: "Just don't be a lawyer, you hear?" And he'd add: "Don't study law, you hear me? The law must not be learned, halleluia!"

Father didn't know what Dr. Amdur's hints about the writer from Beit Komil meant, but the cantor Lapidus, who used to visit our house from time to time, eat sauerkraut, swallow a few raw eggs and then sing Pinchik's "The Mystery of the Sabbath," once told that in the 1930s, a crazy Berliner had lived in this very same apartment, who wrote thin books that nobody wanted to take, even though he distributed them free of charge to anyone he chanced to meet, and he finally took his life in the sea in Tel Aviv. Lapidus had his own version of the identity of the mysterious Komil. For a long time, I had believed that the little brown and yellow flowers of chamomile tea that Mother gargled when she felt a sore throat coming on, were named for him. The cantor said that on one of his journeys abroad, he gave a concert in the home of Mr. Komil, one of the leaders of the American Diaspora, the owner of two gigantic factories — one factory for coconut oil and one for laundry bluing, and when they feasted on the delicacies of the party, Mr. Komil told him that he had a house in Jerusalem, "in the Geula Quarter." Mother wanted to refute Lapidus with solid evidence, but when Father hushed her and asked the cantor to sing something by Sirota or Koussevitzky as an encore, she stood up, offended, and went out to the door to the small front yard.

"A door to the street — a window to the sky," Mother would decree whenever she stood on the curb. Early in the morning, before sunrise, she'd stare enchanted at the packs of dogs, Bedouin sheepdogs, refugees from civilization, who gathered across the border, in the caves at the edge of the Desert, and cut across the still slumbering city, from north to south. She'd wait for the Rebbe of Gur, with the face of a cherub and reddish hair, who'd walk past her quickly. The old rebbe would go out walking on his doctor's orders, accompanied by a pair of students who found it hard to keep up with him, and at the dark street corners, excited Hasids lay in wait for him, to receive his blessing. One morning, after she was widowed, Mother went out to drag in the heavy jugs of milk left by the distributors. The rebbe saw the woman struggling with the jugs and hurried to help her. And ever since, every morning she'd find the jugs next to the door of the shop, the work of the Hasids who followed their rebbe's example and performed a good deed.

On Wednesdays, Mother would anxiously accompany the caravan of old armored vehicles that made its way from Camp Schneller near our house to Mount Scopus, and would wait for them to return in the afternoon, and on the Sabbath, she'd listen in the morning to the singing of the group of Haredim accompanying the bridegroom on his way to the synagogue and she'd say that from the Goyish sweetness of the melody, her ears heard a shepherd's song from the Carpathian Mountains. "Not a shepherd's song," Father would correct her. "The song of the angels who accompanied Our Father Jacob on his way to Padan Aram to find a wife."

On May Day, she'd close the shutters and peep out through the cracks enviously at the demonstrators waving red flags and leaving announcements and red chrysanthemums behind them. And in the springtime, in the evening, she'd try to count the goats of Mr. Bakhur, the younger brother of the five bald virgins who came back from the pasture in the olive grove of the Kerem neighborhood and scattered a carpet of black and brown droppings, the pearls the herd scatters before the jackasses, in Mother's words.

At least once a day, a black cloud, no bigger than a human hand, would rise from the east, from Meah Shearim. "A *levaya*, a funeral," Mother would state, throwing the customers out of the store, shutting the iron doors and going out to the street. Father would join the funeral procession, and Mother would hug me tight, to her apron, smelling of goat cheese, halvah, and fresh milk. "He buildeth his house as a moth, and as a booth that the keeper maketh," Mother murmured the words of Job, while I looked horrified at the surrealist, nightmarish spectacle passing by us — a black mass with a white stripe in the middle, a black mass moving vertically and a white stripe hurled horizontally.

"A door to the street — a window to the sky," were, as I said, Mother's only words of praise of our house. As far as she was concerned, the ceiling was too high, and the hardest thing for her was to get rid of the spider webs spun in their heights. And she wasn't satisfied with the walls either because of the fish scales of the Cypriot *kinstler*, which would drop off, cover the furniture, and dive into the soup. And she was just as annoyed at the roots of the giant casuarinas that undermined the floor of the house and subverted the floor tiles, and not only did that turn the weekly floor washing into a nightmare, but it also tripped everybody who didn't pay attention to the potholes and made them fall face down.

Mother wanted to move to one of the new housing projects Golda Meyerson built in Beit Mazmil. The ceilings there were lower, Mother would relate yearningly after a visit to Ahuva Harris's new home in the popular neighborhood of Kiryat Yovel, and electric wires there were hidden in the walls and the floor tiles were straight. But Father insisted, arguing that he wanted to live in Jerusalem and not the eastern outskirts of Tel Aviv. To that house — a two-story house of pink-tinted Jerusalem stone that became transparent after the rain — Mother brought me from the infant nursery on Mount Scopus one snowy Friday. And here, between its walls covered with fins, I first opened my eyes to that world whose secret I'm trying to touch again, now that the things themselves have been destroyed forever.

I admit that, only after we left that house for good, twenty years later, did the sense that can be called "a sense of place" slowly begin to take shape in me. Against the background of the soft landscapes of the coastal plain, that are more open to heat and trees, Jerusalem and Beit Komil started to put on the mummified and dreamy shape I've wanted to record ever since.

For years I returned to Beit Komil without being accompanied by the well-known sense of a "belated return." I seem to be bound to the practical world and know that the miracle won't happen twice, I'm aware of the pain in store for someone who wants to compare what the child saw with the sights of the present, and instead of fearing the pain, I've tried to derive a dimension of irony from it—both mature and sober. I repeat that all I want is to tempt memory to speak. But it maliciously refuses to grant the modest request. I stand in the place where the things happened, and nevertheless, evasion still prevails. But here, completely by chance, in the Tel Aviv yard, smelling of Lysol and moldy paper, next to the wretched fig tree blooming stubbornly from the crack in the cement, watered from buckets of air-conditioner drippings, surrounded by used books, I smell once again the sauerkraut Lapidus gobbled from his mouth issuing gems, hear the song of the Angels of Jacob sung by the shepherds of the Carpathians, feel the shagginess of Father's coat, see Beit Komil come back to life.

I've often pondered whether it's the stones, the roof-tiles, the floor-tiles decorated with brown-yellow-green—all those details so beloved by devotees of nostalgia—that create the sense of place. Was Beit Komil what it was because of the pink-tinted stone that would become transparent after the rain, because of the grid fence that bracketed the front of the house from the street, because of the roof of orange-and-brown Marseilles tiles? Was it spoiled because of the awful misery of the back of the house (its belly, as Mother put it), because of the floor tiles subverted by the roots of the trees, because of the holes torn by the shrapnel of the Arab Legion shells in the high iron shutters? The whole time Beit Komil was my home, my eyes seem to have been blind to all that. Like every place else, Beit Komil seems to be only the people who live in it, Father and Mother and all the other people around me, whose existence bracketed the borders of my world.

Where are you Mr. Solomon, who before dawn fed breadcrumbs dipped in milk to the pigeons in your dovecote, and in the middle of the afternoon applied leeches and cupping glasses to those who came to you for help? Where are you Mrs. Hilda Zuckerman, owner of the wig salon, whose house later became a lodestone for the Haredi women and a Franciscan monk in the custody of Terra Sancta in the Old City would come to you under cover of night to have his baldness covered with a toupee made of the hair of virgins of the Hungarian Houses? Where is Arn-Barn who would gorge himself on chocolate cats' tongues and petit beurre biscuits and urinate from the balcony onto the passers-by until his father threatened to take him by the *pish* and pull him downstairs and he got scared and stopped?

Many are no longer among the living, others have scattered in all directions—for example, me. For example Reb Yena Ackerman. A few years ago, I came upon him by chance, sitting on the stairs of the synagogue in the old people's home on Allenby Street, selling transistors of dubious provenance. Who will know your life, you who did a big business importing Italian apples to Jerusalem? On the main street of the Mahane Yehuda market, the wives of professors and senior officials from Rehavia and Talbiah would stand in line at your place and buy Delicious and Rome apples, and in your cubicle, under the stairs, you lived like a dog. "He doesn't have one single tooth in his mouth," said the medic Mr. Solomon, and his wife who sold yarn would add, "He doesn't have electricity in his hole either." And once a month, Ackerman wouldn't open the store and instead would polish his room. At dusk, when his work was done, he would pull an electrical wire from the apartment of the neighbor above him and illuminate the little room with a bright light. Mr. Zuckerman, who lived from the labor of the hands of his wife, the Pani, and was free to read German journals and to make friends with the children and with the empty and the frivolous, would lay in wait at Yena's door to see what went on. "After the news, at nine," he'd tell us the next morning, with a lecherous drool on his lips, "a young female came to him on high heels, and didn't leave until twelve-thirty." No doubt Yena would summon a whore to his cubicle. Father and Mother were also convinced of that. Only years later, did we find out by chance that the girl was his daughter.

When rationing came to an end and the orchards of the Galilee began yielding their fruit, Yena couldn't adjust to the new reality and his staff of life was broken. One day he got up, locked the door of his room and disappeared.

"Reb Yena," I addressed him when I saw him on the stairs of the old people's home. "How are you?"

He didn't look at me.

"You don't recognize me?" I asked him.

He was mute.

"We lived together in Beit Komil, in Geula."

"Beit Komil," he waved his cane to drive me away. "There was no such thing."

Years passed. The new tenants of Beit Komil also deserted it. Every apartment that was emptied was sealed by an invisible hand with wooden boards nailed to the locked doors. The window panes were smashed, the shutters, battered by the winds of the Jerusalem winter, were removed or remained hanging by some miracle on a single hinge, rain penetrated through the broken roof tiles and soaked the thick walls and they grew moldy. And often, when I passed by the house on the bus, I was compelled to cast a painful glance at Isaac Karshenti, who bought Mother's grocery store a few months before the Six-Day War, and goes on standing solitary guard behind the display-front refrigerator, waiting for customers and growing old with them.

In the summer of 1988, someone put a colorful sign on the front of the dying house:

ON THIS SITE

BANK MIZRAHI, LTD. AND A SPLENDID SHOPPING CENTER

GEULA CENTER

"They're tearing down your house," a few Jerusalemites told me a year later. They called to tell me that the façade was preserved because that was a strategy used by building contractors to save some percentage of construction costs. But otherwise the building was only a gutted hull.

On the thirteenth anniversary of Mother's death, I went to see the final destruction of our house.

The casuarinas, where Eitan Winestein and I erected play elevators with spools of typewriter ribbon as pulleys, had fallen prey to the axe.

The ceiling of our house, the high ceiling, that, during the shelling, dropped crumbs of plaster, which the child looked at with eyes torn by fear and amazement and decreed "*vayse murashkes*," collapsed under the blows of the bulldozer.

The floor, too, the crooked floor where I'd watch the light movement of the water when Mother washed the house for the Sabbath, was torn up.

And only the façade remained standing where it was, like a

stage set for a photo shoot of an abandoned site, and inside it was Father and Mother's "Tnuva Branch." Isaac Karshenti, who hadn't yet reached a satisfactory arrangement with the entrepreneurs, clung like a caper bush to the crumbling store.

At the entrance to the store, over the right-hand window, is a gray tin board. That sign, with our address, Geula 12, in gigantic letters, Father had put up a few months before I was born, to guarantee that the letter from Kiev, the sign of life from his sister-in-law, who had stayed there with her little daughter after his brother Isaac was executed for the crime of Zionist activity, would reach its destination. The letter, needless to say, never arrived, and the winds and the rain and the sun faded the address until it disappeared altogether.

Isaac Karshenti welcomed me joyfully. He keeps on slicing cheese with a knife that my parents had used, and their scale still stands in its place, trembling at the touch of the halvah. As if inadvertently, I raised my eyes to the ceiling in the south-east corner of the store. Some years before she sold the store, Mother sent for the electrician, Mr. Kaufman, to illuminate the sign on the façade. The electrician was sloppy and when the electric wire came close to the corner, he didn't attach it to the wall but just stretched it and left it hanging in the air.

"Mr. Kaufman, *hot nisht kayn faribl, dos vet nisht haltn,*" that is, "Mr. Kaufman, please don't be offended, that won't hold," Mother complained.

"*Vos hot ir moireh, dos vet yo haltn.*" "What are you afraid of, it will hold," the electrician calmed her.

"*Mecoakh vos vet es haltn?*" "What will keep it up?" wondered Mother.

"*Mecoakh hakurts,*" laughed Kaufman and explained in Yiddish that the electrical wire would hold up because it was short and taut.

Decades have passed since then. Father and Mother are no more. Mr. Kaufman is approaching old age. Beit Komil is destroyed. And only the electric wire, the last chord connecting the present to the past, remains stretched there in the corner of the ceiling, until it is also cut. Isaac Karshenti, who came to some arrangement with the entrepreneurs after trials and pressures, went off someplace, and cleared the way for the artisans who quickly turned Father and Mother's "Tnuva Branch" into "Geula Opticians."

"At long last, I see the needles of the casuarinas again," said Mother, when she put on the new glasses and lifted her eyes to the ancient trees that bracketed our yard from the street. "Everything is so bright now."

Air
That
Never
Finds
Rest

1

Mother loathed Romanticism.

Ever since she had adopted rationalism, after the death of the little girls and the collapse of her first marriage, Mother subjected her internal life to the authority of intelligence and would plan her course with cold, sober logic. But it wasn't only because she was against Romanticism that she closed her heart to the excitement of love and kept her soul from getting swept up in the storms of emotion and imagination, but also because over time a sharp and uncompromising critical faculty ripened in her on the hidden altar of that existence and waged war against what she called Romanticism's dangerous and wanton flirtation with death.

"He's playing with fire, that musician," her face flushed one evening, and she jumped up from the table and furiously turned off the radio. From the beginning of that week, Mother had neglected housework and checking my lessons, and when the store was locked at midnight, and sometimes even later, she sank into a tense reading of the two volumes of *The Magic Mountain* she had borrowed from the B'nai B'rith Library. Father, who had listened to the news in the early evening, went off to the synagogue for the daily Talmud lesson, and had left the radio on, letting the cryptic tones of the string quartet inundate the house. At first, Mother didn't pay any attention to the series of emotional variations, but when a slow funeral march rose from the silence, she let go of the book she had gotten after a long wait, and listened to the tense dialogue between the tempting, demonic lyricism of death and the desperate outcry of life pleading to be spared, until at last she got up and put an end to it.

"Why?" I protested. "That's so beautiful."

"I hate that," grumbled Mother and pounded the closed book, and then she said that, in his impetuous arrogance, Schubert removed the ugly tragedy from the encounter with death, which doesn't let go of its victims, coaxing them with ingratiating words to give him their hand and to go with him, with the maiden pleading for her life, and gives that awful scene a frivolous grace. "Beauty drives him out of his mind," she wanted to convince me, saying that, like all his other romantic friends, Schubert appreciated death, which he saw as a brother and friend whose every intention was pure.

As before, Mother's eyes wandered over my face, trying to discern if I had caught the honesty of her words, and she said that if there was one thing she was worried about, it was the dark charm Romanticism ascribed to death, a charm we young people, who are stupid and inclined by nature to self-destruction and annihilation, eagerly long for. "I'd send all of you to work for a week in the morgue," she wiped the steam from the lenses of her eyeglasses. "And after you have to help the orderly strip the clothes off a dead child, you'd be weaned once and for all from that longing to be gathered into the arms of death."

Mother shifted the book from one hand to the other. And after hesitating a moment, she opened it to the place she had marked with a bus ticket and decided she'd do better to let Thomas Mann speak for her. Because his uncompromising humanism would succeed where she had failed, and at last he'd remove the mask of innocence that Romanticism granted death and would reveal its true face. And so, along with the tarrying Joachim, who fell asleep during the rest hour and didn't hear the bell calling the inmates of the sanitarium to afternoon tea, we too went out to the deserted corridor about a quarter of an hour late. There, coming toward us were three men wearing lace shirts — a gold cross leading the way, then the priest, his eyeglasses on his nose looking serious, and clutching the holy sacrament oil to his heart, and bringing up the rear, the boy with the censer. We stood politely next to Joachim and made a little bow to the holy viaticum, right before the room of the little Hujus girl, room number twenty-eight. And when the boy opened the latch and the priest set foot on the threshold, a cry of despair, a hue and cry, started up inside, like nothing we'd ever heard, three or four times in a row, and then just screaming without a pause or break, like a mouth gaping wide open, with such misery and terror and defiance that it can't be described, mixed with a ghastly pleading, and suddenly it became hollow and muffled, as if it sank into the earth and came from a deep cellar. "But why 'from a deep cellar?'" we heard Hans Castorp ask his cousin in exasperation. "She had crawled under her blanket," Joachim answered him in a dry alert voice. The cross-bearer and the altar boy were stuck there at the door and couldn't get in, and in the space between them, we could peep into the room. It's a room just like yours or mine, said Joachim, and at the head of the bed stood her family, her parents, of course, directing comforting words to the shapeless mass begging and protesting hideously and kicking its legs. And a moment before those who brought the sacrament went inside and locked the door behind them, I saw the girl's head appear for a split second with its wild blond hair, and she raised her gaping eyes, fixing the priest with a stare, eyes so pale, without any color at all, and she ducked back under the blanket.

The fear that inspired the consumptive girl with such great strength as she was dying was indeed contagious, but Mother ignored the menacing sobbing of the clothes closet, whose doors I opened and closed with an uncontrollable compulsion, and kept banging. Most people, she said, are like those hopeless inmates of the sanitarium in the remote Alpine town, and even though their fate is sealed, they go on spending their days drinking afternoon tea and talking trivia, all of it intended to drown out the dark voice of death bursting from the nearby rooms. Mother smoothed the tablecloth, straightened invisible creases, and said that only if your legs took you to the corridors of pain, where there isn't a living soul, would you see at the crucial moment the visions of crumbling and destruction that take place behind the locked door.

Mother leafed through the book that had been felt by so many hands of anonymous readers. As if she were talking to herself, she repeated that while the unscrupulous Romantics are certainly sitting with the mobs of lovable fools and refreshing their frightened soul with those splendid and indecent creations that perversely describe the image of death in stylish and beautiful paeans, writers loyal to truth come from those exceptional individuals who go on a cursed mission no one assigns them so they can come back and write accounts that don't include simpering words and phony enthusiasm for what their eyes saw in the heart of darkness.

Those thoughts of Mother's didn't really surprise me, since she'd often drum them into my ears, just changing the wording to fit the circumstances. I think I heard the first version before she assailed Romanticism, a few years earlier, at the end of summer vacation, just before I entered second grade.

As I said, our house was on the standard route of the funeral processions that made their way on foot to Mahane Schneller, where the charter bus was waiting to take them to the cemetery at Givat Shaul. And on that distant summer afternoon, the funeral procession of a solitary old woman from the old Beit-Israel neighborhood passed by us. When the bustle heralding the approach of a funeral procession was seen in the street, Mother, as usual, closed the shutters of the shop and went outside with Father and the handful of customers to follow it a while to honor the dead. Aside from the pallbearers, this funeral procession included only those who came on it by chance and withdrew from it as soon as they thought they had fulfilled their obligation. And if, in normal funeral processions, the corpse is hidden behind a wall of mourners, appearing and disappearing in turn, the body of this woman, wrapped in winding sheets, was visible all the time. Seeing the small corpse tossed about to the rhythm of the fast pace of the handful of frightened, taciturn men, threatening time and again to slip off the makeshift bier, I was terrified and slipped into the house to hide under one of the beds, as during the shelling of the War of Independence.

For a long time I lay there with my eyes shut, enfolded into the cool, dusty dark, enveloped in the stench of winter house slippers and the reek of the seaweed peeping out in bundles from the mattress, and to calm down, I told myself aloud a story I made up on the spot about Adam and Eve, who instead of eating the fruit of the Tree of Knowledge, were tempted to eat the fruit of the Tree of Life. Influenced by Grandmother's oft-repeated legend of the phoenix, I brought Eve together not with the Serpent but with the Hebrew phoenix, who sang to her the praises of a thousand-year life and enticed her to eat from the fruit that promised her eternal life. God, walking on the paths of the Garden of Eden and catching them *in flagrante delicto*, quickly summons the angels for a consultation and the Angel Michael wonders if, in retrospect, it wouldn't be better to send Eve and her husband the Serpent, the most cunning of all the animals of the field, to tempt the couple to eat from the fruit of the Tree of Knowledge. But God, sitting on His throne and biting His beard, silences him impatiently and says that there's no point crying over spilt milk and they had to think of where to find ever increasing quantities of food for the billions of fools who were going to multiply like flies and would never die.

"You're just like Grandmother," I heard Mother talking to me from far away, and her voice, which surprisingly covered the interjection of one of the angels and silenced him, was drenched with pain and disappointment. For a little while, she stood silent here, next to the bed, listening with pleasure to the exchanges I put into the mouths of Eve and the phoenix, and especially to God's sorrowful monologue. That was pretty much how Mother greeted me when I crawled out, covered with shame and dust, and she added that despite the original, maybe even bold, idea of the story, which my teacher certainly wouldn't like, she couldn't deny that, in the end, my story disappointed her because it showed how much I was influenced by Grandmother. "The weeds she planted in my own flower bed," said Mother, wiping the dust off my clothes, "and only with great toil and incessant efforts did I succeed in pulling them up by the root, are now starting to sprout in your flower bed."

"Death really is frightening to death," Mother didn't let the impression of the event fade even afterward, when she came into the house for the afternoon break. She said that today, when I saw it for the first time, I could understand, more or less, what she was talking about, but I should know that I really saw only its distant and covered reflection. This time, Mother spent the daily rest hours strictly enforced by the municipal authorities cleaning the windows, and thus, from the upper reaches of the room, standing on the window sill and polishing the upper panes, she said that a person isn't known by how he's seen by the world which states its opinion of him, but how he looks inside to the depths of his heart and copes there, all by himself, with the destructive fear of death. There would always be individuals who would dare challenge death openly and protest it at the risk of their lives, and those tests of courage and provocations win them admiration and laurel wreaths. "In my eyes, they're not heroes, but fools at best," stated Mother and grabbing the window frame, she carefully changed direction, and asked if I still remember the

sight of people emerging from the excited Spanish crowd that filled those alleys and stood in the way of the animals stampeding to the bull ring and provoked them. At the beginning of summer vacation, I went with Mother to the afternoon show at the Orion cinema, and the newsreel before the movie excited the spectators around us. They whistled and cheered at the boldness of the men who interfered in someone else's quarrel and shouted in panic when unfortunate people were gored or trampled by the feet of the bulls. Back then, Mother had shrunk in her seat and commented that abuse of innocent animals disgusted her, but now she said that that behavior was simply one of the manifestations of the human fear of death, transformed into acts of provocation and unnecessary risk. And then she looked down at me, and after she tossed the old undershirt to me and asked me to hand her a few sheets of newspaper, she stated that in her eyes, those amateur matadors are no different at all from the "Black Hawk" and his friends, who held dangerous motorcycle races on the slope of Sha'arei Hesed, or those who climb to the top of Mount Everest, and the rafters on the Kon Tiki who were liable to lose their life in the waves of the ocean, gangs of lunatics, in which she dared to include even the paratroopers.

A revolting smell of ammonia, wet newspaper, and muddied dust stood in the room. Mother blew on one of the windowpanes, trying to remove with her breath a stubborn stain that stuck to the glass, and said that most people tend to hide from death. They shut their eyes, and in their naiveté, they hope that if they don't see it, it won't see them either. But that bastard has a thousand eyes like the tail of the peacock and he'll see us all, down to the very last one of us, and nobody will slip away from him.

Mother fixed her sights on the simple stone house of Dr. Israelit, which now that the windowpanes gleamed, was seen across the street, firm and solid, and said that talented writers aren't content to shut their eyes and crawl in panic to secret places, like other human beings, but try to dissolve their fears in the endearing pleasure of tales they make up from their heart, like a person walking alone at night and whistling in the dark.

"That's what your grandmother has done all her life, and now you're following in her footsteps, while I look at it straight in the eye," stated Mother and came down from the window. And she added that she hoped that, when it was time for me to face the test, which will, unfortunately, come sooner or later, I'd gather up all my forces and not lower my eyes.

"Stay here," Mother ordered me about eight years later, at that same early morning hour, when we awakened to the sound of Father's groans and realized he had suffered a mild stroke, the first in a chain of strokes that heralded his impending death, and Dr. Israelit, who was summoned to our house, began examining him. I wanted to get out of there, but Mother put her hand on my shoulder and said that not only wasn't it right to leave Father now of all times when he needed us so much, but that that was exactly what she meant when she talked with me about courage and looking directly.

Helpless, Father was sprawled in the "Electric Fauteuil," and his gaping eyes roved back and forth between us and our neighbor the doctor who tapped his knees with a little hammer and peered into his extinguished eyeballs. After tickling his bare, skinny arms, and turning his head from side to side, Dr. Israelit asked him to repeat after him "Gad, a troop shall overcome him; but he shall overcome at the last." Father tried to do what the doctor said and repeat that blessing of Israel who strengthened himself and sat upon the bed on his sons who were gathered around him before he died, and suddenly he burst into tears and said he had never been Torah chanter in the synagogue because he stammered and now of all times, when he was broken like a Lulav (that image he took, "*vi a tsebrokhener lulav*," will float up every year when I pass by the stands of the four species on the eve of Sukkoth), they ask him to pass entrance exams like one of Kabetski's choir boys. Dr. Israelit smiled in embarrassment, tapped Father affectionately on his drooping shoulders, apologized and said he didn't mean, God forbid, to offend him. That all he wanted was to make sure his speech wasn't affected, and now that he had defended himself as eloquently as Abba Eban, there was, of course, no need for that examination.

When we walked the doctor to the gate of the courtyard, while asking how much she owed him, Mother also asked for his prognosis and whether the stroke Father suffered at dawn today could recur more severely. "I see that madam is already half a doctor,"

chuckled our neighbor, shifted his bag from one hand to the other, and nodded toward me. "Don't hesitate to talk to us freely. You needn't worry about revealing the verdict to the two of us," said Mother resolutely. And then she pointed to the chickens of old lady Wollman, who were running around in the next yard, and added that nobody knew better than he that death is nothing but that big pile of garbage we all peck in, and every single one of us will find his own worms when the time comes.

About two weeks later, when Father seemed to be recovering from the stroke he had suffered and our life was slowly getting back to normal, Mother once again explained the tormenting events of that morning, which had been bothering me almost non-stop ever since. One night, when I came home from a private lesson in math, a vague silence oppressed the house, a silence disturbed solely by Father's angry and uneven snoring. Following doctor's orders, he rested a lot now and went to bed early. Mother was sitting in her usual place in the vestibule, erect and tense as usual when she read, but the library book in front of her under the circle of light cast by the reading lamp on the table was closed, and her eyes lost in the distance were flooded with tears.

"Father! What happened to Father?" I was startled, and barely choking a shout, I tiptoed into the other room where Father was sleeping. Scant bands of light illuminated his face, which was sunk in a drugged slumber, and torments seemed to be stamped in wax, sketching twisted paths all leading to the dark pit of his mouth.

"Don't worry," Mother calmed me when I came out, trying to make her voice sound optimistic. "Father's fine for now."

"So why are you crying?" I asked suspiciously, insisting on revealing the secret she was taking such pains to hide from me.

Mother smiled through her tears and said she had just returned from Mr. Golobin's funeral.

"Is that another one of Father's Russian friends?" I wondered, reviewing in my mind's eye the small group of people from Kiev that included Parhodnik, Sorokin, and Glinka, who sometimes invaded our world.

"Ivan Ilitch Golobin died eighty years ago," Mother chuckled and said in a melancholy voice that if my teachers, whose vapid eyes reflected irreparable stupidity, would relieve us of the need to memorize the kinds of sacrifices and the quantity of flour mixed with oil that goes with them, or the names of the forty-eight states of the United States and their capitals, and would instead inspire us with the aspiration to read the immortal works of world literature, I wouldn't have shown such embarrassing ignorance and I would have known not only who Tolstoy was, but would even bow my head in gratitude at the awesome story he wrote, one of the most brilliant creations ever. What did she have to do with that Ivan Ilitch, that forgotten Russian Gentile, that junior judge, who was promoted after pitiful attempts and received a salary of five thousand Rubles, and was going to die in some provincial city of the czarist realm. At first, she wasn't supposed to feel any sympathy with the utterly simple normal life of Ivan Ilitch, who was devoured by cancer of the intestines, and yet, because of that ingenuous way of telling the story, which was tragic and shocking, and seemingly without any artistic effect, she was overcome by the despair dominating the soul of that man with no one to pity him as he wanted to be pitied, who at certain times, after long torments, needed to be pitied, even though he was ashamed to admit it, as a sick child is pitied, who needs to be indulged a little, stroked, kissed, wept over, as a mother indulges and calms her child. He did know that he was an important person, whose beard was already turning gray, and because of that none of the people around him, not his wife or his children and especially not his fellow judges, could treat him like a child. Yet he needed that badly. And only Gerassim, that plump, young Mujik, his servant during his illness, with his simple, natural, unspoiled feelings, was able to relieve Ilitch's torments. He gladly held the sick man's legs on his shoulders, and that seemed to make Ilitch's pain go away. In that strange posture, the two of them sat and talked with one another, with the sturdy son of peasants holding the legs of the judge and slightly easing the pressure of the tumor spreading in his belly, whispered Mother, and her eyes filled with tears again. That had to be one of the most wonderful human scenes she knew.

She clutched the book to her chest and added in a choked

207

Air That
Never
Finds
Rest

voice that when she was tortured along with Ivan Ilitch in his unbearably oppressive thoughts, when despair overcame him and he knew with absolute certainty that he was going to die, and yet he couldn't get used to it, really didn't understand, couldn't understand it at all, that wasn't the only thing that made her share his dread, but she also knew that all of us would always be condemned to bear that awful fear in our heart; and along with Ivan Ilitch who settles the account of his life running out of his tormented body, she also settled the account of her world, and through his death she imagined her own death, her own end, lying in wait for her around some corner of the future.

Father's snores fell silent and a quiet that seemed to bode evil blew to us from his room. A few times I stood up and after some hesitation sat back down, until at last Mother said she'd better go look at him. She trudged wearily, and at the door she turned her face, leaned on the doorpost with one hand and looked first at me and then at the few books on the table. "That morning, when Dr. Israelit came to examine Father, you set foot in the room of Ivan Ilitch for the first time. That room will forever bear the name of that Russian judge, and only its tenants will change in a row whose rules are hidden from us." And she added that a few years before, when Grandmother's end came, I was still a child who stood on the side and peeped into a realm where he didn't belong, but this time things were completely different, and I had to make up my mind whether I'd be brave and enter it with her, or would choose to remain alone outside. "You have to decide if you want to be like Gerassim, who went into the room and came out of it with such a natural simplicity, or like Vassily, the poor little gymnasium student, the son of Ivan Ilitch, who crept there once and twice, sneaked into his father's bed secretly and looked at him terrified and scared, with an awful blue shadow under his eyes. And that difficult decision you'll make now will be with you forever and won't let go of you for the rest of your life." She fell silent, because I was staring at her with an expression that seemed terrified.

"Father's fine," her voice once again exuded calm when she came out of his room. "He's sleeping soundly. The medicines worked." And after she wiped the dust from the storm clouds El Greco tied in the skies of Toledo and straightened the framed picture hanging at the head of the bed, she returned to her chair. As if she were accepting the judgment, she whispered that every person is the master of his own fate and everyone can choose what battle to risk his life in and what battle to stay out of.

Mother leafed absent-mindedly in the book, and suddenly she raised her eyes to me and said: "Can I ask you something?"

I nodded.

"Do you really want to be a writer?"

"Of course, what a question," I answered impatiently.

"What will you write?"

"Stories."

"And what will the stories be about?"

I shrugged.

"I imagine you'll write about life," Mother expressed her thought aloud. "Everybody does."

There was a degree of truth in that, of course, but the curtain of rancor that separated us was too thick for me to answer her.

"So you'll have to know life. It's not enough for you to be a talented narrator, to have an excellent imagination, know the language. You'll also have to know life from all sides, both the beautiful and the ugly, you'll have to understand it thoroughly, learn the delicate mechanisms that stir cruelty and malice, envy and compassion. You won't be able to get by with talent and sensitive feelings," said Mother, and the organized lecture made it plain that she had devoted a lot of thought to those things, had even formulated them to herself, and was just waiting for the right time to tell them to me. Many years ago, she said, when she was working in blankets and spent a lot of time in the small reading room of the Histadrut Library, drowning her gloom and loneliness in books, she chanced upon a chapter of the memoirs of a Jewish writer from Odessa named Isaac Babel, which was published in a volume of *Ha-Shomer Ha-Tsa'ir*. Babel tells that in his youth he would go to Gorky every day and show him his first attempts at writing. Gorky read the stories carefully and encouraged him to continue, and yet when he realized how weak those immature attempts were, he told Babel to go out among the people and learn to know life as it was before he tried to write again.

"Go out among the people," Mother repeated the experienced writer's advice. "If you run away from life, if you huddle up in your corner and shut your eyes, you'll never write anything worthwhile." And gesturing toward the other room, she added that what was about to happen there was very important for me not only as a son but also as a writer. "Artists create from the pus of life, they don't have any other material." And when she caught the look of horror in my eyes, she didn't relent and said, "That might sound immoral to you, but it's the secret of art, and anyone who is fastidious in his own eyes and things are disgusting in his eyes, had better leave writing alone and study philosophy."

It was late and Father started groaning in his sleep again. Mother turned off the reading lamp and in the dim, turgid light that suddenly enveloped us, she stated that the eyes of the writer did have to be open to life, but there are no schools that teach the art of observing and perfecting the talent of seeing except for the immortal works of true writers. "As far as I'm concerned, don't finish high school, don't matriculate, you don't have to go to university either. The main thing is to read books."

2

To be a child with an inquiring mind born in a house with no books is an awful thing and that's what I had.

In Kiev, Father did have a library with all the best Russian classics, as one of his friends later told me, and he read a lot of them in his youth. But from the day the Bolsheviks murdered his brothers in the interrogation cellars of the Cheka, he despised books and left them to rot on the walnut shelves, to the deep sorrow of the wife of his youth, who thought her husband was foolishly taking revenge on the bedbugs by burning the house down on top of them. When they ascended to the Land of Israel, they left most of the books behind, and the few that Luba insisted on taking with her were scattered to the winds after her death. While most of Mother's library, which she had acquired during her first marriage, remained, as I said, packed up in Grandmother's house, a memento of the iniquity of a past she wanted to wipe out of her memory.

Even then, in my early childhood, I felt the lack of books.

One winter night, Father turned on the radio, and from it came the solemn voice of Shlomo Bartonof reading the Bible chapter of the day. The ancient expanses of the Land of Israel and the torrents of the "Song of Deborah" glowed in the greenish eye of the radio console. The Lord God of Israel set out from Seir, marched from the plains of Edom, the earth trembled, heaven quaked, and the clouds streamed water. A new Genesis, awful and glorious, my eye was opened to a sensual pleasure I never knew before.

When the reading ended, the herds and the river and the necks of the spoilers disappeared and I asked Father if it was possible to read those things again.

"Need a Bible," said Father and turned his face away from me.

"A disgrace for us," said Mother. "A disgrace for us." And pain and helpless indignation for abject poverty filled the room where the three of us spent our days and our nights.

Father stood up and without a word, went out into the night. When he came back he brought a shabby Book of Judges he had borrowed from Mr. Shilem Rotman, the treasurer of the "Akhva" synagogue, and that very night the Lord set out once again on His long road from the plains of Edom toward the Land of Canaan, and all who loved Him like the sun rising in strength.

When I was enthralled by the magic of the printed words and started running in the printed letters, Mother took me to the small neighborhood lending library of Mr. Yehudah Marcus on Yona Street.

Across the street, all my friends congregated at the ice shop of Aharon Broide. Broide, an awkward, childless man, would stand in the heights of his tiny shop like a Roman commander, while his customers waited on the sidewalk, and would pull block after block out of the cabinet with high, heavy doors, put the blocks on a marble slab and brandish a pick to split them in halfs, thirds, or fourths. When he finished his dissection, he would tap the block and slide it onto a slanting tin-coated wooden slab, straight to the hands of the customers, who stood ready, holding tongs brought especially for that purpose. The children watched the work of the ice seller, hypnotized, praying for the moment he'd totter, when a corner of the block would break, and they'd get the ice-cream-of-rationing. "Crystals of ice he scatters like bread crumbs, he sends the cold and the water stands frozen," his brother, Reb Ze'ev Wolf Broide, one of the refugee rabbis of Russia, would preach the biblical passage about him. Reb Ze'ev Wolf Broide owned a rundown grocery, which he left for a little while and went to walk around the street and watch the foolish young people waiting a long time for remnants from the high table.

I, on the other hand, would then visit Marcus's library — the meeting place for the old maids of the neighborhood, bored retirees, and a few young intellectuals, including, as I later found out, Amos Oz. I'd go there two or three times a day, until in time, it became my second home, if not more.

Unlike the other readers, who would exchange one book three

times a week, I was entitled to exchange books whenever I wanted and at any time. And my other advantage there was that Mr. Marcus permitted me to climb onto the high ladder and take whatever books struck my fancy. I'd stand, dusty and sweaty, at the top of the ladder, like Matthew Pascal, Pirandello's hero, and pore over books until one suddenly dropped and fell to the ground. The shop was shocked, a column of dust would rise and two or three spiders would scurry out of it in panic, and the people in the shop would run after them armed with books, to kill them.

Thanks to these extra rights, I developed a systematic method of reading in those days and within two years, I think, I read most of Marcus's books. With an insatiable lust, I read everything that came to hand, without discerning, adventure books and dime novels, children's books and a whole series of "detective" books.

It wasn't until many years later that I found out how I had earned those privileges and why Mr. Marcus liked me better than all his other readers. In an interview he granted to a local Jerusalem paper, Marcus — who later owned a well-known bookstore on Ben-Yehudah Street and a publishing house for books of yoga and American Beatnik poetry — said that in the days of rationing in the early fifties, he had a secret agreement with the owner of the "Tnuva Branch," Mrs. Rakhelevski, my mother: he'd let her son take whatever books he wanted every day and she'd give him more eggs and butter than his ration. "And," he said to Dan Omer, "look what became of her son Chaimke and what became of my son Samson, who is like his namesake." (It wasn't long before all the people operating in that story, Mother and the interviewer, Yehuda Marcus and his son Samson Elam, who, at the end of his life became a holy man with the light of the *Shekhina* glowing on his face, were dwelling in the dust, and I alone remained to tell their tale.)

One Friday, when I almost finished reading all the books of Tarzan and Karl May, Jules Verne and Jack London, Mr. Marcus came down from the ladder, handed me a thick book and said that somebody who has a book by Agnon for the Sabbath doesn't have to bother to take a double portion of bread from the miserable food his library had in abundance in hard times, and added that the book of this clever Galicianer would introduce me to my mother's forebears, those fanatic religious humbugs of the Old Yishuv, who my parents had gotten away from in time, fortunately for me.

On Sunday, before I went to school, I hurried to the library to return *Only Yesterday* and to take a new book to sweeten recess and be saved from the evil hand of the class bullies.

"And what do you think of Agnon's mockery of the B'nai B'rith Library?" asked the book changer impatiently. Everybody knew that the B'nai B'rith Library at the entrance to Ha-Habashim Street was Mr. Marcus's mortal enemy. The neighborhood readers would abandon him one after another and go graze in the fields of the big public library, whose pride was the abundance of books and the cheap subscription rate.

"I don't remember," I confessed candidly.

"Then take the book and read it again, and when you're ready for an exam, come back to me," said Marcus and for the first time since I had crossed the threshold of his library, he refused to give me another book to read.

In the middle of the week, when I returned to him, he asked me to read aloud what Agnon wrote about the B'nai B'rith Library and silenced the bookworms who clung to the shelves so they'd hear the opinion of the writer of *Only Yesterday* about those who sat in that building full of books, and would repent the evil they wished to do him.

In the end, I also betrayed the good and cheerful Marcus and left the crowded shop smelling of almond paste and dust and old paper, where Mother had abandoned me to the charms of books, and preferred the competitor's library. There, too, I'd come and go as one of the subscribers, apparently because of surplus agreements she signed with the introverted librarian who sat withdrawn in her corner with a gauze of eternal sadness in her eyes (her bridegroom, Mother told me one Memorial Day, was killed defending Gush Etzion, where they were among the original settlers, and since then she hadn't set up her own home and lived as a subtenant with Mrs. Hochstein, Yehudi Menuchin's aunt). Judith Robinson let me burrow in the new books that hadn't yet been catalogued and in the repaired books that were returned from the bindery, let me open cases of rare books, which Tschlenow, as I recall, sent as a gift to the Jerusalem library to commemorate his wedding, and I'd go home loaded with popular science manuals, travel accounts, and geography books.

What I weighed and investigated in books, I would deliver in daily lectures. Late in the evening, when my parents would lock themselves in the shop to count the proceeds, to straighten up the shelves that the customers had disturbed and to paste the labels of the ration office with the white of a broken egg, I'd climb the ladder and preach on current events.

From the upper reaches of the shop, so close to the ceiling and so far from the floor, reality looked different to me, surprising and a bit distorted. The florescent fixture flecked with fly droppings was beneath me, the upper shelves that had been beyond my reach before were now visible and covered with dust, and at long last, I saw the logic of the complicated design of the floor tiles. Father and Mother, too, suddenly looked small and helpless.

Father looked at me admiringly, amazed at my marvelous expertise in the solar system, the Milky Way, and the distant galaxies, the names of remote tribes in Africa and Australia, that I knew by heart, and the names of travelers, explorers, and discoverers that would drop from my mouth like pearls. Father used the side of his fist to tap the labels that refused to stick on the sheets of paper, and said that the boy would be Demosthenes. First let him be a human being, decreed Mother and lifted her pained eyes from the accounts she was doing on the back of the party ballots that Father stuffed in his pockets inside the voting booth and that we used as writing paper for a long time after the elections. And as in a dance of marionettes, their heads would come close and go away come close and go away, against the background of the mosaic of colored papers on the counter.

When Father learned that I wasn't graced with a musical ear and a sweet voice, his wish that I would someday be a cantor and continue the golden chain of Kvartin and Pinchik was thwarted, and he wanted me at least to be an orator, whose words would go far. To prepare me for this calling, he'd take me on Friday nights to the synagogue of Zikhron Moshe, to hear the sermons of Rabbi Sholem Shvadron to learn the secrets of the power of speech so I would win people's hearts.

"The whole force of the evil instinct is only in imagination, that's all," the voice of Rabbi Sholem still strikes in my ears from far away. Like all great preachers he had the power to select expressive words instinctively, words that had a coarse and rather primitive persuasive force. "I shall tell you a parable. A villager, a Mujik, who had never seen the cinema in his life, came to the big city and from outside, he saw some hall whose windows and doors were dark and on the wall, as the experts said, pictures ran back and forth. He wanted to see what that was. Well, they told him, buy a ticket. He bought a ticket, he went in, got closer and closer and closer, until he came to the wall. Ah, you understand, he didn't see well. What did he do? He had a big battery in his pocket, he lit it, and he didn't see anything, a blank wall. No pictures, nothing. They started shouting at him: What are you doing? He said: What's this, what am I doing?! I wanted to see better. They told him, What did you do, dummy, here we see only when it's pitch black in the hall. You understand, gentlemen, when the light is lit, the wall is smooth and you don't see a thing. The power of the evil instinct is only a fantasy, a vain imagination . . ."

Rabbi Sholem poured himself a little tea from a Thermos bottle on the windowsill behind him and moved his eyes over the study house that was packed full. An oil lamp hummed in the dark because the electric lights were still out. "Once I was in London. Probably almost five years ago. I went with a few other people. Well, they want to show me and they say: Reb Sholem, here's the queen's castle and there are the king's soldiers walking around in red. Here's a museum and there's a museum. We rode some more, they told me: Here's another museum. What museum is this? They told me some museum that a woman, some French woman made of all the kings from the days of Pharaoh to George V, all of them kings. She made them, of course, from wax, how Pharaoh VI looked, Pharaoh V — I don't know the history. At any rate, then she made the fantasy of how it looked like that. And there was a hat like this and clothes and the sword on his thigh and he's sitting on his throne. How many kings are there, great ministers, yes 250, good, maybe 300. I had to give a talk at a Yeshiva there in London. So something came into my mind, a verse, a simple verse from the Gemara, a wonderful thing, remember, remember, something really wonderful. This verse says: (Rabbi Sholem takes a few sips, delays his words to increase the curiosity in the hearts of his audience) a small town, says the Gemara, is the body, how much is it the body, three measures, and a few people in it, while the organs, the 248 organs, and a great king comes to it, that's the evil instinct, and surrounds it with fortresses and embargos, those are the sins, and comes a wretched man, that's the good instinct, one man, wretched, poor, but wise, who has wisdom, and rescues the city with his wisdom and saves the whole city from the great king. And I asked myself: if there is a small city, why does a great king have to come to it? Let him send three soldiers and let them take care of the small city. Why does he have to come with tanks and divisions and airplanes. And another question, so how does a wretched man, even if he is wise, how does he save the city. With sticks can you fight tanks, divisions, airplanes. When they showed me the museum, a sweet explanation arose in my heart. What can I tell you, gold and silver. As the Bible says: More to be desired are they than gold, yea, than much fine gold; sweeter also than honey and the honeycomb. About that we said: this museum of the kings of wax that the woman made . . . (Rabbi Sholem falls silent, as if he forgot the purpose of his sermon) today that's only entertainment, everybody wants entertainment, there too, in the museum, they entertain. A tall, English guard stands there, must be sixty inches, stands there with a big hat, with wings, people come in and ask, Where I go, he doesn't answer. Why? Because he's also wax, he can't answer, everything's wax. And there an answer to all the questions came to me. The essence of the evil instinct is wax, fantasy, all its force is wax. He wears a crown of wax, and the king himself is also wax, like the guard. Everything is wax. Red cheeks of wax and a sword of wax. Frightening. That king frightens, frightens the people. Tanks of wax, airplanes of wax, soldiers of wax. Everything is wax. But — nobody knows. And therefore, what does the wretched man do? He's wise. He knows it's wax. Knows the secret. All he's got is a box of matches. He doesn't need anything more. He puts a match on the king's hat, another match on the *mundir*, on the medals, (a laugh of relief shakes the audience), all the medals fall. No medals, no king, no nothing. He just lights a few matches, fine, and everything's all right."

"Even Begin and Sneh, forgive me, can have the honor of coming to us in the study house, and learning something from an old Jew," said Father with obvious pride as we went out into the winter night, oozing satisfaction from the experience he had just taken part in. Facing the trees beaten by the wind, he struggled to imitate the preacher's bold mimicry — the twist of his eye shut with mockery, his voice soft as a marshmallow on the tongue, and the prophetic gestures of his arms gathering ghosts to the Torah Curtain. And when he despaired, he said that someone who wanted to prepare himself to be a modern speaker had to take the rhetorical talent of Rabbi Sholem and blend it with general education and expertise in scientific innovations, and that tomorrow we'd forego the visit to Grandmother and the two of us would go to the Town Hall to acquire knowledge and expand our horizon.

In the dusty, badly-ventilated hall on the second floor of the Pearlman Building on Jaffa Road, the regular audience gathered every Saturday morning for the cultural matinee concocted by the Jerusalem city hall for its residents in the late 1950s. Homeless Holocaust survivors hounded by memories sat there along with retired couples, who came for their only weekly entertainment and in its honor they donned their festive attire from the good times before rationing, and mainly lonely women — cooks, waitresses, and those who mended silk stockings and umbrellas — avid for a bit of culture in the stupid Orient, where they had unfortunately wound up. With a precisely repeated formality, they'd use a handkerchief to wipe the chair that had become their regular place over the years, put an old newspaper on it, greet their neighbors with reserve, and stare tensely at the empty podium.

The lecturers were scientists from the university who needed extra income and were willing to tell in popular language about the new tropical fruit that had adapted to the Land of Israel, about earthquakes we had experienced since the early nineteenth century, and about the finds of the archaeological digs in the last season. Rabbis with Zionist propensities also appeared at the Community Center to win souls over to their doctrine, and local journalists whose editors in Tel Aviv were jealous of them and didn't let them express themselves properly in the newspaper, and so they were forced to present their political views and assessments on that platform.

Among all of them, I was the only young person, a precocious child with an inquiring mind. And the anomaly of my presence says more about the wretchedness of the scene than anything else. I would huddle in the first row, facing the platform, determined this time not to miss even one word of the wisdom the lecturers would impart, but it wasn't long before my thoughts would wander as in the Talmud lessons of our teacher Abraham Dagani, and the journeys of Adib Shishakli, the Syrian despot, along with the buxom idols found in Tel Gezer or in Hatsor, were flooded by the quantities of water carried by the national pipeline to the Negev, the barren desert of our homeland. My looks would stray from the lecturer's trembling papers, from his lips twisted with disappointment, from his eyeglasses strolling from his forehead to his near-sighted eyes, to the audience, some sunk in the light doze of a Sabbath morning and others in occupational therapy, that is, making Napoleonic turbans, telescopes, and sailboats from the stenciled pages distributed at the entrance to the Community Center.

Until the day when they would talk about me, I prepared myself as much as I could for my calling. Following Father's guidance, I read Churchill's speeches from World War II, I drank raw eggs and honeyed water and I stood before the mirror and practiced squinching my eyebrows and waving my hands theatrically, and most of all I was careful to kindle the rustling ember of ambition, since, as Father put it, a general's staff is hidden in every soldier's kitbag.

Sitting drearily in the classroom, looking out the window overlooking Mount Scopus, I'd daydream, see myself as Lord Balfour, standing there at the opening of the university, wrapped in a velvet cloak with big sleeves, delivering my words to the nation that had returned to its land. In front of me, on the whitened slopes, among the olive trees, the audience crowded together: Pioneers who had come from the Galilee, laborers in caps who had come down from the scaffolding, rich women swaddled in fur coats on that spring day, and Yeshiva students with their arms folded solemnly — and all of them were listening to what emerged from my mouth.

Behind me, on the stage whose balustrades were covered with carpets from the drawing rooms of the rich residents of Jerusalem, sat the High Commissioner, Dr. Chaim Weizmann, resting his chin in his left hand, Rav Kook in his Sabbath *shtreimel*, the Chief Sephardi Rabbi, the *Rishon le-Zion*, Rav Jacob Meir, proud of the great honor that had fallen to his lot, and Bialik, his face beaming a spiritual pleasure that suited the scene, and their eyes stared at my back with admiration, waiting for me to turn to them. My thoughts and my words seemed to flow by themselves, and now and then I responded to the expectations of the notables and the great men of the Land and bowed humbly to them, while looking at the Judean Desert and the Mountains of Moab, stretching out behind them, flooded with the pinkish light of the sunset, and even the charmed summits seemed to be watching me and were amazed.

I was usually thrown out of the dream and the class to the corridor whose windows faced Gassner's garage, whose presence, smelling of rubber tires mixed with gasoline fumes, enveloped our school. Downstairs, in the yard of the garage, surrounded by wavy tin walls, young workers ran around, groaning under the endless shouts of the foreman, young men whose laziness and simple-mindedness had exiled them from the classroom to puddles of the lubricating oil of life.

Political party rallies used to inspire a real spirit in me. In the days before television, they were held in movie houses, and Father took me to them even though Mother disapproved, since she loathed politics, and especially politicians. Gathering at the doors, bursting inside, running to the first rows to try to get a good seat where you could see Ben-Gurion's rolled-up sleeves or Golda Meyerson's cigarette case, and the violent tension that charged the air — all that was an advance on the account that was settled later, when the mob of idlers turned into the crowd that knew what it had to do, that responded with complete devotion to the simple orders and absolute truths. Suddenly, a person gets up and feels that he is a nation and starts walking, either to make a wicked use of something as in the song — at long last, they're not alone, the poor worms of Jacob in the dusty chairs of the Community Center or the fearful and despised Jews of the great lord who find momentary solace in the parables of the preacher, but are a sturdy organ in a gigantic body that has a head, a very important person, standing on the stage and talking, not from a bundle of shaking papers and tattered cards, or like a tendril weaving in and out of dried-out phrases, but from the depth of the experience and wisdom of leadership crowned with splendor.

Afterward, at home, I'd repeat the bewitched whispers, sowing poison and paralysis, and the shouts that struggle with doubt and logic, preparing myself for my appearance in the school playground. Time and again, I'd try to assemble groups in public, at the edges of the basketball court, and to preach about social and political issues, condemning proportional elections and praising the annulment of the death penalty. But my classmates would all drop away from me, captivated by the contorted soccer-player legs of Itzik Samhiof and by the expertise of Dankner in Ephraim Kishon's humor pieces.

One day, after Father repeated his prophecy that I would be the second Demosthenes, Mother grumbled that not only did Demosthenes have a fine library of his own, but so did Cicero and, not to be mentioned in the same breath, Jabotinsky, and why should I have to make do with less. In the house, we didn't yet have an electric refrigerator, or a gas stove, or a washing machine, but the very next day, after school, I went with Father to Beit Ha-Ma'alot to lay the foundation of my own private library. In one of the apartments of that multi-story building—where, as she later told me, Mother wanted to leap to her death—were the offices of the publishing house Kriyat Sefer, and Father had gotten to know its owners, Mr. Shalom Sivan and his father, when they ascended to the Land in the same ship.

"Today, you'll select a hundred books you want," said Father when we stood at the entrance to the staircase. "And financial affairs you'll leave to me. I'll arrange it with Mr. Stepansky."

Stunned by the abundance of new treasures, I scurried among the loaded shelves, abandoning myself to fresh fragrances I hadn't known in the lending libraries—a smell of printer's ink, polished paper and fresh glue that hadn't yet dried—and pulling out piles of books with an irrepressible lust. The books I selected included the *Legends of the Tanaim*, by Ezra Tsion Melamed, *Bible Commentaries*, by M. Z. Segal, and *The Jordan*, by Nelson Glueck. Mrs. Sivan, the publisher's wife, pulled Father into a corner and asked him if we had gone out of our mind, since only old men are interested in the books the child chose for himself.

"Pnina, he's not a child anymore," said Father, even though I was about ten years old. "Let him take what he wants."

When we returned home, with my fingers red and scratched from the string that tied the bundles of books, Mother's gift was waiting for me — a rubber seal shaped like a cover of an ancient book with my name stamped on it.

One day during the summer vacation between fifth and sixth grades, I made up my mind that the time had come at last for me to write a book too. I bought a thick notebook with seventy-two pages, I drew on its cover a turret of a mosque and some round domes, I surrounded the page with careful drawings of crescents, and in the middle, alternating red and blue letters, I wrote my name and the name of the book: *In the Alleys of Nazareth*.

Within less than an hour, I finished writing the opening chapter, in which, as I vaguely remember, I described an Arab coffee-house, where two men with mustaches and kaffiyas are sitting and preparing an act of vengeance and vendetta. What the plot of the book would be — to tell the truth, I didn't know.

In the afternoon, I wanted to read my creation to my parents. Mother refused and said that you don't show a fool half a work and that the blessing is only in what is hidden from the eye, and the moment I'd bring the words I wrote onto my lips, their magic would vanish and they'd look miserable and worthless, and I was liable, God Forbid, to detest them and not go back to them for a long time, maybe never.

Father dismissed her words and urged me to read.

"Wonder of wonders," he smacked his lips, "wonder of wonders." And when Mother left the room, he said he wanted to show my creation to experts and taste-setters.

The first critic was Reb Anshel Lancut, a Galician scholar, who had worked for many years as a proofreader and a printer of holy books. From the day he had visited his house and seen his rich library — a few thousand books in all areas of Judaism — Father had clung to him lovingly and would pester him with the embarrassing question of why he didn't write his own books but only took care of others' books. "I know how to erase, not write," Reb Anshel Lancut would say, and would denigrate writing books, saying things like, why it is said that when the King Messiah comes, all the trees of the forest will rejoice. They'll be happy, said Reb

Anshel, because then people will stop writing nonsense and will stop cutting down trees to make them into paper. Or the tale he heard from Rabbi Zevin about why the Rebbe of Kotsk refused to write a book: "Let's assume I already wrote a book, when does a person have a free hour to read it? Let's say on the Sabbath, after he prayed and filled his belly with food and drink, that Jew stretches out on his bed and picks up my book and opens it, and right away he's snatched by sleep and the book falls to the ground. For that I should write a book?"

Reb Anshel was a regular customer in my parents' store, and when he came there that afternoon, Father handed him *In the Alleys of Nazareth* and asked for an expert opinion.

And the veteran proofreader took a pen out of his pocket, changed a word, added commas and periods and said that everyone who reads the She'ma and is precise about its letters, is cool in hell. As for content, he refused to say a word, and when Father urged him, he replied that he agreed with Rebbe Levi Isaac of Berdichev who said that the whiteness in the holy parchment is the great illumination on it, and therefore a Torah Scroll with one letter stuck to another is invalid, because the whiteness of the parchment is covered and the illumination is in the whiteness. Father laughed and Reb Anshel added that that illumination in whiteness cannot be attained in this world until our righteous Messiah comes.

At dusk, Mr. Ze'ev Eliashiv came into our store. He was a high-ranking official in the post office, whom Father saw as a representative of Western culture, because he subscribed to the newspaper *Haaretz*, changed his white shirt twice a day, and played the flute. Father brought him into our apartment, which was, as I said, behind the store, and asked his opinion on the opening chapter of the story. Mr. Eliashiv began reading and twisted his lips in an expression of disgust, and then he told Father that the author wasn't faithful to reality. "Nazareth was settled, as every intelligent person knows, by Christians." He sneaked an arrogant look in my direction. "And there aren't any mosques there, but churches."

Outside, in the square in front of the store, Father's friends, simple Russian Jews, sat and chatted endlessly about life and death, politics and gossip, memories of the past, and the future, a typical Slavic chat that confounds everything. Father told his friends what had happened that day. Mr. Moshinski, who owned a building supply shop, called me and said that the words of Eliashiv, the *Hauptbeamter* of the post office, reminded him of the tale of the Jewish immigrant in America who got a job as an echo-from-heaven. "Listen carefully, my young man," Father's friend advised me, "some day this story will come in handy."

"A voice . . . an echo-from-heaven . . . ," giggled those present, but the owner of the building supply store hushed them and said that if they spent less time in empty chatter and had time to read Moshe Nadir's *Jewish Livelihoods*, their ignorance wouldn't proclaim them at the top of the street. And indeed, as is told there, an idler was hired by a farmer to stand at the bridge and work as an echo all day long.

"Understand, please," said the farmer to the employee, "there are people who are great lovers of nature, and they love to hear echoes, and since last year my competitor hired himself a man and stood him somewhere deep inside his farm to make echoes, this year I advertised in the newspapers that on my farm the echoes are even louder, and you, because of your voice, will be my echo."

A little while later, Moshinski continued, the Jew lay hidden between the bushes in the swamp next to the bridge and waited. And someone strolled by whose gestures, as if he were preparing to hunt butterflies and flies, indicated that he was a lover of nature and desired echoes.

At first, everything went without a hitch. The tourist called out once, twice, three times, and the echo answered him and his voice rolled throughout the farm. For a moment, silence reigned. The echo lit a cigarette and then the man asked "How are you?" "Thank you," replied the echo, "I'm all right, how are you?"

Half an hour later, the former echo held two dollars and forty cents, his salary, and the farmer pointed to the railroad station.

Mr. Moshinski looked at me and at Father and at the members of the group who were drinking boiling cups of tea that Mother had poured for them, and asked if I understood the moral of the story.

I moved my head from side to side.

Father's friend smiled and said that Mr. Eliashiv's words about the fidelity the writer is obligated to shouldn't make me faint of heart, God forbid, because I had to know that only the echo has to be faithful.

Mother stood on the side smiling, her hands in her lap, and didn't interfere in the men's conversation, but afterward she remarked that I'd be wrong to ignore Mr. Eliashiv's criticism and be led astray by the conclusion of Mr. Moshinski, who knew all there was to know about screws and nails, but wasn't one to establish hard and fast rules in matters beyond his ken. Literature is indeed made-up, and yet the more precise and faithful to reality is the realistic base of the story, the higher the wild imagination of the creator can soar and devise incredible plots. "And at any rate," she said, "an author has to be faithful, at least to himself."

3

Amazing as it may seem, only in retrospect did I become aware of the extent of Mother's influence on me as a writer. ("Never be tempted to call yourself an author," she advised me after my first prose chapter was published in the literary supplement of one of the newspapers, and people started preceding my name with the desired title; "you better be satisfied and say you're a writer." In her opinion, you should act like that not only out of modesty, but first of all because everybody who boasts of being an author walks around puffed up with his own importance, like a cop on the beat whose uniform makes him stand out too much, and he doesn't see what he should see, while the modest writer slips in invisibly, like a member of the secret police and nothing escapes his eye.) Not that Mother concealed her persistent attempts to shape my literary vision, which would, she believed, guarantee me a foothold in reality, which would be even firmer than the one I'd gain from science (she saw religion only as empty magic and belittled its importance), but she was too wise to obscure that interference, and impressed her thoughts on me so much that I incorporated them into my awareness without feeling it.

Only three years before she died was it all revealed to me as if innocently. I found her standing on the closed porch of our house, which I used as a study, and leafing through a book of essays by Graetz, which she had chanced to see on the desk. Mother murmured the long, twisting sentences of the great historian as if she were caught red-handed, they were beyond her, but the letter he wrote to the person who translated his literary work into Hebrew, thrilled her because somehow it was addressed especially to her. Mother read me Graetz's words revealing his firm opinion that the hand of God ruled the course of the history of the Jewish people, and yet that hand must not always be presented openly, and the historian should only hint at it as a finger of God, like the author of the Book of Esther, who presented the miraculous rescue without divine intervention. And then she said that that was how she also wanted to act, to be present in my world in everything and yet, as much as possible, to remain hidden from view. All her life, Mother admitted, she had admired the restraint with which Miriam had acted when she appeared on the bank of the Nile and watched as taut as a string as her baby brother was hurled on the water, and she also overcame her instinct to interfere as much as she could when she saw the rickety arks of bulrushes, where I floated the first children of my mind, struck by reeds, and was careful not to disturb chance encounters from working their unexpected effects on me. "The king's daughter coming down to wash in the river may always appear by chance," Mother concluded, "and with an instinct of curiosity, she'll stretch out her arm to the child and take him to the palace."

Now, when my mind wanders back and forth among mounds of memory in a meaningless attempt to capture her fluttering image, I see her standing on the side, leaning on the door frame, and tensely watching Father boasting to a group of his friends about the essay I wrote about the first jet of oil that burst from the off-shore drilling. Reb Anshel Lancut took the essay out of Father's hands, raised his glasses to his forehead and brought the page close to his nearsighted eyes contemptuously, yearningly and curiously, the way old rabbis examine reddish spots on the panties of women to determine if they are clean. His nose sniffed my hesitant lines, and then, with a twist of his lips, he said that this time he wouldn't repress the truth in his heart and would have his say, an apt remark, since, two weeks before, when he read *Alleys of Nazareth*, he had made do only with hints. "I beg your pardon, Mr. Rakhelovski, not everybody who wants to take pen in hand does so," he said, very slowly stroking his beard. "And not only should a Jew be an expert in the Holy Tongue in which the world was created and the Torah was given, but he also has to know at least how to distinguish between masculine and feminine and singular and plural and needless to say he must teach his fingers calligraphy, which is called penmanship by the sages of the Talmud, and not put the twenty-two holy letters on the page like fly droppings, Heaven Forbid."

Those cruel words of wisdom were cut off by Father's friend, Reb Shlomo Tellingtor, who had sat still the whole time, silent, fiddling with his snuff box. The old man, one of the important Hasids of Boyan who made a living from a small shoe polish factory he had in the Akhva neighborhood, tapped the relief of the wings of the sphinx on the silver box, and said that, with the help of God, he had also produced quite a few books and so he could confidently say that all the defects in me that Reb Anshel enumerated, were trivial, could easily be corrected. And then he took a pinch of snuff, inhaled it with a snort, and added that the Holy-One-Blessed-Be-He brought those defects down to the world only to spare all those proofreaders and editors and to grant them a suitable living, otherwise, they would have starved to death long ago.

Reb Anshel flushed like Father, turned to his interlocutor and asked him if it wasn't enough for him to blacken his shoes with his greasy polish, but he also wanted to blacken his face in public. But Reb Shlomo didn't give in and said that, even though Reb Anshel was infected with heresy and became a third or a quarter Zionist, he couldn't shake off the ignorance of the Zunz Hasids, and committed an unforgivable sin against me by suppressing the divine spirit of creativity granted me by Divine Providence. "If the young man's spirit falls and he becomes weak, he is liable, God Forbid, to despair of writing and perhaps will never again dare to try his hand at what his soul has destined for him."

The proofreader dismissed my essay and said that he wasn't surprised at Reb Shlomo, who praised ignorance to the skies, since the head of his dynasty, Reb Israel of Ryzhin, was a total illiterate, and from the mouth of a reliable man, the bookseller Reb Lipa Shvager, he heard that the Rebbe of Ryzhin couldn't even sign his name and his treasurers would sign his letters for him.

Father cast a scared glance at the Hasid, but Reb Shlomo smiled, amused, and announced that that was a well-known secret throughout Brod, and Shvager, who was a Husyatin Hasid, heard it from Reb Feybush Mordechai, the son of the Rebbe of Ryzhin, and he himself told that explicitly in his book *The Glory of Israel,* which was published the week I came into the world and he gave it to Father as a gift when he came to my Brit Mila. And indeed, the holy rebbe did write little, and as usual, all his letters were written by his associates, and when he had to sign, he'd sign with big letters, and in vain did the notorious scholar Yossl Perl try to mock him and even presented his manuscript in the window of his school in Tarnopol to show the passersby the Rebbe's inability. Reb Shlomo got up from his stool, retied his belt, closed his eyes, and quoted from memory the words of the rebbe: "When Father departed from the world, I was a child and I had no rebbe, I got my Torah only from life itself (*mayn toyre hob ikh mkabel geveyn fun chai hachaim aleyn*—his words are engraved on my heart in Yiddish) and the Torah you get from life itself even the Messiah can't renew."

"The Ryzhin rebbe is a fool," Reb Anshel decreed and asked Mother to go into the store with him and give him the white bread and lean cheese his wife had ordered that morning, and then he turned his back on the excited group of men and added that anyone who wanted to make good use of his time shouldn't get into a debate with those idlers, who go on running after the royal chariot of that good-for-nothing who sanctifies ignorance.

When he came out of the store, passing by them without a glance, Tellingtor called after Reb Anshel, "*a geshtrofter galizianer*," a punished Galician, and said that until the sun of the Ryzhin rebbe shone on them, their land had stood desolate and was a heap of ruins and a desert with no human being.

Until the store closed, Mother walked around among us like a dove, humming with a clenched mouth and not saying a word, but when the three of us were alone, she gave her tongue free rein and tormented Father for his disgraceful custom of bragging about my essays to the rabble that assembled every day in the small square at the entrance. The blessing is found only in what is hidden from view, she repeated as usual, and he who in his foolishness reveals things prematurely, as they are taking shape, prevents them from the possibility of growing which is always done in secret and hidden, while he was like an impatient child who takes the dirt off the peas he planted in his garden bed to see if they've already sprouted, and thus condemns them to destruction. Father put on his hat, growled that she wrapped me in cotton like an Ethrog and tried to protect me from criticism that forges and matures, and went off to the synagogue in a fit of pique.

"A man's pride shall bring him low," Mother whispered at the slammed door, and then asked me to help her wind the skeins of green yarn she had just bought from Malka Abramson and hadn't yet had time to prepare for knitting. She undid the braid of strings swathed like a pigtail, wound them on my outstretched arms and started moving rhythmically back and forth around me. And as the taut strings between my wrists quickly grew smaller and the ball in her hands grew bigger and thicker, she said that this afternoon, as she listened to the argument between our two customers, to her amazement, she was filled with affection for the defamed rebbe. "A Litvak soul like me isn't suspected, God Forbid, of a Hasidic tendency," smiled Mother, and yet she felt sympathy for that orphan who was left in his mother's care after his father died, for mobilizing all the forces of his soul to turn the defect that had afflicted him since birth — a defect that could have overpowered him — into an effective instrument for building his spiritual force that won him admiration far and near. "The ability to turn a weakness into strength is the most important trick in life," Mother summed up the moral she had learned that afternoon, and thrust the end of the string in the skein of yarn.

When she finished her work, Mother said softly that, the next day, the idlers who gathered in front of the store would wrestle without us because she intended to go with me at that time to Weinstein's office supply store next to the central post office. For about half a year, she went on as if she were revealing a secret, she had been saving under cover, so as not to rouse Father's wrath, adding one penny to another, to buy me a typewriter. "For a person whose occupation is writing, that's not a luxury," she decreed at the sight of my expression of surprise. "It's a vital tool — just like a hammer and a saw for a carpenter and a plunger for a plumber." And as she spoke, her hands hovered like an anxious bird over the wicker basket where the balls of greenish yarn flecked with black rested like new laid eggs. Then her look grew veiled and she said that, as a girl in the Hungarian Houses, she left her parents' home a lot and went to Mrs. Ticho's studio to watch the artist at work, and she noticed that from time to time their neighbor left the paper or canvas stretched on the easel, took a few steps back, and examined the drawing. "An artist has to get away from his handiwork for a little while to get the proper perspective," she quoted the painter and said that only later did she understand that that dimension of distance was vital not only for painters but for everyone involved with art. A person who writes also needs to get away a little from what he has written so he can examine things objectively. "When you see your story typed neatly and not in a handwritten manuscript full of erasing and additions, you can judge it more sensibly as if you were a stranger reading it," Mother concluded, and then, as if she recalled something important that had been forgotten for some mysterious reason, she added that about a year earlier, even before she had thought about the advantage of the typewriter, she had accidentally discovered the secret quality of that tool for deriving the mysterious rhythm of poetry.

It was in early summer, on Lag b'Omer, I think, when she went to visit her sister in Ramat Gan and didn't find her at home. To kill the time until Aunt Miriam came back, said Mother, she wandered to the Yarkon River and strolled in the drowsy streets of the neighborhood of old-timers. In the evening calm that descended on the residential suburb, the sound of typing came from one of the one-story houses and blended with the feverish singing of the many birds preparing for sleep in the treetops. The pounding, which sometimes sounded hesitant and perhaps even stammering and sometimes stubborn and belligerent, fascinated her, and she stood there, in the shade of a tree listening to it, until a young woman and a red-headed boy came out of the house to the lighted porch and then she hurried away before they noticed her. She had no doubt that through the metallic sounds she heard the heartbeats of a mean man praying, expiating his sin to his Creator, pleading for his life and the life of those who sent him, and his heart was torn and turbulent.

(One Yom Kippur, a few years before, when her obstinate atheism seemed to crack for a moment, Mother admitted that even she couldn't deny the resemblance between poetry and prayer. When I came home from Father's synagogue in the afternoon, I found her sitting and gazing with red eyes at the flickering flame of the memorial candle she had lit during the day in memory of her many dead, and in her lap was Grandfather's old prayer book. On the Days of Awe, Mother preferred to stay home and not go to the synagogue, which annoyed Father, who suspected her of taking revenge on him for immortalizing the wife of his youth in the name of the synagogue. "For a moral stock-taking, I don't need all the *yentas* around me, whose bad breath and the perfume they sprayed on themselves knocks me out, along with their empty chatter about cheap Parisian couturiers they brought to their houses and the fabric they were lucky enough to buy." That's how she'd answer him when he related his sorrow to her and told her that the sight of the orphan chair in the women's section grieved him very much. Mother then inquired if fasting wasn't too hard for me and then she asked if I had read the prayer "Let us now relate the power" properly, and without waiting for my reply, she started reading from the book that was consumed here and there by her paralyzed father's saliva, in a cracked, restrained voice, without any melody: "A man's origin is from dust and his destiny is back to dust, at risk of his life he earns his bread; he is likened to a broken shard, withering grass, a fading flower, a passing shade, a dissipating cloud, a blowing wind, flying dust, and a fleeting dream." And without pausing after the ancient words, which according to our family tradition had been written, as I have said, by our ancient ancestor Rabbi Kalonymos ben Rabbi Meshulam from the words of Rabbi Amnon, who appeared to him in a nocturnal vision, on the third day after his death, she said that with those deafening words, a person wants to cross the endless plains spread out before him and to meet the God within him, just like the bothered and tormented person who tosses and turns in his bed at night, and he gets up and picks up a book and leafs through it until he suddenly finds lines that express his situation at that moment and he reads them to himself in a whisper and he thinks he has succeeded in leaping over the gaping abyss of his loneliness. "But it's all emptiness and vanity," commented Mother with a skeptical smile; for by now she had reverted to her traditional positions and said that in their innocence, or perhaps their foolishness, both the worshipper and the poet think that words are strong enough to make some change in the world and in reality. And then she decreed that since I wasn't yet thirteen years old and was exempt from fasting, I should slip off to the kitchen and strengthen my heart with food and drink.)

Mother rolled one of the bands that had encircled the skeins of yarn into a kind of hollow tube, put it to her eye, closed her other eye, and looked through it at the constantly shrinking and expanding green eye of the radio, and said that only a week earlier she had accidentally discovered the identity of that man whose hidden prayer on the typewriter she had listened to as she wandered in the neighborhood of old-timers. "It was none other than Uri Zvi Greenberg, the poet," she had a hard time hiding her pride at her sharp sense of observation. She had realized it at dawn on Wednesday, when, as usual, she perused Mr. Harlap's piles of newspapers. Our neighbor opened his small notions shop late and the distributors would put his newspapers in our shop for safekeeping. Mother would then take advantage of the fact that there were few customers to indulge in a furtive scan of the newspapers, from the Communist *Voice of the People* and the right-wing Revisionist *Freedom* to the progressive *Times* and the Aguda's *Herald*. She saw that as the perfect way to review events from many perspectives at the same time and to shape her own view. That morning, next to the bundles of *This World*, she had come on the first issues of the new magazine called *Pomegranate*. The journal caught her eye mainly because of the color photos she had previously seen only in foreign magazines, and primarily because of an article about men who grew breasts like women after they had eaten chicken injected with hormones, an article that pleased Mother because it supplied her with a new and rather convincing argument to justify her vegetarianism. As she was leafing through the magazine, she also came on a photo report about Uri Zvi Greenberg, whom she remembered as an excited, red-haired bachelor in the 1940s, who sublet a room in the Yevins' cellar on Strauss Street. Mother lingered especially over the photos of the woman he had married since then, a young woman in a summery striped dress, shown hanging up laundry in the yard or reading a story to her son, and suddenly she recognized her as the woman she had seen that evening in the Old-Timers' Neighborhood in Ramat Gan coming out to the lighted porch with the red-headed child. "Even the secret prayer house I told you about was immortalized in the article," Mother claimed greatness and waved the journal at me. She had kept it among her papers, open to the page where the poet was seen

sitting on a sofa, bent over a typewriter on a low table, and surrounded by a child's stroller, diapers and toys. "That's the kind of
typewriter I want to buy you tomorrow," she announced and
added, squelching a smile, "You see, poets are also first and fore-

most human beings."

The disgraceful thought that authors and poets are in fact animals settled in my heart when Father's Russian suitor, Mrs. Olga
Parhodnik, showed up in our house and put a pack of playing
cards on my sickbed. "All the distinguished people of our nation
came to pay you a sick visit, *zeeskeyt*," Aunt Olga rolled her tongue
and turned to Father, taking advantage of his wife's absence to
plant a juicy kiss on his lips.

Herzl, Nordau, and Pinsker looked at that time like heads of
yeshivas who had succumbed to depravity, while Jabotinsky and
Trumpeldor looked serious, in visored caps like a pair of firemen
who had reluctantly put down their axes and hoses and sat for
the painter of the cards a little while. On the other hand, the
quartet of authors looked like a menagerie, and for a long time
after the red fogs of the great scarletina of my childhood had
dissipated, Feyerberg with the face of a consumptive sparrow,
Berdichevski sporting his Nietzschian sea-lion mustache, Tscher-
nikhowsky looking like a lion, and the furious Brenner like a barren bear—all of them went on roaming in the endless fields of
my imagination.

On the opening evening of the Twenty-Third Zionist Congress
—the first one held on the soil of Zion—reality came and undermined my childish images, which Mother had hinted at when she
handed me the first issue of *Pomegranate*. Father, who, as I said
before, thought that one of his obligations as a Jewish father was
to expose his son to the major events of our nation at that time
of the beginning of deliverance, took me, to Mother's distress, to
the convention hall at the entrance to the city.

For long hours we stood on that distant August evening of '51
under the national flags flapping at one another, disappointedly
watching as the indifferent and official delegates crossed the
stone square that was flooded with winds, and were swallowed up
in the doors of the entrance hall, whose ceiling was studded with
light bulbs, to the solemn scene in which we had no portion or
inheritance. Father, who had spent his life studying the faces,

speeches, and customs of the great men of our nation from their blurred pictures in newspapers, celebrated whenever he succeeded in recognizing somebody.

"Here's Aaron Zissling," Father cheered, leaning on the police barricade, at the sight of the suntanned and sturdy man who seemed to have been brought here straight from behind the plow in the fields of Ein Harod. "And here's Shragai, the mayor," he had caught sight of the Mizrahi activist walking smugly and pinched my arm to keep me alert. "When you go to school after summer vacation, you can boast that you saw them." In the slowly emptied square, three figures were suddenly seen climbing up toward us, and the silvery illumination of the spotlights linked glowing halos around them. In the middle was a man with a silvery mane blowing in the west wind, and on either side of him, supporting him as it were, strode his serious escorts, fitting their steps to his. He was waving his arms as if he had the word of the Lord, and his two companions, holding concealed basins, were trying not to let a single pearl from his mouth fall to the ground. "That's the poet Shlonsky," Father decreed knowingly. "And those are Ya'ari and Hazan, the leaders of Mapam." But I was convinced that in fact they were Aaron and Hur climbing to the top of the hill of Rephidim to fight Amalek, and between them climbed the Master of the Prophets with the staff of God in his hand.

Thanks to Mother, I met a living poet for the first time and even talked with him.

Every Thursday, when she went to the market at Mahane Yehuda to buy saltwater fish or carp to satisfy Father's longing for meat, just a little, Mother would first visit the nearby tinsmith's shop of Zerah Ha-Levi, and leave me there so my impressionable child's eyes wouldn't see the carp fluttering in the net of Matthes High Priest, Father's friend, and the scale-covered hand of Corporal Epstein, his steward, brandishing a cleaver over them, and a lust for murder wouldn't enter my heart.

Reb Zerah's shop was black and mysterious like the cave of Elijah in the rock of Carmel. Graters, mugs, lamps and Hanukkah lights, all made of tin, were hanging in clusters on the invisible walls, and he'd sit among them, his eyes glowing and pained from the smoke and the eternal gloom.

"Reb Zerah is a poet," Mother would coax me, when I'd insist on going with her to the fish store. "And they even publish his poems in the newspapers." And the little tinsmith, who had known Mother since childhood, would hold out a tin Hanukkah lamp to me and a brush dipped in aluminum paint and say with a bashful smile, waste not want not.

And as I'd sit there putting a hesitant layer of paint over the labels of the canned goods factory that indicated the original use of the tins, and Reb Zerah would work the bellows or cut out circles and rectangles from the squares of tin, the store was filled with his stories, which now, far away in time and place, float up again in strips like the remnants of tin that dropped from his big scissors.

From his memory, he'd cut the portraits of his ancestors: his mother's mother, who sold milk to make a living in this world and washed corpses to increase her earnings in the next; her father, Reb Zerah Isaac, nicknamed the "Messiah" because of his concern with mysticism, whose splendid Sukkah in Mazkeret Moshe would smell like the four methods of Bible interpretation, with a succession of the plain, the symbolic, the homiletic, and the esoteric; and his paternal grandfather, who was "snatched" by the Czar's army in his youth, was redeemed after several adventures and attended the Gymnasium in Kiev, immigrated to the Land of Israel, and earned his living by writing addresses to begging letters of the soup kitchen for the poor and teaching foreign languages to the young people of Jerusalem, and in the dead of night, he'd compose a new interpretation of the Zohar—a manuscript full of mysterious drawings, which was burned during the explosions on Solel Street when it was left in the home of his uncle, Mr. Isaac Levy, the famous official at city hall, agent and merchant.

When I persisted in coming to his shop, Reb Zerah became more candid and also told about his father, the tinsmith, who at Hanukkah 1918, after the English entered the Land, roamed in the abandoned battlefields around Jerusalem, gathered up shell casings and made them into household and kitchen implements. "Isaiah's prophecy came true: 'They shall beat their swords into plowshares, and their spears into pruninghooks,'" said Zerah Ha-Levi, and told that the eternal lamp made of burnished brass that hung in the "Tiferet Israel" synagogue in the Old City until Gentiles came to our inheritance and desecrated our holy tabernacle, was his father's handiwork. And his vessels were so wondrous that even Professor Boris Schatz and Mr. Bar-Adon and their students at Bezalel art school came to visit him in his workshop in Zikhron Tuvia, talked with him and praised his handiwork. And even though his vessels were splendid, and the machines for washing wheat ordered by the flour mills and the iron tanks for roasting coffee were the pinnacle of expertise and perfection, and his knowledge of soldering metals won praise for Zion from the German engineer of the railroad station, even so, he was poor, for the Sages have said, "poverty follows the poor" and his son inherited his wretched poverty.

His speech, which flowed easily when he told of his forebears and their deeds, grew agitated when at last he dared tell me about his own life, the life of a Jerusalem youth of the Old Yishuv, who wanted to rebel, but out of pity for his parents and because of his soft nature which shied away from dissension, he didn't pursue his idea. He told, and his somewhat albino face flushed, about his work as a faithful servant in his uncle's store — he spent three years there working hard, and he stealthily read textbooks imported from Germany for the Ezra schools — and about his short term as a student in the Shulamith music school which ended when his father, who was terrified that the "treasurers" of the Orthodox communities who were in charge of the "distribution" of charity money, would discover that boys and girls sang together in that institute. His service in the Hebrew Brigade, where he fled from his uncle's store, was a chapter in itself. Time and again, views of the tent camp at the foot of the Carmel were spread out, rowing in the sea of Haifa, which almost ended with the boat capsizing, guarding Zikhron Ya'akov, a Lag b'Omer bonfire in Atlit, when an old farmer sang them "Zion, Zion, *mayn heylige land*," and the episode of the drowning of Corporal Shor in the waters of Tira always kept recurring like a festering wound — end of happiness, grief.

One day when he put down the bellows, took off his apron, and put on his hat as if he was preparing for prayers, I knew that our friendship, a Thursday friendship, no longer needed proof. With his black and wounded hands, he took sheets of paper out

of the inside pocket of his suit and read me a thoroughly polished poem about a magic chandelier, the torch of the King in
Heaven, and at dawn he beheld in it the darkness of the town, a
chandelier whose candles winking fire and flames in the nests of
sparks scatter springs of glory and sources of life. And all at once,
the shop turned into a celestial tabernacle, and the tin vessels rising on the tables of the poor became brass. And all the yearnings,
all the pains, all the poverty of the stunned lad who got out of
the army and the same day was hastily taught the craft of tinsmith
by his father, a backbreaking craft he hated with all his heart,
now knocked timorously on the locked doors of rebelliousness
and compassion of words.

The works of other poets he refused to read. "The Book of
Psalms is enough for me," he said and blew on the dying embers.
"And if I want something new, Yehuda Ha-Levi and Ibn Gavirol
support me comfortably." To the edge of possibility, he aspired
to be original, not to be influenced by anyone—that's what he
repeated to me when I asked him time and again what poetry he
loved. To put an end to his proud and innocent obstinacy, on my
last visit, I came to him armed with *She Holds an Almond Branch*
and *Warm Human Voices* and forced him to listen to some poems
by Yitzhak Shalev, who in those days had taken the hearts of
poetry readers by storm. He crouched in his corner, his hands in
his lap, hidden in the lining of his apron, and not a muscle
moved in his tortured face.

"That's the poetry of the fish," he hissed, rejecting with a rebellious thrust of his chin the books I wanted to leave with him,
and then he said that if I went to Rapoport's shop, right behind
our wall, and looked closely at the fish swimming in the pool
there, I'd see that their lips are constantly moving. "Ask Reb
Matthes, your father's friend, and he'll tell you that fish too, like
all creatures, speak poetry." The old tinsmith wiped his cracked
lips with the back of his hand once and then again and said as if
to himself: "But their voice doesn't reach us."

Zerah Ha-Levi's words infuriated me and since then I avoided
visiting him, and when I saw his stooped figure passing by our
house at noon, pushing an old baby buggy loaded with tin objects, I'd hide from him. Once Mother inadvertently witnessed
my evasion. From the corner of my eye I saw her amazement, but

before it turned into words, the amazement died out on her lips and left only a spasm of pain. And that day and the days that followed, I felt her disturbed look lingering on me an instant more than usual, like a person who discovers something new and threatening in someone he thought he knew inside out, but she refrained from questioning me about what had happened between me and my friend the poet.

I thought the matter was forgotten, but it rose up in a hint about a week later during an exchange between Mother and Father. Father, who discovered that Mother had secretly made up with Ahuva Harris and even visited her, despite the big fight that had erupted between them, teased her about her inconsistency and made fun of her for not keeping her vow not to talk with the stupid goose either in this world or in the next. "That's none of your business," Mother silenced him, and then she turned to me and said she didn't know whether to be angry at or to envy young people who so easily, without any sense of loss or feelings of guilt, could turn their back on those who were their friends and now they don't need them anymore, and can wipe them out of their lives, as if they never really existed.

4

The first time Mother read anything of mine was only a few days before my first work was published in the newspaper, and even then she wouldn't have dared change her practice if I hadn't asked her explicitly to do that because of the circumstances. In retrospect, it is beyond my understanding how she managed to suppress her curiosity for eight whole years, but the fact is that from the time we left Weinstein's shop together with me proudly carrying the new Remington in a solemn triumphal procession in the streets of Jerusalem, Mother made a firm decision to retreat backstage, and only permitted herself to listen from there to the timid echoes of the typewriter keys that often rose from my work place, but never did she ask me about what I was writing, and of course she never asked to read my work.

Like someone who clung with all her might to the image of Miriam, Moses's sister, who stood at a distance, Mother thought, as she was to whisper to me on one of those days — may their memory be wiped out forever — when we sat in the corridor of the oncology department of Beilenson Hospital waiting for a radiation treatment, and she was in a hurry to tell me things before death brought down a screen between us, that her ostensible indifference to my writing was intended to guarantee my creative freedom. She clutched to her chest the results of the blood test and said that any outside interference, even the slightest, could confound my attempts to seek my own ways of expression and maybe even put an end to them. Often, she said, she was afraid I'd mistakenly put a negative interpretation on her disregard and see it as a manifestation of a lack of interest and maybe even alienation. Emotionally, she was even willing to accept that, but to her surprise, I never expressed either complaint or criticism, but on the contrary, accepted it quite naturally.

"I want you to know that, back then, instead of wasting my time and energy on unnecessary interference, I made sure you had as much free time as possible," she said and carefully ran her transparent fingers over her bald head, her temple, and the lid of the empty eye socket, and as she did she emphasized the four crosses the radiologist had marked there to complete the square of radiation; and she added that only someone who is free and exempt from chores other people set for him, someone who has the luxury of not doing anything, only he can ultimately come to terms with cosmic and human mysteries. And indeed, Mother did invest her creative talents in those years in writing notes to the school authorities, using various and sundry diseases and pestilences and fictitious family events to excuse my repeated and recurring absences from school.

I devoted the blessed mornings she put at my disposal to writing and reading and to frequent visits to the used book shops, which were, to use the expression coined by Gorky, my university. Here, halfway between the closed privacy of the workrooms of creators and researchers and the chilly public spaces of libraries and the lecture halls of colleges; here, in a place which is thoroughly intimate, I felt the tremor of the breath of culture. And not only did those visits merit encouragement in Mother's words, but she even opened the meager cashbox of our shop and urged me to take whatever sum they demanded.

My ideal was the bookstore of Bamberger and Wahrman, which was famous in those days as a meeting place for all the great men of Jerusalem, after Reb Michal Rabinovitch passed away and his store, "The South," was destroyed in the explosion on Ben Yehuda Street just before the British left the Land. Time and again, I'd come to the shop on Solel Street, next to the printing press of the *Jerusalem Post*, but the clerk who sat at the entrance, would reject me with a letter opener in his hand and say that they didn't sell textbooks to Gymnasium students. When I'd persist and say that I knew very well what the books offered for sale here were about, he would give me a grudging smile and decree that my appearance indicated that I didn't have enough money in my pocket for their rare books. And so, rejected and offended, I'd peep through the dusty window and look with disappointed eyes at a scholar sunk in contemplation, standing, his eyeglasses on his forehead, burying his face in an old book, or at a group of sages whispering together and telling secrets beyond the flaming sword which turned every way. The sights I saw, but the smell of the place I learned only many years later when I read in Agnon's *Shira*: "The smell of old books came to his mouth, a smell of dust, of old paper, of leather, of cloth, with the additional smell of all the generations that had used the books. It was like a spirit of yearning and turned into a spirit of lust that can't be sated by all the books in the world."

From the store for ancient books, where I wasn't allowed to set foot, I would plod, sullen and angry, to a shop called "The Light," whose owner, Reb Abraham Rubenstein, would greet me warmly, as I told earlier, and from there I'd go on to other stores to the west. Across from the drugstore of Sar-Shalom Deutsch, who, according to Grandmother, discovered the book of remedies hidden by King Hezekiah, was the bookstore of Sheinberger, the brother of Shaya Sheinberger, the late "foreign minister" of Neturei Karta. Sheinberger, a redhead who had turned white, with a black caftan and unkempt sidelocks, sat in the middle of his shop, where there were neither shelves nor tables, surrounded by hedges and hedges of books, like a brood hen sitting on her chicks. He didn't let anyone into his shop, and you had to yell at him what you wanted from the door. He didn't usually sell very much, but sometimes, after I'd appear with my hair cut, without the arrogant pompadour of the secularists, he'd be pleasant to me because he had known my grandfather, and after he'd investigate and inquire if I still observed the Sabbath and laid tefillin every day and wasn't irreligious, he'd pull a book out of the heaps, usually books from the first Jerusalem printing presses, and say he was interested in selling this book today.

I think that the most rigorous of all those colleges was that of Reb Yosef Dov Shtitzberg and his son, Reb Zelig, up Meah Shearim Street, next to the Geula post office. Outside, the bookshop of the father and son looked neglected and forlorn. Strips of cloth were still criss-crossed over its display window to protect the glass from the shells of the Arab Legion in the War of Independence, and on them were tatters of announcements about journeys to the graves of saints, about grapes without any fear of abomination, and about a saint coming to the city. The door was closed and it was hard to open it and it creaked. Inside, you'd find yourself in one of the best arranged and neatest bookstores in the Land of Israel, whose like I saw years later only in the streets around the British Library. The shelves, stretching along the walls, were crowded and crammed, and rose up to the ceiling. The room was unusually high — maybe fifteen feet. On the side, leaning on the card catalogue, sat Reb Zelig, a short man with a sharp and observant eye, and a pointed grayish beard. He dressed in the garb of the Gur Hasidim — a round black hat, trousers stuck into stockings and black slip-in shoes. His voice was soft and polite, as a person who had acquired his courtesy in the metropolis called Warsaw before the War, yet his manner was that of a strict bank manager, who demands that applicants for loans prove with clear evidence that in fact they could also get along without them. Shtitzberg Junior expected his customers to show expertise in the book they wanted to buy before he deigned to sell it to them. His questions were learned and sharp, and he continued his investigations and inquiries until he was convinced — and it was hard to convince him. When he was kind enough to part from three books without asking me about their content, I knew for sure that I had completed my required courses with him and had received superlative grades and that the way to the desired doctorate was open to me at long last.

Just as she protected me on weekdays from the prying eyes of the school authorities, so Mother persisted in spreading her wings over me against the anger of Father, who refused to accept my increasingly frequent absences on the Sabbath. "Lord God, what wilt thou give me, seeing I go childless, and the stewards of my house are the grandsons of Reb Nathan Wasserman," I heard him bitterly protesting to God when I slipped out of the house one Sabbath in the middle of the meal. He swallowed his tears and asked Mother if his iniquity was so great that I abandoned him not only when he went to the synagogue, where, fortunately, he found consolation in the offspring of the author of *Shakris*, who wanted to be near him because his pockets were full of fruit toffee, but I also added insult to injury and took off from the meals of the day, leaving them, my aged parents, to rot in their loneliness, turning their joy into a eulogy.

"Don't get in his way," Mother scolded him, rejecting his

attempt to get her on his side, and said that as parents they had to recognize their son's right to leave them whenever he wanted without calling him to account for it.

"If only I knew at least where he disappeared for half the Sabbath," Father grumbled and Mother poured him another bowl of soup and said with an imperturbable confidence: "To places he loves, where his feet take him."

And as for me, almost by themselves my feet would lead me to the sides of the roads, to Nabi Kimer, beyond Beit Sima Balilyus, to peep into its moldy gloom, flooded with greenish rainwater, of a buried world, where legendary Moslem heroes who had fallen in battle against the Crusaders slept the sleep of eternity, to Ha-Nevi'im Street swooning with heat, and to the deserted expanses of the Russian Compound.

In the sun gleamed the soft yellow hewn stones of the old Russian Orthodox convents that had once housed the abhorred police cells. Through the slightly open door I stole a glance at the vestibule. Above, over the entrance, was an icon, with spots of mold blooming under the glass on it. A smell of non-kosher dishes — pork stewed all night on the stove in the inner rooms, cooked with bread and cabbage — was absorbed in the thick walls. At the window, with a simple glass vase on display holding an acacia or pine branch on its sill, a broad stone sill, I lingered a little while. Not until years later, when I read on the title page of *Eugénie Grandet* the dedication to Mary, whose portrait, says Balzac, is "like a branch of sacred box, taken from an unknown tree, but sanctified by religion and kept ever fresh and green by pious hands to bless the house," did I understand what I had seen that Sabbath afternoon in the window, where a torn and dusty lace curtain hid what was going on behind it from the passersby.

From there, I'd turn to the pine grove where all the trees leaned eastward, on the slope going down to Musrara, would wander among the rounded and truncated concrete pyramids, the "teeth of the Dragon of Albion," as our neighbor Har-Sheleg used to call the tank barriers that remained from the Bevingrad fortifications, I'd crush the chamomile flowers that grew there and smell my fingers, which smelled like a pharmacy.

At the back windows of the laboratories of the Hebrew University, which were housed in the days after the War of Independence in the Russian Consulate at the beginning of Shivtei Israel Street, near the Mandatory prison, where Feinstein and Barzani clutched the grenade to their chests and blew themselves up, I'd linger to savor loneliness. Along with the dread, the attraction and repulsion, I'd inhale the smell of little guinea pigs in the layer of sawdust lining the bottom of their cages blended with the pungent aroma of the ailanthus, that wild tree with elongated leaves, that increased in the courtyard packed with the barbed wire accordions of the central prison, and I still don't know that the energy emanating from the sights and smells, from the pain and beauty, an energy amassed in those delicate and fleeting moments, will ever be expressed someday.

At the end of these aimless wanderings, I'd always come to the border. At one end of the world, at the place where old communications trenches and tangles of rusted barbed wire arbitrarily cut deserted yards, a collapsed wing of an abandoned building or a pale strip of road where wandering mold broke out of its layer of asphalt, I'd stop reluctantly, my soul staring ahead, at the other end of the world. The sense of danger from mines planted here so close and from the unseen snipers, their heads wrapped in red Kaffiyahs, peeping in a flash from behind the sandbags of the positions, would intensify the yearning to approach the forbidden city beyond the heaps of ruins of no-man's-land. The honking of cars and the shouts of the peddlers in the distant markets that disturbed the silence of the Sabbath seemed to me like the bleating of yearnings of the other end, but, as Rebbe Nahman of Braslav said, we are now at the edge and end of Israel, in a place where the border of Israel ends, and the city of Mother's forebears I will not reach, because everything has an edge and an end.

How far Mother went to protect the blocks of time she conquered for me in those years I learned by accident in one of those short remissions of her disease, when her headaches relented and she returned to her old habits of reading. While leafing through a new collection of writings of the bibliographer A. M. Haberman, her curiosity was aroused by a chapter with a long list of essays whose authors had condemned them to be hidden or burned. She was intrigued by the struggling soul of the writers, tossed between regret, depression, and humility, as expressed in "what are we and what is our life," on the one hand,

and arrogance and excessive pride explained in the sayings "for whom do I labor" and "the generation is unworthy." For a long time she sat withdrawn in my study, and her one eye made its way between smoky bonfires, heaps of torn strips of paper and open graves, where corpses and manuscripts are lowered, in an attempt to decipher the dark secret of those who slaughtered their own creations. A proud laugh put an end to the silence, and she asked me to listen carefully to what happened to the author Jacob Rabinovitz. Rabinovitz, as Mother called him, decreed that an author is commanded to write every day, even on the Sabbath, and he did that, but the next day, on Sunday morning, he burned all the forbidden writing he did on the Sabbath so that he wouldn't enjoy the work of the Sabbath. Mother turned here and there, like Moses smiting the Egyptian and burying him in the sand, and when she saw that there was no one in the house except us, she said: "It's lucky that on that Sabbath, a year after Father died, you didn't do what he did. So, at least, you still have the poem about Father, and if you had destroyed it, your whole life wouldn't have been enough time to regret it." Even though my desecration of the Sabbath was exposed, I tried to deny it by raising my voice angrily, but she hushed me, quite offended, and said that at least now, before the end, maybe the time had come at last when our relations would be clean of the dust of righteousness and pretense. Even today, although many years have passed since then, she said, she still saw me coming home with great fatigue, much concentration, and internal tension on my face. "I guessed I was witnessing the revelation of a new poem," she said as if to herself, and from the mirrored lenses of her sunglasses, which she had put back on, the double image looked at me, scared and frightened. And after a short silence, she added that she hurried out of the house on some pretext so that her presence wouldn't be an obstacle to me if I was overtaken by the wish to write down a poem, even though it was the Sabbath. "I knew, even though I never wrote, that at moments like those the distance between existence and destruction is thinner than a hair's breadth."

That Sabbath, in the winter of 1964, I sat foreign and alienated in the small synagogue Father had established in the memory of his first wife. About half a year after his departure, all that remained of his spirit there were the tablecloths he had sewn from Luba's sheets, a florescent bulb flecked with fly droppings that immortalized the memory of his parents, and the new Ark of the Covenant, an Ark of the Covenant on wheels, which Mother and I had donated to commemorate his death.

I was tired and worn out from humiliating duty at Training Center 4 and was not reverent. Shalom Gad Brinker filled the classroom of the Sephardi school for boys, which became a temporary prayer house on the Sabbath and holidays, with his sweet voice describing the Dreamer thrown into the pit in Dothan and his coat of many colors his father made for him dipped in blood, and with growing exhaustion, I looked forward to the end of the prayer and the concluding Orphan's Kaddish, and suddenly Tamar covered in a veil appeared before me, wrapped herself and sat in an open place which is by the way to Timnath.

At "in an open place," I was gripped by a dazed fever. "In an open place" — what a unique phrase! — and I turned instinctively to Rashi's commentary and read that our Rabbis interpreted it as an open place of Abraham, whom all eyes expect to see. And all at once, the figure of Father arose in me, whose weary bones soaked up the rains of rage and were now sprouting weeds that would pop up when spring came from the cracks between his tombstone and the whitening earth of the Mount of Quietudes. I saw him sitting like the aging Abraham, and waiting for a son who refuses to be born, sitting in the doorway of his shop on the Geula Road at the entrance to the army camp, Mahane Schneller, and waiting for customers, helpless and hopeless.

Even before the prayer came to an end and without saying Kaddish, I fled to the streets and wandered around unaware, muttering like a lunatic the words that were joining together with one another, converging into a poem. In the afternoon, when I got tired of walking, I went home.

On the windowsill, in a deep ceramic bowl that looked like the floor of the sea, rested pomegranates, shriveled summer pomegranates. With growing rage, I stabbed the pomegranates that Mother had bought a few days before his death, and none of us had wanted to eat. All of them, every single one was rotten.

By the time of the afternoon prayer, that original impulse for harmonic self-revelation, described so well by Nadezhda Mandelstam, who was an eyewitness to the poetic labor of her husband

Ossip, an impulse that cannot be artificially faked, or hurried or delayed, was finally consummated. Nothing could any longer stop the flowing internal voice, not even the ban on writing on the Sabbath. And while the voices in the prayer houses clung to the plea "Bless us all, Our Father, with the light of Your Countenance," transparent and wavering, like the dim light of the sun, I sat and wrote "Like Abraham."

> Like Abraham
> my father in the distant days
> would rise up early morning after morning
> and wait for angels
> in the open place.
> He knew they
> bore tidings for him
> as a father who bears his son
> the whole way.
> But the day permeated one of the mountains
> and the evening appeared above it
> like three angels who didn't come.
> Light sown
> in the furrows of his cheeks.
> Another purple grain set
> in his temple that looked like
> a pomegranate seed.

Mother returned Haberman's book to its place, at the top of the heap of new books piling up on my desk, and said that even though her hostility to religion had moderated over the years, that was, of course, no reason to conclude that her basic position had changed regarding the artist's freedom of creation, that, in her opinion, he doesn't have to obey anyone, and certainly not the rabbis and teachers of Halakha, but solely the command of his own heart. With ostentatious impatience, she drummed her fingers on the edge of the table and remarked that I mustn't forget that it was I and no one else who told her, back when I was finishing high school, the brave and skeptical words of Alexander Uri, the saint with the sweet and spiritual eyes, who worked as a janitor in Dr. Wallach's hospital. When I was about to cross Turim Street on my way to the draft office, I was approached by this acquaintance of Father's, who in his youth had been a member of Ha-Shomer Ha-Tsa'ir, and he talked to me about literature and writers, as I have told at length in my book about Bialik, Brenner, and Agnon, and said among other things that Agnon was a great artist who didn't have God in his heart, but a God of his creation.

"There is no God in his heart," Mother was moved and started straightening the books on my desk, grumbling that it was like a decree of fate that her constant struggle to free up time for writing for me was entwined and interlaced from the beginning with the other struggle, the struggle to extricate me from the bonds of faith, that time and again I had foolishly shackled myself in them, out of a fickle response to the gang of agents of The-Holy-One-Blessed-Be-He. Thus, she tried to minimize the damage of the yeshiva students that Father had brought home, thus she tricked me away from the gravitational pull of a group—half underground and half establishment—founded by a Haredi building contractor who subsequently became an important political figure, and if not for her, not only would I have been enlisted in the violent struggle they carried on against Christian religious institutions, but I would also have been tempted by their coaxing, would have left school and joined one of the yeshivas, and thus she even forbade me to set foot in the home of Rabbi Kipnis after we visited him during the week of Sukkoth. On that visit, Father bragged to his venerable rabbi, that a poem I wrote was to be published in the children's newspaper. Our host twisted his mouth with loathing and asked Father if he remembered the Hornostapli synagogue in Obruch, at the end of the Street of the Butchers, on the border of the old cemetery. Father nodded and wanted to cling to his memories, but the Rabbi nipped nostalgia in the bud and said that according to the elders an ancient synagogue had stood there before, about three hundred years old, which was founded by the first Jews who had settled in the district. In that synagogue, Rabbi Kipnis told, a young man always sat at night, one of the learned young men, and between the pages of the Talmud, he wrote his heretical words, until once his candle set fire to the Torah Curtain of the Ark of the Covenant and the whole building burned down. "Ever since the days of Mapke, authors bring a strange fire into the Tabernacle and a flame to the house of Israel," said the Rabbi and charged Father with not letting me squander my talents in vain, but with making me give bulwarks to Torah, and someday I would write "*sforim*" and not "*bikhlakh.*"

"That story is one more of the lies the pious use to put the fear of God into us," Mother's face flushed and she said that, just as I would some day have to tear the mask off the real face of those activists who shirk military duty with the basest kind of hooliganism, so I would have to refute that Haredi legend. (In retrospect, it turned out that the words of Rabbi Kipnis were essentially true. In 1850, the synagogue of the butchers in Obruch burned down and after the fire, Jacob Shmuel Ha-Levi Trachtman, a nineteen-year-old scholar, fled the city and found shelter on a farm, and for about thirteen years he worked as an administrator and book-keeper for its Jewish owners. The articles and books of Tracht-man — who wrote under the noms de plume of "A Simple Man," "A Loyal Man," and "Jacob Didn't Die" — were published from the early 1860s to his death in extreme old age in 1925, in all literary forums, including *HaMagid, HaMelitz,* and *HaCarmel,* and even in the Jerusalem *Havatselet.*)

The anti-clerical tempest subsided with the same suddenness as its shaking and threat to storm the whole world, and with measured, calculated movements, Mother again rummaged in the pile of books, seeking a story or article that would win her heart. I took advantage of the lull to ask how she knew that the poem I had desecrated the Sabbath with was the poem about Father.

"The pomegranates gave you away," she whispered and explained that in my poem she rediscovered that sliced fruit, as she had seen them when she returned home after the Sabbath, and the sight of them went on rolling in her memory ever since like split skulls in the blue bowl on the window sill. And yet, now, in their poetic metamorphosis, sealed with the seal of eternity, they beam and glow much more than before, even though, in truth, no change had taken place in them that was visible to the naked eye.

"If I'm not mistaken, Sherlock Holmes also caught one of his most careful murderers only because of a hair or a crumb of tobacco the culprit mistakenly left behind at the scene of the crime. It's all a matter of sensitivity to details, as you know," Mother waved away — either with a chuckle or with the joy of the victor — the expression of surprise on my face when I heard her revelation, and then she added that I had indeed acted wisely when I decided to include that poem in my book of poems, even though it was pale — "Come on, let's not fool ourselves, an embarrassing mist of flaccidity arises from it, as from wet trees when the sun shines on them after the rain." My poetic image would indeed have benefited if that lovely youthful poem had gone on moldering among the pages of the forgotten journal where it was first published, Mother claimed, but the human side of me would have gone on nursing the offense of the poem with maternal devotion for a long time if I hadn't corrected the wrong by reprinting it.

And indeed, that poem, which was intended to complete the first group of my published poems, had caused me only heartbreak when it was published quite a few years earlier. When, with trembling hands, I leafed through the new issue of the journal where it appeared, I was alarmed to discover that the editor had wielded his pen over the pair of words "open place," which was, as I said, the initial impulse for writing the poem, and had corrected it to "opening of the house." At that moment, the revolting act drove me out of my mind, and instead of making do with restoring the gouged-out eyes to their sockets, in a foolish, infantile rage, in a ceremony of self-punishment, I erased my name wherever it was mentioned in the journal — from the first page, from the table of contents, and from the poem itself, as if repudiating the poem would also cancel and remove the shame cast on it by such caprice. At any rate, I mourned my own death too much, and even when grief replaced wrath and groaning replaced weeping, I still denied my poem and avoided telling anyone about it, most of all Mother, whose very tactful disappearance from the house had allowed it to see the light of day.

"Father is now going up and down among the seven heavens, and in his regular hideout, in the lining of his sweaty Borsolino, swathing his bald head is the poem you wrote about him," Mother greeted me with tears of joy when I came home from the army on a weekend pass one Friday, about a month and a half after the poem was published. She waved the copy of the journal that had fallen into her hands, convinced that it would be a happy surprise for me, and said that through the screen of weeping she imagined she saw Father running around there, above, among his many acquaintances, all those who had ostracized him in the long years of his childlessness, and bragging about his only son who was not only a poet, but who had now even engraved the letters of his wretched fatherhood into a song of grief.

"Did I say something wrong," Mother was shocked when she noticed my stubborn silence. As I said, I didn't let her in on my secret, and reluctantly I was forced to admit the grief the published poem had caused me.

"Even in the most expensive Persian rug, you'll always find some error," she said and explained that the weavers deliberately damage their carpets, inflicting on them some mistake that ruins the perfection. When she was very young and often went to the home of Mrs. Ticho, Mother said, one afternoon, she sat in the parlor of the artist's house waiting for her to finish boiling and sterilizing the surgical instruments of her husband the doctor, and gazed for a long time at one of the colorful tapestries, until she noticed a tiny asymmetry between the edges of the right and left sides of the rug. Mrs. Ticho was moved by the young girl's sharp eye and said that it was indeed not an optical illusion or an unintentional error, but a deliberate blunder. She had found out about it, she said, on one of her visits to the Albertina. The curator of the Viennese museum, an expert in the art of Asian weaving, showed her the almost hidden flaws in every model of the carpets and explained it as the artists' desire to defend themselves against the envy of their competitors and to ward off the evil eye. But, here in Jerusalem, in her husband's eye clinic, added Mrs. Ticho, she had met an old Jewish weaver from the city of Kashan, who laughed at the curator's practical explanation and said that the reason was much more spiritual, as pure and simple as only inspired artists can express it: With the flaw in the rugs, the weavers declare their inferiority to God, who is the symbol of perfection, and admit that those who dwell in clay houses will never be equal to Him and will never reach His level, because the net of error is spread over all life and no one will escape it.

Spellbound by the modesty of the artists of Asia Minor, Mother tried to prove her point with the example of the homes of Mssrs. Davidoff and Tsufiof in the Bukharan neigborhood. The splendid buildings of the silk and pearl merchants, she declared with a soupçon of solemnity, had lost some of their glory because the architects or the owners decided to deliberately damage the perfection of the creation by setting unequal intervals between the windows, thus distorting the symmetry of the façades and expressing their belief that man will never achieve divine perfection.

"Soon it will be the Sabbath, and I'm standing here and pestering you with Persian rugs and Bukharan palaces," laughed Mother and said that in fact the example doesn't suit this case. "The poem about Father is touching even after the bad editing." She almost whispered, weighing every word, and said that someday, when I published a book of poems, I'd be able to correct what was damaged: "Words, unlike human beings, can always be brought back to life."

5

For nearly two years I kept on knocking on the doors of the editors of literary sections, and my total capital was a sheaf of poems, and the shorter they were, as Isaac Babel writes in his memoirs about his youthful stories, the more arrogant they were. The editors' secretaries wanted me to leave the "material" for perusal; they didn't let me into the inner sanctum, and promised I'd get a reply in the mail. And so, every single day, I wasted my time waiting for the mailman. Only once during that whole period did a piece of mail arrive with my name on it, a letter from the editor of *Hatsofe*, and the thickness of the envelope did not bode well. When it was opened, a painfully familiar packet of pages fell out along with a compensatory note from the editor's assistant saying that even though between the lines I had clearly learned my stuff, my poems weren't fit to be published in the journal founded by Rabbi Meir Bar-Ilan, because they were devoid of piety. I quickly condemned the letter to four legal deaths, tore it up and burned it and scattered its ashes in the toilet and flushed them down, but that word "devoid," I couldn't seem to destroy, and it surfaced now and then from its hiding place flooded with the sewage of insult. At the bottom of the letter, the assistant had added the handwritten comment that said, approximately: the period of the Enlightenment, Praise God, has passed away, so why do you want to dance attendance on the secularists? Isn't that why we took pains to establish such splendid educational institutions and placed teachers and educators in them?

Seven years later, when I brought Mother my book of poetry as soon as it came off the press, I realized that, from her hiding place, she had attended my formal execution of the letter of the religious newspaper. "Pity those who were lost but not forgotten,"

Mother laughed and inhaled the fresh smell of printers' ink and the paste of the binding, and said that if you succeed, when you look back, there's nothing more bracing than the letters of rejection you got in your youth.

And yet, one day, after I had despaired of becoming a published poet, I got a note from *Davar* that Ezra Zussman, the newspaper's literary editor, wanted to see me.

On a Wednesday afternoon, I went to the editorial office on Sheinkin Street in Tel Aviv, and with faint heart, I climbed up to his narrow office, loaded with books, on the fourth floor. Zussman was one of the most noble, restrained, and enigmatic poets, who walked around like an angel with drooping wings in that center of Hebrew literary activity. Even though he was in his mid-sixties at that time, Zussman was restrained in writing and still delayed collecting his poems in a book in the belief that he hadn't yet refined and shaped his works properly.

He sat on the edge of the chair, far away from the desk, on his lap were newspapers and mail — I noticed that he lifted his legs a bit and changed their angle to keep the papers from falling — and he absent-mindedly tore a gray paper band wound around *La Nouvelle Observatoire*. Even though it was his office, he seemed to be just as much a stranger there as I was.

"And I am just a passer-by / passing between the gates / gate after gate and no one opens — / and where is the keeper of the gate?" I would read a few years later in his first book of poems, published in 1968, and which ironically I helped get into print as a junior editor at a publishing house.

Well then, he said in a Russian accent, well then . . . And he amazed me with his big, solid nose, which pulled him, his tortured face and his ascetic body down, and with the sleeve of his blue shirt, which was much bigger than his suntanned, bony, thin arm, the arm of a poet and farmer — well then, he said, I read, fine, so . . . And he fiddled with his straw hat, picked it up and put it on the pile of manuscripts on the desk, which didn't look like his desk, a straw hat that looked at that time like the hat of a French vineyard owner. Well, if so . . . we'll print it.

Zussman spoke into his shirt collar, one minute hesitant and cautious, and the next confidently, he spoke as if in an unclear manuscript that still had a lot of blank spaces that needed consideration, erasing, and writing, shifting the transgressions to other pages.

From time to time, somebody came in, waving a typed page and said: Ezra, for God's sake, it's impossible to go like this! Let's see, said Zussman, let's see, and chewed on his glasses, what I wrote here, let's see . . . he said, embarrassed and shy, and the glasses in his mouth roved back and forth. Some time later, after I'd gotten to know him, I learned the meaning of the frequent entrances of the agitated people. Ever since Zussman discovered the wonders of the typewriter, his manuscripts had become a constant nightmare for the typesetters and proofreaders. He'd type his literary articles and his theater criticism on paper of varying widths he chanced upon in the press or the editorial office, but he couldn't fit them to the restraints of the beginning and end of the line, and so part of the words were typed on the platen of the typewriter and not on the page.

Well, then, said Zussman, and wrote something in the left hand corner of my poem. Fine . . . we'll print it.

Did he understand that I wrote the poem after a case of unrequited love? Did he fully understand the metaphors? Did he sense the pain and disappointment that were crystallized and turned into words? Did that soft vague man know the mysteries of love?

Not until years later, when I read "Here my heart loved and here my heart failed, and in its failure it awakes and sings," did I ask forgiveness in my heart for the dullness and arrogance of that fledgling poet who thought he was the first living creature.

Zussman talked a long time. I didn't know when to go, finally I stood up.

"You're going," he said and I didn't know if that was a statement or a question or a request. When I stood at the door, half out into the corridor, I gathered my courage and asked: "The poem — that is, the poem, my poem, do you like it?"

"I read it," said Zussman and looked at me in amazement, probably wondering if I really understood him. (Only years later did I know that that was the greatest grace a poet could get from his fellow man.)

About a week later, I was summoned to the proofreaders' office.

"Fiksler's looking for you," they told me on the phone. "It's about the poem."

The small office, which seemed to be hanging over the noisy typesetting room halfway between the press and the editorial offices, hummed at that hour of the morning like a Lithuanian yeshiva during seder, when all the yeshiva students sit together in one big room and study aloud with a partner. Two junior proofreaders were reading the texts of advertisements to one another (we owe good proofreading to anyone who pays money to the newspaper — that is, the advertiser — not to someone the newspaper pays royalties to — that is, the writer — Shapiro, the director of the press once said furiously). On a wooden carousel that served as a telephone stand in an opening between the two rooms, leaned a dignified Jew, with a Wolfson beard, and roared into the receiver: "Tell him Lang says 'candlesticks' and not 'cendelsticks' in so many words." In a corner, next to the window, sat a white-haired man with black sleeves on his arms, his shirt buttoned up to his neck, marking galleys with a foppish ritualism.

"You don't know vowel markings," he growled at me. I think he was sucking a cough drop at that time. Then he swallowed and said in a voice that still bore the traces of a Transylvanian yeshiva student's melody: "A poet has to know vowel markings."

Isaac Fiksler was the uncrowned king of the proofreaders' room. He was the only one who proofread the articles of the important authors and essayists who contributed to the paper, including Shazar, Dov Sadan, Sh. Shalom, Eliezer Steinman, and David Zakkai. That was his bonus. Later on, when I worked with him, and Fiksler asked me to proofread Zakkai's "In Short," I knew we had become friends.

Many people would come to him for his expert advice, and he never replied without first checking the Bible, Jastrow, *The Complete Lexicon* or *Mishpat ha-Urim*. In an emergency, he allowed himself to glance at the dictionary of Yehudah Gur. "Grazovski," he called him familiarly. He left Even-Shoshan's dictionary to "those with empty noggins." "I don't rely on a dictionary I could participate in composing," said Fiksler alluding to the immortal wit of Groucho Marx.

Like a genuine scholar, his whisper was a fire crackling and all his words were like coals hissing, and he derived a rather perverse pleasure from a sharp and delicate teasing of the Mapai activists who would dispute at length about Zionism and socialism on the pages of the newspaper. Once a party leader came to him, who had written a flattering article about Golda Meir at the time when she was secretary of the party, and asked him if he was entitled to write that the aforementioned party member had arbitrated that issue thoroughly for seven clean days. "At her age?" replied Fiksler in dismay. "What, is she Our Matriarch Sarah?" Lang and Pesakh Milin burst out laughing, while the political journalist, who didn't know the Halakhic expression about counting the cleanliness of a menstruating woman, slipped out ashamed and went up to Zakkai to ask him to explain the obscure answer of the irascible proofreader.

"You don't know vowel markings," Fiksler repeated to me in our first meeting and handed me the manuscript of my poem, with its vowel markings corrected in green ink with a fountain pen.

"Do you know what Agnon says about that? Agnon says, 'Poems need vowel markings. Poems without vowel markings are like a wedding without dancing,'" and his rather metallic irritable laughter suddenly broke off as if his vocal chords gave out.

Every Friday, I'd get up early in the morning and go far away to the newspaper kiosk that sold *Davar*, open the paper with trembling hands and learn that the poem wasn't printed.

At first I explained the delay by the long line of poets, but when a long time passed, I secretly cursed all the poets who published a new book of poems, celebrated an anniversary, or even passed away into the beyond.

About once a month, I'd sneak into the press and, unobserved, would open the heavy drawer where the lead lines of my poem were placed, tied with wire. The lines were indeed set there, but additional blocs of poems were piling up all around, threatening to choke my little poem, the poor in Manasseh. At night I'd have nightmares that the cords grew weak and the lines of the other poems got mixed up in the lines of my poem — and that's how it would be published.

Later, Yossl Birstein told me what happened to his first poems, which were published in a trilingual Jewish newspaper in Australia. On Friday when, like me, he opened the paper with shaking hands, he was glad to find his debut work in it, but when he started reading, he was stunned. Interspersed between his lines were lines he didn't recognize. He waited impatiently all weekend, and early Monday morning, he lay in wait for the editor at the street corner. At nine o'clock, the editor appeared, a tired, bitter, old Jew. Birstein tugged at his sleeve and told him of the tragedy that happened. "I know, *yunger man*, I know," said the editor and invited the young poet into his office, and there he told him that he had also written poems in his youth, poems no one wanted to publish, and ever since then, they had lain sadly in his desk drawers. The poems he really couldn't publish because they were immature poems and didn't suit his years, but when he came across a young poet and published his poems, he added to them some of his bashful stanzas that still needed correction.

On the days after my nightmares, I'd return to the press and lay in wait for Aryeh Lerner, Ezra Zussman's assistant on the editorial staff of the literary supplement. Lerner, the first one to translate *The Little Prince* into Hebrew, would show up at the editorial office at unlikely times, slip inside wearing his biblical sandals and carrying his heavy leather briefcase, filled with bottles of cognac and pamphlets of poetry, which almost dragged him down, would look around with the eyes of a hunted animal, an extinguished cigarette in the corner of his mouth, and would spend hours at the press, at the lay-out cart.

First, I'd ask him about the fate of my poem, as if it didn't make any difference as far as I was concerned, then I pleaded with him, begged, and finally, after nine months, after I had tormented myself, pondered whether he and Zussman had changed their mind, whether they were disgusted with the poem and didn't like it anymore, whether they had forgotten it, whether they were hatching some plot against me, I came to Lerner and demanded that he give me back the poem.

"Come to me at the press on Wednesday morning, when I lay out the newspaper," said Lerner and evaded giving an answer for the nth time.

On Wednesday, at the press, I found him standing docile and disciplined next to Isaac Furman, the master typesetter of *Davar*, who moved blocs of lead in his big, open, and overflowing hand from the trays to the lay-out cart.

"You see how we work?" said Lerner. "First we lay out the articles, then we fill the cellar with a story or an essay." Lerner talked and Furman carried out what he said. "Now, as you see, we have windows left in the page . . ." I still didn't know what he was getting at. "And the hollow windows I fill with poems." And the assistant editor pointed to a brown cardboard folder stained with colors of ink and sweat, crammed with sheets of poetry, and said, "And now I measure the length and breadth of the window and look for a poem that fits it."

I was dumbstruck.

"When I've got a window that fits your poem, it'll be published. Not one week before."

Tears filled my eyes. In his eyes, I was nothing but filler. And yet I didn't say anything and went on standing there like a fool. Suddenly Lerner was called to the phone. Isaac Furman put his arm around my shoulders, there was something very paternal in that gesture of his big, sweaty, blackened arm.

"Next week you'll get into the paper, I don't care if I have to crop the tail of one of those graphomaniacs." Furman leafed through the calendar and said that I'd get into the last issue of the year, "By 1965 you'll be a seasoned poet."

"And what will Lerner say?" I asked anxiously.

"Pooh, down here, I'm the editor," said Furman and added that if I didn't believe him I could ask Nathan, and he meant Alterman.

And that's indeed what happened, but after the first of the week, at the end of the obstacle course, the final invisible hurdle was still in store for me, separating me from the goal. On Wednesday afternoon, when they took longer than usual to finish laying out the page of the weekend edition and the New Year's edition which was to come out on Sunday, and the veteran Lerner rushed to his office so as not to have to come back to the pressroom until the next Wednesday, Furman took me from the proofreaders' office, where I had begun working secretly, without the permission of the army, and pushed me into the arena.

"Your time has come to rule, buddy," shouted the leader of the typesetters in a loud voice, and as he did he took out of the page that had been set just a little while earlier the poem of some noisy modernist the deputy editor was fond of, and sent it with his adjutant to the land of cut-out, to be abandoned to the hazards of time.

"Zalman," — this time he meant Shazar — "once told me that one angel doesn't carry out two missions," chuckled Furman and sent his second adjutant, another obedient lad with a mustache, one of the students of "Working Youth," to the storage cabinets to bring my bashful poem.

The lord of miracles, who lowers this one and raises that one, rubbed his hands with glee to instruct me that here, in his kingdom, his breath alone works mighty deeds, makes news, sows righteousness, sprouts salvation, but my joy vanished at the sight of the apprentice typesetter standing erect between the open drawers and waving his hands desperately to inform me that my lead lines with vowel markings had disappeared as if the earth had split open and swallowed them. The impatient Furman who joined in the search had no ideas either. When the galley sheets that were supposed to be kept in the file of the literary section delivered to the press weren't found either, I was sure a malicious hand had been sent to take the poem out of the world.

"Just don't get paranoid," my benefactor encouraged me when he saw my defeated stare at the blind lead window, and said that only last week Lerner and Zussman had lost a manuscript of Sh. Shalom. He drank from the glass of milk that was handed to him, licked the crust off and imbibed it with a noisy grunt, and said that if I found him the manuscript of the poem by three o'clock, he himself would make sure it was reset and inserted into its place, as if nothing had happened. "If Furman promises, Furman delivers!"

All my attempts to write the disappeared poem from memory came to naught. And since the only copy of it at that moment was in Jerusalem and there was no phone in our house, I forced myself, even though it was very unpleasant, to use the emergency arrangement meant solely for trouble and summoned Mother to the phone in the house of our neighbor, Mrs. Israelit. Frantic and gasping, Mother listened to what had happened to me at the press, obediently repeated my instructions of how to find the poem among my many papers, and fifteen minutes later, from

Mr. Ribicoff's pharmacy, word by word she dictated to me the words of love I had whispered to the girl who had rejected my suit in a matter-of-fact, precise, detached voice.

On Friday, the twenty-seventh day of the month of Elul, 1964, the poem was published and it seemed to me that the whole world was waiting for that with bated breath. But nobody said a thing about it.

"How's the poem?" I assaulted Mother when I came home on leave Friday afternoon.

"Unfortunately, I haven't read it yet," she apologized and told of her anger at the customers who almost drove her crazy because the challahs were too pale.

"But you read it on the phone two days ago," I said incredulously.

"On Wednesday, I only dictated it to you, today I'll read it," and she said that in the morning she had managed to buy five copies of the paper to send to those wicked teachers, who in her opinion didn't appreciate me enough. Finally, as expected, Mother didn't go through with her idea, and the newspapers remained lying in reserve in the clothes closet, under the sheets, next to the photos of Yael and Tovele and the American visa.

All that Sabbath, Mother kept rereading the "City of Gold" until she must have known it by heart, and on Saturday night, before I went back to Tel Aviv, she said that the girl I wrote about in the poem didn't deserve that honor. I told mother that I still loved her, even though she didn't want me, and maybe, I added, it was precisely because she was so terrific that the poem came out good enough to be printed in the newspaper of Berl Katznelson and Moshe Beilinson. "Nonsense," said Mother. "That's how it always is — the higher the mound of garbage, the more beautiful the flowers growing on it."

And whenever Furman met me at the press, especially when I went down to get my work card signed, he'd ask, "Well, did they pay you yet?"

Two months later, I got a royalty check.

"They paid me," I told Furman that day.

"How much?" he asked, and I made some answer.

"Come on, let's check the calculation," said Furman and passed his hand over his big forehead. He multiplied the number of lines by the price of every line according to the rate and then he said: "Go to the accountant's office and tell them Furman said they robbed you."

"How?" I asked.

"They didn't pay you for the double space between the stanzas."

Isaac Furman was a credible man, and without suspecting him, I went to the accountant and demanded more.

Comrade Tomer Peretz burst out laughing and told me to go to hell.

Tears filled my eyes again.

The next day, when I met Furman, I asked him why he had misled me and made me the butt of a joke, didn't I have more than enough bitterness because of that poem.

"I did that so you'd know that a poet is also paid for his silences."

A grimace of pain passed over Mother's face when I told her that, after his offense had faded somewhat and his moral lesson was no longer in doubt. She clenched her lips and didn't say a thing.

"You don't think Furman's right?"

"That's not what's bothering me," she said slowly, and explained, choosing her words carefully, that, as far as she knew, writing a real poem is such a complicated and delicate thing that depends on doing so many things at the same time. So she didn't understand how I had any energy left over to get involved in peripheral matters. "You should do your work. Sometimes that by itself is too much for a person."

Similar words, steeped in pain and disappointment, she repeated to me about six years later, when the date for the publication of my book of poems was approaching.

For two summers, the sun had roasted the galleys of my first book, waiting on the shelf next to the window in the offices of Am Oved Publishers, for its turn to be sent to the press. Every morning, when I came to work as a junior proofreader at that publishing house, I'd secretly visit the sheaf of poems, smooth the bulges stamped in the paper by the lead lines when the hand press went over them, wipe off the dust that collected between the pages, and glance with damp and docile eyes at the commanders of the publishing house, hoping their heart would soften and they'd at last deign to print my poems.

In those days, my whole world was bound up in that thin pack of papers, wrapped in a blue rubber band that was cracked by the heat—the essence of my pains and delights and memories, which had donned the firm cloak of words.

One day in the month of Nisan, when tiny spiders and spring-time bookworms filled the shelf of page-set books with new life, my sheaf suddenly disappeared and left behind a bright spot on the galley sheets of the book beneath it.

The head of production, who told me the good news that afternoon, was practical as usual and advised me to think about the cover, in order to prevent further delays. "You must have thought of something already," he either asked or stated. He spoke to me softly, wanting to reward me for the long grief, and said that the publisher would grant my request even if the cover was drawn in color and would cost more than usual.

After some hesitation, I called a young artist, whose drawings I liked in those days, and asked if she'd agree to draw the cover for my book of poems.

The joy in her voice flattered me, and we arranged to meet during the week of Passover in a small café at the end of Dizengoff Street. Our talk delighted her, and when we finished, the artist collected the bundle of galleys in her bag and said we'd talk again in a week, when she finished reading the poems.

On the day of the appointment, I called her back. If I had been more alert, I would certainly have sensed some reserve and fear in her voice. "We should meet," she said. "Why don't you come to our house when you're in Jerusalem. By the way, my husband"— and here she said the name of a rather well-known critic of poetry—"also wants to talk with you about the poems." Excited, I quickly set a date to meet.

At night, I came to their house on the slope of one of the streets winding down to the Valley of the Cross. The husband, a stocky fellow, with a repulsive, unshaved face, let me into the gloomy house. A tiny table lamp cast a circle of light on my sheaf of poems, which was put in a ceramic bowl along with some rotting Valencia oranges. His wife had to go out of town on urgent business, he said without raising his eyes to me, moved his tongue over his gums, trying to gather up the remnants of food that were stuck to them, and when he succeeded, he chomped the crumbs with a grunt. "We read your poems," he said. "No doubt you're an epigone of Aaron Shabtai. You took a lot of material from his book *The Teachers' Room.*" I was drenched with sweat. I said that I had indeed read Shabtai's book and loved it, but I took the material of my poems from the experience of my own life. "I'm not talking about love," said the critic coldly, burped, and a strong smell of smoked fish, mixed with bad breath, filled the unventilated room. "I'm talking about taking, about stealing." The syntax, he argued, is Shabtai par excellence, the family materials like the grandmother and the aunts, and even the opening of one of the poems, "In the Early Fifties," flowed into my poems straight from *The Teachers' Room.* He thought I had reached the peak with the use I had made of "Tin Buckets." That's a typical Shabtai phrase, and how did I dare to use it. "Why didn't you write 'copper buckets' instead of tin buckets?" suggested the artist's husband. I very foolishly tried to explain to him that in the years I talk about in my poems, the 1950s, there were only tin buckets in our house. Copper buckets, the buckets of the inheritance, had been lost or sold, and plastic buckets hadn't yet come into the world. In our house, as in other houses, there were tin buckets, "all-purpose" buckets we bought with the Dov Yosef's ration coupons. "Nonsense," said the critic and continued the monologue which was all erudite arrogance, contempt, and hatred.

As if my body were penetrated with the venom of a viper, I sat across from him for a long time and heard insults, and couldn't pull myself together and get up. "If you don't weed the conspicuous influences of Shabtai out of your book, I won't be able to recommend to my wife to draw the cover," he concluded in his Polish diction, as he led me to the door.

I left his house, scolded and depressed, holding the sheaf of poems. I hated them. I hated myself. Later, when the young and promising artist and the aging poetry critic split up, I was to realize that I had fallen victim to the turgid and suspicious relations between them. The hot-tempered artist cuckolded her husband a lot, and he suspected that I was one of those who got into her bed. She denied that vigorously, and he demanded that she prove it by refusing to draw the cover of my book and letting him take care of me in his own destructive way. But when I left their house, naturally, I didn't know all that.

All night long I wandered around like a sleepwalker in the dew-covered streets of Jerusalem, regretting my life, wanting my soul to die. And on the first bus, where some early-rising soldiers were dozing, I returned to Ramat Gan. Mother was sitting on the fence in front of our house and waiting for me. Without a word, she listened to me as I wept and told her what was happening to me. When I finished talking, she poured me a cup of coffee and said that a poet has to write poems, that's all—not to worry about the covers of his books and not to meet with taste-setting critics and literary scholars to try to promote his case. Each one should do his own task.

"And now, we've talked enough," Mother shook herself out of her consolation of mourners and went into the shower to see if there was any hot water, and when she came back she said: "You can take a shower," and she added that to that day she was proud of two practical habits she had succeeded in passing on to me in my childhood: how to tie a knot that can always be undone and how to climb on a chair. "Lean the back on the wall so that when you get down, you won't hit it and fall," she'd repeat to me and explain that everything designed to make life easy is ultimately what trips you when you come down.

6

Mother's pride and joy, which increased when my first book appeared, quickly died out and was replaced by grievous disappointment. It was hard for her accept what she saw as the endless aftermath of the publication, and more than anything else, she despised the tortuous calculations with those who didn't deign to promote it with the favor it deserved, and the claims against those who praised it whom I considered stingy with compliments. And so she suffered from the weekly expectation with which I had infected everyone around me with the appearance of the Friday newspapers whose literary supplements would determine whether the day of rest was either a feast and a joy or a eulogy, to baldness, and to girding with sackcloth. What was mainly disgusting in her eyes was my compulsory fiddling with file folders of reviews and the requisite thank-you notes sent to me by poets and authors to whom I had proffered my thin booklet with overly enthusiastic dedications. "Like all the men in our family, you also prefer to turn your eyes back instead of looking bravely forward," Mother tormented me when she could no longer restrain herself, and she even scolded me for becoming more and more like that beaten-down Gladiola, her dead girlhood friend, whose son, who inherited not only her gladiola height, but also her madness, was one of the great luminaries shining in the firmament of Jerusalem basketball. All the years, Mother's friend hadn't gotten any pleasure from her son, who, as soon as he reached adolescence, had smoked openly, chased after women, curled his hair, strutted, and groped with his eyes — in short, an empty reckless boy. The Gladiola often complained to Mother that the varicose veins at the top of her legs came from standing so much at the closed doors of the principal's office and the teachers' room, when she was called to be reprimanded for her son's deeds. Until one day, that excellent young gentleman was imbued with the rage of basketball: He joined a local team, reaped applause, was lauded, and even the Tel Aviv newspapers started contacting him. At the same time, his mother left the corridors of the school with a sigh of relief and started spending her mornings in Mr. Harlap's small shop, where she carefully surveyed the newspapers and bought every issue that contained a mention of her son's name, either good or bad. In those days, their house looked like the Maccabi dressing room in the "Hero's Hall" in the courtyard of the Lemel School. When we went there we saw nothing but sweaty cotton shirts lying on the chairs, the dining room table, and the counter, and hanging on the window handles. Balls and springs to strengthen muscles had rolled into the corners, and gym shoes were all over. Mother wrinkled her nose at the smells, and seemed to ask casually if the time hadn't finally come for the young man to turn his hand to a useful trade. And yet, unlike her humility and perpetual sadness in the pre-basketball era, Gladiola now felt good. She'd place before us office folders stuffed with newspaper clippings cut out with a loving hand and pasted onto blue or pink sheets of construction paper, and as she followed the guest's leafing hand, she'd make sure it did not skip even one newspaper clipping, she'd try in vain to bounce one of the balls like a player, and as she did she'd recite again the praises lavished on her son on the radio. One day, when Gladiola was bad-mouthing some contemptible journalist who had slandered her son, her dear son burst into the house like a hurricane. "Kiss my ass," he silenced his mother, and after he had decanted a bottle of milk into his guts and blurted a series of farts while hopping lightly in place a few times, he announced that instead of wasting his time on the sheer nonsense they wrote about him in *Sports News*, he'd hurry back to the gym and train for the derby on the Sabbath.

"If the Torah were not given to us, not only would we learn modesty from the cat, robbery from the ant, and nakedness from the dove," Mother extracted wisdom like the preachers, "but we'd also learn to distinguish between wheat and chaff, from the champion who farts and jumps." And with those enigmatic words, Mother tried to get me back on track, to persuade me to drop all those peripheral issues like pursuing honor and winning a seat at

268

HAIM
BE'ER

the Eastern Wall, and to go back to my desk. But with the dissipation of the last veil of euphoria about the publication of my book, the bitter truth was revealed in all its ugly nakedness—an incomprehensible malignant silence of an inconceivable intensity permeated me and paralyzed me completely.

Mother, who discerned that immediately with her alert senses, didn't hesitate to change her position, and a few weeks later, as if by chance, she decreed that, all in all, silence isn't a catastrophe, but is the internal, less visible, aspect of speech. Silence and speech, she said, are like a reversible garment worn sometimes on one side, sometimes on the other, as need be, just like the cowboy jacket I got from America for my bar-mitzvah, a jacket with one smooth waterproof side and the other side covered with lamb's wool. And ignoring my uneasiness at discussing the muteness that had attacked me, she added that for someone who writes, dry periods are just as important as flourishing periods, of course, as long as you don't flinch from them or fear them and don't attribute a destructive significance to them, but let them fill their function.

"In point of fact, it's more correct to say that this is an incubation period," a sudden softness poured into her voice, and she gathered into her lap the stuffed chick that Roni, her little granddaughter, had left on the sofa the day before, and said that every creation required a minimal period of hatching, and warm privacy, a secret lair hidden from sight, before it sallies forth into the world.

"I didn't imagine that writing is a disease in your eyes," I didn't bother to hide my anger, hoping that would make her leave me alone at long last.

"And I saw in my imagination the darling chicks that filled Uncle Jacob's incubator," laughed Mother and ran the soft down of the toy chick over her cheek and remarked that if it was hard for me to accept that comparison because of the sick association it evoked in me, she'd try to convince me with a more positive tale. Just before I got married, when she was looking for fabric fit for a dress she could wear under the wedding canopy, she heard Yoskovitch, owner of the fabric store, tell someone who came to his shop a story about the rabbi, "Sefat Emet," a story etched in her memory mainly because of the moral in it. Once, said the merchant, who was a kinsman of the Rebbe of Gur, when the Tsaddik was about to go to the healing springs in one of the spas and the Hasids accompanied him to the border, one bold yeshiva student hung on the window of the train as it started leaving the station, and asked the Rebbe to grant him "*letzt gelt,*" that is, to tell him words of the Torah as a parting gift. The Rebbe pointed to the puffing locomotive and said more or less: "Do you know, young man, where the locomotive gets the strength to pull all the cars? Because it confines all the steam inside itself . . ."

Mother handed down her opinion in praise of restraint and waiting, and went back to the traditional image of Miriam, the sister of Moses, standing at a distance and watching him, trying with all her might to keep her eyes off my still bleeding wounds of muteness. And yet, when I found it hard to hide from her my harsh envy of the success of one of my acquaintances whose new novel excited both readers and critics with its sophisticated structure, its teasing and surprising plot, and the linguistic sparks, which were like worms to a corpse in my flesh, she didn't hesitate to assert her judgment about the book and its reception, and in the process she also hinted at an explanation of my long silence. "Believe me, it's a superfluous book that will quickly sink into oblivion." She wanted me to put my trust in her literary taste, which hadn't disappointed thus far, and she added that the book that was keeping me awake was a smug book, a performance of self-satisfaction and nothing else. A real book isn't a noble cultural act as outside observers who aren't experts might think, but something wild, unbridled, written out of compulsion. "That's a compulsion that has nothing to do with peace of mind or the artificial sophistication that gave birth to that book." She said that and pushed away the book that had been given to me by my friend with a warm dedication in the hope that I'd write a sympathetic review of it in one of the literary supplements. "If you think about it objectively," she stared at my orphaned desk and at the pile of dust-covered papers on it, "you'll have to admit that it takes quite a bit of nerve to burst out of your private niche and demand that the world stop and listen to what you've got to say." She stood up, paced back and forth in the room, and said that in her eyes the closest thing to writing a book was the custom of delaying the reading. Everybody is entitled to delay the reading in the synagogue, just as everybody is entitled, even if he has no talent, to sit down and write a book, and yet only rarely does one of the worshippers dare to get up, pound on the *bima* when the open Torah scroll is placed there, and demand that the congregation halt the reading because he has something he must protest, an act of iniquity that cannot be passed over in silence.

"You must surely remember Mr. Eliezer Eliner," said Mother and her eyes flashed, and without waiting for my answer, she added that that pious scholar, who used to come to our shop from time to time, about ten years ago, moved heaven and earth not to deport Dr. Sobol from Israel. The man, a Jewish psychiatrist, who was accused in the United States of spying for the Soviets and sentenced to life imprisonment, had fled here and asked for political asylum, but the authorities quickly granted the American demand and decided to deport him there. Eliner, said Mother, didn't flinch from coming on the Sabbath to the bourgeois synagogue of Heikhal Shlomo, where the Minister of the Interior Shapiro worshipped, and started a turmoil during the Torah reading, with the demand, stemming from a profound moral conviction, not to give in to the brutality of Ben-Gurion and not to turn a man who fled over to the hands of his pursuers. Mother examined whether I had correctly understood the comparison of preventing the reading and said that only when a person has something really important to say will he sit at his desk and write what's in his heart, and not a minute before.

About three years later, Mother surprisingly violated her firm resolve to avoid any open interference in the silence that descended on me. It was at the height of the very dreary winter after the Yom Kippur War, when my second leave from the army ended and I had to go back over the Canal.

That whole Sabbath, I tried to calm my family and I delighted them with stories about the infantry command I was assigned to, in the trenches of the camp for decoy Egyptian missiles in Jenifa —about the target practice held by the master sergeant and his pair of assistants, shooting eggs and tomatoes at mock targets in the wadi going down from ancient Jebel Ataka; about the gluttony of the brigade rabbi, a paratrooper with a ruddy face and eager for battle, for cheese triangles and anchovy paste; about the helicopters passing over us every morning on their way to the negotiations at kilometer 101, and about the personal servant of the CO, a bald, feeble-minded fellow who walked behind his master wherever he went, carrying an easy chair looted from the Egyptians so he could put his weary behind on it. Mother listened to my stories with clenched lips and a frightened look expressing total disbelief. In the late afternoon, when my wife took the children to the nearby playground, Mother took advantage of our time alone together to say that my extinguished eyes and the apathy I had shown during my previous leave, about two months before, worried her less than the jubilation I was trying to present today. "Your eyes are telling completely different stories," she had trouble suppressing her feelings. "You can tell me the truth. You know I'm as silent as the tomb."

In the fading light, I told her things I had sworn not to tell anyone, and then when total darkness enveloped us, as on those distant Sabbath nights in the Hungarian Houses, when Grandmother sat in her corner and softly sang *"Got fun Abraham, fun Isaac un fun Jacob, hit dayn folk Israel,"* and the two of us whispered together, I could no longer help revealing to her how one day, in Zir Tartur, not far from the Lexicon Junction, a lone Egyptian bomber attacked our convoy, and an oil tanker in front of us exploded. Fragments of it flew in all directions, and we ran, pale and drenched in sweat, to look for the driver. On a sand dune, among shell casings and some low desert bush I saw an arm — one arm torn off, suntanned, hairy, with a big steel watch on it, a very virile watch that had stopped.

The next day at dawn, Mother appeared at our house to go with me to the bus. We walked in the rainy gloom — at night there had been a sudden downpour — and she fought with me to take the heavy kitbag, persisted in carrying it to the bus stop, and murmured that I'd still have many chances throughout the day to drag it myself. All alone, we stood silent in the shed, watching the pesky drizzle. "If only you have rain like this across the Suez," she said at last, and as if she had overcome internal obstacles, she added: "That arm, the arm you saw there, you'll write something about that." And without waiting for the bus to come, she kissed me and hurried off, and the grayish light of the morning that was struggling to rise illuminated her as she walked.

So it's no wonder that my plan to surprise Mother failed a year later when I came to her holding a sheaf of pages I had just finished writing, something I had secretly been working on diligently ever since I had been released from the long reserve duty in the Sinai. Her room, overlooking the tops of the cedars and sandalwood trees of the small park behind her house and the mountains of Judah turning blue beyond them on the horizon, was filled for a moment with the reflections of the deeds that yielded to the force of my imagination, and with the familiar images that had shrunk to dialogues, gestures, and vistas of longing. Expanding and contracting at random, with arbitrary movements, that deliberately cut themselves off from their rhythms and from their real durations, the flashes of this imaginary biography of pain blending the lighted days of the child with the nightmare times of the adult were cast on Mother's attentive face, as if it were a taut screen.

"I didn't have even a shadow of a doubt that when your period of paralyzing despair came to an end, you'd write mature prose, just like you learned to read when you were a child." Those were Mother's first words when I finished reading her the sheaf of pages, reminding me of how I learned to read after both the teacher and Father despaired of me and thought I'd be illiterate.

After I reread the essay that would later be the opening chapter of *Feathers*, Mother suggested a series of corrections, including the recommendation that I give up the uninspired name I had given that chapter and call it "Circle Circle Cranes," as in Mattityahu Shelem's poem, as the angry mother hums incessantly, holding her son's hand on their way home from Bahira Shechter. "The round movements of the birds' hovering without a sound, high in the sky," said Mother, "evoke the internal rhythm of the story." And she suggested that I send the story to one of the literary supplements, maybe the editor would like it and would print it in the Passover issue.

I won't deny that ever since this block of prose began taking shape in me, the fear that Mother would be angry at me has lodged in my heart, or that at least, she'd be unhappy that there are too many lines of resemblance stretching from her and Father to the parents of the narrator in the story. And that fear, which grew more intense as the work of writing came to an end, reached its peak when I sat before her and read the words. But the delicate mimicry of her face, her eyes shrinking with pleasure and the occasional peals of laughter that were hard for her to stifle, quelled my fears so completely that before I parted from her, I dared to reveal them to her. Mother, who was leaning on the ledge of the balcony and examining the crests of the sandalwood trees that glittered and dyed the park a coral red as it woke up from its fall of leaves, straightened up, turned to me and said with an implacable force: "You and I know that Father isn't Father and Mother isn't me, and what your Aunt Ayala will say or our real neighbors in Jerusalem, really doesn't interest me, but I'm worried about you because that question does concern you." Then she leafed through the pages, which she asked me to leave for her to read that night ("You have to read a book with your eyes, not hear it from announcers or intermediaries," she once refused my invitation to join me at a reading. "In this private meeting I don't need intermediaries") and commented, with disappointment blended with pain, that the time had come for me to be immunized at last from the demands and extortions of those around me. My destructive tendency to think too much about the world, she said, would make me betray the internal truth of the story. "You'll feel an obligation to refine and improve the characters of the father and mother in the story and you'll remove the demonic and grotesque bases in their personalities, so no stain will stick to me or your father, God forbid, until your story will fit the literary anthologies they teach in the Mizrahi schools."

"So, you're suggesting I change everything to the third person?" I asked in despair.

"Are you crazy? You don't touch a story like that," she laughed. "I'm suggesting that in the next chapters, you put us in, me and Father, as secondary characters, not especially important ones. Ayala and the neighbors will be glad to find us there, glorious and beautiful and mainly optimistic and filled with love of our fellow man, while you'll be free to make your hero's father and mother into whatever you like."

Her solution, so simple and yet so brilliantly sophisticated, surprised me.

Mother caught the flash of joy that lit up in my eyes and said that Tellingtor, the one who had a shoe-polish factory in Akhva, used to say that the work of the Lord should indeed be done out of great innocence, but to get to that level of innocence, you have to be cunning as a fox.

I could have gone on for days telling of the many events that come together and split apart in a blend of times and places, but even the delightful charm, which seems to be the essence of engaging in these deals, couldn't wipe out of my memory even for a short time the knowledge that this life, whose freshness and original splendor I wanted to restore has already been destroyed in fact, has sunk into nothing, has perished. Moreover, the more the rebellious remnants of memory responded to my whispering and came together into some image, even if partial, the more palpable and certain has our lord Death, whose shadows were cast on the narrator from the start, become, and his reign is poured over everything and his is boldness and dominion.

A few days after "Circle Circle Cranes" was published in the Passover edition of *Ma'ariv* and I was already writing the next chapter, Mother was afflicted with lethal headaches and blurred vision in her left eye. After running around by herself to doctors, who quickly dismissed her complaints as acute migraine or a well-known symptom of emotional distress, one morning she showed up in the emergency room of Beilinson Hospital and announced that she wouldn't leave until they found the cause of her torments. We learned all that at lunch that afternoon. Until my dying breath, I will continue to be tortured by the disheveled hair, the blazing face, and the eyes frenzied with the dread of death, that appeared in the door of our house when she returned from the hospital. She threw herself on the sofa and for several minutes wept horribly. Dr. Aravit, a young and wise neurosurgeon, the first one who examined her properly, she told between sobs, discovered a tumor in her cortex that was quickly bursting into the eye socket and pressing on the visual nerve, so they had to operate at once, that week.

About half an hour later, we reluctantly returned to the table. Mother stunned us with how quickly she managed to regain control of her feelings. She washed her face, combed her hair and wanted to join us in our truncated lunch. "I haven't eaten anything since morning. I'm starving to death," she said in her usual way. As she was bounced around in the two buses from Beilinson

Hospital, she told us, she decided that this very afternoon, she'd go with the two grandchildren and buy them gifts — a wristwatch for Roni and a tricycle for Memmi — so they'd remember her fondly, since you can never know what kind of broken vessel with a twisted face would come off the operating table.

She rejected the applesauce and preferred a cup of tea instead. "When my time came to go out into the world, the angel sent me to God to get my allotment of years from Him," she said, trying not to lose her grip on the reins of humor. "And it turns out that in the end He's no more than the greengrocer: He puts seventy apples in my bag, one apple a year, but I was foolish and gluttonous as only a little baby can be, and I asked for more, so He bent down to the crate of bad fruit under the counter and added another three rotten and wormy apples. Now, it looks like I'll have to eat them up too."

The last two and a half years of her life were a series of hospitals, operations, radiation and chemotherapy treatments, and nevertheless she tried with all her might to live the rest of her life to the full. "I'm not a sick woman," she looked straight at the social worker of the oncology department who came to probe her character. "I've just got a meningioma." And just as she didn't give up on herself, so she also kept on demanding that I go on working on the novel — even though I was worrying about her health and the trouble we had with her — so that I wouldn't lose touch with writing again.

Of course, I was free to write only in the remissions between the eruptions of the disease, when we were foolishly tempted to believe for a while that the bitter death had been removed. "Everything you and I go through will finally go into the book," she apologized with an embarrassed smile when I found her bending over the bathroom sink, fishing out strands of hair that had fallen out from the radiation. "Just like the shrieks of the seagulls went into the poems of Dylan Thomas." I admired her expertise in the details of the biography of the Welsh poet whose poems she had never read, but she explained that in the early months of my army service, when the silence and solitude of the long winter nights became almost too hard for her to bear, she alleviated them by reading. And then she read somewhere that Dylan Thomas told that often, when he sat in his small, isolated house, stuck to the steep cliff of the rim of the bay, and wrote a poem, the seagulls would pass over him with their hoarse and ugly shrieks, and those seagulls were immediately fixed in the picture of his poem, like a chance passerby who winds up in someone else's photo. After her death, among her many books, I found *In That Awful Wind*, and between its pages a postcard I sent her from basic training marking the experience of a visit of Yehuda Amichai in the wild vistas of his beloved poet.

During those remissions, which unfortunately grew shorter with time, I would come to her house almost every evening and read her the pages of the book that was being written. And even though we knew that, in that race, death would ultimately overtake us, that daily ceremony filled her, and why deny it—me, too—with a pitiful joy of triumph.

When I read to her for the last time, Mother, as usual, sat straight up in bed facing the window and was fascinated watching the clouds borne on the east wind, the mountains in whose bosom she would find rest at the end of that summer, and she listened to the story of the narrator and his father walking in the middle of the night to the scene of the blessing of the sun on Mount Zion. That whole night, before dawn on Wednesday, the twenty-third day of the month of Nisan, 1953, the day when the sun, according to the calculations of the ancient astronomers, completed its great twenty-eight year cycle and returned to its place in the firmament, at exactly the point where it was hung on the fourth day of Creation—the father stayed awake, fortifying himself with black coffee and cigarettes, waiting for the appointed hour. At two o'clock, he turned on the lights, caressed the child's face and told him that if he didn't want to miss the sunrise, they had to set out.

A greenish light from the street lamps that filtered through the treetops shading them cast transparent needle-shaped shadows that moved not only on the stone walls, to the rhythm of the breathing of the wind, but also on the night table next to Mother, and on the white Styrofoam mannequin in the shape of a faceless human head with a graying wig, that stood among vials of medicines, Thermos bottles, and pictures of her grandchildren. The father held the child's hand and asked him to etch in his heart the memory of that night and that walk, because he had no doubt in his own heart that it would float up frequently "and I won't be here beside you."

Mother clutched the hot water bottle to her breastbone and still didn't take her eye off the skittish sky, as the boy and his father went outside the settlement and a cold wind struck their faces. The father put his jacket on his son's shoulders, and it came down to the child's ankles, and he laughed and told him not to be sad because the next time, in another twenty-eight years, he'd be the one to take off his jacket and put it on the shoulders of his son as the two of them walked together to see the sun renewed.

"He was in a good mood and acted capriciously, leaped on the cobblestones and the stories poured from his mouth. Never was I so close to Father as at that hour," I went on reading from my papers, but Mother signaled to me to stop. She shut her one eye and said quietly that her heart tormented her suddenly for being so hard-hearted to the two of us back then, and by mobilizing all possible arguments—the early hour, the cold, and the danger of the border—she prevented him from taking me with him on his walk to Mount Zion, as he had been preparing to do for several days.

"At least now you can repair that sin," her chin trembled, where bristles of hair were turning gray at the bottom. "Too bad I never tried to write. Someone who writes can live his life over, but for me it's late, too late," and she sat up straight again, opened her eye and her head rising from her nightgown was bald as an eagle's.

At the end of the month of Adar, the last remission came to an end. She sat in the dark, supported by pillows, and ate her meals in silence. A few times, she tried to get out of bed and go to the bathroom to wash her linen with her own hands, but when she fell more than a couple of times, she stopped that too. Most of the day, she'd doze and when she'd very slowly open her eye, she'd talk to me in Yiddish (as her disease grew worse, the language of her childhood encroached on the place of Hebrew). When she started calling me "father," it was clear to me that she was slipping away from us into that unknown realm steeped in the chiaroscuro of her childhood.

(In Room 42 of the Tate Gallery in London, in the early 1980s, I found something astonishingly similar to those days I don't dare erase from my heart. In the corner of the room devoted to Surrealism and full of the works of Max Ernst, Miró, and Salvador Dali's telephone with a gigantic red lobster on the earpiece, and next to the door hung a small painting by René Magritte. It's apparently a painting that isn't highly regarded because the museum administration didn't bother to make a postcard or a slide of it, and it doesn't appear in the deluxe albums of that popular Belgian artist. But "The Mathematical Mind" sent a sharp pain through me. After all the merciful Madonnas carrying an adorable baby on their arm or in their lap, Madonnas that have populated Christian art for twenty generations, here is a reverse Pietà: an adult with the plump and impassive face of a baby carrying in its arms a diapered baby with the face of a grownup woman. He means me, I am the one cared for by a sick, old mother. The stinking fruit of modern medicine, which extends a person's life but can't grant him a minimal quality of life, and that throws into the arms of the sons sick and stumbling parents who need somebody to help them and carry them on their shoulders. And the sons still see themselves as children who haven't yet tasted life.)

On the evening when you examine the house for leaven before Passover, four months before she turned to dust, Mother lost consciousness. That afternoon, I put clean sheets on her bed and a white ironed cloth on her table, and I showed her the flowered robe my wife had bought her for the holiday, and said she would inaugurate it by wearing it at the Seder. And then she shut her eye and seemed to sink into sleep again. I left the house quietly. When I came back about two hours later, her bed was empty. I found her in the kitchen, leaning helplessly against the sink, holding a box of matches in her hand. "Don't get mad at me, don't get mad at me. I didn't make a fire," she murmured as I carried her in my arms and laid her on the bed. Her hands were sooty and her jaws were clenched. I gave her something hot to drink and kept asking: "Why, Mother, why?" But she didn't answer. In the room, pillow cases and stuffed plastic bags were piled up around the sewing machine, whose drawers were emptied. In my absence, she had managed to stuff into them spools of thread, needles, DMC threads, sewing patterns, Burda pamphlets, skeins of yarn, knitting needles, photos and newspaper clippings of my poems and writings. Everything was packed and ready as if for a journey. On the kitchen counter, dozens of candles cut in two were arranged, and in the sink, packed carefully in newspaper, as if ready to be thrown in the garbage, were the wig, a corset, an old teapot, combs, the sole of a shoe, the medicine tray and the new bathrobe. Many matches, most of which had gone out right after they were lit, were scattered around, the margins of the newspapers were singed and small strips of soot hovered in the air of the kitchen. I wanted to straighten up the mess, but Mother, with the last of her strength, lifted her hand off the blanket and signaled to me to stop.

Mother's final torments and her death that I impetuously granted to the character of the mother in the book I went back to writing after she passed away, I now wanted to take them out of there and copy them here now, where they belong, but her shining face, which accompanied me during the two years since I started groping for what Ruhama Weber declared to me — that one day I might make some resurrection — suddenly grew dark. What echoed in my ears was, "We interpret 'Thou shalt not steal' different from usual," the moral lesson she preached to me when she noticed that I had embedded in one of my literary texts some sections that had already appeared in my earlier books, in another context. "We interpret 'Thou shalt not steal' as thou shalt not steal from yourself."

7

One Sabbath morning, not long before she got sick, the two of us were alone at home. Mother was reading a book, and I was watching the wind play with the edges of the two curtains, covering and revealing in turn the glow of the old bauhinia tree blossoming outside our window. A small, silly sparrow, who had slipped away in his flight and passed between the waving cloth sheets, suddenly found himself trapped in the room, and by the time I threw the pair of windows wide open, he had banged himself time and again on the lintel, and then he dropped helplessly onto the sofa beneath him.

Mother, who followed the small turmoil from her armchair, commented that for some reason it reminded her of one of my private Talmud lessons, in which she had been a coerced silent partner. The yeshiva student Father hired to deepen my religious education took pains to teach me the problem of the ownership of the wallet that was thrown into a house through one door and came out through another door. As it flew through the house, did the wallet become the property of the owner of the house or not? And the answer to this question, as he tried to teach me, depended on determining whether something in the air that never finds rest is like something resting, yes or no. "That great phrase, air that never finds rest, thrilled me so much," said Mother, "that that whole talmudic discussion didn't interest me anymore." The yeshiva student, who despaired of his explanations ever getting through my thick skull, decided to demonstrate the issue of the wallet in a kind of solitary reed of air, passing like cellophane in the house, and waved his own wallet and put it in the air. Its contents scattered over the whole room, and it made us laugh so hard that the Talmud lesson ended early.

"We also pass, each of us, into the life of another, like those flying wallets," said Mother and fell silent.

A little while later, a sparrow came in again between the two ends of the curtains that were beating softly against each other, passed through the room, and went out the window on the other side.

"I wonder if that's the same bird who was here before?" I mused.

Mother was still silent a while and then remarked as if casually: "How can you recognize anybody?"